TWO TALES OF THE EAST INDIES

Paperback edition published in 2000 by Periplus (HK) Ltd.
ALL RIGHTS RESERVED

ISBN 962-593-628-9
Printed in Singapore

Publisher: Eric Oey

Distributors

Asia Pacific
Berkeley Books Pte Ltd.
5 Little Road, #08-01
Singapore 536983
Tel: (65) 280-1330
Fax: (65) 282-6290

Indonesia
PT Java Books Indonesia
Jl. Kelapa Gading Kirana
Blok A14 No.17
Jakarta 14240
Tel: (021) 451 5351
Fax: (021) 453 4987

Japan
Tuttle Publishing
RK Bldg. 2nd Floor
2-13-10 Shimo-Meguro, Meguro-Ku
Tokyo 153 0064, Japan
Tel: (03) 5437 0171
Fax: (03) 5437 0755

United States
Tuttle Publishing
Distribution Center
Airport Industrial Park
364 Innovation Drive
North Clarendon, VT 05759-9436
Tel: (802) 773 8930
Fax: (802) 526 2778

Preparation and publication of this work were supported by the Translation and Publication Programs of the National Endowment for the Humanities, the Foundation for the Promotion of the Translation of Dutch Literary Works and the Prince Bernhard Fund, to whom acknowledgment is gratefully made.

TWO TALES OF THE EAST

THE LAST HOUSE IN THE WORLD
By Beb Vuyk

THE COUNSELOR
By H.F. Friedericy

PERIPLUS

Contents

Preface to the Series

This volume is one of a series of literary works written by the Dutch about their lives in the former colony of the Dutch East Indies, now the Republic of Indonesia. This realm of more than three thousand islands is roughly one quarter the size of the continental United States. It consists of the four Greater Sunda Islands—Sumatra, larger than California; Java, about the size of New York State; Borneo, about the size of France (presently called Kalimantan); and Celebes, about the size of North Dakota (now called Sulawesi). East from Java is a string of smaller islands called the Lesser Sunda Islands, which includes Bali, Lombok, Sumba, Sumbawa, Flores, and Timor. Further east from the Lesser Sunda Islands lies New Guinea, now called Irian Barat, which is the second largest island in the world. Between New Guinea and Celebes there is a host of smaller islands, often known as the Moluccas, that includes a group once celebrated as the Spice Islands.

One of the most volcanic regions in the world, the Malay archipelago is tropical in climate and has a diverse population. Some 250 languages are spoken in Indonesia, and it is remarkable that a population of such widely differing cultural and ethnic backgrounds adopted the Malay language as its *lingua franca* from about the fifteenth century, although that language was spoken at first only in parts of Sumatra and the Malay peninsula (now Malaysia).

Though the smallest of the Greater Sunda Islands, Java has always been the most densely populated, with about two-thirds of all Indonesians living there. In many ways a history of Indonesia is, first and foremost, the history of Java.

But in some ways Java's prominence is misleading, because it belies the great diversity of this island realm. For instance, the destination of the first Europeans who sailed to Southeast Asia was not Java but the Moluccas. It was that "odiferous pistil" (as Motley called the clove), as well as nutmeg and mace, that drew the Portuguese to a group of small islands in the Ceram and Banda Seas in the early part of the sixteenth century. Pepper was another profitable commodity, and attempts to obtain it brought the Portuguese into conflict with Atjeh, an Islamic sultanate in northern Sumatra, and with Javanese traders who, along with merchants from India, had been the traditional middlemen of the spice trade. The precedent of European intervention had been set and was to continue for nearly four centuries.

Although subsequent history is complicated in its causes and effects, one may propose certain generalities. The Malay realm was essentially a littoral one. Even in Java, the interior was sparsely populated and virtually unknown to the foreign intruders coming from China, India, and Europe. Whoever ruled the seas controlled the archipelago, and for the next three centuries the key needed to unlock the riches of Indonesia was mastery of the Indian Ocean. The nations who thus succeeded were, in turn, Portugal, Holland, and England, and one can trace the shifting of power in the prominence and decline of their major cities in the Orient. Goa, Portugal's stronghold in India, gave way to Batavia in the Dutch East Indies, while Batavia was overshadowed by Singapore by the end of the nineteenth century. Although all three were relatively small nations, they were maritime giants. Their success was partly due to the internecine warfare between the countless city-states, principalities, and native autocrats. The Dutch were masters at playing one against the other.

Religion was a major factor in the fortunes of Indonesia. The Portuguese expansion was in part a result of Portugal's crusade against Islam, which was quite as ferocious and intransigent as the holy war of the Mohammedans. Islam may be considered a unifying force in the archipelago; it cut across all levels of society and provided a rallying point for resistance to foreign intrusion. Just as the Malay language had done linguistically, Islam proved to be a syncretizing force when there was no united front. One of the causes of Portugal's demise was its inflexible antagonism to Islam, and later the Dutch found resistance to their rule fueled by religious fervor as well as political dissatisfaction.

Holland ventured to reach the tropical antipodes not only because their nemesis, Philip II of Spain, annexed Portugal and forbade the Dutch entry to Lisbon. The United Netherlands was a nation of merchants, a brokerage house for northern Europe, and it wanted to get to the source of tropical wealth itself. Dutch navigators and traders knew the location of the fabled Indies; they were well acquainted with Portuguese achievements at sea and counted among their members individuals who had worked for the Portuguese. Philip II simply accelerated a process that was inevitable.

At first, various individual enterprises outfitted ships and sent them to the Far East in a far from lucrative display of free enterprise. Nor was the first arrival of the Dutch in the archipelago auspicious, though it may have been symbolic of subsequent developments. In June 1596 a Dutch fleet of four ships anchored off the coast of Java. Senseless violence and a total disregard for local customs made the Dutch unwelcome on those shores.

During the seventeenth century the Dutch extended their influence in the archipelago by means of superior naval strength, use of armed intervention which was often ruthless, by shrewd politicking, and exploitation of local differences. Their cause was helped by the lack of a cohesive force to withstand them. Yet the seventeenth century also saw a number of men who were eager to know the new realm, who investigated the language and the mores of the people they encountered, and who studied the flora and fauna. These were men who not only put the Indies on the map of trade routes, but who also charted riches of other than commercial value.

It soon became apparent to the Dutch that these separate ventures did little to promote welfare. In 1602 Johan van Oldenbarneveldt, the Advocate of the United Provinces, managed to negotiate a contract which in effect merged all these individual enterprises into one United East India Company, better known under its Dutch acronym as the voc. The merger ensured a monopoly at home, and the Company set out to obtain a similar insurance in the Indies. This desire for exclusive rights to the production and marketing of spices and other commodities proved to be a double-edged sword.

The VOC succeeded because of its unrelenting naval vigilance in discouraging European competition and because the Indies were a politically unstable region. And even though the Company was only interested in its balance sheet, it soon found itself burdened with an expanding empire and an indolent bureaucracy which, in the eighteenth century, became not only unwieldy but tolerant of graft and extortion. Furthermore, even though its profits were far below what they were rumored to be, the Company kept its dividends artificially high and was soon forced to borrow money to pay the interest on previous loans. When Holland's naval supremacy was seriously challenged by the British in 1780, a blockade kept the Company's ships from reaching Holland, and the discrepancy between capital and expenditures increased dramatically until the Company's deficit was so large it had to request state aid. In 1798, after nearly two centuries, the Company ceased to exist. Its debt of 140 million guilders was assumed by the state, and the commercial enterprise became a colonial empire.

At the beginning of the nineteenth century, Dutch influence was still determined by the littoral character of the region. Dutch presence in the archipelago can be said to have lasted three and a half centuries, but if one defines colonialism as the subjugation of an *entire* area and dates it from the time when the last independent domain was conquered—in this case Atjeh in northern Sumatra—then the Dutch colonial empire lasted less than half a century. Effective government could only be claimed for the Moluccas, certain portions of Java (by no means the entire island), a southern portion of Celebes, and some coastal regions of Sumatra and Borneo. Yet it is also true that precisely because Indonesia was an insular realm, Holland never needed to muster a substantial army such as the one the British had to maintain in the large subcontinent of India. The extensive interiors of islands such as Sumatra, Borneo, or Celebes were not penetrated, because, for the seaborne empire of commercial interests, exploration of such regions was unprofitable, hence not desirable.

The nature of Holland's involvement changed with the tenure of Herman Willem Daendels as Governor-General, just after the French revolution. Holland declared itself a democratic nation in 1795, allied itself with France—which meant a direct confrontation with England—and was practically a vassal state of France until 1810. Though reform, liberal programs, and the mandate of human rights were loudly proclaimed in Europe, they did not seem to apply to the Asian branch of the family of man. Daendels exemplified this double standard. He evinced reforms, either in fact or on paper, but did so in an imperious manner and with total disregard for native customs and law (known as *adat*). Stamford Raffles, who was the chief administrator of the British interim government from 1811 to 1816, expanded Daendels's innovations, which included tax reform and the introduction of the land-rent system, which was based on the assumption that all the land belonged to the colonial administration. By the time Holland regained its colonies in 1816, any resemblance to the erstwhile Company had vanished. In its place was a firmly established, paternalistic colonial government which ruled by edict and regulation, supported a huge bureaucracy, and sought to make the colonies turn a profit, as well as to legislate its inhabitants' manner of living.

It is not surprising that for the remainder of the nineteenth century, a centralized authority instituted changes from above that were often in direct conflict with Javanese life and welfare. One such change, which was supposed to increase revenues and improve the life of the Javanese peasant, was the infamous "Cultivation System" *(Cultuurstelsel)*. This system required the Javanese to grow cash crops, such as sugar cane or indigo, which, although profitable on the world market, were of little practical use to the Javanese. In effect it meant compulsory labor and the exploitation of the entire island as if it were a feudal estate. The system proved profitable for the Dutch, and because it introduced varied crops such as tea and tobacco to local agriculture, it indirectly improved the living standard of some of the people. It also fostered distrust of colonial authority, caused uprisings, and provided the impetus for liberal reform on the part of Dutch politicians in the Netherlands.

Along with the increased demand in the latter half of the nineteenth century for liberal reform came an expansion of direct control over other areas of the archipelago. One of the reasons for this was an unprecedented influx of private citizens from Holland. Expansion of trade required expansion of territory that was under direct control of Batavia to insure stability. Colonial policy improved education, agriculture, and public hygiene and expanded the transportation network. In Java a paternalistic policy

was not offensive, because its ruling class (the *prijaji*) had gov-
erned that way for centuries; but progressive politicians in The
Hague demanded that the Indies be administered on a moral
basis which favored the interests of the Indonesians rather than
those of the Dutch government in Europe. This "ethical policy"
became doctrine from about the turn of this century and followed
on the heels of a renascence of scientific study of the Indies quite
as enthusiastic as the one in the seventeenth century.

The first three decades of the present century were probably
the most stable and prosperous in colonial history. This period
was also the beginning of an emerging Indonesian national con-
sciousness. Various nationalistic parties were formed, and the
Indonesians demanded a far more representative role in the administration of their country. The example of Japan indicated to
the Indonesians that European rulers were not invincible. The ra-
pidity with which the Japanese conquered Southeast Asia during
the Second World War only accelerated the process of decoloni-
zation. In 1945 Indonesia declared its independence, naming Su-
karno the republic's first president. The Dutch did not accept this
declaration, and between 1945 and 1949 they conducted several
unsuccessful military campaigns to re-establish control. In 1950,
with a new constitution, Indonesia became a sovereign state.

I offer here only a cursory outline. The historical reality is far
more complex and infinitely richer, but this sketch must suffice as
a backdrop for the particular type of literature that is presented in
this series.

This is a literature written by or about European colonialists in
Southeast Asia prior to the Second World War. Though the literary techniques may be Western, the subject matter is unique.
This genre is also a self-contained unit that cannot develop further, because there are no new voices and because what was
voiced no longer exists. Yet it is a literature that can still instruct,
because it delineates the historical and psychological confrontation of East and West, it depicts the uneasy alliance of these antithetical forces, and it shows by prior example the demise of Western imperialism.

These are political issues, but there is another aspect of this
kind of literature that is of equal importance. It is a literature of
lost causes, of a past irrevocably gone, of an era that today seems
so utterly alien that it is novel once again.

Tempo dulu it was once called—time past. But now, after two world wars and several Asian wars, after the passage of nearly half a century, this phrase presents more than a wistful longing for the prerogatives of imperialism; it gives as well a poignant realization that an epoch is past that will never return. At its worst the documentation of this perception is sentimental indulgence, but at its best it is the poetry of a vanished era, of the fall of an empire, of the passing of an age when issues moral and political were firmer and clearer, and when the drama of the East was still palpable and not yet reduced to a topic for sociologists.

In many ways, this literature of Asian colonialism reminds one of the literature of the American South; of Faulkner, O'Connor, John Crowe Ransom, and Robert Penn Warren. For that too was a "colonial" literature that was quite as much aware of its own demise and yet, not defiantly but wistfully, determined to record its own passing. One finds in both the peculiar hybrid of antithetical cultures, the inevitable defeat of the more recent masters, a faith in more traditional virtues, and that peculiar offbeat detail often called "gothic" or "grotesque." In both literatures loneliness is a central theme. There were very few who knew how to turn their mordant isolation into a dispassionate awareness that all things must pass and fail.

E. M. Beekman

The Last House in the World Beb Vuyk

Introduction

Although a product of the present century, Beb Vuyk's prewar writing has a direct link to the genesis of the Dutch colonial enterprise. Emotionally as well as aesthetically, she has a closer affinity to the mariners and other enterprising individualists of the seventeenth century than to her own generation. The essence of that affinity is contained in what was once the luminous concept of "adventure." In Vuyk's earlier work adventure is a positive experience, though it is always besieged by conformist society.

In her study of *The Origins of Totalitarianism*, Hannah Arendt noted that there was a difference between colonialism and imperialism, between "the old adventurers" and the imperial bureaucrats. The original impetus of colonial trade was "to facilitate the exchange of the treasures of the world." Though, to be sure, this was not a charitable enterprise, earlier colonialism had "no ambition for permanent rule or intentions of conquest, decimation of the native population, and permanent settlement." The latter activities, which for many critics help define imperialism, became the norm during the course of the nineteenth century and the first three decades of the twentieth. That earlier less culpable era is often misinterpreted, possibly because, as Arendt notes, "the real influence of pre-imperialist colonial enterprise and overseas settlement" on the development of imperialism was rather small. The history of imperialism is, of course, far more complicated. But what is important here is the realization that there is a significant difference between the two eras, including different mental outlooks and different experiences of reality.[1]

In that earlier time of mariners and marauders, reality still seemed remarkably close to romance, and romance was far sturdier than fantasy. The romantic desire for adventure could still have practical consequences, and commercial enterprise still had an air of bold inventiveness about it. Adventure was not consciously pursued by those seventeenth-century individualists. The accounts of their tribulations were tales of adventure that might entertain, but that were primarily intended to be utilitarian and were meant to instruct. They provided those who came after with practical sailing information and geographical details, they investigated the mercantile potential of foreign regions, and they spoke to the next generation of seafarers with the voice of experience.

That earlier age of colonial trade was peopled by independent spirits. Arendt's "old adventurers" had "stepped out of society," were "enterprising beyond the permitted limits of civilization," were individuals of "their own making" who lived, in Conrad's words, in "a world of hazard and adventure." That age with its recalcitrant spirit of adventure perished and was replaced by an institutionalized imperialism in the form of the huge bureaucracy of the colonial civil service. Hazard was replaced by administrative necessity, adventure was negated by legislation and boundaries of the mind as well as the map were no longer limitless but were instead carefully circumscribed by governmental directives. The colonial empire was not interested in individuals but found its strength in numbers, its reward in diligence. One could summarize the development of colonialism from the seventeenth to the twentieth century as a gradual transition from an age of heroism to one of prudence. To be sure, the myth of excess, luxury, and romance persisted, and the tropics could still attract some of the best spirits of the usurping nation. But they inevitably discovered that chivalry, nobility, and bravery were no longer viable in the political reality of imperialism. They had become, in Hannah Arendt's words, "the tragic and quixotic fools of imperialism."[2]

Beb Vuyk's narrative of her personal experiences represents an anachronistic retelling of that earlier age within the context of the harsh and antagonistic twentieth century. Her acceptance of life as adventure is neither innocent nor intellectual. On the contrary, she experiences adventure as if a tonic and knows that it stimulates the best in a person. And yet to a present reader Vuyk's avowal may seem quixotic, and, though she lived her adventures less than a half century ago, they seem to be part of an antique world of unaccustomed clarity of vision and purpose. Hence an examination of that world as it is presented in *The Last House in the World* and in some of her other work is not only a specific exegesis, but also an interpretation of adventure in terms of literature as well as life and, indirectly, a description of that vanished era of colonial history that preceded imperialism.

At the heart of adventure is movement, as Robert Louis Stevenson wrote, about a half century earlier. "For my part, I travel not to go anywhere, but to go. I travel for travel's sake. *The great affair is to move;* to feel the needs and hitches of our life more nearly; to come down off this feather-bed of civilization, and find the globe granite underfoot and strewn with cutting flints."[3] For Beb Vuyk too, the most characteristic element of adventure is motility, in both a physical and an emotional sense. When she lived with her husband on a tea plantation in central Java—described in her first novel, *Thousand Islands* (*Duizend eilanden*, 1937)—she felt hemmed in by an ordered existence with its mundane incitement of "promotion, bonuses, and salary increases." Life was "canalized" and needed to break out of its demarcations and move like a "river that flowed unfettered between banks covered with wild forests." She felt "enclosed by the monotonous tea [shrubs] and the dark forests" (434),* corralled, as it were, by the unyielding and ponderous mountains. She felt a claustrophobia that was imposed both by the landscape and by her husband's life as a company man, and she began to yearn for "a wider land and an existence that was less hemmed in, for the freedom of much water and the joy of the sun" (435). Ironically, the confinement she felt was reflected in the Javanese name for the volcano that blocked her view of open spaces. It was called *Kemulan,* a name derived from "kemul," which means to cover or to enshroud.

When her husband lost his job in 1932 they gambled: rather than live "a careful existence in Java, in semi-poverty," they

---

* Page references in the text to works other than *The Last House in the World* refer to the original text in the single volume edition of Vuyk's collected work which, though not inclusive, is the most convenient. Beb Vuyk, *Verzameld Werk* (Amsterdam: Querido, 1972). All translations are mine.

chose to leave for the Moluccas and "leap into adventure" (437). To hazard a risk is fundamental to the experience of adventure because, as Beb Vuyk knew, it meant breaking out of the living death of inertia and safety in order to give oneself to the flow of uncertainty that can revitalize existence the way the stirring of the wind provides a tree with what it needs to keep its branches supple and its wood healthy. They gambled, preferring, in Stevenson's words, "galvanism to acquiescence," and they won.[4] And the life they led for eight years on the island of Buru in the Moluccas is called an "adventure" again and again like an iteration of joy.

Existence, according to Vuyk, can only be an adventure if it is energized by motility. Her favorite simile for this freedom is water, but she means a body of water that is not stagnant, not harnessed by man, that is still dangerous and free. When Vuyk and her husband arrived in Buru she exulted about the "broad, vivacious water, with the light, green land around it. Leksula [a town] was dead, here everything is alive." She had escaped the confinement of the Javanese mountains for the liberation of the living, moving water of the Moluccas. Although she first experienced life as an adventure when she went to the Indies, far from the confining society of Holland that distrusts adventurers, the well of this regenerative water is located in that very same country of origin. It was in the Netherlands that she became used to "a flat land, shining and astir with a great deal of water" (434, 435). And after Beb Vuyk left Indonesia in 1958, she did not go to live in a Dutch town or even near one, but bought a boat in order to live "on the open, always moving water, which is the best part of this country" (445). It is this geographic particularity that links the Indies to Holland for her, while the association is also emotionally consistent, because the open water was part of her personal mythology. Beb Vuyk was born in the harbor of Rotterdam, close to the spot where the pilgrims set sail for America on the *Mayflower*. This atmosphere "of water and houses, of old ships and small wharves" was an "atmosphere of adventure and romanticism" (422).

The opposition between movement and repose, activity and quiescence, between stream and closure, is central to Vuyk's work. This antithesis is evident in the smallest details, in what seem the most ordinary interstices of her prose. But it also contributes to more profound dimensions. In the sixth section of *The*

Last House in the World, she develops the process of oxidation as a metaphor for the moral condition of Dutch colonial officialdom. She uses it in a transitive sense of the corrosive influence the colonial experience can have on an ordinary citizen from Holland, making a modest and unpretentious man become quickly rusted solid in his own unwarranted importance. In other words, he becomes inflexible; weighed down by his presumed stature, he is no longer endowed with emotional or moral motility. The momentous change of moving from the European continent to the Asian archipelago was not an act of progression but one of retardation. Inflexibility is the same as motionlessness, be it physical or psychological. The irony of the passage is that this is said to happen particularly in the "outer possessions," those islands farthest removed from centralized authority in Java. In those outer regions, such as the Moluccas, a colonial official had a great deal of freedom and could practically ignore the strictures of the colonial bureaucracy. Vuyk asserts that it is precisely in such freedom that the person with the least mental agility becomes the most intransigent and inflexible.

This contrast finally refers to the most fundamental issue: life is movement, stasis is death. This is implied rather than adduced, and most movingly so in section eighteen, which describes the birth of the narrator's second son. Pregnancy means confinement, imprisonment by one's own body. It reduces the narrator's activities and sets her apart from the adventure of life on Buru. She feels backed into a corner, a more immediate physical equivalent of the claustrophobia she felt in the mountains on Java. Incarcerated in her own flesh, a mere custodian of the unborn child, the inactivity torments her with thoughts of death. She is afraid that she will die while giving birth, and ponders the different ways men and women die. This too is done in terms connoting the world of adventure. Men can die in a dramatic fashion; for instance, from the "gruesome bite of the crocodile," or from a wound received while chopping down trees. But women and children die more prosaically. "There are many ways for a man to die, but small children die because they are overfed and women die in childbirth." She also resents the fact that her condition forces her to reconsider civilized society. She has rejected that society, has opted for the adventure in the tropics, but now, in her susceptible and perilous situation she can't help thinking of Holland where there's a doctor "in every street, and in every fourth street . . . a hospital with drugs and instruments and the mercy of painkillers," while in her present situation there's often "eighty miles between life and death."

That her ordeal is ineluctable makes her the victim of a searing loneliness, while the passivity it enforces traps her in thoughts of dying. This experience cannot be shared. "Now I am beyond all mankind on the desolate, arctic plain, the rigid, cold loneliness of death." She finally emerges victorious from this lonely vigil, but this is not realized until a crocodile (*buaja* in Malay) has gone after the placenta which, to prevent it from being used for black magic, had been tossed into the sea. With that cry of "buaja, buaja," activity opens up her life again. Along with the deliverance of the child, she too has been set free. Commotion is now all around her: the shouts of the Malay, the shots her husband fires at the crocodile, the dogs' mad running around the house. She breathes "rapidly" again when she knows that "the child is born and I am alive," and once again she is back in the "wild, primitive ecstasy of the adventure that is life." When, as if by magic, a doctor happens to be on board the ship which stops at the island only once a month, she takes the opportunity to consult him. He lets her listen to the fetal heart and its rapid flutter grants her the first reconciliation. "He lets me listen to the child's heartbeat, a small, quick heart. This is the first tenderness. The small, quick heart of a child."

After she has exulted over life like this, the beginning of the next chapter describes how her other son, Hans Christiaan, fell seriously ill on the island of Ambon. The few terse sentences are constructed around images of immurement, and once again this implies an association with death. For four weeks she stayed with the boy in a hospital, "completely cut off from the world, in a small isolation ward with no other view than the morgue." Coming right after the nativity passage this short section seems like a reminder that the lot of women and children remains always precarious, quick to imprison them in a living death. Mother and child surmount the threat once more, and the text proceeds to rejoice with its most extended passage, describing a long voyage by *prao* to the island of Ambelau. The importance of the cluster of images referring to movement, travel, water, sun is evident in that this experience is repeated in the story "Journal of a *Prao* Voyage" ("Journaal van een prauwreis," 247–57).

Except for the exotic locale, the text of *The Last House in the*

World seems to contain little of what is now vulgarly demanded of adventure literature. The material is far from lurid and there is little "action." But, as Paul Zweig pointed out in his study *The Adventurer: The Fate of Adventure in the Western World,* the present age has trivialized adventure. It once constituted "an ancient and widespread subject matter" because adventure "plunges [the reader] into essential experience."[5] Robert Louis Stevenson, one of the masters of the art of adventure, made similar claims for his subject matter. He felt that novels which want to address all mankind "must leave off to speak of parlours . . . and begin to deal with fighting, sailoring, adventure, death or child-birth. . . . These aged things have on them the dew of man's morning; they lie near, not so much to us, the semi-artificial flowerets, as to the trunk and aboriginal taproot of the race."[6]

All the primordial experiences Stevenson mentioned are evident in Vuyk's work, if not essential to it. Robert Kiely's assessment of Stevenson's work applies to Vuyk's as well, because for her too "adventure is immutable and universal" and has "a kind of sacred purity"[7] about it. Adventure was far more readily experienced in the colonial tropics, whereas it was stifled or emasculated in the civilized societies of Europe. This is one reason to argue for a link between colonial literature and the literature of adventure, as well as for a close affinity between colonial literature and romanticism. And even though Beb Vuyk's work is modern, it contains the essential experiences of adventure, including a mythological dimension.

It was already noted that in the present text childbirth is presented as an essential confrontation between life and death. Furthermore, the passage that makes this connection is placed in the narrative in such a way that it acquires the same luminosity as that of the more readily acknowledged adventurous episodes of the perilous sea voyage or the extended struggle to carve out a living in a dangerous and alien land. In this manner, the occasion of childbirth is granted an epic measure. This is confirmed by the sinister presence of the crocodile.

The *buaja,* both the reptile itself and a mythic beast larger than life, is worthy of an epic contest. The present work is, of course, a modern description of a pioneering existence on a remote island, and one won't find an epic combat here such as Beowulf fought with Grendel. But the subtlety of Vuyk's literary art finds a way to intimate the larger dimension. The book opens and concludes with the crocodile. At the end of the very first paragraph the mud and the presence of crocodiles make the coastal mangrove forests inaccessible, and at the end of the last paragraph of the book the "gruesome crocodile" is said to abide on Buru. This is meant to be negative because the crocodile regains supremacy over its domain after the De Willigens have been defeated by the injustice of the Dutch colonial administration. Where other privations—illness, death, poverty, a poor soil, and Sisyphean labor—could not succeed, the inhumanity of bureaucrats can prevail. Symbolically, their heartlessness is transferred to the *buaja,* because the awesome beast suggests death in all the negative connotations that were mentioned before.

The first place where the De Willigens encounter the crocodile in the Moluccas is at Leksula, while they are still on their journey from Java to Buru. For the narrator Leksula was "dead," and this is emphasized by the fact that on a walk through neglected coconut plantations they pass a stagnant pool that is overgrown with weeds and "stinks of crocodiles." In a later passage describing a coast of mangrove forests, their *prao* becomes entangled in the excessive vegetation. They are forced to strike sail and have to paddle up a river. The vegetation is described in terms of weapons and the more mobile leafy trees have been "driven back" by the dark *nipa* palms that thrive in mud like crocodiles. This terrain is then described as "a prehistoric landscape, transfixed, bigger and stronger and crueler, that oppresses us while we flee through it." According to Vuyk's own symbolism, this desolate landscape invokes a strong feeling of claustrophobia because it is motionless.[8] This primordial region is the realm of the *buaja:* "the crocodile has his paths here on a slope that goes from the forest down to the river, and they have been sanded smooth by his stinking belly." This prodigious landscape is the land of death. Such a demonic beast as the crocodile is the ultimate opponent for either adventurer or epic hero. Such a place and such an adversary have to be, in a literal sense, extraordinary. And so must its opponent.

Such a man was Heintje who, despite the diminutive, was the couple's most powerful ally on Buru. Heintje Limba came originally from the island of Ambon and was the companion of Captain De Willigen, the narrator's father-in-law. As described in the opening paragraphs, the time when these two came to Buru to work the fifty *kajuputih* stills was a time of legend. To inhabit such a legendary time one must be a prodigy, in order to be a match for it: Heintje is described as "a great hunter, a tremendous drinker, and a reckless adventurer." Heintje and the captain engage not only real dangers but also translunary ones: the *suanggis* who are the "courtesans among the hundred ghosts of the Moluccas." Together the two men "drove the forest and the *suanggis* back with their axes and machetes," and it is only natural that two men who fight such a fight no longer acknowledge the mundane restrictions of quotidian society—such as differences of race, social position, or religion—because they have "something far nobler and otherworldly: the bond between two men who fight a lonely battle, back to back." This is Beb Vuyk's finest formulation of Stevenson's sacred purity of adventure. Serving as a preamble, it gives the book's celebration of adventure the appropriate dimension of legend.

After the captain has died from an all-too-human disease, it is Heintje who becomes a hero figure for the captain's sons. His literary affiliations are just as important as the man himself, since the De Willigen boys see him as the personification of heroes created by such past masters of adventure literature as Captain Marryat *(Masterman Ready),* Scott *(Rob Roy),* and Cooper *(The Last of the Mohicans).*[9] And Heintje is equal to the task because "he was the fastest hunter and the most skillful fisherman." But he also had another necessary gift of the adventurer. Heintje was a good storyteller and "knew the latest news as it traveled from *kampong* to *kampong,* grievances, intrigues, and the evil that is about at night." Once the heroic stature of this Ambonese adventurer has been established, it is clear that he will be able to face the most formidable foe: "By day he used to shoot crocodiles where they lay sunning themselves on the dry sandbanks when the tide went out, while at night he'd shoot at the red light of their eyes between the roots of the mangroves."

One night the *buaja* monster infiltrates the compound of his adversaries, getting closer and closer to the narrator. First, the monster destroys the idyllic freedom of adventure. Its dangerous proximity to the house makes it imperative that people no longer bathe in the river, but use instead the bathroom which, up till then, had not been used, and "Batuboi lost one of its charms." Ordinary reality is powerless against the monster: it bites through the best shark hook they have, those made of the finest English steel, and ordinary bullets cannot harm it. But Heintje knows better. One needs a hook made from the antlers of a stag to catch it and, if that fails, dumdum bullets. It is not the "civilized" staff who notice the monster first, but the more "primitive" Alfurs, the erstwhile head-hunters from the heart of the country, the Moluccan equivalent of what the colonial Spanish in South America called the *Indios bravos*. Heintje prevails over the crocodile, but throughout the account are intimations that the animal has powers superior to ordinary mortals. After lead bullets, dumdum bullets, lances, a noose, and a coup de grâce, it still manages to escape during the night, the appropriate hour for this demonic shape from darkness. And when it has finally died the narrator ends the passage with a shudder of apprehension at the might of this beast because she has no doubt that it is "infinitely more horrible and repulsive" than its kin, the gigantic snake that also inhabits this as yet still legendary island.

During the later childbirth scene, the *buaja* surfaces again, now perilously close to the narrator when she is most vulnerable. First its essential power is mentioned again. Its "gruesome bite" is one of the dramatic ways a man can die, because it inflicts a wound that is precisely described as extending "from the groin to the knee on both sides of the leg." This time the scene is entirely nocturnal, and when the moon rises, the *buaja* goes after the placenta. There is no doubt any longer about its elemental manifestation as death. And at precisely this point, Vuyk carefully insinuates its hellish association. The native population, she informs the reader, consider the placenta the twin of the newborn child. They call it *kaka*, or "the elder brother," who must die in order to grant life to its sibling. In Ambon, Heintje's country of origin, the placenta was used in black magic to invoke the devil. To prevent such use, the Europeans have the afterbirth tossed into the sea, but not far enough, and the red of the crocodile's eyes becomes the birth blood on the waters. When the cry of "buaja" is heard, it is the narrator's husband who assumes Heintje's role as the dragon slayer. But it is significant that, though he fires both barrels of his shotgun, no mention is made of a kill. And yet, although this dragon can never be slain, it is overcome. And the victory does not belong to a man, no matter how "right" such a man as Heintje is, but to a woman. Even if she seems most assailable in her condition, she possesses greater might than a weapon. The *buaja* attacked something that was part of her, to be sure, and came dangerously close to his intended victim. But as if tricked by a decoy, its power was diverted by something that died in order to give life, by *kaka*, the elder brother of legend. Like a support system that is no longer needed, the placenta was expelled *after* it had fulfilled its mission of feeding a new life. The monster was foiled by a sacrificial death and the woman, spent but exulting as after an epic contest, has overcome a foe men could not vanquish. She triumphed over death with the weapon of life. Perhaps this is the greatest meaning one can grant adventure, that it is an essential experience that is truly immutable. For surely the ultimate adventure is the struggle between life and death.

After this triumph comes the reward of the long *prao* journey to Ambelau that is sustained by all Vuyk's positive symbolism. But the last three words of the book are: "the gruesome crocodile." It has prevailed. The narrator won her fight óver the dragon in the arena of existence, but the adventurer's greatest adversary, organized society, is found to have collaborated with the enemy. It is appropriate in this context to mention that the crocodile also symbolizes hypocrisy, that in ancient Egypt it was said to represent governmental tyranny, and that in Malay *buaja* is a slang-word for the criminal element of large cities. The identification of the crocodile with the colonial government is bitter but, in terms of Vuyk's work, inevitable. "It's all over, the vision and the labor. On the large plain, weeds will grow again and vermin, the giant python and the gruesome crocodile."

All the romance of adventure in the tropics, if not the pure joy of life in an anterior world, was summed up by Beb Vuyk in the beautiful synesthetic phrase: "the wild green scent of adventure." This expresses imaginatively what the colonial experience should have been and seldom was, except perhaps in the age of mariners and marauders.

Beb Vuyk used the synesthetic phrase first in *The Last House in the World,* at the outset of the climactic childbirth scene, and offered it twice more in the "Journal of a *Prao* Voyage." The phrase also provided the title for a collection of her stories that appeared in 1941 in the Indonesian capital, then still called Batavia. Clearly it felt like the right formulation to her, as indeed it was—until the Second World War.

The phrase distills the essence of Beb Vuyk's fictional world, both in a general and in a more personal sense. "Adventure" is the magic lodestone, and to it cling the modifiers "wild" to recall the motility of adventure, "green" as the predominant color of the Indies, and "scent" for the olfactory experience that is unique to these tropical regions Rimbaud called "les pays poivrés."[10] But the phrase is also a distillate from more private and aesthetic materials.

In most of her work, and especially in *The Last House in the World*, color is a dominant force.[11] Beb Vuyk's Moluccan world is a brightly lit one, burnished by the sun. As opposed to the dour, pluvial mountains of central Java, this sparkling island realm can be an adventure for the eyes alone. And by force of repetition the two main colors, green and blue, almost seem to aspire to heroic stature in their own right.

Green is the color of sensation, and that is what adventure is all about for Beb Vuyk. But the color also had a personal significance for her. Although in her youth she had associated green with a fearful atmosphere (423) and had found in Java that it could be oppressive, on Buru it becomes exuberantly positive. It cures, it heals, it is energy and promise, and, in the final analysis, it is the color of good fortune because it is associated with nature and with the distillate of the *kajuputih* leaves. There is no doubt that Vuyk's expressive image of adventure is meant to evoke that aromatic oil. At the beginning of the second paragraph of the book she uses similar adjectives to describe both the oil and adventure. This alliterative echo is lost in translation, but is clear in the original.[12] Yet there is an irony here. *Kajuputih* means "white wood." These trees are not very tall and somewhat resemble a cross between scrub oak and birches. The curious thing about the *Melaleuca leucodendron* is that one tree—called the mother (*ibu* in Malay)—sends out roots in expanding circles from its trunk. From these roots, every thirty feet or so, new growth shoots up to about the height of shrubs. These diminutive *kajuputih* trees are called children (*anakan*) of the mother tree, and it is from the leaves of the *anakan* that the fragrant oil is distilled. Hence one could say that Buru's erstwhile modest wealth was based on an arboreal matriarchy, a theme that, though never obtrusive, is of considerable importance.

The oil that is distilled from the *anakan* leaves is a dirty white.[13] The characteristic green color of *kajuputih* oil was due entirely to the verdigris inside the copper still head (or *kepala*). Oil that was the original color was not acceptable; what made it valuable was the color that came from the green rust. The adulteration that produced this prized aeruginous green has a positive connotation and is quite the opposite of the moral oxidation that made Dutch officials rust solid in their vaingloriousness. But the oil was also in jeopardy because in order to increase or preserve its valuable green color fraudulent practices were rampant, corrupting it until the original pure product could hardly be found anymore. And while moral corruption is said to pollute the humanity of the colonial officers on their way to the Indies, the purity of the *kajuputih* oil was adulterated "during the long hot journey to Europe," turning it to a drab brown. And brown for Beb Vuyk is at best the color of domesticity, but most often she associates it with death.

The green scent of adventure is as assailable as the green aromatic oil that is the quintessence of the verdant tropical island. And both should remain "wild" because civilization—interloping European progress—will want to control and thereby corrupt it. Such progress restricts initiative, restrains exuberance, regulates hazard, and domesticates adventure. By desiring to make risk safe and effort an equal opportunity, organized colonial society made individual enterprise suspect. Regulatory controls reduced the speculative aspect of existence but this also devitalized the energy of individual endeavor. In Beb Vuyk's prose written prior to the Second World War, work is still an adventure. The De Willigens work very hard on Buru. They are fully aware of the hardships they must face, but all adversity is mitigated by the intoxication of their knowing that they are forging their own destiny, and not laboring mechanically for an obscure purpose dictated by remote control.

This working for the joy of it is an activity that provides fulfillment and that, though it wants a return, is not done for profit margins. Their pioneer existence is "a vision of work in the hot days of the eastern monsoon, or in the wind and rainstorms when the monsoon changes. This is a poor country, almost infertile, but rich in the mercy of labor for this day and for all our days to come." The "mercy" of labor has an unusual and archaic ring to it. Present society is unable to identify work as romance, unable to experience daily labor as an adventure. And perhaps because it is an idiosyncratic effort, there is a dimension of selflessness to this toiling. The "vision" that Beb Vuyk associates with work is similar to Kipling's. In what was once one of his best-known poems—"L'Envoi," the last poem in *The Seven Seas*, a volume Vuyk read (439)—Kipling sang of an age when "no one shall work for money, and no one shall work for fame; But each for the joy of working."[14] What angered Vuyk was that when the people who believed in this had finished the hard, dirty, almost heroic work of changing a wilderness into productive terrain, they were tossed aside as outmoded and replaced by the company men who felt no allegiance to a dream or a vision. To them such feelings of loyalty were signs of debility or, at best, remnants of an antique innocence. The usurpation of individual effort by the colonial bureaucracy is a tragic theme for Beb Vuyk because it destroyed individuality, and infected the old pioneers with the sickness of loneliness, a disease far more virulent than isolation in a hostile environment because it was caused by ingratitude and human betrayal. Work becomes mechanized and "personality is eliminated. Java is becoming modern. Java is becoming so inhabitable that it is almost uninhabitable" (115; see also 108–10, 118, 136).

But Vuyk had one gift that her enemy, the unknowing allies of the *buaja,* could never rob her of. While they could only write progress reports or tool a bloodless rhetoric for official declarations, she had "memory as an exciting story" (254). Adventure is worth talking about and the best adventurers are great storytellers. This essential link between literature and adventure was also emphasized by Paul Zweig. "Adventure and storytelling have always gone hand in hand. The great adventurers have not only been great doers, they have been great talkers, like Odysseus returning from the magic countries with his essential tale, or Gilgamesh engraving his adventures on a stone tablet."[15]

Heintje Limba has this essential gift in order to make him complete as the consummate adventurer. He tells hunting stories when he gets older and his life becomes slower, while earlier, when he wandered along Buru's coasts with the captain, the two men listened many an evening to the stories told by old Alfuran chiefs around smoky fires. In a subsequent autobiographical text Beb Vuyk emphasized that joy of going up and down the coast of the island when "in every *kampong* [there] were people who could tell stories" (439, 435). Listening to tales about hunting, drinking, strange events, and also to tales about work, she realized that the origin of literature was "the story, the event, the anecdote told by one [person] about another." And whereas in her youth she had experienced the adventure of life by proxy from books (similar to the character in her story "Way Baroe")[16] she lived the tale in reality in the Indies. There she felt privileged to experience such a life as "a book that originated directly from the reality of life" (436).

After this return to the origins of literature, she felt like writing again and her work became, in her own words, "romantic and realistic at the same time. No longer the romanticism of the imagination, but that of immediate reality" (439). This was possible because reality was still romance, as it had been for the early mariners and travelers. One must remember that from a European point of view, ordinary life in the tropics was extraordinary. To be able to report a quotidian detail as the following is incredible: "a giant snakeskin hangs drying in the wind; it's twenty feet long and almost four feet wide in the middle."[17]

In the introduction to his collection of tales *Within the Tides*, Joseph Conrad provides us with his own evaluation of this same contradiction, and he does so in terms remarkably similar to Beb Vuyk's.

> I am speaking here of romanticism in relation to life, not of romanticism in relation to imaginative literature, which, in its early days, was associated simply with medieval subjects, or, at any rate, with subjects sought for in a remote past. My subjects are not medieval and I have a natural right to them because my past is very much my own. If their course lie out of the beaten path of organized social life, it is, perhaps, because I myself did in a sort break away from it early in obedience to an impulse which must have been very genuine since it has sustained me through all the dangers of disillusion. But that origin of my literary work was very far from giving a larger scope to my imagination. On the contrary, the mere fact of dealing with matters outside the general run of everyday experience laid me under the obligation of a more scrupulous fidelity to the truth of my own sensations. The problem was to make familiar things credible. To do that I had to create for them, to reproduce for them, to envelop them in their proper atmosphere of actuality.[18]

Beb Vuyk's "problem," too, was "to make unfamiliar things credible." She did this by enlisting the aid of adventure literature because it allows even the most incredible events to be part of the narrative norm. That is its sustenance and its lifeblood.

In 1893, Robert Louis Stevenson wrote Sidney Colvin about his dissatisfaction with his novella *The Ebb Tide:* "there seems such a veil of words over it; and I like more and more naked writing; and yet sometimes one has a longing for full colour and there comes the veil again."[19] It seems understandable that incredible events and places would ask for grandiose prose, matching hyperbolic style to hyperbolic event. And as Paul Zweig notes, such "a veil of words" was indeed used by writers like Conrad, T. E. Lawrence, and Charles Doughty. These modern writers of adventure literature "tell tales of splendid courage and exotic actions in a style which secretes complexity and slowness, until the actions recede and become a background for the elaborate frescoes of style."[20]

This is not the case with Beb Vuyk. Her style is "naked," sober, and scrupulous, which is not to say that it is a natural style, as inevitably artless and candid as that of the early books of travel. Vuyk's naked style is a deliberate technique meant to convey a particular vision. There is an intentional restraint in her work that allows the text to present a greater range of symbolic possibilities instead of clouding the reader's perception with a gorgeous veil of words. Beb Vuyk would agree with Stevenson's outcry from 1883 that "there is but one art, to omit. O if I knew how to omit, I would ask no other knowledge. A man who knew how to omit would make an Iliad of a daily paper   . He learns it in the crystallization of daydreams; in changing, not copying fact."[21] And Beb Vuyk did so and fashioned a small epic out of a modest life on a remote island in the Indies. Her own achievement is best expressed by a comment she made about the way an ordinary man told her about his sick child. "He tells the story in simple words that hide the emotion and transform this particular case to an instance of universal fate."

There remains one final paradox. Surely Paul Zweig is correct when he acknowledges that, in a general sense, adventure literature is "unrelentingly masculine," that it "is a form of initiation into the emperion of the masculine." But Zweig also recognizes the paradox that, though this may be true, the adventurer as well is subject "to the enveloping influence of the feminine which haunts adventure tales in subtle but definite ways."[22]

At first one gets the feeling that Beb Vuyk also wanted to be a member of that emperion. Willem Walraven—another fine writer of Dutch colonial literature, who knew Vuyk in Java—mentions that she told him that as a child she wanted to be a boy.[23] In a subsequent biographical text Vuyk admits that she longed for male friendship because "men are truer and simpler in their relationships among themselves" (435), and dreamt of becoming a "ship's captain or forester, planter or governor" (432). She wrote about such men at the beginning of the present book: men like the captain and Heintje Limba, ennobled by "the bond between two men who fight a lonely battle, back to back."

Her admiration for men like these did not diminish but, it seems to me, Beb Vuyk subtly altered the tenor of the adventure tale until she showed that the generative power of woman is victorious in life's ultimate adventure: the confrontation with death. She did not accomplish this rather unique inversion of the genre in a strident fashion, but rather insinuated it by means of the cunning composure of her style. Perhaps this was possible because, as Zweig points out, the modern development of the tale of adventure has "displaced the substance of adventure inward" and is now created on the basis of "the interior rhythm which the adventurer imposed upon the world of his experience."[24] And when it is said that adventure alone seems capable of "restoring values which have been worn thin by domesticity" —because, after all, adventure deals with life in extremis—then gender turns out to be quite irrelevant. Due to this shift in emphasis "adventure will no longer be a form of travel literature, but of autobiography."

Beb Vuyk has always made it clear that most of her work is autobiographical. Texts such as *The Last House in the World*, "Journal of a *Prao* Voyage," "My Grandmothers" ("Mijn grootmoeders"), and "Fulfillment and Return" are entirely autobiographical, and in most of her other work the autobiographical element is only slightly altered to suit aesthetic requirements. When one reads about Vuyk's youth and family, one would think that the masculine world would have the strongest influence. Her paternal grandfather sailed to Java around the middle of the nineteenth century and did not return until forty years later.[25] He worked on coffee and tobacco plantations until he was independent and responsible only to himself (425). He married a woman from Madura and had two sons and a daughter. Vuyk's own father was born in the Indies but came to Holland when he was five and never saw his country of origin again. He became a shipbuilder in Rotterdam, where Beb Vuyk was born in 1905. Both the paternal and maternal lines of her family were connected with the sea in one way or another, and it would seem that such escape routes as adventure, the Indies, and the sea would be associated with men.

Gradually the opposite emerges as the truth. The men turned out to be closed and silent people who were estranged and wounded by a loneliness that knew no cure. Death, too, was associated with men. As a small girl she once saw two men digging up graves and the remains were not "the scraped-clean, bleached white and shiny skeleton of a doctor's office, but brown, with remnants of rotting flesh and withered hair." Another metonym for death were her great-grandfather's false teeth which his wife kept in a brown chest in the attic. It is not surprising that by extension death is "brown and does not move" and that it would assume the outline of her great-grandfather not as a ghost but as an aggregate of chunks of bone and filthy flesh (430–31, 425).

On the other hand, the women in her family came to assert themselves as symbols of defiance, courage, and the Indies. The daughter of her paternal great-grandfather and his Maduran wife died young. There was a picture of this aunt whom Vuyk had never met. She was told that people from Madura were trustworthy but also quick to draw a knife because they were proud and easily insulted, "I began to identify with [both] the portrait of this aunt who had died so young, and with the unknown, reliable, proud grandmother who was so quick to pull a knife" (426). This identification across the ages was emphasized when Beb Vuyk realized from the reaction of the jeering and pestering students that she looked different from other Dutch children, that she had the alien and uncommon looks of her Maduran grandmother. This physical fact isolated her even more. But the sphere of feminine influence won out, and the world of the tropics, with its life of adventure, came to be identified with her grandmothers. "Java, Sumatra, the jungles of Borneo, the distant islands of the Moluccas. The worlds of my two grandmothers began to come together; strange and adventurous and at the same time one's own as a far and familiar fatherland" (433). And though she was still a girl, this discovery made her determined to become a writer and go to the Indies.

The alliance of woman, Indies, and adventure extended further into her life. On her way to the Indies in the fall of 1929 she

met a man by the name of De Willigen whom she married. He
was of mixed parentage: his father was a retired officer in the
Dutch colonial army and his mother was an Indonesian from the
island of Ambon in the Moluccas. In 1930 Vuyk made her literary
debut and two years later she married and moved with her husband to a tea plantation in central Java. Six months later he lost
his job due to the Depression. This experience is faithfully described in her first novel *Thousand Islands.* In 1933 the De Willigens moved to Buru and lived the life narrated in the present
work.

It is curious that there are few clear and direct references to her
husband in her work. One does get the sense of a reliable presence whom Vuyk asserts is "sensitive, true, and pure" (437), but
it is in Walraven that one finds De Willigen described as a physically and emotionally strong man, one who is intelligent, a
woodsman, and a hunter.[26] He was the model for Carl van Waer-
laarden in *Thousand Islands,* for Hajo in *Bara's Wood (Het hout van
Bara,* 1947), probably for Hermans in the story "Story of an On-
looker" ("Verhaal van een toeschouwer"), and he is, of course,
Fernand De Willigen in *The Last House in the World.* One does not
feel that he is ever fully realized as a character, but rather that he
is an accumulation of abstract qualities that, though admirable,
fail to assume a memorable shape.

The eight years Beb Vuyk spent on Buru were the happiest of
her life (440); but a change came soon, a change that was drastic
and irrevocable both for her own life and for her generation. In
1940 she was in Java enjoying a respite from Buru, the island that
Walraven liked to say was inhabited by "ex-cannibals and con-
sumers of dogs."[27] Holland fell to the Nazis in May 1940, and the
Dutch East Indies surrendered to the Japanese in March 1942. For
six weeks Beb Vuyk was a prisoner of the Kempeitai, the Japanese
equivalent of the Gestapo, and she spent the rest of the war in
concentration camps. Her husband was also imprisoned and
wound up in Thailand. After the war they experienced the horrors of Indonesia's struggle for independence, and when it became a sovereign state, Beb Vuyk and her husband assumed Indonesian citizenship, which in those days represented an act of
courage. In the beginning of 1958 she went back to Holland and
has lived there ever since.

A better world died in the Second World War. Within half a
decade an era had vanished with such swift inevitability that by

1945 it seemed a distant and antique epoch as remote as the Middle Ages. Hannah Arendt had a similar feeling about this break that was so ruthless and final that one can only call it a historical amputation. "We can hardly avoid looking at this close and yet distant past with the too-wise eyes of those who know the end of the story in advance, who know it led to an almost complete break in the continuous flow of Western history as we had known it for more than two thousand years. But we must also admit a certain nostalgia for what can still be called a 'golden age of security,' for an age, that is, when even horrors were still marked by a certain moderation and controlled by respectability, and therefore could be related to the general appearance of sanity. In other words, no matter how close to us this past is, we are perfectly aware that our experience of concentration camps and death factories is as remote from its general atmosphere as it is from any other period in Western history."[28]

Beb Vuyk understood this amputation very well. Her style changed in order to register it. This is not to say that her literary mastery was diminished, but that the content and tone changed in order to accommodate the horror of a world where the *buaja* not only flourished but was far more fearful than she could ever have expected. When a day was no longer an adventure but a contest for survival, the hard life on Buru suddenly looked idyllic. Whereas *The Last House in the World* had been written from a "surfeit" of joy, her subsequent work dealt with "the fear of human cruelty that had penetrated into one's own life" (444). Her work became shorter, far more temperate and extrinsic, and written in a style of "tense resignation" ("gespannen gelatenheid," 445).

Although the literature written about events that occurred in the Indies after 1940 does not properly belong to the genre of "colonial literature," it should be mentioned that those few ruthless years severed a world from its former inhabitants with such violence and finality that it gained an incommensurate vitality as ghostly as a phantom limb. By 1945 Beb Vuyk's ante-bellum life on Buru was suddenly much closer to that of the mariners and travelers of the seventeenth century than it ever could have been before the war. This strange and fearful perspective foreshortened the immediate past and made it seem to be on the same plane as what was heretofore considered a dim and distant time. But that augmentation had at least the consolation of myth. The legacy of the Second World War and what came after it can never grant such comfort. It is the reality we still live today.

I

When my husband was still a little boy, his father, a retired officer, bought fifty stills for manufacturing *kajuputih* oil on the island
of Buru[1] with Heintje Limba, a young Ambonese,[2] a great hunter, a tremendous drinker, and a reckless adventurer. In those
days the KPM[3] ship docked once every two months at Kajeli, the
old settlement of the Company, which at that time was still the
seat of government and also the home of a missionary. But the *kajuputih* concession, called Batuboi, was further down the bay,
four strenuous hours of paddling,[4] even if you had the current
and wind with you. It was a vast terrain, about two thousand
acres of steep hills covered with light green *kajuputih* shrubs; a
stony, barren landscape that, *tjot* after *tjot*, became higher and
bluer toward the interior, until it merged with the mountains of
Central Buru. A wide river basin, overgrown with *alang-alang*[5] as
tall as a man, divided the concession into two halves. A narrow
strip of forest along the banks of the *kali*, small clumps of trees in
the small valleys branching off to the side, and for the rest nothing but hot fields of *alang-alang* between the steep, bald hills.
From the farthest still, Tubahoni, that marked the boundary in
the west, it stretched for twenty-four miles to the stinking tidal
forests on the shore, hardly accessible because of the mud and the
crocodiles.

Scattered all over the hills were the stills, primitive distillation
machines to extract the fragrant green *kajuputih* oil. In order to
strain the oil and pack it for shipping, a place had to be found

house. Such a place could not be found in rugged Batuboi, with its wide edge of mangrove forests, its many *agas* and mosquitoes, but an hour's rowing away was the *kampong* Namlea, diagonally across the bay, on a level strip of land along the coast. They hacked a clearing in the tidal forest of a small *tandjong* that jutted out into the water, and built a temporary iron *gudang* and a primitive house of *atap*. The shore curved outward here, and *praos* could always find safe anchorage behind this *tandjong*, even during the time of year when the wind blew straight into the bay and produced the violent surf, the feared *air putih*.[6]

The beach was wide and white and without mangroves. *Ketapang*[7] trees with leaves that turned red with the change of monsoons provided the afternoon with shade. The soil was poor, but not stony, and the wind kept the trees and the flowers alive even in the hottest hours. It was the most beautiful spot of Kajeli Bay, and the healthiest: no *agas* and no mosquitoes, the wind from the sea by day and the "sibu-sibu," the wind that blows from the interior, to cool the nights. But on moonlit nights the *suanggis*[8] danced on the beach, and the *suanggis* are the courtesans among the hundred ghosts of the Moluccas, which is why the local population held the place in ill repute. Old Captain De Willigen and Heintje Limba drove the forest and the *suanggis* back with their axes and machetes, and built their headquarters there. This was where they received native chiefs and Chinese merchants for endless conferences, and it was from this spot that they shipped the first big lots of *kajuputih* oil, while the KPM ship that had come this far to pick up the new cargo rode at anchor off the *tandjong* and sent its *praos* to the primitive pier. And on this spot their friendship grew beyond a master-servant relationship, to one no longer admitting a difference between two races, one that became something far nobler and otherworldly: the bond between two men who fight a lonely battle, back to back. When the house and the surroundings had become a little more livable, Captain De Willigen went back to Ambon, where he sent his two eldest sons to Java and took his wife and eight small children to Namlea. It was a child's paradise. The primitive house and the new yard hacked out of the tidal forest looked more like a bivouac than a permanent home. Some corn and vegetables had been planted behind the house, and deer were shot there when they made a detour to nibble at the young shoots while they were on their way to the sea for their afternoon dip. Sometimes the dogs would bark loudly when they chased a wild boar straight through the seed beds.

The *kampong* Namlea consisted of five or six houses, and the road to it led through a swamp that was dangerous because of crocodiles. There was no *pasar* and even the usual staple foods like rice, *pisang,* and coconuts were not regularly available. They caught their own fish and they hunted deer and pigs in the hot hills.

They lived a real pioneer existence. Everything had to be tried out and accomplished with little money, many children, many worries, and tremendous courage. Fruit trees were planted, vegetables sown, and a coconut grove was begun. The children went looking for driftwood along the beach and built houses and fortresses in the forest. They went swimming in the shallow water between the reefs, and looked for mussels for lunch when the hunters had failed and the fish traps were empty. Later, when a permanent dwelling was being constructed, they helped build it. They'd row a *prao* loaded with pieces of coral from the reef to the beach, collect shells to be burnt down to lime, and braid threads of *aren*[9] into ropes that would tie the *atap* to the rafters. They got their education in the afternoon and during the long tropical evenings.

After two years my husband was sent to Surabaja[10] to go to school. But throughout the years, in the school and later, when he worked as a planter in eastern and central Java, he kept longing for far-off Buru, for the house they had built themselves, for the gardens they had planted, for a life white from loneliness but completely independent.

Business on Buru was very good during the war, but it was followed by a recession and a big blow at the same time: a case of neglected diabetes made it mandatory for the old man to go live on Java. They held an auction, the *kajuputih* concession was leased to an Arab and the captain took his wife and the remaining children to Java. The big yard, already shaded by many fruit trees, the house, and the *gudang* were left in the care of Heintje who had been given the yield of a few stills to keep everything in working order.

The old man died and the children went to school and were scattered in various professions all over the Indies. Those were the good years. There was money to be made everywhere and it would have been foolish to risk a good and safe existence for an adventure on a remote island.

The tide turned once again. We had been married five months when the blow came that changed our lives completely. It was the usual story in those days: the oldest employee with the top salary was kicked out to be replaced by a youngster who they could pay a pittance of a hundred guilders. We were even treated rather well when compared to others: they gave us three months salary, paid the vacation bonus, and gave us half the passage back to Europe.

We spent a whole night making plans, scared and excited and very worried about the baby that was still to be born, but also secretly elated with the great adventure of our lives. We didn't have to talk about it very much. We had been fantasizing about something that would happen out of the blue to make us rich and allow us to go to Buru. And now, just when we least wanted or expected it, we hadn't exactly become rich but at least we'd been freed to a certain extent. Life, which seemed to have been channeled between promotions, bonuses, and salary increases, burst the dikes, broke loose like a *bandjir* and turned into a river that flowed unfettered between banks covered with wild forests.

We exchanged our passage to Europe for tickets to Buru. We withdrew our money from the bank, sold our furniture, and stocked up on a huge supply of provisions and all kinds of other things. We took our leave of civilization, of electricity and refrigerators, of taxis and cinemas, milk, meat, and vegetables on demand, in order to go back to the most primitive form of life: homemade bread and homegrown vegetables, furniture you've made yourself and fish you've caught yourself, back to illness and the fear of a most painful death, with the nearest doctor a day's sail away and available only once every two weeks.

II

We begin our journey and we are happy that we are able to leave. We go on board ship and a hidden fear travels with us. Two months in a big city without a job have made us timid and embarrassingly humble, and we are inclined to think that all people with a decent salary and a good position are superior to us.

My husband can escape from this pressure: he is going home,

to a land he loves, where all troubles will end. He can be happy like someone who has finally managed to escape. I am not more of a coward than he is, but there is a fear I don't dare talk about. Sometimes I cry about the child, the child that has to be a son and who will be named after Andersen, Hans Christiaan.

I often think of the emigrants I saw as a child, passing through Rotterdam on their way to the harbor and America. And now I am traveling like them: cut loose, confused, dazed from anticipation. Our friends get out an atlas when they hear we are going to Buru. After a long search they discover the island to the west of Ambon, with the deep bay on the northern coast, where Namlea is. The journey will take ten days from Priok,[11] and we'll spend three of them in Macassar,[12] waiting for our connecting ship.

The first port of call in the Moluccas is Leksula.[13] It has high wooded mountains and a narrow shiny beach with small overgrown islands in the white surf, remnants of a broken coast. The houses lie half buried under the abundant green, and a fleet of small *praos* comes shooting toward us even before both anchors have rattled down. The passengers who traveled on deck jump on the swaying companion ladder with all their *barang*[14] packed in cans and bundles. The rapid Malay of Ambon, larded with Portuguese and Dutch words, hits us like a surf of sounds.

The first mate comes to ask if we want to go ashore with him, and I jump for the first time on the swaying companion ladder and into the launch that rises and falls on the waves.

Copra lies stacked in bags in the middle of the beach. Three Chinese are talking next to it, and a group of children, thin and yellow with bellies swollen from malaria, also hang around there. The KPM brings its own coolies along in the Moluccas: *badjos*,[15] small solid Macassars. With heavy bags against their necks they come down the sloping beach at a trot, and into the sea that comes up to their waists where the loading *prao* heaves up and down. We walk around a bit in the *kampong*.

Outrigger *praos* have been dragged on the beach and are lying, clumsy as crabs, under the *ketapang* trees that are shedding their leaves. The houses stand on the left-hand side of the road, the *gaba-gaba*[16] is bleached with age and the *atap* on the roofs looks frayed and disheveled: an abandoned, poverty-stricken *kampong* built on sandy, sterile soil. The road beyond runs through neglected coconut plantations, alongside a small pool that, overgrown with weeds, stinks of crocodiles. A coconut tree has fallen straight across the path. It has been completely hollowed out by beetles. We walk back along the beach, looking for small shells and red organ-pipe coral.[17] My husband skims a piece of *karang*[18] across the water, and says cheerfully: "Namlea is like this."

This is the last country in the world, not even a country really, but loosely scattered islands thrown carelessly into a blue, burning sea. Withered and desolate and gnawed by decay.

Two days latter we arrive in Kajeli Bay in the late afternoon. When we wake up, we find ourselves sailing along the low coast of Tandjong Kajuputih,[19] which juts out far into the sea. On the other side the Moluccan Sea is smooth as a pond, its color a rapidly changing, transparent green. Then Tandjong Karbouw catches our attention, a high green shore with scattered *kajuputih* trees, gray and slim as poplars—a Dutch dike, somewhere between Arnhem and Nijmegen on a warm drizzly afternoon in August.

It rained that morning. A watery sun shines on the mangrove forests along the beach on the other side of the bay. Behind them the steep hills seem green and lovely because of a great deal of young grass.

At this point the bay curves inward on both sides, and Namlea appears on a small plain along the coast, just before the high shore rises and breaks off in the hills. The hatches are opened and the derricks are turned toward shore. The journey is over, the anchor clanks down for the last time.

Uncle Heintje arrives with the first *prao:* a meager, already aging man. He addresses my husband by his old name from childhood, "Little Brother Sinjo,"[20] and he calls me "Nonnie." He is visibly moved. The business has been idle for twelve years and he has rented the house to others. But now, at last, one of the ten children has come back to his old plantation to stay. He tells us about the situation in Namlea. The price of *kajuputih* keeps going down and Bader has shamefully neglected the concession. He is always fighting with his still workers and almost every year a part of the foliage is burned. This looks like a bad start, but it hardly matters. The broad, vivacious water, with the light green land around it. Leksula was dead, here everything is alive. We are going to live here with our little boy. We are going to work here. The ship stays in the stream and we are taken ashore in the launch that also pulls the *praos* with our *barang*. People are pushing and shoving on the pier and around an iron shed. The government office is behind a magnificent *waringin* tree,[21] with a big Chinese *toko* on one side of it and the KPM *gudang* on the other. What a difference between this thriving place and desolate Leksula.

This is the one ship per month from Macassar that drops anchor in Namlea. It carries the goods that have been ordered, important mail, money shipments, the latest news, and business associates on their way to Ternate.[22] That's why every Chinese has put on a jacket, the Arabs wear their finest embroidered fez, the Ambonese parade around in stiffly pressed trousers, and the Binongkos[23] in brightly checkered *sarongs*. Even those who have nothing better to wear than a torn pair of pants or a dirty *kain* still flock to the customs shed to enjoy the one-day party that is celebrated once every month.

Heintje stays behind to look after our *barang*. The way home runs along the beach between *praos* pulled up on the beach, large Chinese *tokos* and small *kampong* houses. There used to be a swamp here but the government drained it, with the result that the mosquitoes decreased and human beings increased. The new *kampong* has been built up almost to the *tandjong*. The district officer's large white house is built a little inland, past the *kampong*, at the bottom of the hill. Its front lawn slopes slowly down to the beach and behind it coconut trees move against a background of dark *manga*[24] green, the coast bends outward to form a small cape.

We walk quickly along a narrow sandy path between coconut trees and *melati*[25] bushes. We can see the roof now, and soon the front of the house itself.

Enggeh and her children stand waiting for us on the big porch. They're all wearing stiffly pressed clothes. We're home.

A brown house, brown like the earth, and a green garden, alive and moving because of the wind. A sandy path and a wide bright beach under low *antjak*[26] trees and the red foliage of the *ketapangs*. On the other side is a dark line of mangrove forests, on the shore behind the exhausting blue water, and then the green and blue of the mountains behind it.

The KPM ship has drifted somewhat, and now lies athwart our *tandjong*. We can hear the winches rattle. The launch zips back and forth between the ship and the beach. Then we hear the first whistle. A heavily laden *koleh-koleh*[27] is slowly paddled to our beach. The *prao* runs aground in the sand. A few Binongkos appear from the backyard to help Uncle Heintje unload. Crates are carried into the house and opened. Yesterday, when we were in

Ambon, we bought a cupboard for storing food, and a table and four chairs of unpainted wood. Our bed is put together in the small bedroom. We fill the oil lamps and pump up the blue flame until it becomes a bright white light. And the work goes on.

Enggeh has prepared the evening meal and comes to announce that it's ready. Dry rice with fresh fried fish and *pisang goreng*.

We hear the ship's whistle for the third time, a low and melancholy sound over the dark water. The rattan chairs we brought along as deck chairs have been put out on the lawn beside the house. We smoke a cigarette there after our meal and listen to the rattling of the anchor chain when it is pulled up.

Enggeh and Heintje are squatting next to us. They ask about the old lady, Nonnie Marie, and Sinjo Frank, about all the children who lived and played in this house.

The ship is leaving now. We watch the red lights on top of its masts slowly disappear behind our own trees. Because we have come home to the last house in the world, we have run into port forever in a distant bay.

III

The next morning we are awake with the first light of dawn. The sun rises behind us, above the Moluccan Sea. The water in the bay is still gray, but the first light is falling on the mangrove forests on the other side, which look a brighter green and seem very close.

For five months I lived high up in the mountains of central Java, where we looked up to other slopes from our own, all squeezed in a ring of mountains. I have escaped from their coercion forever and I shall look every day now across this living, vivacious water. We have a house here to give us shelter, a garden to feed us, a bay where fish jump out of the water in glittering arcs, and hills where deer run free and fast. Only those who know the loneliness of poverty in a rich and densely populated country feel that they have escaped and finally achieved security outside the dwellings of men.

Enggeh brings the morning coffee. Willem, her oldest son, begins to sweep the yard. The big bamboo broom makes the fallen leaves of the breadfruit trees[28] crackle like paper that is ripped up.

We walk around the house under the big *manga* trees. Crabs

run away from us; they have undermined the entire yard around the front porch with their holes. They are horrible animals, little more than a head and claws, faintly orange in color and incredibly fast. They are completely out of reach in their holes which, dug several yards under the ground, branch off into corridors in all directions. Neither flowers nor grass can grow on the front lawn anymore, and the crabs have undermined the foundation of the house on one side, making it tilt a little.

Twelve years is a long time for a house to last in the tropics. The strong roots of the big *manga* tree have grown up through the foundation and burst through the floor in two places. An earthquake tore the bathroom sink and white ants are eating away at the *gaba-gaba*. But Heintje has made a new *atap* roof and changed the *gaba-gaba* of the walls, and now the house stands brown and broad and safe on the beach, almost untouched. The windows are small, high, and narrow, with sturdy shutters and no glass. They dim the light in the rooms and fill the house with a cool twilight which, in practical terms, is a bit of a nuisance. But the dark inner hallway leads to a big open gallery that has only a back wall built of *gaba-gaba*. The side walls are no more than low cement walls, with ironwood poles every six feet to support the roof. It is light in here and open, and a cool wind blows despite the heat.

Gaba-gaba is the midrib of the leaf of the sago palm.[29] The leaves, which are more than ten feet long, are cut down and stripped until only the thick midrib is left, about two inches wide and between twelve and fifteen feet long. This is then dried until it begins to turn brown. In order to use the *gaba-gaba* it is cut in strips of equal length and, pressed together by means of bamboo pegs, it is fitted into wooden frames until it is a shiny brown wall that is tight and compact. It won't let in wind or rain but it will bend when an earthquake shakes the houses. The foundation of the house is made of coralstone, joined together with cement. The low wall, less than three feet high, that supports the *gaba-gaba*, is made of the same material. The attic is also made of *gaba-gaba*, and it is topped by an *atap* roof, with a gentle slope to it.

Atap is also made from the sago palm. The part of the leaves that is stripped from the midrib in making *gaba-gaba* is not thrown away but is carefully folded around bamboo slats, about six feet long, and tied together with rattan thread. When they are put tightly over each other and tied with *aren* fiber, these strips of leaf make a cool, brown roof.

As soon as breakfast is over we go with Heintje to inspect the garden before the day gets too hot. Over the years the trees have changed more than the house. They used to have slender trunks but now the house stands in the shadow of their ample foliage. They were planted too close to each other, and for years they have been waging a continuous battle, without battle cries or the sound of blows, visible only in the mutilations that have occurred during their growth. A coconut tree bends its trunk like a gas pipe and the big *lubi-lubi*[30] has grown only to one side, pushed away by an enormous *sukun*.[31] Soursop and papaya are pining away under the heavy shadow of the *manga,* but the *djeruk nipis*[32] on the beach stands in full sunlight, with a harvest of small yellow lemons scattered all around. We walk deeper into the garden, although "garden" is too civilized a concept for this almost worthless, impenetrable wilderness. Heintje has to use his *parang* to hack a path through the *alang-alang* that reaches up to our waist. We keep making new discoveries. Everything is growing helter-skelter, cloves and nutmeg, *kapok,*[33] *pisang,* lemons, and pomegranate.

Corn has been sowed in a clearing. A few bushes with *terongs*[34] grow along its edge, and a few meager beans grow in the middle of the corn. There are no other vegetables in our garden. There is a small field of *kasbi*[35] a little further on, and *pisang* and coconut trees are growing so closely together on the other side of the *tan-djong* that we can't muster the courage to enter. There's months of work to be done here. Everything has to be hacked open, branches must be pruned, and trees rooted out. Our first priority is a plot to sow some vegetables, and on the way back we keep our eye out for a suitable clearing.

We cross a small plot of grass and go to the sheet-metal *gudang.* It still looks in remarkably good condition. Heintje has turned it into a house by adding a porch made of *gaba-gaba* and a kitchen made of *atap.* A big outrigger *prao* lies on the beach in front of the house, the last survivor of a fleet of five that succumbed one after the other. It is damaged and cracked at the edges, full of old scars, but built from long-grained *bintangun*[36] wood and therefore still seaworthy for years to come. We sit on Heintje's front porch on small low bamboo stools. The chickens run away from us, but a very old dog comes to rub its head against our knees.

"He was still small when Tuan Captain De Willigen and his wife and children went away," says Heintje slowly, in a flat voice.

Heintje's life is divided into sharp divisions: his youth on Ambon, his work with the Tuan Captain, and the lonely years after that. This is a new beginning for him.

He was a young man, hardly twenty, when he struck down his opponent in a fight in Rumahtiga[37] and was forced to run. Captain De Willigen gave him a job. Heintje heard later that his opponent had not been killed, but he did not go back to Ambon. He belonged to a well-to-do Ambonese family, and he owned *dusuns*[38] and a family home in Rumahtiga where life moved at a slower pace. Boil sugar and beat sago, fish on a moonlit night when the tide was rising, and for amusement church on Sunday and the endless family quarrels and *kampong* gossip. It was a life fit only for the old and those born lazy. Sometimes that life would burst open in a drunken feast and a bloody brawl. The best of the young people signed up with the Company and fought in Atjeh[39] to escape the apathy of a country where sago grew in abundance and working made no sense.

But before Heintje thought of signing up he had finished his last fight and had found his goal when he was on the run. Together with the Tuan Captain he roamed along the coast of Northern Buru, as far as Bara.[40] They slept in a damp bivouac in the woods, on the bright beaches, or in the leaky houses of the Alfurs.[41] They shot deer, driven to them by the beaters who shouted at the top of their lungs, cut the red meat into thin strips to dry it until it became *dendeng,* and sat around smoky fires and listened to an old Alfuran chief tell them how his ancestors used to hunt up and down the slopes before the Company sent its ships, and long before Ternate sent its conquerors.

Heintje learned to respect the faith of his Muslim brothers and did not eat pork in their *kampongs*. He also learned to respect the small *pemali* houses of the pagan Alfurs, where they kept the skulls of their ancestors in bowls of Chinese porcelain and voc-blue. Those were the years before the district officers had enough courage to go on an inspection tour here and exchange the bowls for worthless presents and a friendship that would soon prove worthless too.

Heintje got to know all the roads that went up into the hills from the bay. He bought *kajuputih* oil from the Chinese retailers, helped to set up a coconut plantation on Butonleon, supervised the still workers on the concession, and directed the fire fighters when fire threatened the big plain. He no longer had to drink away his boredom or exhaust his strength in useless fights.

Later, when the journeys were restricted between the *tandjong* and Batuboi, he married Enggeh, and their children grew up together with the De Willigen boys who saw in him the living hero from their books. He was Masterman Ready, he was Rob Roy, and he was the Last of the Mohicans. They looked with awe at his long-barreled muzzle loader, his bullets, his powder horn, and the big hunting knife he used to finish off the wild pigs he shot.

By day he used to shoot crocodiles where they lay sunning themselves on the dry sandbanks when the tide went out, while at night he'd shoot at the red light of their eyes between the roots of the mangroves. He caught the glittering, white *bubaras*[42] that snapped at the shiny rooster's feather and swallowed the steel hook in the foaming wake of a fast sailing *prao*. Sometimes he only pulled in the head, because the jaws of a shark had struck faster than his hand had been able to reel in. He was the fastest hunter and the most skillful fisherman, but he also knew the latest news as it traveled from *kampong* to *kampong*, grievances, intrigues, and the evil that is about at night.

But something of the old uselessness returned when Tuan Captain went away and the house stood empty. There was enough to eat and some money to buy clothes, the sun provided warmth, the moon, light, and the earth, sago. His life slowed down and he began to tell his children about his old hunting trips. He had not been part of the *kampong* for years, and the *tandjong* had become an abandoned fortress, with just one old soldier standing guard for nothing.

Then we came and now we sit on his small front porch. "Sinjo," says the old man both familiarly and respectfully. "Heintje," says my husband, with both respect and the old love of a child in his voice.

The yard around us has almost been reconquered by the wilderness. The red climbing roses on the front porch are dead and beetles have got to the coconut trees in front of the house.

None of it matters. The yard could have been better kept by European standards, and it could have been exploited to greater advantage. What difference does it make?

Heintje has lived all those years for this one moment. The solution has arrived and work can begin once again.

IV

We have two months before we have to go to Ambon because of the boy. We have to furnish the house, clear the garden, plant vegetables, settle with Bader, and investigate the state of the *kajuputih* business. Bader is in the back woods and will be back in a week. His son pretends not to know anything about the business in Batuboi. We start getting our house in order.

We were not able to take our own furniture along, because the KMP freight charges were incredibly high. We did pack our glass and stoneware in crates, along with our kitchen utensils, a bed, and a few odds and ends. We took some reed chairs along to use as deck chairs and in Ambon we bought a table, four chairs, and a cupboard. But we already had given the matter of furniture some thought while we were still on Java, and had had crates built which could be easily transformed into open cabinets.

We ask a simple *tukang* for help. There are three of them, which seems rather a lot for a small place like Namlea, but it is far too few because they work only in extremely rare instances, when they can't get out of it.

Taxes were collected last month and the corn is yellow and heavy in the beach *kebons;* there really is no need to earn anything at all.

So Jesaja and Obednego won't work, but Wimpie Tasisa is Heintje's brother-in-law and he comes to our aid out of a sense of obligation. He only knows the roughest kind of work, but my husband teaches him how to join wood and works with him all day long. Once Wimpie is working, it goes quickly, but the problem is to get him to start every day, because he is a fanatic hunter who is used to tracking game at night and sleeping by day. But Heintje has paid his most pressing bills twice already, and Wimpie tries to get up on time, five days in a row. And by then the cupboards are finished and he can go back to his old ways.

We paint the table, the chairs, and the cupboards a shiny red, transforming them into a dining-room set. We order a writing desk from the Chinese carpenter. We need it badly and it will be done in a month. The *tukang* is a tall Chinese, yellow and emaciated from smoking opium. He can't work without his evening pipe, and every week he comes to beg for a small advance. When he finally delivers our desk half a year later, the advances have equaled his fee.

Five Binongkos live in our backyard, in the old coolie quarters. They place their fish traps behind the *tandjong* and haul them up every other day. The water is full of fish here, but it doesn't bring in much money. Hardly anybody buys fish except the three European families and the wives of the Javanese soldiers. It would be ridiculous to spend good money on something you can get yourself without any trouble at all. Fishing doesn't take much time. They throw the *bubus*[43] out at night and dive for them the next morning. Sometimes they have to repair the traps or the old *prao* but they spend most of the day gambling with dice under the lean-to roof of their house. They hawk their fish in the *kampong* in the morning, and in the evening they squat for hours talking and smoking around a smouldering fire of coconut bark, while smoking the remaining fish.

Their leader is La Djanihi, an old still worker who used to work for my father-in-law. One evening he squats down next to us and tells us about life as it used to be among the Tuan Captain's stills. He accuses Bader, the Arab who has been renting the concession, of all kinds of wrongdoings and complains about the price of fish that keeps going down every day. We ask him if he and his four *kontjos* would clean up the yard for us. They show little enthusiasm, even though they are badly off. They discuss the matter for a long time in their own language, until La Djanihi switches back to Malay. They'd much rather go fishing, but in order to help the Sinjo Tandjong,[44] they are willing to take turns working in the garden; every day two of them will work while the other three fish. The next morning two of them start beating down the grass in the backyard. They clean up the coconut tree, cut the dead branches, and crush the ant nests that leave a deep scar in the trunk. They weed the corn, cut down the useless, pink *turie*[45] trees, and remove the weeds that curl around the young *pisang* leaves. We make our own seed beds for the vegetables, and Heintje helps with the *patjolling*.[46] We seed the simplest vegetables: *bajem*,[47] beans, and cucumbers.

And then there is still the problem of domestic help. Heintje's wife helps with the washing and the cooking, but there is a lot to be done. Bread has to be baked, wood cut, charcoal burned, and the yard swept. Her full name is Enggelina Barends. She comes from a quadroon family of liberated slaves who took their master's name after they converted to Christianity. She has lived here for years, right next to the big house, but it doesn't show at all.

She is just as dirty and lazy, and yaks just as much as any other woman in the *kampong*, but she makes great bread, is very loyal, and is tied to us for life.

Willem, the oldest of the four children who are still at home, looks very much like her. He is a dark strong boy, and has gone to school[48] for nine years and has made it to the third grade. He will be home for good next month and I suggest that we train him as a houseboy. We sit down with Heintje one afternoon to talk about it.

Working for pay is a disgrace in the Moluccas. Working for a wage either in a house or in the fields is only done by the descendants of slaves. A free man, who owns his own land, works his *dusun*, beats his sago, and goes fishing. He helps his neighbor build a house, and he will go with another neighbor to boil sugar. He doesn't get paid for that, just his food and at best a share of the harvest or the catch of that day. If he has been to school he will look for a job as a clerk or as a *guru*,[49] and if he is a sturdy man he will sign up as a soldier. But otherwise he stays home, goes fishing in the bay, and beats sago in the forest. It takes three days to crush the marrow of a sago tree and wash the flour out of it, and a family that consists of a husband, a wife, and two children can live on that for a month. There is always fish in the bay, and coconuts and fruit in the yard; red sugar,[50] *kenari* pits,[51] and cloves bring in a few guilders a month to buy coffee, petroleum, and sugar. Working is not a disgrace, but to work for pay for strangers is.

But we live on the same soil, the big house and the *mandur* house are one. Willem will help in our household, just as in a big family all the children help with washing clothes, cooking food, and looking after the yard.

Since he is an *anak piara*,[52] a son of the house, he'll receive food and clothes, and a little pocket money now and then. But because it has only been three years since I left Europe, where all relationships are ruled by money and law, I insist that we open a savings account for Willem and that we deposit something in it every month.

Heintje has to think this over for a moment, before he gives his permission. When he is gone my husband explains: "The old man only approves because he understands that you don't know yet how things are done around here. He feels that every monetary reward is pointless because he knows that he can count on

our help in case of illness, poverty, or death, for all the calamities
of life. That's worth more than a fixed sum every month."

We walk up and down the small path along our house. Evening
rises purple from the ground between the trees. I think: "He be-
longs here and I am a stranger. Or was I so deeply humiliated in
Europe that I am ashamed to accept the help of an ordinary human being?"

V

Some time later visitors begin to stop by, visitors who differ in
color, looks, and social status. There are respectable Arabs, ven-
erable like the patriarchs from a children's Bible, Chinese merchants with ample jackets flapping around their emaciated
opium bodies, and old women from the *kampong* who used to
work for my mother-in-law. She used to help them when their
labor was difficult or when they were seriously ill, and now they
come to tell me about it while sipping sweet coffee and munching
on native cookies. Muslim women wear short *kabajas* and batiked
sarongs.[53] Christian women wear *kabajas* that come down to their
knees, with such long sleeves that the lower part has to be folded
back like a cuff. Respectable people, like the wives of *gurus* and
mantris, wear white *kabajas*, and ordinary folk wear lightly colored
kabajas with a small tip or a little flower. There are special patterns
for men and for women, for Muslims and for Christians.

My in-laws lived on the *tandjong* long before Namlea became an
administrative center and this meant that people came to them
for all their problems. They went anywhere if a child was expected or when somebody was dying. They went to weddings
and funerals. There was no doctor yet, not even a *mantri* nurse.
People came with the wounded after a bloody fight, with old,
neglected wounds, or with overfed crying babies, but they also
came with inheritance problems and land business, or to borrow
money for covering up a deficit (which they never paid back).

They called him Bapak Captain and Tuan Tandjong,[54] and now
they address my husband with Sinjo, the name from his childhood, and they call me Nonnie. Those names stick. We are still
called the "Sinjo and Nonnie Tandjong," and we are known as
such as far away as Ambon. When my husband went to visit the
administration's offices in Ambon, the assistant resident's at-
tendant announced him as "Sinjo Tandjong."

The chiefs also come to visit—the *radjas*[55] of Lilialy and Licela and the *hinolong* of Kubalahin. The *radjas* are the official native administrators, while the *hinolong* is the real chief according to *adat*.[56] At the time when the Company took possession of Buru, the island was still some sort of colony of Ternate. The Sultan of Ternate had his representatives, Muslims who levied a tax on the pagan population. As usual, the Company tried as much as possible to keep things as they had always been, and it looked upon those representatives as the local chiefs of the population, even though they were really strangers in terms of both religion and origin. Things remained that way for three hundred years. The Alfurs along the northern coast mixed with adventurers who had come from elsewhere, such as the Binongkos and Sulanese, and became Muslims. On the southern coast, where the Utrecht Mission[57] is still active, many have converted to Christianity. But in central Buru, in the mountains around Rana Wakolo, live the Hindus and the pagans, and the *radjas* have little power there in questions of *adat*.

One of those old Hindu chiefs was a friend of my father-in-law. His successor remembered the old relationship and informs us of his impending visit. His messenger is a scabby fellow with a mass of wild hair, wearing a torn, dirty shirt, but he bears himself with dignity and moves nobly and quickly like a stag. He delivers a letter: a piece of rattan with eighteen knots in it. Heintje explains its meaning. We have to untie one knot every day, and we can expect the *hinolong*'s visit when all eighteen knots are gone. And so, on the eighteenth day, we send the *prao* to the other coast to go get the great man, because the Alfurs are mountain people and don't own any boats.

I have a lot of coffee ready and have made *wadjik,* a kind of glutinous rice mixed with coconut milk and boiled with red sugar. The next morning the *prao* comes in with the tide. The *hinolong* sits in the back, a tall man with one eye who is naked except for a pair of dirty shorts. He quickly gets out of the *prao* and walks to the *gudang* without looking at us. Behind the door he changes into his ceremonial robes, a pair of pajama trousers with colorful stripes and with a waistband that, after it's tied, comes down to his knees, a white jacket with buttons in the shape of a W, and a belt with red and orange stripes that he tightly winds a couple of times around his body.

We exchange greetings on the open porch. The *hinolong*

doesn't speak Malay, or perhaps he pretends not to, for some political reason. One of the other Alfurs acts as his interpreter.

Years ago my father-in-law had gone hunting in the Wa Apu
region[58] on the other side of the bay and he had met the predecessor of this *hinolong* on one of those trips. During the long evenings after the hunt the old Alfur would tell him about his people,
about their habits, their customs, and their unwritten history
from the days before the Company. Later on my father-in-law
managed to get the government to make the *hinolong* of Kubalahin a *kepala soa*,[59] which gave him some official status as an old
adat chief, even though he remained under the *radja* of Kajeli. The
old *hinolong* remained grateful for this all of his life, and even
though he was already an old man, he addressed my father-in-
law as *Bapak* and gave him the Fud Fadid, a mountain behind Kubalahin. A more practical businessman would immediately have
taken advantage of this relationship. It is not difficult to obtain a
damar[60] concession once you have secured the main chief's ap-
proval. The Alfurs are really primitive people, shy as animals, but
they trusted him completely and he accepted the present without
filing the appropriate papers because he was a better friend than a
businessman. He left Buru sick and almost penniless, but the old
stories are retold for the benefit of the son who resembles him
most in character and appearance.

And now we have met each other and are sitting on the front
porch. The *hinolong*, my husband, and I are sitting on chairs;
Heintje is standing behind me, and the Alfur interpreter behind
the *hinolong*. We inquire after each other's health and the health
of family and children. We ask if there's been good hunting. We
thank him for his gifts: a small basket filled with *tutupola* (sago
rolls) which were not baked in a stone mold, but in fresh green
bamboo, which gives them a different taste, a can of *katjang* or
peanuts, and two piglets in a bamboo crate. The *hinolong* praises
the old days and complains about the present. Neither the *damar*
nor the rattan from his forests is worth anything, *atap* and *gaba-
gaba* give the women some cottage industry, but hardly bring in
any money, and they've learned the value of money during the
last few years. In the old days they lived their own life, they
hunted deer and pigs with their long spears, set traps along the
game paths in the forest, and dressed in bark. But when the price
of *damar* went up they got used to many things they hadn't
known before: *sarongs*, trousers, headcloths, enamel pans, and

stone plates. In the past they only valued civilization for its salt and the occasional red loincloth, but now their needs have increased, and so have their desires: they want petroleum, sugar, soap, coffee, and cheap cotton dresses from Japan. That's why they began to distill *kajuputih* leaves in the hills behind their *kampong*. It is a kind of work that does not agree with them. When the *kajuputih* leaves have been plucked and tossed in a heap to ferment for two days, they have to be fired on a particular day, and the Alfur is not used to doing things on specific days. He hunts deer and pigs in the hills, beats sago in the forest along the Wa Apu, the big river, he scratches here and there in the dirt with an iron bar in a badly cleared field and drops a few kernels of corn into the opening, he defoliates the sago palm and dries the midrib while the women sew the leaves into *atap*. The Alfur is a free man and only works when he feels like it. And it happens quite often that the *kajuputih* leaves rot in the *blubur* or that he stokes up the fire too much and too carelessly to get the oil quicker because the sun is shining on the slopes on the other side where his brothers are hunting the big stag. And then there is the Chinese, who always insists on being paid, who goes looking for them in the *kampong* and pursues them to where they beat sago in the forest. When they first began to distill they built the primitive still themselves: two wooden vats, one with a cast-iron bottom for the fire and the other the cooling vat. The distilling vat fits on top of the oven they built from clay and stones from the river. But they didn't have enough money for the still head for cooling: the copper *kepala* pot. So the Chinese gave it to them as an advance worth forty guilders, equal to one hundred bottles of *kajuputih* oil. And now the young men, who'd rather hunt or roam in the forests, have to work to deliver a hundred bottles of *kajuputih* oil.

There is much *kajuputih* behind Kubalahin, and more stills could be put there. What price would Sinjo Tandjong ask for the *kepala* pot?[61]

We consult each other. This is going to be our first transaction. We come up with a price and figure out how much the monthly installments will be. The interpreter translates and the *hinolong* agrees. But much later, when we are drinking our fourth cup of coffee and he is eating his eighth piece of cake, he suddenly asks: "How many months are there in a year?"

We patiently explain it to him all over again. He seems to be bothered by either scabies or lice.[62] He rubs himself back and forth against the rattan chair, takes a leaf and *pinang*[63] nut from his belt and shakes a little lime on it from a hollow bottle-shaped gourd. He is a tall man, well built with broad shoulders. His face with the short goatee looks at the same time sly and very child-like. He lost his left eye in an old fight, but with the right one he looks around cunningly[64] and suspiciously.

Marmot, my little dog, comes in wagging its tail and jumps over our feet. The *hinolong* picks it up, scratches its thick fur and indicates that he would like to take it along with him. But my husband is able to make it clear after a while that this little dog is my special pet, but that in a little while he can choose among our hunting dogs. Only partially satisfied, the Alfur puts the little dog down again. A little later his eye catches a batik hanging on the wall and again he indicates that he would like to have it. My husband quickly tells him that we can't possibly part with that *kain*, since it's *pusaka*.[65] I'm becoming somewhat uneasy. How are we going to keep on finding excuses in order to deny him his wishes?

It's getting very hot on the open porch, and the conversation drags on endlessly, Malay sentences with the Alfurese transla-tion, the Alfurese reply and its precise translation into Malay. Enggeh creeps up behind my chair to tell me that the Binongkos caught a lot of fish. Perhaps I should buy everything, since the Alfurs are likely to stay as our guests for a few days. I buy the whole catch and offer it to the *hinolong*. He motions a few boys from his retinue to accept the fish and to clean them on the beach. That diverts his attention. The *hinolong* and his interpreter turn their heads so they can keep an eye on the boys, because fish is a rare treat for mountain people. When the boys have left the beach and have lit a small fire in the backyard, our important visitor fi-nally rises after a few more idle questions.

That night we almost have a rebellion on our hands. The Bi-nongkos refuse to sleep in the same house with the Alfurs and we refuse to let our guests go to the *kampong*. Heintje finally comes up with a solution. The Binongkos are going to sleep in one house and the Alfurs in the other, but since the fishermen still don't trust the pagans being that close, La Golo, who comes from Bu-ton and whose younger sister is married to an Alfur, will sleep with the Alfurs.

The arrangement remains in force for four nights. Then the Al-furs leave and we give the *hinolong* some presents to take to his wife: sugar, salt, coffee, scented soap, and a little dog.

VI

Our yard borders on that of the district officer. We pay him a visit on one of our first nights in Namlea. He is a small powerful man with the neck and shoulders of a farmer. His wife and I talk about domestic matters, the price of fish and how hard it is to get vegetables. We drink lemonade and eat homemade cookies and sit on chairs that have been rubbed and rubbed until they shine.

My husband asks about the state of the *kajuputih* business, but he only gets short superficial answers. We talk about our plans to revitalize the old man's neglected concession. This is a matter of the highest importance to us, and it is also very important for the subdistrict of Buru, but the man in charge shows little interest.

We realize that we have not been given any important information when we walk home along the wet muddy road, but we do know for sure that we have little in common and that any topic would be exhausted within ten minutes.

Two weeks later we meet them on the beach. His wife is walking ahead of him and we talk a bit until he catches up with us. "Come," he tells his wife, "we have to go this way." And they climb up the hill along a narrow path, almost without a greeting. The next morning my husband goes to the district officer with the papers for the concession. He wants to know if the old conditions are still valid. "What would you like me to do for you?" the man in charge asks him, as affable as a king. My husband is amazed: "You don't have to do anything for me, I just came to get some information.

From that day on we listen very carefully to what our visitors have to say about the district officer. The Arabs and Chinese praise him because he is so helpful, but the Binongkos have an interesting story to tell. When it's time to collect taxes, he summons the people who can't pay to the district office. Then the gong is beaten throughout the *kampong* and the merchants are told that they can get laborers at the district office if they are willing to pay the outstanding taxes. The Chinese pays the taxes and he has one more coolie, and the district officer will see to it that the coolie won't run away. It sounds like a serious complaint, and one that might explain his conduct toward us. But the man is transferred before we can get to know more about this business than some rumors from the local population.

When he auctions off his goods, the Chinese and Arab merchants openly show how much he has accommodated them. His old hat fetches forty guilders, and his cane ten. The shiny chairs have been packed and put on board the *kapal putih*,[66] but the rest of the furniture along with various odds and ends are sold for 4,600 guilders. His successor, a young man who obtained his degree in colonial administration[67] only two years ago, is left with a stack of contracts in which the careless population of Buru lease their stills to the merchants in such a way that they remain their property in name only.

The lieutenant lives with his family on the other side of the *kampong*, by the *tangsi*. One of his children has developed an inflammation of the middle-ear, and the wife has taken the sick girl and her two sisters to Ambon. The lieutenant himself is on tour a lot. But he's home a couple of days before the boat from Java is due and we become acquainted. He is a very tall man, an officer in the Dutch army, but assigned to service in the Indies for five years. And perhaps that is the reason why he doesn't have the typical colonial attitude. Almost everybody who comes to the Indies to find employment has begun to change before he gets off the boat. The unassuming man who embarks in Genoa has become several degrees more important by the time he disembarks in Priok. It is an oxidation process of the soul that nobody can escape. The Company has taken over the rights of the native chiefs, and for three hundred years now every newcomer upon arrival in the Indies has become automatically a chief, a leader, a very important person. He has become a European as soon as he leaves Europe.

On Java this sense of inclusive leadership can now be found only in the hinterland and on isolated plantations. Life in the big cities here is much the same as life in the smaller cities in Holland, except that it is even more boring. But in the outposts, on the rubber plantations in Deli,[68] along the rivers of Borneo, on the hot and barren islands in the Moluccan Sea, behind the mosquito-infested swamps of New Guinea, in such places every European is still a representative of Authority, a person and a symbol at the same time, and this symbolism proves to be fatal to most of them. In such places the importance of Europeans is in inverse proportion to their numbers, and the dangerous oxidation process is much accelerated where those numbers are down to one or two. He becomes rusted solid in his own importance. The simpler the environment he comes from and the less educated he is, the faster this process takes place. Though seldom recognized as such, it is an illness that is far more real than most diseases.

No matter what position he is assigned, be it a civil servant or an officer, a missionary or the manager of a remote plantation, if his self-criticism is silent he won't find anyone else to criticize him. His personnel kowtow to him and the native population tells him what he wants to hear. There is no friend to give him advice, nor an enemy to mock his stupidity in public. He is alone among thousands who look up to him as if he were a king. Opposition remains hidden for him: the gossip that's whispered around mosquite fires, and the anonymous letters that his boss throws contemptuously into the wastebasket. In the end he loses all sense of discrimination and exchanges his own insignificance for the importance of the Authority he represents. Only a few are destined by their nature and character to withstand this corrosion of their own eminence. Be he missionary or official, planter or lieutenant, the people run to him whenever disaster strikes, be it fire or flood, earthquake, sickness or death. And once they have lost their names forever in a lonely grave or in an overpopulated country, the story of their lives is told somewhere in a *prao* waiting for wind, around a smoky fire, or by the light of a small petroleum lamp.

This lieutenant does not belong to those rare ones who have peopled their solitude. He is not an exceptionally gifted man, but for five years he has managed to stay free of colonial pomposity, vanity, and prerogative. The few evenings he's staying in Namlea we spend in each other's company. His youngest daughter had been in bed for days with a high fever, before the doctor could get from Ambon to Namlea. The diagnosis was inflammation of the middle-ear, and it had to be operated on as soon as possible. But the Papua boat was late and they had to wait for two days with their cases packed and their clothes ready. The boat whistled them out of their sleep on the third night, the feverish child was rolled in a blanket and carried to the motorboat that rode on the river. It took them a few hundred yards across the choppy water and then they had to maneuver the jump onto the companion ladder. He came back an hour later, alone. But the doctors in Ambon did not dare perform the dangerous operation, and so the mother left the two oldest girls with acquaintances and went on to Java, alone with the delirious child in a small cabin, hot as an oven.

The story makes a big impression on me: the long wait, the boat that came late, and then the long journey until they were finally ready to operate in Malang.[69] I imagine myself on a journey like that with my unborn son, a deathly ill, delirious child, traveling for days with no medical assistance.

But the operation was a success and the child is alive. The father tells us about it while we sit outside, smoking a cigarette. He tells the story in simple words that hide the emotion and transform this particular case to an instance of universal fate.

Hundreds of children have been ill on these islands, far from any medical help, screaming, with their voices distorted by fever or the onset of death.

Above us are the same stars that are over Ambon, where the doctor lives. Once every two weeks a ship sails to Ambon through the Straits of Buru, across eighty miles of water. Sometimes there are eighty miles between life and death.

VII

Bader returns from the backwoods, and comes to talk business. He is a big man, graying already, with a friendly face and a very dignified posture, a crook and a bloodsucker, but he looks completely trustworthy. He reminisces about the days of Tuan Captain and he inquires about the old Lady, the boys, and the girls. He is an old friend of the family, his voice is soft and friendly. He complains about his stokers and about business in Batuboi. He rented the concession in order to help his friend, the Tuan Captain, but he hardly made any money during all these years.

We remember accounts that were never in order and never on time; we also remember 1928 when a *pikol* of *kajuputih* oil got a hundred and fifty guilders. He has swindled his friend for years and now he's trying to swindle his friend's son in that soft voice of his. Does the Sinjo want to start for himself? Would the Sinjo then pay the land rent and taxes for the past twelve years? Bader has operated Batuboi for twelve years, and for twelve years he has paid the land rent and taxes. We get out the old contract; it does not contain specifics about land rent, so that is the concessionaire's responsibility.

"But why didn't Tuan Bader deduct that rent every year?"

"Business has been so bad the last few years that the income did not cover the land rent that was owed."

He shows us old bills. Three stills operating in January, two in

February. He probably had six or seven going, but it couldn't be checked all the way from Java. If we want to work Batuboi we will have to settle this old debt first.

We talk for an hour. The debt represents an enormous drain on the little capital we have. We talk for another hour. After three more conferences we come to an agreement a week later. We'll pay off half of the debt, and work half of Batuboi. Bader generously allows a choice of terrain to the right or the left of the *kali*.

We set out two days later with the morning sea breeze. It is a cool day, with rain clouds hanging low over the gray water. The sky is light blue between patches of fog, washed clean after days of rain. A school of small fish jump out of the water, chased by a big *bubara*. The tide is coming in. Chickens are busily looking for mollusks on the last reefs that are still dry. Only the roof of our house can be seen through the *antjak* leaves. Namlea lies on a small plain in a wide shining curve of the bay. Right behind the *kampong* the land suddenly rises some sixty feet, a green, slightly undulating savannah with *alang-alang* grass, *kajuputih* trees, and *kajuputih* shoots.

The bay lies before us, the broad swell of the sea rising and falling as regularly as breathing. High blue mountains descend to the beach in a green row of hills, and a wide belt of mangrove trees closes the last slope off from the water. The wind turns a little and we make straight for the *kampong* of Lain: four houses and a narrow beach hacked open among the *mangi-mangi* roots.[70] We bend down to put the boat about and we get so close to the hills of Batuboi that we can clearly see the dark spot where the *kali* flows into the light green of the mangroves. We take the sail down and four men start rowing, but we approach the mouth of the river very slowly. We are now traveling on the quiet water between a small island and the coast. The water is shallow here and we can see the bottom clearly. Coral grows in the white sand like dark forests on a bright plain. We can see red organ-pipe coral and brain coral[71] with its many twists, moldered green, and fine *karang* coral that looks like petrified ferns, immobile, graceful flowers. Small brightly colored fish dart through these coral lanes, a gray *tatu* with red and purple stripes, and goldfish with black spots and big fins on their backs and tails. A pale blue starfish lies on a small clearing. The light is diffuse, filtered through half a yard of blue water, moving and hesitant, quivering from the light swell. Somewhere a shadow falls as of a dark cloud: a big fish swimming fast along the surface. New forests and new gardens, new lanes and small paths, and another starfish lying flat on a smooth stone.

Suddenly the reef breaks off, the bottom lies deeper now, a lonely desert of sand. We're getting into the off-shore swell. The mangroves stand in the water up to their underarms, their leaves are rocking up and down. Behind us the heat rises from a burning blue sea. We slide into the river that's carved into the scorched land like a dark moist groove.

The tide is at its highest now and floods the mangrove roots, as well as their stench and decay. The banks look like flooded land, with only the tree tops still sticking out above the water. The mangrove forest becomes narrower as the river curves. Forest trees stretch out toward each other, behind the low *mangi-mangi*. We slide past lianas hanging down like cables, past dead branches and a vine with yellow flowers. Near the second bend our mast gets stuck in the plants that hang down from the trees. We lower the mast and paddle deeper into the green tunnel. The banks are getting higher, with *nipa* palms[72] which, though their sheaths have been broken and hang down in a slovenly manner, hold their giant leaf blades high like weapons. The banks belong to the *nipa* palm trees with their small dark leaves on thick smooth ribs. They grow some eight yards high out of the mud to form a movable tree roof above our head, and have pushed back the low bushes and forest trees with their small leaves that are never still. The crocodile has his paths here on a slope that goes from the forest down to the river, and they have been sanded smooth by his stinking belly.

This is a prehistoric landscape, transfixed, bigger and stronger and crueler, that oppresses us while we flee through it. We moor near the stump of an old bridgehead and we make our way through the *nipa* forest by jumping from one trunk to the next. Then we are blinded by the sun and we wake to the glaring day of the plain.

The *alang-alang* waves over six feet high, sharp as a knife and toothed like a saw, all the way to the hills which, long and very steep and overgrown with the same grass, with new *kajuputih* growth and thin *kajuputih* trees, rise up shadowless.

We walk along a narrow path that has been trampled down in

the *alang-alang*. A chicken runs cackling in front of us and a dog begins to bark. We find the still at the foot of the hill. Under a broken roof of *atap* an old man is making an oven with stones from the *kali* and clay from the river. His left cheek bulges with a large tumor. His speech is unclear, as if he is pushing a big wad of tobacco behind his teeth. He has made his *baleh-baleh* under the lowest part of the roof. It has a dirty pillow and a couple of torn *kains*. There is a cooking pot between three stones, and there are a few plates and bowls on a primitive table. That's all the furniture in a dwelling that is both house and factory at the same time, made from a lean-to roof and some *nipa* leaves that have been put loosely against one side of it to form a wall.

Heintje chops a joint off a long bamboo, just below the node. He takes it into the forest that grows beside the hill along a small *kali*. Well water drips between stones covered with green moss. We drink from the bamboo. The water is cold and tastes of grass and moss. We pour the rest over our face and hands.

Behind the still is a path that leads to the forest where Lamana's two sons are making a *pantjoran*[73] out of bamboo that has been cut in half. This will take the water from the well to the cooling vat. But the path that leads through the plain is overgrown with *alang-alang* that, more than six feet tall, cuts your face.

I am going back to the *prao*, together with two of the rowers. My husband and Heintje will use their machetes to hack a path to the still at Pohon Bulie in the next valley. There are forty stills in Batuboi, the trip is going to take two days.

VIII

Kajuputih trees grow all along the northern coast of Buru, from Ilat to Ajer Buaja.[74] Thin white trunks are scattered over the plain and have climbed the ridges of the hills where they are outlined in black against the red evening sky. The young shoots, sprouting from the roots, cover the slopes around them, gray as the mist on mornings during the west monsoon, and green and lovely an hour later, under a glaring sun, as if they were the slopes of a more fertile country. But where the leaves have just been torn off to be distilled, the poor red soil protrudes between the bare twigs and the hard grass. And the bare bushes along the road glisten on the rusty earth as white as bones when the *alang-alang* has withered away in the hot months, when the heat bursts out from the soil, comes blowing across the water, and is cast back by the blue, merciless sky. The light bark of the trees, thin as paper, glistens even brighter now that the color of the grayish-green leaves has evaporated in the hard blue of the motionless sky and the surface of the water that is forever in motion. Men and women walk through the young growth in all seasons with tall baskets, tearing off the leaves that will be heated in a primitive contraption until they yield the green fragrant *kajuputih* oil. That oil is still little known in Europe; it is used in some patent medicines and occasionally in the perfume industry. In the Indies it is a panacea for all illnesses, internal and external: a few drops on some sugar will cure a stomach ache, and it is rubbed on the skin against rheumatism or lumbago. The strong smell keeps the mosquitoes away, and a few drops in a bowl of hot water will loosen a cold. This green medicine from Buru is the remedy for everything in the brown houses on every island, places where a doctor comes only once a year and where people are more afraid of him than of death itself.

This oil has not been in use all that long. Rumphius[75] knew of a medicine made from bruised and pulverized *kajuputih* leaves, but he doesn't mention the oil. Almost a hundred years ago Assistant Resident Willer[76] traveled around Buru to study the possibility of European colonization of the island (sounds very appropriate for those days). His extensive report, which was later published as a book, contains a detailed description of the preparation of *kajuputih* oil. Among other things, he describes the method of distillation and provides a cost estimate, and what is remarkable is that neither the method nor the price have changed appreciably over the last hundred years. But the situation of the natives has changed completely. When Willer visited them, they only had stills on the slopes behind Kajili, and these stills (they call both the place where they distill the oil and the vegetation around it "stills") belonged to the population of Kajili, Ambonese Christians who have lived there since the days of the Company, as well as a few Muslims.

Willer mentions the Wakanos, the Serhalawans,[77] and a number of other names that are familiar because their children and grandchildren are still living in Kajili and Namlea. But they now own only one still, and it is heavily mortgaged. All the other stills have passed into the hands of Chinese and Arab merchants.

In the past the wind from the West would bring the high *praos* from Macassar to Buru once a year, and the *kajuputih* oil was exchanged for rice, coffee, petroleum, *sitsjes*,[78] plates, and pans. The Buginese[79] built a small house of loose *atap* on the beach, where they opened a *toko*. At night they slept in their *praos*, with poops as high as the castles on the ships of the Company. They rode at anchor only a few yards away from the shore, because the roadstead of Kajili is open and the water has the broad swell of the sea. But then a Chinese came and built a *toko*, and from then on *kajuputih* oil could be exchanged all year round for the merchandise that before had only been available for a few exciting weeks. At first this improvement seemed to make life a lot more pleasant. The people of Kajili were given ample credit and they didn't worry about it because they had never learnt how. Thoughtlessly and carelessly like children they took away every month many more guilders than the value of the oil they delivered. Their advances quickly added up to several hundred guilders, with the result that the Chinese merchant wanted papers, which they signed without ever questioning them. They couldn't sell their land, the agrarian laws protected them from that, but they did rent their stills and surrendered their rights to harvest the *kajuputih* leaves, until such time as that rent would have paid off the debt. But the debt was never paid because they blithely kept on buying things at two or three times the normal *kampong* price. The stipulations of the contract were completely in favor of the merchant. The fee for firing the still was paid by the month or for that part of the month during which the still was actually in operation. The owner himself was not allowed to distill any more than that and the merchant would only work the still when it suited him, and it was very often to his advantage to leave the still idle. And so debts kept on rising, as did the prices of the goods that could be bought on credit.

Judgment day came slowly but surely. They lost their stills, their houses were neglected, and their children became impoverished. Since they owned land, it was a disgrace to work for others or for a wage. Now and then one of them would manage to escape into a respectable job as a *guru* or *mantri*, and the other members of his family would live off him like flies off carrion. Most stills have been taken over by Chinese and Arab merchants in this way, but there are a few large concessionary plots that are rented out by the government, which bought them from the local

population at a decent price and collects a considerable tax on
them each year. The government does not collect any tax from the
land operated by the Chinese and Arab merchants, and their
managers are not restricted by any regulations. And so the un-
lawful occupants manage to stay ahead of the concessionaire who
has acquired his land honestly.

The merchant never operates the stills himself, he rents them out
to groups of stokers, mostly from Sula or Buton. Six or seven men
agree to work a still together. They pay for this privilege and, furthermore, they are required to deliver their oil at a fixed price and
buy their food and clothes from the merchant, also at a fixed
price, which is two or three times higher than the one paid in the
kampong, with the result that after a few months their debt is
greater than the advance they started out with. The carefree Sulanese especially have become more or less the slaves of their merchants and they never recover their freedom. One or two will run
away now and then, and the debt will have to be written off, but
even that is not really a setback, because the high sum is largely
fictitious, consisting for the most part of the merchant's excessive
profit. The situation would have become impossible years ago, if
the distillers themselves hadn't found a way out. They are required, of course, to deliver all their oil to the merchant, but it is
very simple to keep a couple of bottles and sell them to another
merchant at the higher market price. There is a flourishing black
market in *kajuputih* oil, and everybody takes part in it. Merchant
Ong will buy the oil from merchant Kie's workmen, just as Kie
will buy the oil Ong has been cheated out of. One cheats the other
and they both know it, but they get on well together anyway. The
Chinese merchant exploits the stokers, but they are part of the
family in his *toko*. They sit there half the day, squatting and playing dice, and they sleep between the counter and the shelves and
snitch *katjang* from the jars.

You lie and I cheat, so why shouldn't we stay friends? And we
won't think of revenge until the dry season comes. That's when
accounts are settled, without any form of negotiation. August,
September, and October are the dry months. A scorching wind
blows inland from the hard blue sea. At this time of year the
nights are red from the fire that runs across the plain, rattles
down the slopes like a blazing train, and stands by day above the

hills like a dark pillar. At times a fine rain of ashes is blown into the houses and a light gray smoke hangs over the water like a tardy morning fog. When the fire flares up at night on the hills by the shore, the dark water washes the glow before our feet, red and horrible, as if the sun was going down again in the wrong place, and this time forever.

The *alang-alang* that grows among the young *kajuputih* growth has withered away to sharp hay, and a small spark is enough to set the whole plain on fire. Sometimes the fire starts in a clearing that has been burnt down carelessly, and sometimes it is caused by Alfur hunters who set the *alang-alang* on fire because the green shoots that sprout up a few days later attract herds of deer. But in most cases it is a cigarette butt that has been carelessly thrown away in just the right places. There's nothing to it, nobody will ever find out, and there are so many reasons to seek revenge.

There is, for instance, the still owner, locked in furious argument with his merchant about the contract; the only satisfaction he can get is with a fuse and a small flame a quarter of an hour before the wind rises at night. Then there are the stokers who owe a lot of money, who are forced to work and get deeper and deeper in debt. When the fire has gone through the hills the still cannot be worked for ten months, and for ten months they are reprieved from slaving. There are also the arguments between two owners of the same still. Hardly any still is registered and nobody knows exactly where the border is. It can happen in Buru that the same still is sold twice, which leads to all kinds of fights and most often to a court case. But when the verdict is pronounced and the still has been assigned to one of the claimants, his *kajuputih* leaves are sure to be burning come the first dry month, and nobody will be able to prove a thing.

There are also fights among the workers themselves, about their share in the earnings, about women or gambling debts. These fights are settled with a fire that devastates many acres of leaves. There would probably not be a single *kajuputih* tree left on Buru if the tree itself wasn't so well suited to survive fire. Its thick bark consists of several layers of cork on top of each other, which makes for natural insulation. For three days after the fire the hills look black and desolate in the bright light. The leaves on the lower branches and bushes are dead and golden like autumn leaves, and the fire has branded its mark in the bright shining trunk of the *kajuputih* tree. On the fourth morning the new *alang-*

alang begins to peep through the ashes, and after a month the new *kajuputih* sprouts begin to grow from the old roots. At the edge of the wild forest where the fire burned a broad swath, the *kajuputih* has conquered a new terrain, and so the trees penetrate farther and farther north and south along the coast and deeper into the hills.

IX

Hans Christiaan is twelve days old when we come back to Namlea. The chief mate's first born is the same age, and he claims the right to carry Hans Christiaan down the swaying ladder that hangs over the side of the boat, while the launch bobs up and down below it. This is the time of year when the wind blows straight into the bay and causes a tremendous surf, the dreaded *airputih*. The launch rises and falls with the waves, we risk the jump and when we are level with the platform of the ladder again the chief mate hands the boy to us. We remain standing while hanging onto the hood of the engine. The water slams over the people on the benches when the launch makes a turn in order to pull up in front of the ship where the loading *praos* are. The waves smash to a white foam on the low reefs. It was still raining when we left, but the East monsoon is early this year. The day is taut and clear, the sky and the water a hard blue, the tops of the coconut palms and the leaves of the *pisang* trees are the same green between the bare yellow beach and the bare yellow hills. When we get into calmer water behind the *tandjong*, the merchants tell us about the big fire in the hinterland, pointing to the smoke that hangs above the hills like a dark cloud.

We have come home, forever, with our sweet boy. We have been delivered from pain and fear now that we have left the world for this sanctuary. Our house stands wide and brown and safe in the green garden, by the narrow beach of the *tandjong* behind which the water has lost its strength. But there are five different fires in the hills that evening, and we feel as if we are living in a besieged fortress surrounded by the enemy's guard fires.

We managed to get half of Batuboi out of debt, but if it burns down we won't be able to work it for a year. It burnt down eight times during the twelve years when Bader was in charge, and the fires followed each other so quickly that in some places the shrubs have almost no leaves. If we want to have a chance at keeping the fire away from our land, we will have to start up the stills as quickly as possible so that there'll be people to help us fight the fire when it reaches the border.

There are enough people who want to work the stills. They squat in front of Heintje's door in the evening. They have heard that the Sinjo is going to work the stills again. They only owe fifty guilders to the merchant, and they will be free if the Sinjo pays. But Heintje warns us not to take on old debts, whatever we do.

We ask them how they got themselves in debt, and we listen to their endless, monotonous complaints. They pay twenty guilders for a *pikol* of rice that costs five everywhere else, and forty cents for a *katti* of salt, which is about three times too much. They're unjustly fined. Didn't Bader once keep twenty-five guilders of their money because they ate the corn they grew themselves, instead of his expensive rice. We tell La Bunge, La Kamba, and La Baru that we are going to work Batuboi ourselves, and that we shall see to it that our people don't get into debt. We will pay every month, and so they will be able to pay off their outstanding debt in monthly installments.

They stay and talk about it in their own language, and then ask permission to leave and talk to their friends about it. The next evening they are by Heintje's door again. They have heard that the Sinjo will pay for the oil at once. They are used to settling accounts with their merchant once or twice a year. They really want to work for the Sinjo, but it is customary to get an advance when they take on a new job. Won't the Sinjo give them twenty-five guilders? Then they can pay off the old Chinese merchant and pay the rest of their debt every month. When we refuse they ask permission to go and talk about it with their friends.

They are back a couple of days later, and again there are endless negotiations. Now they only want an advance of ten guilders, which means that a team of six workmen who are going to work a still together will start out with a debt of sixty guilders.

We have been negotiating for almost a month. The gong is beaten three or four times a week, there is a fire every night on a slope or in the plain. Finally, Halik Ternate decides to rent one of our stills and work it together with his brother and two nephews. We discuss the conditions in more detail: the rent for the still and the price we are going to pay for the oil they will produce. He is Sulanese, with a small, clever, rat's face, long arms and legs, and a back deformed from rheumatism. He is known as a thief and a cheat, he has debts everywhere and nobody will give him credit any more. He brings his perennially pregnant wife and five children to collect *atap* to build a still house. The whole bunch of them must have been written off by the merchant, because nobody comes to protest when they get to our still. For that matter, they won't be distilling any oil in the next few weeks. They have to build the still house first: a roof of *atap* and two walls made from the same material. They put the *baleh-baleh* on one side and wall it in with *atap* to make a kind of bed, while the *bluburs* are on the other side: bins in which the plucked leaves are kept to ferment for two or three days. In the middle of the house, directly under the ridgepole, they build the *tungku*, the oven, with clay and stones from the *kali*. The *tungku* reminds one of a baker's oven, with an opening for stoking the fire and where the wood is shoved in. There is also a round hole in the upper part of it, where the big cooling vat is going to be placed. Normally it takes five to seven days to build a still house and a *tungku*. Halik takes a good three weeks because first he has to use a lot of hocus-pocus to pick a favorable day and then, when he just gets going, a relative dies and he has to take his wife and children, his brother and nephews inland for the *slametan*.[80]

We always find him squatting by Heintje's door to ask for coffee, rice, and *pisang* for his youngest child, for a quarter to buy some fish, and for two and a half guilders as a contribution to the *slametan*. Now that he's working for us he considers the *tandjong* his home, and comes to pick *djuruk* and breadfruit and his children go looking for driftwood on the beach.

By the third week my husband finds only the still house ready, the *tungku* hasn't even been started yet and when he has given the Sulanese a piece of his mind about their work and their diligence, Halik asks again for rice, because the breadfruit on the Sinjo's tree is so small. But after this discussion Halik does know where he stands. There will be no more rice, coffee, money, or *pisang*. The Sinjo will be back in two days and the *tungku* will be ready by then. My husband and Heintje go down to the plain, following the tracks of the deer, but before they are back home Halik appears on the *tandjong* with three of his thin hungry children, and asks me for rice. I give them ten pounds.

Two days later he's waiting for my husband by the still, his rat's face one big smile: "Tuan djahat tetapi Njonja hati baik,"[81] and my husband bursts out laughing, because the *tungku* is really ready this time, and the real distilling apparatus can be set up.

The Sinjo stays two days at Halik's still, to get to know what's going on. He helps install the boiling and the cooling vats and he sees to it that the fire is kept going and that the oil gets distilled.

The boiling vat is fitted into the round hole in the upper part of the *tungku*. It is made by tying a number of staves together with tight rattan ropes around the *kuali:* a round iron pan without handles that serves as a bottom. They fill the cracks between the staves with wet strips of *kajuputih* bark. During the distillation process this bark secretes a tar that seals the structure even more tightly. Next they close the vat with a big wooden cover that has a round opening of about sixteen inches in the middle. The cover is seamless, carved in one piece from the trunk of some forest tree. The *kepala* pot, the most important and most expensive piece of the whole installation, fits into the opening of the cover. This pot, which is needed for the cooling process, resembles a red copper helmet. The first cooling takes place there by means of the outside air. The helmet has a copper drain pipe attached to it, the *trompong,* that ends in a drum that stands next to the boiler vat, and that is completely filled with water. The *trompong* emerges again through an opening at the bottom of the drum and the mixture of water and oil, which is still boiling hot, drains into a square gin bottle that has been put into a small pail filled with water. A tiny hole has been made in the bottom of the bottle, so that it works somewhat like a retort. Although the equipment is ridiculously primitive, it is completely effective, and, except for the metal parts, it can be assembled entirely with materials from the forest.

While Halik was building the *tungku,* his two nephews had been cutting wood in the forest: short pieces to start a good fire and long trunks to keep it going. Heintje hustles the boys into the forest early in the morning during these first days, because a lot of wood will be needed while the *tungku* is still moist. Hamba, Halik's brother, is working on the *pantjuran*—the long bamboo conduit that brings the water from the forest wells to the still. There is no getting away from work now that the Sinjo stays by the still all day, but on the second day Heintje shoots a deer and they sit around a small fire in the evening roasting the red meat and are almost happy. The next morning they all go out to pick leaves.

They tear them off the low bushes and throw them into a basket that, when full, is emptied into a bag. The picking is easy, all you need is a pair of calloused hands. The hard part comes when you have to pick leaves far from the still and then have to carry the full bag down a steep, slippery slope, and sometimes drag it up another one and down again along a steep ravine. Halik is forty, an old man by local standards, and his brother Hamba is probably a few years older. The two nephews are young men, unmarried; but the older ones are hardly more responsible than the younger men. A bunch of kids, driven to work by hunger, but preferring to put it off as long as possible. They are Sulanese who came over from Mangoli.[82] And even though they have lived here for thirty years, they are, according to *adat*, still foreigners and are not allowed to cut down trees in the sago forests. They complain because they didn't get an advance, complain because the Sinjo didn't let them get as much food as they wanted, which would have enabled them to put off work a little longer, and they feel ill at ease because the Sinjo has come to look after the still himself, something that the Chinese or Arab merchants would never do. But when they heard Heintje's shot they ran outside, carried the deer to the still, helped skin it, boiled water and cut the meat into pieces. For three days they are happy because of that night's unexpected feast and they work hard. But my husband stays with them until they are ready to begin distilling oil.

X

That morning Halik has filled the boiler of the still with leaves through the opening in the cover and tamped them down well with a wooden cudgel. After some four hundred pounds of leaves have been squeezed into the boiler, two pails of water are added. Next the *kepala* pot is firmly secured in the opening with a strip of wet bark and after that they begin to feed the fire. Hamba goes off to pick leaves on the hill on the other side of the forest, together with his wife and nephews. Halik's oldest daughter washes rice under the stream of water from the *pantjuran* because, since there's been some good work done, the rice bag has been opened. Halik has trouble with the fire, which doesn't seem to want to burn in the wet *tungku*. The others come back about ten o'clock, empty their bags into the *blubur*, stick their sweaty heads under the stream of water from the conduit, and light cigarettes. When the worst of the heat is over this afternoon, they will all return to the forest to chop wood.

The fire begins to draw better and the first oil begins to drip into the bottle, three hours after the boiler was filled—almost an hour too late. Halik has little to do after this. Occasionally he stirs the fire, pushes the long trunks a little further into the oven and stacks the new wood on the edge of the *tungku* to make it dry. Later, when the bottle is almost full, he pours out the oil. The distilling process will be finished by eight, but then the hardest part of the job begins: taking out the red-hot leaves and refilling the boiler again for the evening round. Until that time Halik sits curled up on the *baleh-baleh*, smoking a cigarette and eating pieces of *kasbi*. His wife has gone into the forest to look for vegetables, and Hamba and the big boys are asleep. It is a very hot day. Only the children are playing in the full *bluburs*. Halik sleeps while his wife keeps an eye on the fire. The others go into the forest around four. When they come home again at nightfall and drop the wood from their shoulders, Halik has just stirred up the fire again and shoved two long narrow trunks inside. The last oil drips away. The yield is bad because the *tungku* is still wet and the leaves could even be too old. Four hundred pounds of leaves yielded a mere two bottles, about three pounds of oil. Darkness has fallen when Halik cautiously unties the *kepala* pot, pulls away the steaming packing, and jumps back from the hot steam that escapes from the boiling leaves. The cover itself remains closed. They use the opening in the middle, where the *kepala* pot stood, to pry the pressed leaves loose with long two-pronged sticks and throw them on a pile behind the still house. It's heavy and hot work, and Hamba helps his brother with it. Except for small pairs of torn shorts, they are naked, and the sweat runs down their skinny bodies. An hour later the boiler vat is empty. Hamba goes to bed and Halik fills the vat again. Filling seems easy after the hard work of emptying it. Halik walks back and forth between the *blubur* and the vat with a big basket in his hands. The boys are asleep on the floor; they stir restlessly because they are plagued by mosquitoes. Later the evening wind rises and rustles loudly through the valley in the forest.

Halik leans against one of the posts of the house, blows on a piece of charcoal until it glows and lights a cigarette. The cold wind dries his wet naked torso, he shivers and goes inside. The small oil lamp is smoking. He turns the wick down and pushes the last leaves into the boiler vat, winds the packing around the copper *kepala* pot and pushes it into the stokehole. Finally he stirs the fire.

One of the children is dreaming and wakes up crying. A woman calms it down. The wind has blown the mosquitoes away. The boys have turned on their sides and are breathing loudly and deeply.

Halik pulls a *sarong* from a bundle of clothes and wraps it around his shoulders. The fire is burning well now, but the wind moves up between the steep slopes of the valley and makes the *tungku* drafty. Halik falls asleep, leaning close to the warm earthen wall of the *tungku*, tucked into his *sarong* like a bird in its feathers. Two hours later the oil begins to drip into the bottle. He's awakened by the sound or maybe it's just instinct. He checks the bottle, puts the last piece of the bamboo conduit at a somewhat steeper angle, and adds wood to the fire. Soon he dozes off again, but wakes once more with a start, pours off the oil and throws more wood on the fire. Branches crack somewhere in the forest where a herd of deer is pushing toward the water. Halik lies down on the *baleh-baleh* and sleeps through the last hours of the night, until dawn. The fire has slowly burned down. The last drops of oil drain into the bottle. He opens the *kepala* pot in the first morning light. His oldest nephew helps him empty out the boiler.

On the third day the boiler easily yields three bottles each time it's filled. The *tungku* is beginning to dry out. Hamba and the boys hang around the still that morning. The day rises straight up, blue and bright and fast as a bird. In two hours the heat will be reverberating between the hills and the sky. The pickers have to go out as soon as they can in order for them to return before the naked stones of the worn path burn their feet. But the boys don't want to eat the cold roasted *kasbi*, and wait for the rice to boil. Hamba goes off looking for his machete. It is well past eight when they take off for the hills and it is already as hot as in the afternoon. When they come back after three hours their bags are barely half full. In the afternoon they stay around the still and lie down in the shade of the lean-to. The ship will come today, and the Sinjo and Heintje have gone down for the mail. The still is no longer in operation when Heintje comes back two days later. All the leaves in the *blubur* are gone and nobody has gone picking.

That night the plain behind Namlea burns. The frontline of the fire is one hundred yards wide, a red line, alive and roaring like an animal. The gong summons the people from the *kampong*. Soldiers have been called out to help and they mow down the *alang-alang* and the *kajuputih* shrubs with their *klewangs*. But the wind blows the fire across the road, down to the foot of the hills, where it is beaten out. The next morning the narrow strip of land between the bay and the Moluccan Sea is scorched black from beach to beach.

Halik and his family kept watch on the border of Batuboi and helped fight the fire when it got down to the hills. The fire has been overcome. Heintje distributes rice. That morning they sleep, black and scorched, in the shadow of the still house. Halik waits two full days before he fills the *tungku* again. They work an entire week and then walk down the hill to get paid.

In the afternoon they appear on the *tandjong*. The boys squat on the beach under the *antjak* trees. Halik's wife, big with child, sits on the outrigger of the *prao* that has been pulled on the beach. The little ones are looking for mussels in the sand. On the stoop of the back porch, the Sinjo and Heintje square accounts with both men.

It's been more than a month since the posts for the still house were driven into the ground, and since we advanced them half a *pikol* of rice after a great deal of talking back and forth. But they have kept coming back for small amounts of money. During those five weeks they have eaten more than they could earn in ten working days. There is a small debt left, a little more than two and a half guilders, but it bothers us because we guaranteed that our workers would not get into debt. But it does not bother Halik and Hamba at all. They immediately increase their debt by asking for an advance. All they get out of us is some rice, and they set off for the *kampong*. They hang around in the *kampong* for three days and then they work the still ten days in a row. This time there's a surplus and it is paid out to them in cash.

XI

The next month six Butonese come to see us who want to rent a still and work it together. Lamani is their *anachoda:*[83] he is in charge and will do the distilling. The others will pick leaves, chop wood, and take care of the conduit.

We made one condition: "no advances," but Halik and his family managed to get into debt almost immediately. It is better not to stick to principles too rigidly as long as we have to operate this way. We'll come to another better arrangement later, when we will know all the advantages and disadvantages of the traditional method. In the meantime we have to help these people a little with money and rice. It takes about seven days to build a house and a *tungku*, so we give them ten days' worth of rice and half a guilder each as an advance.

A week later we get two more groups from Buton. They are dark powerful men with broad shoulders and hard muscles. They travel east from Buton and the surrounding islands which are all barren and without sufficient water. They look for work in the coconut plantations of Halmahera,[84] the oil refineries on Bula,[85] and the new concessions on Papua. They are a diligent and sober people who save all their money on workdays but who turn into reckless dice players on holidays, and fanatic bettors at cockfights. They wander from island to island, their belts with clinking coins pulled tight to keep their stomachs small, and then gamble half a year's work and hunger away in one mad night. They come with the west wind from Buton, some with the KPM but most of them in small rickety *tembangans*.[86] For a few guilders they are allowed to float along the coast, huddled close together, with a few handfuls of corn for food and a carefully measured water ration. They are honest men, hard-working and true to their word. Now and then they settle on the coast and marry into families from Sula and Buron. But when they lose their wanderlust they also lose their best qualities. They become lazy and mendacious like the coastal people and they learn to eat sago.

Only one of the groups has done well after a week of building. Three of Lamani's men are in bed with a bad case of malaria, and the others don't feel like working twice as hard, so they wait until their mates are cured. The third group hasn't even come to take a look at its still yet. The sister of Ladjenihi's youngest nephew got married and the whole group went to the wedding with the rice and advance. Not until two weeks later is Odeh's still finally going, are Lamani's sick pluckers strong enough to work again, and do the wedding guests return asking for food because they've lost everything playing dice. They are amazed when we refuse and hardly angry. They have to work another ten days before they can begin to deliver the oil, and if they don't eat they'll get weak from hunger. They accept the scolding and the half *pikol* of rice silently and set off for the hills on the very same day.

We've got four stills working now, out of forty, scattered over some four hundred acres. Every morning at six my husband goes to the concession in a *prao*, and comes home with the evening wind, usually around seven, but sometimes later. He gets to know the lay of the land, the big river plain that is marshy but has good drainage, which makes it good for growing coconuts, the small valley next to the plain, where the forest has made the soil fertile, and the sloping grounds on the other side of the *kali*, where one day he hopes to plant rice. The stills are hours away from each other. The *anachoda* rakes the ashes out of the fire, while the sweat runs down his body from the heat of the fire and the heat of the day. Out on the hills the pickers pull the leaves off the shrubs.

This morning the Sinjo dropped in unexpectedly to check on the work. The water splashes out of the *pantjuran* in a wide stream into the big cooling vat. But now the Sinjo has that water collected in a drum first, and then conveys it from that drum into the bottom of the cooling vat. The cooling water becomes less hot that way, and the yield increases. Some time later he has ribs put around the *trompong*, [87] which increases the cooling surface, and the yield increases again, almost one extra bottle per day.

The *anachoda* gets more and more annoyed with the Sinjo for coming to check, even though he also profits from the increased yield. The Arabs and the Chinese rarely check on their stills, they stay in their *tokos*, busy with their books. Ladjenihi silently watched the change of the conduit, but he protests when it comes to improving the cooling vats. He has been an *anachoda* for forty years, and he has always worked a still his way. Why does the Sinjo Tandjong, who's been back on Buru only a couple of months, think that he knows better? And those ribs around the *trompong* are a nuisance, they keep breaking all the time. The Sinjo comes to watch again but Ladjenihi would rather work the still without being checked on, so that he can always have thick coffee ready in a grimy pan and listen to passing friends who come to talk for half a day and bring him the latest news about playing dice and fires and about Bang Liong who pays fifty cents for a bottle of oil if you take it to him in secret, after dark. How can Ladje-

nihi sell oil to the Chinese merchant if Uncle Heintje and the Sinjo
come to check the still every day?

He resents these visits as a personal insult. They have rented
the still and they're paying for the right to work it. They can work
the way they want to, and they can work as much or as little as
they want to. It's all so simple. When there are no leaves left in the
blubur the still stops for a few days until the pickers have brought
in enough leaves again, and when the wood is gone the *anachoda*
lets the fire go out and waits until a new supply is stacked up.
And there are the many *slametans* for weddings, births, and cir-
cumcisions. They're used to attending every funeral, every feast,
and every *menari* night.[88] But now the Sinjo wants them to get
permission first, and wants the *bluburs* to be full and for there to
be enough wood, and he insists that they leave a man behind to
finish boiling the leaves.

The oil is brought to the *tandjong* on Saturdays. It is checked,
measured, and put through a sieve. In the evening they play dice
with the money they earned. That evening Odeh Mahdi loses all
his own money, the money of his men, his big gamecock, and the
clothes in his trunk. The next morning he enlists Heintje's help to
get an advance out of the Sinjo, and when that doesn't work he
finds a Chinese *toko* in the *kampong* where he buys a new *sarong*,
rice, fish and petroleum, promising to pay it all back in oil.

The following week the yield of Odeh's still drops from four
bottles to barely three. But when Heintje keeps watch for a day,
the still is back to its old yield again. Heintje has heard about the
dice game, has seen the new *sarong* and the bag of rice under the
baleh-baleh.

It's Saturday again and Odeh squats by the back porch. He is
wearing a new pink shirt and a green checkered *sarong* rolled up
around his hips. He has a pleasant open face, is neither shy nor
ashamed. He spreads the fingers of his left hand and says in a serious, almost disapproving voice: "Why does the Sinjo want to
do everything different? People are used to delivering oil in exchange for merchandise and some change. When we pay cash in
the *kampong* the Chinese merchants ask for oil." That evening,
after dinner, we sit on the lawn in front of our house and smoke
cigarettes. Crabs are rustling away in their holes. The wind has
chased all the mosquitoes away, and the leaves and the shadows

are moving in and out of each other. Heintje sits on the edge of the stoop. We are going to order rice from Ambon, and coffee, sugar, *katjang idjo*,[89] and petroleum, and we are going to supply our workers with all of this. This is no defeat, merely a tactical retreat until we can achieve a complete victory.

XII

Pohon Bulu, Odeh's still, is no longer profitable after two months, and Odeh and his people are going to the Pohon Kwini still. They take the whole building down, take the *atap* from the roof and the side walls and carry it for an hour across the plain until they get to the new still. Then they ask for five days' leave to visit their family. Accounts have been settled for the last time and they set off, their belts bulging with cash. A month later we send Heintje inland to look for them; it takes him a week to round them all up. They don't have a cent left and ask for an advance of petroleum, coffee, sugar, and rice. It takes another three weeks before the still gets going. Seven weeks have been wasted due to hanging around and not doing anything.

We have been given a trial order from Europe for a drum of oil. It has to meet all the requirements of the Dutch pharmaceutical industry. Pohon Kwini is one of our best stills, with a high yield in oil and a high weight per volume. We had counted on this still but it was started up too late and we can't deliver on time. We try to buy oil. Heintje makes the rounds of all the merchants with his aerometer,[90] but they aren't used to being selective about their oil —quality is not important for the Macassar market—and we don't find the good grade oil we need. The drum is sent a month late.

The wedding guests have also finished with their still. Ladjenihi asks for another one and Heintje assigns Prahu Honi to him, but they are not happy with it. Prahu Honi is a still close to the beach, and the leaves from the plain yield only three bottles per still. They want Tubahoni, the still in the mountains, which yields more than five bottles. They refer to Odeh's people, who are now working Pohon Kwini, where every filling yields six bottles. The Sinjo explains that they just left a still that yielded five bottles and that it is fair that they get now a three-bottle still, because Odeh's people first worked a still that barely yielded three bottles. They have to take turns working a good and a moderate still. But they keep on refusing and they leave toward evening and Hong Liong gives them each an advance of two and a half guilders and a *sarong*. Satisfied, they set off for the hills and a day's journey to where Liong has a still he never checks on. They have already gambled the money away and the new *sarongs* hang carelessly from their hips. They carry a bag of rice through all the hot hours of the day. They got it on credit for twenty guilders, which is three times the normal price.

It's getting close to *puasa*.[91] The scum of the *kampong* is working Halik's still now: thieves and arsonists, Saleh Kau who has only one eye, Mohammed Kabau, and Umar Ternate with his whole family. They need credit for the *slametans* and for the new clothes they have to wear on the holiday, after the fasting is over. So they are willing to work for Sinjo Tandjong for a few months, because he pays them in cash and never forces them to buy rice when they have enough of their own bread, fruit, and *kasbi*. Halik has been suffering for weeks from rheumatic fever. He looks after his youngest child while his wife helps with the picking and Hamba takes care of the fire. On Java the festivities to mark the end of *puasa* last three days but on Buru the stills are idle for almost three weeks. Lamani's crew finish with their still shortly after the beginning of the fast. They have been ill a lot, have taken a lot of pills, and earned little. They are looking for another merchant who will give them a sizable advance and a new set of clothes in exchange for their promise to work one of his stills after *puasa*.

Odeh's people don't fast. They distill the last leaves just before *Hari Raja* and then go to Ambon for the festivities, with their belts full of cash. Odeh leaves with his new gamecock on his arm, and promises to come back for sure, as soon as his money is gone.

The *puasa* began at the end of November and the deer hunting season starts on the first of December. We haven't heard from the *hinolong* in months. We saw his men in the *kampong* a couple of times, selling chickens and *atap*, but they never brought us *kaju-putih* oil to pay off the debt. We send the Alfur gardener to the Wai Apu to ask about the promised oil, and we send a length of rattan along, with ten knots in it: "In ten days the Sinjo and Uncle Heintje will be in Kebulain."

The *hinolong* has repaired the roof of his house, slaughtered a chicken, borrowed cups and plates from all his sons, and spread a white tablecloth over the table. It's true that he can only deliver ten of the fifty bottles of *kajuputih* oil, but it would be impolite to notice such a small difference, since the reception is so friendly. There are deer tracks along the bank of the *kali* and every night pigs come to feed on the leftovers in the stand of trees where the young men beat sago.

They make plans for a big hunt. Heintje knows the right *adat*: all the game is for the guests, but it is expected that everybody with a rifle receives a free shot of powder. There are six usable rifles, including the Sinjo's and Heintje's, but the beaters have also come armed. They repaired their broken muzzle-loaders with bits of wire and rope. They all come to ask for a shot of powder.

For two days they hunt in the hills and in the sago marsh along the river. The women cut up the animals and roast them over a small fire. On the third day the Sinjo and Uncle Heintje help to make *dengdeng*. They have brought salt and saltpeter along. Five deer and seven pigs have been shot. The whole *kampong* is fed for two days and even then there's almost a *pikol* of *dengdeng* left that is packed into empty tins. The last pig is wrapped in fresh bamboo and roasted over the fire; men, women, and children are bloated with meat.

Tonight the men sit around the small fires where they slowly smoke the remaining meat in bamboos so they can keep it even longer. Uncle Heintje has made a big pot of coffee and he passes the tin of sugar around. They talk about hunting as it is today and the way it used to be in the old days. Later the *hinolong* talks about the days of the first *hinolong*, who divided the hunting grounds and gave the mountains and the rivers their names. After a few hours of sleep, the Sinjo and Heintje leave early the next morning. They present their host with the leftover powder. Two sons help carry the *dengdeng* down and the *hinolong* has promised to come to the *tandjong* next month, to deliver the oil. He made thirty knots in a piece of rattan.

My husband will be gone for six days. This is my first night alone. The day has gone by like all the others. The lieutenant and the district officer are both gone on tour, there's only the child I speak

Dutch with. Hans Christiaan is seven months old and he makes
bird noises.

It is evening. I eat under the big lamp on the open back porch.
The tablecloth looks very white in the bright light. A fruit drops
somewhere in the garden, and the surf beats against the reefs,
regularly like breathing. The maid brings a small lamp into the
bedroom and closes the doors. I select a book for the night. As
long as the child is drinking I'm not alone. He looks at me, his
eyes are wise and serious and without fear. The wind rises when
I put him back in his cradle and the curtains are blown into the
room. A bright, metal moon is screwed into the night, and the
shadows of leaves and branches grow into the room against the
klambu of the big bed. There is a communion of poetry, a union in
loneliness that transcends the words and that consoles like music. I read Rilke aloud:

> In this village stands the last house,
> lonely as the last house in the world.

> The street the small village cannot hold
> goes slowly further into the night.

> The little village is only a passage
> between two distances, full of misgiving and afraid,
> a road along houses, not a pathway.

> And those who leave the village wander a long time
> and perhaps many will die along the way.[92]

XIII

This *puasa* is a holiday. Hans Christiaan is trying to pull himself
up in his box under the big *manga* tree. Heintje puts the last strips
of *dengdeng* to dry on old pieces of zinc. A bird of prey is circling
high in the air, the big air rifle stands ready to shoot. The garden
has been hacked open weeks ago; the trees pruned, the coconut
palms cleaned up, and the torn dead *pisang* leaves cleared away.
We have sown spinach and beans in the vegetable plots. Now
that the first rains have come my husband turns the plots over
once again and transplants the first cabbage and the first toma-
toes from their seed beds. When the day gets too hot he comes inside and works on the books. These days we swim every morning
in the small bay in front of the house, where there seems to be no

danger of sharks, but where one shouldn't really swim alone. A *sero*, a big fish trap made of poles with bamboo mats between them, has been set up all along the reef that runs from the *tandjong* a great distance into the sea. At the end is a platform that has been made for the men who come to empty the *sero*. We swim to it, pull ourselves up, and look out over the water. The mountains fold their shadows over the hills, and the heat rises from them like blue vapor. A *tembangan* with red sails slowly rounds the *tandjong*. We hear the ropes and the woodwork creak when it goes about, then the sails catch the wind again and in a stately manner, as if sliding down a long slope, it runs ashore behind the *kampong*. We swim back, the tide is high, a final wave shatters powerlessly against the *antjak* trunks. We are lying in the water that, though calm outside the surf, is restless with sun and shadow under the yellow *antjak* leaves. Our house looks at its best from the sea, low and wide under a safe, brown roof. We touched up the plaster and built a small low wall around the porch. The house now looks like a country house, a farm house in the country with its shutters, painted green and yellow, fastened to the walls. On one side, the bougainvillaea we planted not so long ago reaches for the roof. I called it "The Last House in the World" when we sailed by it in the launch with a group of passengers from the Papua packet. It was early morning and still a little foggy and the white house by the shore seemed to be floating in the gray morning light. A few people laughed, but a tall engineer from the BPM[93] said seriously: "This has to be the last house at the end of the earth. The world begins again after Ternate."

But there is no loneliness today. We are lying next to each other on our own beach under our own trees and Hans Christiaan, naked except for his white hat, is crawling toward us across the first few feet of wet sand.

In the afternoon we play tennis with a couple of Chinese merchants and the clerks of the district office. Sometimes we talk and smoke cigarettes afterwards in the little house on the courts. It is good to know about their joys and worries, it breaks the loneliness Europeans live with, as if under a bell jar.

We are also invited to their parties. The first one was the wedding of Liem See Kie's daughter. She was sitting in front of a high bridal bed in a dress of green Chinese silk, her eyes lowered, her small face powdered white and surrounded by a white tulle veil that hung down in a strange fashion. We ate at a long table on the front porch, together with the district officer, the lieutenant, and the most prominent Chinese who had left China not that long ago. When they slurped a little too much, the host patted them on the back in a fatherly fashion. There were all kinds of delectable soups, shark fins and edible birds' nests that tasted like spoiled jelly, fried fish innards and ten-year-old eggs, pale brown with a fairly strong taste and with dark centers like kidneys. In between courses we chewed on melon pits and drank beer. When a large ant had drowned in my glass, our host fished it out with the fashionable long nail of his left hand.

Ambonese sergeants, clerks, and less respectable Chinese were in the inner gallery. Behind them was the *toko* where *mantris*, attendants, and lesser merchants slurped their soups, under the bright hot light of Petromax lamps. But in the outbuildings slaves and Binunku coolies, half naked, played dice crouched next to plates of food. Outside a flute orchestra of schoolboys played their latest hit, "It's a Jolly Holiday in Zandvoort," while inside the record player coaxed people to "Come with me to Pasadena." The bride was still sitting in front of her bed when we left, long past midnight. She got up and shook hands and said thank you in a high pitched voice, then she arranged the veil around her chair again before she sat down, a small Chinese bride in a European dress. We had eaten too much strange food and felt sentimental.

Months later I went to visit a Chinese family that had lost a child. It was the only son and the mother had stopped having children five years ago. She sat in the *toko* with her head on the counter and sobbed rebelliously and uncontrollably, the way I would have done. Her husband carefully slid his arm under her head and pulled her inside with him, the way my husband would have pulled me along. Later they went to China and bought a son. "Children are cheap in China these days," her mother-in-law told me. It was a sweet little boy with a bright intelligent face, about Hans Christiaan's age. I praised the child and said it was bigger than mine. She smiled politely but her eyes remained hard.

In the evening we go fishing in the small *prao*. We leave before the land breeze starts blowing, at the hour when the sun goes down, and we don't know what to look at first: the red and gold and purple evening sky above us or the coral groves below where orange and blue fish dart between red pipe coral in water so clear and unruffled that we can see our shadows move across the light sand. We fish with *kumang*, [94] hermit crabs that spoil the air and the water with their stench and attract fish from afar. We move from one to the other of our usual spots when we have no success at the first place we try. The light vanishes and the sky quickly loses its color. But when all is dark a streak of light lingers over the mountains of Way Lua like a faded scar. We fish with rod and line, or with a hook, but without a float. The catch varies a lot: sometimes six or seven fish within fifteen minutes, and sometimes it takes an hour before we catch our first one. We can tell what kind of fish we are dealing with from the way it bites. There is the *garova*, with immense jaws, sucking very carefully on the bait, and there is the clever, gold and purple-striped *tatu*, [95] a coffer-fish who pulls the line under the coral where the hook gets stuck and we lose it. The *sibu sibu* rises an hour after sundown, a turbulent wind that makes the water unruly and makes the outriggers of the *prao* beat the water on first one side, then the other. We go home about eight, sailing with the *sibu sibu*, or paddling if it stays away too long, while Uncle Heintje whistles for wind. Sometimes the moon draws us a shining white path, cold and aglow like ice that has not been skated on. But the most glorious trips home are on dark nights, when there is neither moon nor stars but the sea is lit and the fish dot fast tracks through it, the paddles and outriggers hit the water in a spray of silver drops, and we sit hunched forward and see ten thousand candles shining in the dark halls under the sea.

XIV

Every evening we sit out in the breeze together and try out new plans for our workers. The old system is no good, because it forces them to start out in debt. A group of men has to work at least ten days before they can earn anything, and they can get plenty of credit during that time that has to be paid back when the still gets going. For the simple, carefree people of this country the time when they don't earn money is more advantageous than the time when the still is working, because that means they have to pay off their debts. They don't rest after the work is done, enjoying the money they have saved, but they rest before they start working, enjoying the money they get as an advance and the clothes they buy on credit.

Immediately after *puasa* we have a big still built on Wai Senga, with a double oven and a pipeline for the water, and Wimpie Tasisa builds a dorm behind the still. This still will work all year. Leaves can be picked for it in such a wide radius that the first leaves will have grown again when the last leaves have been picked. This way stills won't have to be assembled and then taken down again, which is a useless and time-consuming affair. We would have preferred to build a big central installation, but the terrain is too difficult and too extensive. We're beginning with this one still for the time being, and we are looking for a place to build two more. Only Halik and Hamba continue to work the small still at Walsut, which hardly yields three bottles and earns next to nothing. But they refuse our offer to come and work on the big still for a picker's wage, and to bring the members of their family along. The Sinjo's new plan is a folly far greater than all his previous mistakes. They have always rented a still and worked it the way they wanted: they have plucked leaves whenever they wanted and chopped wood when they felt like it, accumulated a large debt with their merchant and stolen oil to get some cash. They are content with their freedom and twice three bottles per day when the still is producing. The big still and the new living quarters don't appeal to them at all, because Heintje will be there all day to check that the fire is kept at the right temperature, that the oil flows smoothly, and that the terrain around the still is kept clean, and the Sinjo is talking about experiments and ways of macerating the leaves before they go into the still. Walsut is on the border of Batuboi, and once the Sinjo has started his experiments, he won't have much time to come by very often, and there is a high hill on the other side of the *kali,* where there are enough leaves to yield five or six bottles. It is very simple to let the boys pick there in turn and to keep the Sinjo happy with three bottles. And so Halik and Hamba spend three weeks building a small rickety still at Walsut and Uncle Heintje leaves for Ambon to look for workers. A month later he comes back with fifteen people, all from Buton. They have never worked on Buru before, they have never picked a leaf and have never operated a still before, which means that they also know nothing about arson or stealing oil. The still and the living quarters are ready. They can start. We

have been able to persuade La Bunga Itam, one of the oldest distillers, to become *anachoda* for a fixed wage. We give him La Endo,
one of the new people, as an assistant, since the job of *anachoda*
has become much more difficult, because the still has to be filled
twice and emptied twice. Double fires must be maintained as
well. Three people volunteer to chop wood, the others go picking. The first morning their fingers have red scratches from the
flaky twigs they tear the leaves from, but their hands are calloused and the problem disappears after a few days. The group
goes off into the hills at six in the morning. Heintje weighs the
leaves between ten and eleven, and they pick for another two
hours in the afternoon. Pay is computed per hundredweight of
leaves for the pickers, and per cubic yard for those who chop
wood. This way the people who work the still are no longer af-
fected by a high or low harvest of leaves, and that cancels the
preference for certain stills. Nor do we rent the stills anymore.
The workers get paid for the leaves they pick and we do the distilling and accept the advantages and disadvantages of running
the business.

Two ships later we send Heintje again to Ambon and have a
double still built on Pohon Kinar, one and a half hours deeper
into the hills. Four Butonese want to rent a small still on the other
side of the *kali.* Halik and Hamba are still at Walsut and they work
an average of three days a week, even less when it rains hard. But
in spite of the rain that makes the slopes slippery, and the wood
that is still green, and the inexperienced pickers, Wai Senga
keeps operating for months at a time. With new people we must
eventually be able to get a regular production every month,
which is impossible under the old system. Only with steady cus-
tomers and a steady production can we keep a regular business
going.

The price of the oil is low, as is true of other products, and there
is a lot of swindling going on to increase the small profit. Coconut
oil and gasoline can easily be mixed with *kajuputih* oil and there
are complaints from everywhere that there is almost no unadulterated Buru product left. These adulterations happen frequently
and are difficult to prove: when the oil is cloudy and impure it
loses its specific green color on the way to Europe, and with it part
of its commercial value. The bright blue-green color of *kajuputih*
oil comes from the verdigris in the copper distillation apparatus.
Some of the boilers lie far away from the *kampongs,* sometimes a

journey of many hours on foot. The oil is carried down from the stills in old petroleum cans a day before the ship is due to sail. The iron from the can separates the copper during that journey in the hot sun; the rustier the can and the hotter the sun, the redder the oil becomes. Sometimes it's just a little yellow discoloration that can only be spotted in a glass tube but sometimes the oil turns a bright orange. But green or black or red, all colors are accepted on the market in Macassar. Yellow and green oil are mixed, and colored with a chlorophyll preparation when the result is not green enough. This gives the oil a dark and cloudy look. But during the long hot journey to Europe the iron rust keeps on working and discolors even this green to a turbid brown.

Theoretically we are in a very good position. We have our own production of very good oil, we check and buy all the green oil from other merchants, unadulterated oil of good grade. We are able to cream the crop here, to select the best kinds, and to leave the rest, the inferior and discolored oil of suspicious mixture, to the market in Macassar.

But before we increase production with a third still, we build a primitive construction, half house and half *gudang* on Pohon Bulu. We use it to store rice and petroleum, sugar, coffee, and dried fish. Oil is delivered here every night, put through the sieve, checked and measured, and left to settle in glazed pots. The house stands on poles, the floor is made of woven bamboo and wobbles like a primitive suspension bridge, the roof is made of *atap* and the walls are made of woven *nipa* leaves. When the house is ready we stay there for two days with the boy. Four men paddle us across the bay and up the wide *kali* between mangroves with their bright green, fleshy leaves and the messy *nipa* palms with their sheaths broken down along their trunks.

We have to walk for half an hour from the jetty along a path made of tree trunks through a marshy plain, and up a narrow path into the hills. Behind a stand of *windhout*[96] from which red and green screeching parrots fly, a garden that was planted with *pisang* and papaya begins. An open kitchen and a bathroom have been built next to the house, and a bamboo pipeline brings in fresh water from a well in the forest. Life here has reverted to its most primitive form. We eat rice with *dengdeng*, dried meat, and *tjolo-tjolo*, a sauce made from onions, vinegar, and water for dipping raw vegetables. We sleep on the *baleh-baleh* in this green house that still smells of trees and leaves. When we open our eyes in the afternoon to a light that is sieved through the greenery, it seems as if we are waking up enchanted in the hollow of a reed-stalk. The next morning we leave at six to go to the stills on the other side of the *kali,* two hours away. Coconut trees are growing on the beach near the still Prahonie. We drink the water from the young nuts and scrape off the soft meat with a small spoon cut out of the tree's bark. We go back in a long detour that brings us to the stills in the forest. When we get to Pohon Samama we find the *anachoda* squatting by the fire. Two workers are repairing the water pipes. They cut us a cup from a piece of bamboo and we drink the cool water from the well, which tastes of earth, moss, and herbs. We go down the small tributary of the *kali,* jumping from stone to stone, on a shortcut through the forest, until we get to a dry *kali* bed, a wide road rustling with dead leaves. The doves are cooing in the flowering *waringins,* there are deer tracks on the path, a flower blossoms with stiff red leaves, and a vine hangs down from a tree in clusters of flowers that resemble broom, except that they are pink and much more abundant and fragrant. The sun shines directly down on us when we get to a forest meadow overgrown with the stiff leaves of the *kunjit.*[97] Then we go down again to the bed of the *kali,* where the side of the rock rises steeply next to us, astir with green tresses.

We drink lemonade at home, the boy puts the rice on, softens the *dengdeng* in water and cooks the *kankung*[98] for Hans Christiaan. We walk down the path to the *kali,* about a hundred yards below. The water is brackish and muddy in Namlea, but in Batuboi a small clear river flows rapidly over dark stones. There is a wonderful place to bathe, right behind the house, between the bamboo trees. To make sure that nothing can happen a bamboo fence has been built across the *kali* so that the crocodiles, who lie sunning on the protruding mangrove roots at the mouth of the river, can't attack us. After the hard hot walk in the morning we cool off for an hour in the fast flowing water in a pleasant, green twilight. And after that we take our siesta. Maybe we'll get *pisang goreng* with our tea, or else sweet potatoes that grow abundantly here. They are cut into very thin slices, baked until crisp and eaten with sugar. The shadow of the high hills falls pleasantly across the plain. We walk through the plantation, looking for a place for the new seed beds, count pineapples, and collect the papayas that are ripe. After that we take a look at the piglets behind the house of the Alfur gardeners. There are seven of them. One morning the three Alfurs were on their way to the *kali* when they suddenly heard a fierce grunting in a stand of sago trees. The boys let out an old battle cry in unison, and went at it. Both mothers ran away, but the piglets sat there trembling, paralysed, as if enchanted, huddled in the *alang-alang*. Obednego bent down and picked them up as if they were shells on the beach. He put nine of them in his shirt, and two managed to get away. Now they're in a small bamboo cage and eat sago and corn, and sniff our fingers like puppies. Yesterday they had their ears cropped, which means they have graduated to domestic pigs.

Evening comes when the sky changes to red and gold in the west and a cool wind blows through the wide valley and chases away the heat of the day. We have our chairs put outside under the wild *manga* tree. The moon begins to rise and two owls are hooting by the river. Our *mandur* slowly walks down the road to keep watch in the stand of sago. The boy fries eggs for the *nasi goreng* and brings us our coffee. The night is almost cold now.

The *kajuputih* grows on the slopes, and the plain stretches from the mangrove forests on the beach to Tubahoni, the still that marks the border: two hundred acres of *alang-alang*, a swamp that is full of mosquitoes in the rainy season and an inflammable reed field in the dry months. A fire that burns on this plain cannot be contained, because it's all withered *alang-alang* that grows yards high and quickly becomes fuel in a valley that sucks up the flames like a chimney. If it were well drained this soil would be eminently suitable for a coconut plantation, and that's why we filed for long-lease tenure on it. We sit and talk about the day's work, and about the work of the days to come. Later, when the *kajuputih* business will no longer absorb all our energy, we'll plant *kapok* and coconut trees and we'll breed cows to keep the grass cropped.

People are crying out for work all over the world. There's work here: we have oil to distill and we have to teach a people how to work in more honest circumstances. It's a heavy task by day, and a dream at night. To hack open the forest, drain the swamp, put in seed beds, dig holes for plants, and weed the crops until the dangerous plain has been transformed into a fertile garden. A vision of work in the hot days of the eastern monsoon, or in the wind and rainstorms when the monsoon changes. This is a poor country, almost infertile, but rich in the mercy of labor for this day and for all our days to come.

XV

A giant snakeskin hangs drying in the wind; it's twenty feet long and almost four feet wide in the middle.

Buru is a country of gigantic snakes and the snake is the sacred animal of the Alfurs. Legend has it that the population is the off-spring of a princess and a snake. Behind Kajeli, the old settlement of the Company, is a mountain with a very sharp peak, the Gu-nung Kukusan. The tales say that the top is hollow and that there must be a fortune in old porcelain in its depths, but this sacred hidden heirloom is guarded by giant pythons.

We have also heard stories about ordinary snakes. Shortly before we arrived two little sisters were attacked on their way to school by a giant snake. The older girl began to scream and when the men came running they found the corpse of the younger one, completely crushed, with not a bone left unbroken.

One night Uncle Heintje heard the fearful scream of a pig be-hind our house in Batuboi, and a few hours later, in daylight, they discovered a wide track in the *alang-alang* as if a *prao* had been dragged through it. The Alfur gardener knows the explana-tion. A snake caught a pig and went off into the bushes to digest it while it slept. He immediately gets his long lance and takes off into the *alang-alang*, followed by Heintje, who doesn't feel very safe even though he is armed with a double-barreled shotgun. The snake has gone to the river where the soil is marshy and the sago trees stand close together. Later the tracks circle back and make a big turn by the house, and when the pursuers step out of the shadow of the tall *alang-alang* they find the python in the mid-dle of the road, no more than fifteen feet away from them, rolled up like a hawser. The Alfur tickles it with his lance and it shoots up into the air like a spring. Heintje misses the first time, horrified by the terrible head that's ten feet above the ground, but the sec-ond shot smashes the cervical vertebrae.

After work that afternoon, they throw the beast in the *prao*, and row down the river and across the bay to the *tandjong*. It's Sunday afternoon, we are drinking tea on the lawn when the *prao* runs ashore. The snake takes up the entire bottom of the *prao*, but we have to wait until it is stretched out on the beach to see what an incredible beast it is, over twenty feet long from head to tail and almost four feet thick! In the middle bulges the stomach and you can clearly see the outline of a pig's body. Willem is sent out to buy a roll of film and he rouses the whole *kampong*. First appears the Chinese healer, who puts in a bid for the gall bladder, but other people come rushing up before the bidding is over. Such a snake has not been shot in years. With great interest the skin is cut open and the pig rolls out of the snake's stomach the way Lit·tle Red Riding Hood came out of the stomach of the wolf. The pig is still intact, a young almost full-grown animal. They proceed with cutting the snake open on the beach, looking for the gall bladder. It gives off a sickening stench and we have both the snake and the pig weighed down with stones and thrown into the water behind the *tandjong* as soon as possible. But the next morning, when the reef emerges at low tide, an Alfur retrieves the pig, roasts it, and asks a few friends over. It must have been quite spoiled by then: even the Alfuran intestines can't take it. It works like castor oil, and they spend the rest of the day on the beach.

A snake is never alone; somewhere in the dark sago forest its mate must still be crawling around.

We don't get to shoot another snake, but we do get something else soon afterwards. One evening an Alfur boy walks to the spot where we bathe, to wash some clothes in the river, and he almost steps on a crocodile. The animal is lying right behind the bamboo fence, it must have come from upstream. Fernand also decides to put an end to our carefree bathing in the *kali*. The bathroom in the house, which was never used, is put in order and Batuboi has lost one of its charms. The Alfurs put out a shark hook with bait on it, and the next morning we find the hook—made of the best English steel—bitten off and dangling from the wire. Heintje maintains that you can only catch a crocodile with a hook made of deer's antlers.

Even before a stag is shot, the fight takes place in a small tributary *kali* that's almost dry. Again the Alfurs are the first to notice the crocodile and they send word to the house to alert Uncle Heintje. He happens to be weighing leaves at the moment, and a whole group of workers goes to the *kali* with him. The animal is still in the same spot, partially submerged in the thick mud, its head and the upper part of its back clearly visible. The old hunter empties both barrels at it, but the lead bullets are crushed flat against the horny skin. The animal does take off, however, and flees in the direction of the big river. The boys run shouting through the forest, trying to cut it off at one of the bends. They make bamboo lances and chase the crocodile back to the fence.

This time the gun is loaded with grooved bullets which pierce the armored skin and enter the heart. The crocodile raises itself on its short front legs, bellows like a bull, and opens its immense jaws as wide as it can. The workers push it back, most of its strength is gone and it can only put up a weak defense. The Alfurs throw a noose around its head and drag it home, where they give it the coup de grâce, though even that doesn't finish it off. The crocodile tries to escape again in the middle of the night, dragging the long bamboo pole it has been tied to straight through the tomato beds. Nobody is asleep, there are no grooved bullets left and ordinary ones have no effect. When it is finally dead, they put the animal in a *prao* and take it to the *tandjong*. It is infinitely more terrifying and revolting than the snake.

The left half of our garden on the *tandjong* turns out not to be very fruitful; neither work nor manure has been able to improve the quality of the soil. The chalk keeps coming through a thin layer of earth. The only thing that will thrive there is *alang-alang*. If we put a sturdy fence around it, it would be a good place to keep pigs. One day we hear that three pigs form part of the "tanate" that has just been delivered, and we decide to buy them. The "tanate" is a kind of tax that Alfurs have to pay. When Buru came under the direct rule of the Dutch East Indies government, the Alfurs were told that they had to pay taxes, which they promptly refused to do. They had never paid taxes before and, being conservative by nature, refused to do so on principle. But they had to admit that they used to pay a yearly tribute to the sultan of Ternate, and it was finally agreed that from now on this tribute would be paid to the Company, since the Company had taken over the sultan's rights. The tribute, which should never be considered a tax, is called "tanate" and it is paid in *atap, gaba-gaba, katjang,* sago, millet, pigs, and chickens. All this is taken to Namlea, put up for auction, and accounted for, and that's how we got our pigs.

They are ordinary Alfuran pigs, that is to say wild pigs, which were caught when small and domesticated. Their ears have been cropped to distinguish them from their kind in the forest. Two boars and a sow is not the best possible arrangement, but the second boar is not fully grown yet and we are thinking of buying a few more females in the *tangsi*. A *tangsi* in the Indies is quite different from a barracks in Holland. Only professional soldiers are stationed in these outposts. They live in large sheds, with their wives, children, chickens, parrots, and dogs. Because there is often very little in such small places, each *tangsi* has its own vegetable garden and its own stables for pigs and goats. But we discover that our breeding plans will most likely come to nothing, even before we decide to acquire some military pigs. An old Chinese tells us that both boars have been castrated, so we should really buy a breeder in the *tangsi,* but when we ask the sergeant who is in charge of the stables to find one for us, he comes up with a five-day-old piglet. All the others have been castrated to put a stop to their incredible proliferation.

For the moment at least our pig farm won't be expanding, because there are no pigs for sale in Namlea, which is a predominantly Muslim *kampong.* From time to time a Chinese will fatten an animal he got from the Alfurs for next to nothing, but you can't say that they really breed them. We have placed an order for a full grown boar with the Alfurs, but they still live in a timeless world, and what they promise to do in half a month is usually delivered in half a year.

We spend a week looking for a pig boy. The Christians are too refined for this kind of job, and the Muslims won't go near a pig. Fortunately an Alfur appears, a respectable murderer who has done his time and wants to enjoy the blessings of civilization in Namlea a little longer before he retires to his mountains. Having two kinds of pigs turns out to be a problem. The *tangsi* pigs are used to cooked food, but the Alfur piglets are raised on leftovers of sago and cassava roots and refuse cooked food. We can't get sago refuse in Namlea, and although everybody has *kasbi* in his garden, nobody is willing to sell it. Our backyard is full of *sukuns* with big fruits that used to keep shipwrecked sailors alive on uninhabited islands. They are very good for pig fodder and the *tangsi* pigs love them, but the Alfur pigs won't touch them. The problem would have solved itself after a few days, but the Alfur boy sides with the Alfur pigs. He thinks we are cruel and stupid and he expresses his disapproval in every way. But we win the battle against the Alfurs, the pigs, and the boy. The pigs are given corn and breadfruits, and the Alfur rebels scream for a week, but after that they eat along with the others. And suddenly a breeder appears, after all. One morning we discover the tracks of a wild boar around the pen. We try to think of a way to get it inside without letting the others out. On the third night he divides his attention between the sows in the pen and a row of recently planted cassava. The next evening he is fatally shot.

XVI

There are more *tokos* in Namlea than ordinary homes, but their number doesn't matter since they all sell the same things. They all cater to the needs of the still workers. Anyone who owns one or two stills also runs a *toko* and pays for the oil in merchandise.

There are also three or four big shops and they, too, are very similar. They stink of cockroaches, Chinese medicine, and *kajuputih* oil. Newly imported merchandise is stacked high: cotton fabric, tennis shoes, beautifully striped shirts, red pants, enameled dishes and plates with red and yellow flowers on them. But the most incongruous objects appear from dark corners and bottom drawers. Before the Depression they used to make big money here. In 1928 *kajuputih* oil went for one hundred and fifty guilders a *pikol,* and the nights weren't long enough to spend the money that was earned during the day. Those were the days when they imported the beautifully lacquered shoes, the watches, alarm clocks, and expensive brands of cognac. Then the market fell, and the merchants were stuck with all their pretty stuff, and since they considered a sale uneconomical, they stashed everything away until better days. But the better days never came. Instead came the invasion of cheap Japanese goods and as a result the expensive stuff was moved to the back of the shops, where it stayed, gathering dust. If you want pointed shoes with lacquered toes, you can get them up here for a song, and the same goes for swollen tins of butter that has turned into shoe polish and alarm clocks that have rusted through. But sometimes you find merchandise that has aged well: a box of Sunlight soap, a little moldy and the wrappers faded, but you can get it at half price; or a bottle of excellent port that has profited a great deal from isolation. Browsing is an exciting and entertaining affair. You stumble from one miracle to another. But you shouldn't object to scurrying cockroaches and can't have too fancy a nose.

This refers to the imported merchandise, but you can also find native products such as the dark-grained *salmudi* wood, heavy beams of ebony, and dried python skins ranging in length from ten to thirty feet. The martaban jars[99] are fragrant with *kajuputih* oil, and one can smell it everywhere.

Once every four weeks the big ship arrives: the KPM ship from Macassar. That is the most important day of the month. Normally the boat anchors in the bay from sunup to sundown. We eat on board, we receive visitors, and for a day we are part of the world. As soon as we have heard the anchor chain rattle, we run to the bathroom, trying to get to the ship with the first launch. The first-class deck has been scrubbed clean, the beer and the orange crush are deliciously cold. The Chinese merchants have set up shop downstairs on the middle deck. They travel the East from Macassar all the way beyond Ternate and along the coasts of Papua and Halmahera. Their merchandise travels in gigantic crates, and everything is stacked during the journey: hundreds of cotton prints —with small patterns for the long *kabajas* of the Ambonese women, and patterns in bright colors for the Muslim ladies—bright green and pink checkered *sarongs* of the kind the Sulanese and the Binongkos wear, thousands of velvet *toppies*, shirts, shoes, knives, plates, blankets, mattresses, and fake Boldoot eau de cologne.[100] I do my shopping here around Christmas, when we have to buy presents for our Ambonese servants: cloth for pants and *kabajas*, leather sandals, towels, and broad-rimmed hats for the men.

You can also buy things when the *tokos* have an auction: tins of oatmeal, boxes of soap, milk, ham, and jars of jam of the most varied kinds and makes. It's just that you never know what you're going to find. One month I'm looking for jam and come home with soap, and the next month I need oatmeal and there is only an immense supply of baby food, or a choice selection of toilet mirrors. Every month brings a different surprise, but the bustle and the stench remain the same. All merchants stock up on the ship, and when it returns two weeks later from its journey to Halmahera they pay their bills with *kajuputih* oil which is brought on board in stone *tempanjangs*[101] and old soybean oil crocks, the way it comes from the stills, and is taken along to Macassar, unchartered. Every day has its own adventure. Sometimes there are fishermen from the Philippines who dive into the sea from their small narrow *praos* and overcome big fish with their steel arrows They wear next to nothing, just their goggles and a pair of shorts. The arrow is hurled from a kind of catapult that looks like a gun and the fish is retrieved from among the coral on the bottom. The fish are bright green or fiery red, but there are also spiny lobsters and small octopuses, called *guritas*,[102] and sharks, which are hit behind the head with steel arrows. It's fun to sit on the beach on the driftwood and buy brooms, sago, eggs, and coconut oil from a man in a leaking *prao*. He looks like the dwarf in Nils Holgersson,[103] but his name is Makararu, "Eclipse of the Moon." This morning, after breakfast, we heard somebody call "ikan, ikan," and a small *prao* with a square sail from Ceram rounds the *tandjong* and quickly runs ashore under the big *ketapang* tree. I am sitting on a somewhat bleached tree trunk that has been washed ashore, and the man displays his wares for me: live fish just caught in the mouth of the Wai Apu where crocodiles like basking in the sun on the sandbanks when the tide is out and where there are so many sharks that the fishermen often pulls up on the head of his catch because the shark strikes faster than a man can pull. I haggle for a quarter of an hour, time is irrelevant. Finally we come to an agreement: eighteen *tonkols*[104] are counted out on the beach in front of me—a small kind of tuna with delicate, fat meat. I pick a couple of beauties for ourselves, and the still workers will use the rest for *ikan asar*,[105] smoked fish. For this purpose the fish is cut open, gutted, salted, and smoked over a small fire of coconut shells. We have a big family and have to feed forty still workers, so we often buy fish by the *prao*-load and smoke it all ourselves, because it's a hot trip to the place where the *kajuputih* is distilled. Sometimes *praos* will bring *djulung*,[106] a kind of seapike which the people from Negri Lima on Hitu catch while deep-sea fishing. The fish is meant to be smoked and gets a good price in Ambon, but now and again the fishermen bring a *prao* full to Namlea to get some cash. We can hear them coming in the distance, in a big *orembaai* paddled by twenty men to the beat of their own song and the beat of the rower in the bow. The *prao* becomes bigger and the sound of the voices becomes more distinct. They round the *tandjong* and the wind blows the words of the rowing song toward us:

> Kole kole
> Orembaai, kole
> Radja patih tanah barat
> Orembaai, kole.
>
> Undure, undure,
> Djangan kami undure
> Apa datang dari muka
> Djangan kami undure

("Kole, kole Orembaai, kole. Powerful king from the west [the west wind], Orembaai, kole. Go back, go back. We won't go back, no matter what the dangers are ahead. We won't go back.") Everybody runs to the beach because the fast exciting song has made us all restless. People gather on the jetty in the *kampong*. There soon will be a big fight because the *djulung* is cheap and there hasn't been any fish for days. We, on the *tandjong*, don't stand a chance because we are a fifteen-minute walk from the jetty, so I send the gardener out in the small *prao* to wait for the *orembaai*. The song stops and the *djulung* is counted out, a thousand for three guilders, a *prao* full of green glistening fish. The drumbeat is heard again, and the people push and shove on the jetty in the *kampong*. Now the work begins for us. Everybody wants to help, because there are always a few fish left at the end. Heintje, his wife and children, the gardener, everybody rushes in. Bamboo is split and woven into small racks. The fish is soaked in salt water and then pressed to the small racks by means of a few crosspieces. The small racks are placed side by side on a piece of chicken wire with a small fire under it, a small fire that produces a lot of smoke. One boy stays behind to keep an eye on things, the others go back to their usual jobs. Sometimes a flame leaps up, immediately extinguished with a handful of coconut fibers. At night it is a marvelous sight with everybody busy under the tall *manga* tree behind the *mandur*'s house. The place is lit by a petroleum lamp suspended from a protruding branch; the lamp produces a restless light, because the landwind has risen and makes it swing back and forth. When the work is done people stay around the fire to roast more fish, breadfruits, or cassava. Somebody gets up to turn the *djulung* over and a child stumbles sleepily into the house toward its mat. This is a life of uncommon intimacy.

Somewhere is a line that divides us into ordinary people or adventurers. Ordinary people will never understand the happiness or the charm of this life. They miss the comfort of the cities, the ice machines, electric light, schools, doctors, and the movie theaters where for one evening they can enjoy the romanticism of a desolate island, but from a comfortable chair.

One can talk to adventurers. They understand the pleasure of a trip in a leaky *prao*, the excitement of an unexpected shot and the scream of a dying animal, the discomfort of the rains, a leaky roof, and rivers that *bandjir*. If one's life has been lightened by the grace of adventure there is a feeling of nostalgia in cities and inhabited places and a slight irritation at an inglorious existence, safe and without risks. Such were the lost sons who set sail and died and the colonies became their legacy. But the colonies have become overseas territories where they prefer to exclude adventurers. Luckily there are still some lonely places and hidden islands left where a fool can live and be grateful for the grace of his exceptional existence.

XVII

The festivities for the queen's birthday have started by sunrise, otherwise the overloaded program could not be taken care of in twenty-four hours. It's barely six when the schoolchildren file past in a long row. Each school has its own banner, but the children also wave small flags and play their bamboo flutes. Most of them wear blue shorts and new white shirts. The Muslims wear black *sonkos*,[107] a kind of fez, and the Chinese boys wear white suits and big caps that make them look both serious and sly, like the portraits of their famous generals. All the children stop in front of the district officer's house, they serenade him with the national anthem and the smartest child quickly rattles off a speech in High Malay, which it understands as much as a schoolchild in Holland would understand Middle Dutch. They get cookies and pink syrup drinks before they march off to the jetty where the *praos* are now lining up for the race.

On Ambon, with its hundreds of *praos* and its many experienced rowers, this is the main event of the day. Any settlement of even the slightest significance has sent its *orembaai*, with twenty rowers and a man in the bow to beat the rhythm. The boats are built especially for the race, very slender and very fast, with a bow and stern curving up into a sharp point. They have trained for months and a lot of money is bet on them. With the racing *praos* come the revelers. First the *radjas* in an *orembaai* decorated with coconut leaves and flags, accompanied by gongs and flutes and the loud singing of male voices. The *praos* sail to the city of Ambon from all over, and give the bay a festive appearance with their music and their flags. Here on Buru we get only a smaller version of the big feast in Ambon: there are no *orembaais* with sharp lines, high bows, and well-trained rowers to compete for the prize. We only have some *koleh-kolehs* and outrigger *praos* manned by still workers and fishermen, which hurry between the beacon and the jetty. But the air is still cool above the bright water, and people with happy faces and festive clothes are everywhere along the shore, in the *praos*, on the beach, and in the trees that spread their branches over the water.

A church service follows a hurried breakfast. The *guru* waits for us at the door and takes us to our seats. The church has been whitewashed like a barn, and the congregation sits on low bamboo chairs except for the Europeans, who are only expected to attend this one day and for whom a row of wooden chairs has been reserved right under the *guru*'s lectern. We're sitting there as if we've been punished and the entire congregation stares at us. The small group of shrill flute players that replaces the organ in Moluccan churches has been reinforced with the excellent orchestra from Kajeli. The psalms sound splendid with this accompaniment, threatening and imploring impetuously like a Negro choir.

After the service we are expected at the district officer's to pay our respects, a parody of the solemn Public Audience that is now customary in the Indies in places like this. After that we take some time out to bathe and change, and the flute band is already waiting on the doorstep to escort us. Together with the district officer, the military commander, and the Javanese doctor, we walk to the district office. Chairs are waiting on the big open porch, the schoolchildren are lined up on the front lawn and every school presents something. The girls from Wamlana dance around a Maypole, the Waplau school gives a demonstration of gymnastics, Chinese boys and girls sing a song translated from Dutch in shrill Mongol voices, but the most interesting presentation is the war dance, the *takalele*[108] performed by Alfurs from the Wa Apu region. They appear while *tandakking*[109] in a wide circle, dance twice around the open space, and then each one jumps at his adversary. They fight each other two by two with small wooden swords to the beat of the *tifa*, a drum made of deerskin, and ward off the blows with a long wooden shield. They wear red loincloths and a red cloth has been casually tied around their unkempt hair like a ribbon. Their *guru*, a man from Ambon, didn't think that the red loincloth covered enough, hence they wear black cotton swimming trunks under it, accented with red and green stripes, which make them look silly. The *tifa* is beating faster, their feet go faster too, the blows sound hollow on the wooden shields, they jump forward and avoid each new blow with an increasingly faster tempo.

It turns out to be the big success of the morning and the rest of the day they walk around in the *kampong* with happy faces. They're Alfurs from the mountains and hardly speak any Malay; they are as shy as animals, but today they are the most important participants. They will be back next year, of course, and with a new *guru* who will have managed to find a better solution to the problem of nakedness. They will wear trousers and a kind of sleeveless jacked made from the bark of trees, their *adat* dress, which is not worn any more on Buru. There's nobody left who knows how it should be made, only some old woman remembers anything at all. The dancing clothes should not be compared to the old dress in any way, because these are coarse, made of long fiber, and disintegrate very quickly. But it is a good solution to the clothing problem: you can't very well go to the "Feast of the Thirty-First"[110] with only a red loincloth to cover the scabies on your stomach.

After the performances, games are held under the supervision of the *gurus*. Those who win get to choose first, but there is a prize for everybody. The boys' prizes are wrapped in pink copies of the *Haagsche Post*,[111] the girls' prizes in ordinary newspaper: pieces of cloth, cheap *kains*, belts, and towels.

In the restaurant under the *waringin* tree Ahmed puts the first *sate*[112] on the charcoal grill. Once a year Namlea can boast of a restaurant. Ahmed came to Namlea as a *djongos* and stayed here after his *tuan* was transferred. He comes from Batavia and is a carpenter, a bricklayer, a cook, and a gardener. He knows everything, has heard of everything, and tries everything. He has the gift of gab, is not too honest and not too reliable, but he's an energetic person and a real adventurer.

A few days before he went to all the notables, told them of his plans, asked them if he could count on their business, and borrowed small tables and chairs. By noon a tent of *atap* has been constructed—a large open space decorated with young coconut leaves and paper garlands—where we find our chairs around our tables.

Ahmed leaves his *sate* in order to greet us, we admire his set-up and examine the kitchen where all that good stuff is cooking in borrowed pans. We nibble on *krupuk*[113] and *katjang goreng*[114] and

Ahmed rearranges the seats into one big circle and takes our orders. Cold beer and lemonade are brought from the canteen and the first course is served: *soto*, a kind of chicken soup from Java. After that we eat *sate kambing*, goat's meat skewered on little sticks and roasted, with a hot sauce of Spanish peppers, lemon, and soja, and served with *lontong*, rice cooked in *pisang* leaves. The variety of dishes is limited, but they taste wonderful and it's quite an affair to eat in a restaurant, even if it is no more than a Batavian *warong* where you'd never find a European. But people are feasting today all over the Indies, and we're also part of it, and so is Namlea.

In the afternoon there is a soccer game between the most important clubs in Namlea: *Oranje* and the military team. Soccer has very little to do with sports in the Moluccas, but it is a nice opportunity to settle general and particular grievances. Most games end in a fight or are the cause of another one that sometimes isn't settled until weeks later. The game on the thirty-first is the most important one, and months later the losers still look at the winners suspiciously and vengefully. The best thing to do would be to drop the game altogether, but because a former district officer contributed a silver challenge cup when he left, it means that they have to play for this trophy every year, and there will be no peace in Namlea until one club has won it three years in a row, and nobody knows how many years will have to pass before the shame and the revenge of the other clubs will be forgotten.

Then there is only the evening left, the *dansi-dansi*[115] in the big shed. The administration has put up the money for it, and the district officer acts as host. Everybody who is not a coolie or a still worker has been invited: all the Chinese and Arab merchants, the regents and other local chiefs, the *gurus, mantris,* and attendants. The shed has been decorated with Chinese lanterns and coconut leaves, chairs and benches are lined up against the walls, and bottles of beer and lemonade are waiting on a big table. They found a couple of respectable-looking murderers in prison, put them in white jackets, and made them waiters. The first people arrive a polite hour late. Most women are wearing white *kabajas,* with the wide sleeves drawn tight around their wrists and buttoned with small gold buttons. They wear silver pins in the hair knots in the nape of their necks, ornately embroidered church slippers appear from under the folds of their *rokkis*[116] and flowered *kains* with ironed pleats. The men are wearing their white church *kabajas* and

cloth trousers, and instead of jackets *sitsen baniangs*[117] with small
blue or purple flowers on a white background. The *baniang* has no
collar, hangs open in front, and looks like a bolero jacket that has
turned out a bit too long. The flute orchestras from Namlea and
Kajeli sit on tables and chairs at the back of the shed. This morning they provided the music for the psalms, and tonight they'll be
playing old waltzes. Immediately after the first glass of beer, the
couples take their places for the quadrille. Josua, the fat *mantri*,
leads the dance with his big accordion and he calls out the figures.
He waves his fat hand and the couples bow and part, come together for a couple of waltzing steps, then bow and part again.
Now all the women stand still, and only the men dance, and then
the women step toward each other. "Senangalé" *(chaîne anglaise)*:
the arms are held high in an arch and, on the tips of their toes,
they exchange places, on and on. Josua shouts such unintelligible
sounds as: "senangalé, agoos, mulinékrois." My husband translates: "chaîne anglaise, à gauche, moulinette à quatre." People
are dancing in a proper and dignified manner, the stiff *baniangs*
creak, a *rokki* fold rustles, the men dance barefoot, and the wom-
en have also already kicked off their slippers for a fast waltz. The
best dancers found each other, regardless of race or rank: the
lieutenant's wife is dancing with our *mandur*, the district officer
with the wife of a servant. This dance takes more than an hour,
the movements succeed each other in endless variations, and
when the final notes have been played and the ladies have been
escorted back to their chairs with a bow, the men light cigarettes
and the women giggle behind their white handkerchiefs. Then
the *tifa* begins to sound and the *menari* lovers form a circle.

The *menari* is a typical folk dance from pagan times, and though
it is no longer danced as in the old days, it still is honored at all
Muslim celebrations. But it is pagan, Alfuran in origin. The first
Moluccan Christians wanted to shed their Alfuran past as fast
as they could. They took the names of their Dutch masters, forgot their old pagan dances, lost their language and their entire
culture, learned to speak a mixture of Malay, Portuguese, and
Dutch, went to church in black clothes, and danced the quadrille.
That's why the Christians still dance the old genteel dances from
the days of the Company, and why the Muslims have kept the Alfuran *menari*. People who have seen the beautiful subtle dances of
Java are soon bored by these *menaris*.

The *tifa* pounds. While bowing, men squat next to women with downcast eyes. They stretch their arms and twist their hands back and forth. The man dances around the woman in wide circles that quickly become smaller and smaller, like a rooster around the chicken he desires, until the *tifa* stops with a final resounding blow. The flute orchestra starts up again after a little while and Josua plays his accordion to call people together for a new quadrille. It gets stiflingly hot in the shed, the dust from the dirt floor is swirling around, and the coconut oil in the hair of the women begins to smell unpleasantly rancid. Day has come when the *tifa* is silent at last and the smallest boy in the flute orchestra stumbles home, drunk with sleep.

XVIII

It is Hans Christiaan's birthday. He is standing on the lawn beside the house, wearing a pair of shorts embroidered in yellow and blue. We got him a small deer for a birthday present. We had a lot of rice cooked, in bright festive colors, with all kinds of herbs, and roasted chickens over small charcoal fires. Everybody at our place has to eat with us.

We've known for two months that Hans Christiaan won't be an only child. My husband is primitive enough to be happy in spite of the worries but I cry at night because I hate this child. I have a secret fear that it will kill me because of that. I want to keep him hidden like a shameful secret. I can't talk about it to anyone, not even at home. My mother writes to me how worried she is about my sister who is expecting her first baby. But in Holland you can find a doctor's house in every street, and in every fourth street there is a hospital with drugs and instruments and the mercy of painkillers. I don't want to ask for money. I am married and I have a husband to take care of me. If you have children you pay for them either with money or with death. I pay for it, the full amount, with all the horrors of an incredible fear.

Hans Christiaan was born on Ambon, but we can't even think of going to Ambon now, there is neither time nor money. My husband goes to the concession four or five days a week, and he spends his nights in the *pondok*. We also took over the other half of Batuboi. The whole concession is operational now, to keep the taxes and land rent down and to keep our operating costs as low as possible. The demand for oil of good quality remains a fiction of the Trade Museum and the Experimental Station in Buitenzorg.[118] There's only demand for cheap oil, quality is secondary. Our oil is beginning to be known: we can get rid of everything we have, but we want a better price for our superior quality and that usually is the end of a deal. Communication is another problem. The mail boat comes directly to the island once a month, there is also a connection via Menado,[119] but that is highly irregular and not very reliable. We can receive telegrams, but they can only be sent from Ambon, and only every two weeks does a boat go to Ambon.

Prices go down every month. Profit is a thing of the past. We are subsisting on our capital, even though we live like the local people on rice and vegetables and on what can be shot or caught. The other merchants make no profit either, but the problem is simpler for them: they increase the price of their staple goods and make some more money on rice and petroleum until this also comes to an end and then in the following few months the flames leap up.

The nights are bright with fire. From the Sula islands, Buru looks like a red fog. I have never seen it burn as it does this year. The whole coast is burned black like a mine shaft; Batuboi and the narrow strip of coast near Namlea seem green islands on either side of the bay. The borders are guarded every night, because every day brings the threat that the fire will jump from the adjoining acreage to our land. Only when the rains begin is the greatest danger past. In some places along the border a slope has been scorched black, but no fire has been set on our land. This proves what we keep on trying to explain to the colonial administration: ninety percent of the fires on Buru are the result of bad working conditions. But the people themselves want to keep things that way. They don't want to stay with us; every time the boat comes we have to get new people from Ambon as replacements because every month our people go over to the Chinese. A man who has worked almost a full year wants to quit and we ask him why he wants to leave. His answer is typical of his people's thinking: "Bajaran bagus, makanan murah, tetapi tita terlalu keras,"[120] that is to say, the pay is good, the food is cheap, but the rules are too bothersome. To him "tita" means that he has to begin his work on time, that he has to take medicine when he is ill, that he has to have his living quarters checked for cleanliness, and that he has to work under supervision. And most of the others think the way he does. We can rarely keep people more than a year: they either have saved enough to go back to Buton, or they didn't get enough of an advance and then the Chinese looks very tempting again. There are a few exceptions. Odeh Madi returned from Ambon with six friends. La Runga never wants to leave us again, though a couple of times a year he will ask permission to roam around for a month, but he always comes back. La Endo and La Kini and a few others have also decided to stay with us, and those crooks Halik and Hamba work little, but consistently. Some day we will have the nucleus of a work force, but during these months our troubles are almost unbearable.

I am alone with Hans Christiaan and this new child I do not know nor love, that has neither shape nor name and who has backed me into this corner. I live in a cool house, in a big garden that provides us with coconuts, fruits and vegetables, chickens and eggs. Sometimes the *prao* comes home unexpectedly with a pig tied to the outriggers or a haunch of venison tied behind the mast. Those are the good things of this life, the green, wild scent of adventure. If the new child wasn't there I would be able to enjoy it, without a care, unharmed by loneliness, and rarely worried by money because I am essentially in search of adventure, and money only torments the bourgeois.

But who is going to take care of me when this new child is born? I know that this year's budget for the district of Buru includes a doctor and a small hospital. If it had been a position in private industry it would have been filled in a few months, but a bureaucrat never hurries. It takes two cells forty weeks to grow into a child, but the promised doctor only materializes two years after the child has been born.

A fall from a roof, pneumonia, a wound from an axe, or the horrible crocodile bite from the groin to the knee on both sides of the leg. There are many ways for a man to die, but small children die because they are overfed and women die in childbirth. "Tuan Allah punja mau,"[121] God's will, say the people of this country, the Christian, the Muslim, and the pagan Chinese. A piety that is blasphemy! Smile for God's sake when there's a fire, an earthquake, death, bad harvests, or a raging flash flood, but leap up like a flame at the evil people will inflict on you, be it from injustice, laxity, bureaucracy, stupidity, or neglect of duty.

A *kapal putih* docks unexpectedly at Namlea. It has a health officer on board who finds everything in order. He lets me listen to the child's heartbeat, a small, quick heart. This is the first tenderness. The small, quick heart of a child.

Five days later I wake up with the first vague pain. Both Hans Christiaan and my husband have a fever. The *kebon* brought ripe pineapples. I bathe the boy and give him aspirin and I cook syrup and jam from the pineapples. Everything is ready in the guest room. It's going to happen this night. I am not scared anymore, only a little bit excited and very clear-headed, as if taking an exam.

The pain returns at noon. Hans Christiaan still has a high fever, he begins to rave in the evening, and it's ten o'clock before he falls asleep. We let the lamp hang high in the guest room. The boy has boiled two cans of water. We walk arm in arm on the narrow path in front of our house. The clerks from the district office are shooting at bats on the other side of the fence, by the flagpole. The animals that are hit scream like tortured children. We walk up and down until I no longer dare stay outside.

The big lamp makes the small room very hot. I am lying on the narrow bed, and Fernand gets a low chair. We both have a book. I try to read while the pains come faster and I recite aloud Marsman's[122] beautiful poem "In Memoriam P. M.-S." A cloth hangs over the lamp. My pillow is in the shadow, but the light falls on my hands and the blue book. Fernand drops off to sleep. I put my hand on his thigh, I feel the fever burning through the thin pajamas, and then there is a new attack of pain. I am lying on my back, I'd rather be on my side, but I don't know if that is advisable. The pain ebbs and then rises again.

"Fernand."

He sleeps on. I am lying right under the open window, I pull the curtain back a little and I feel the salt taste of tears in my mouth, not because of the pain but because of the terrible loneliness. Now I am beyond all mankind on the desolate, arctic plain, the rigid cold loneliness of death. Things get confused after that, there is the pain and the cold that well up from the heart, but at the same time my burning head soaks the pillow. I fall asleep for a moment, wake up from the pain, and fall asleep again. This will go on at least until morning. It was about midnight when we went inside. It is still dark outside, a foredawn[123] moon rises. I wake Fernand to ask him what time it is. He switches his flashlight on and goes to the inner gallery to look at the clock. One thirty. This had been going on for only an hour and a half.

"Wake Enggeh and tell her to make some coffee."

He walks out of our house, crosses the little lawn to the *man-*

dur's house, and rattles the shutter.

The pain pushes me back, four, five contractions right after each other. Something soft and warm that seeps away. I try to grab the curtain so I can look outside, and fall back again. Fernand is standing in the door.

"Why didn't you come sooner?"

The wind rises and blows the newspaper off the lamp. I throw my arm over my eyes and over my mouth. Then the child cries.

"Lie still."

He sits on the edge of the bed, ties off the umbilical cord, and wraps the child in a towel. A gust of wind blows the curtain up against the ceiling. Enggeh stands by the door and says: "How can it be here already?"

"Come here," I say, "take it."

"Is it a *sinjo?*" she asks.

Fernand holds the child in his arms, still rolled in a towel. His face is pale and tired and very tender. He says: "I didn't notice." He unfolds the towel. "It's a boy." The people of this country call the placenta *kaka*, the elder brother. They imagine that two children begin to grow at the same time and that one dies at birth so that the other may live. They use this *kaka* to prepare medicine and magic charms while invoking the devil, all done according to the proven recipes of Ambonese black magic. That's why we dare not bury the placenta and instead have it weighed down with stones and thrown into the sea. Willem, the houseboy, was probably too lazy to push the *prao* off the beach, and threw the package into the water while still standing on the shore. The water quickly assumes the smell of blood.

Both the baby and I have been taken care of, the big lamp has been taken away, and my husband is drinking a cup of coffee outside. The moon rises. Suddenly somebody on the beach shouts very loudly: "Buaja, buaja." A chair falls down in the office when my husband grabs his double-barreled shotgun, and shortly thereafter there are two shots. The dogs run around the house, barking like crazy.

I sit up straight in bed and understand: a crocodile went after the placenta. I am panting and I breathe rapidly.

"Buaja, buaja." The child is born and I am alive. It's all over: the fear, rebellion, and loneliness; there's only this wild, primitive ecstasy of the adventure that is life, this hard, lonely life in this remote, this blessed land.

XIX

Hans Christiaan fell ill while we were staying in Ambon, and because they were afraid it might be polio, I spent four weeks in the military hospital with him, completely cut off from the world, in a small isolation ward with no other view than the morgue. But he returned to us safe and unharmed from the fevers and delusions. His little brother can walk when we get back to Namlea. Children grow so fast into life, the elder is four years old and the younger two, and we take them along on all our trips. This time we rented a big *prao* and are going to sail to Ambelau where we want to hire woodcutters. The children play in the empty boat for two days, and they are so excited they can hardly get to sleep. It's a big outrigger *prao* over twenty-five feet long. A small deckhouse was built over the closed hold, consisting only of four sidewalls and an *atap* roof. There is room in it for two small mattresses, and when we sit up straight, our heads touch the *atap*. They've put a platform across the outriggers, almost four feet wide. It supports a primitive stove made from an old petroleum can to be used for cooking. It is just three o'clock in the morning when we go aboard, and the night is very dark. The lamp is hung in the big *ketapang* tree. The tide is high and the *prao* pulls impatiently at the thick anchor rope as it rides on the dark choppy water. We squat in a small *koleh-koleh* that gets us to the boat with a few strokes. A cock begins to crow in a *manga* next to the house, confused by the bright light. La Runga and Odeh Madi row the heavy *prao* out past the *tandjong*. When the sails are hoisted and we are slowly floating out on the current, Odeh calls out for good winds with the loud voice of the big gong. We wait for an hour before the mouth of the Wai Apu. There is a heavy swell and the empty *prao* is tossed violently up and down. The day starts with a slight discoloration above the tops of the hills. The children are asleep and sometimes I sleep too.

When I am fully awake, the water is running away behind us with a clear sound. The landwind picks up and we sail out far beyond Kajeli, close under the high shore of Tandjong Waät. My husband tends to the primitive rudder, which consists of two big paddles, one to the left and one to the right of the bow. Uncle Heintje is standing by the jib, the two Binongkos keep the *prao* balanced on the outriggers, and Fillipus, our Alfur houseboy, squats by the stove to make the morning coffee. The wind is cool and the light is still gray. A slight morning fog hangs over the Moluccan Sea. Heavy forests grow at the foot of steep hills, but the wood gets sparser toward the peaks and an *alang-alang* field shines as green and lovely as a meadow in the Alps. The children have woken up and they each unwrap a *ketupat*.[124] The wind washes the sleep out of our eyes, we drink hot coffee and eat *ketupat* with a *sambal*[125] of ground fish. Life is an ecstatic adventure.

The cape where the northern coast curves southwest is called Tandjong Kajuputih. It is a dangerous point, the sea has a broad swell here and the strong currents of the Buru Straits cause whirlpools and eddies. The *prao* is bounced up and down and we are all seasick. Each of the children lies in a corner and I am lying in between, too miserable to be afraid of the dangerous current and the white surf between the reefs. We go about for the last time, the rigging creaks, and the Binongkos jump from the leeward to the windward outrigger. We quickly run inland with a wide turn. With the landwind diagonally behind us we come into calmer water close by the shore. The sea recedes very far at low tide. There are few reefs, the beach is wide and bright. Trees grow along the low shore: *ketapangs, antjaks,* and the bright green beach tobacco.[126] Mists cover the sun and the wind stays cool. We sit on the small quarter-deck and look out over the water, the green hills, and the yellow beach. We steer for the shore just before we get to Ilat, a spot where a wide *kali* rushes out against a shingle bank. After we have bathed in the wide river we send our people out to look for young coconuts, chickens, and eggs in the small *kampong*. The wind has fallen completely, we eat and board our ship again. The Binongkos have to row or we would get too far off course, and we are lying in the deckhouse, head-tail, head-tail, like sardines in a can. When I wake up my husband has taken the helm again. The weather has deteriorated badly. The wind has risen again and it is blowing squarely against us. We are right in front of the round Tandjong of Ilat, the sails are lowered and the rain blows in from the south.

The downpour gets to us when we try to row out of Tandjong Ilat's current. The *prao* is lifted up and thrown down again. The rain comes in right over the bow. We pull the sheets off the mattresses to protect the front of the deck house and a wave breaks across the bow, straight through our makeshift curtain and over the sleeping children. Hans Christiaan looks around with amazement, but little Rudi begins to cry. We are at the mercy of the violent rainstorm for an hour. The rain penetrates the *atap* roof, and two or three times a wave comes in. We have rolled up the mattresses, changed the children, and put them on top of the mattresses, covered by their capes. We can't see anything because of the rain. Flashes of lightning show Ambelau like a low mountain in the fog. The wind has turned again and is now blowing from the left across the bow and we try to tack. I see nothing but a wavy line of water that keeps on going from my eyes to my stomach. I am seasick again.

My husband is at the helm, the Binongkos row in the front, and Heintje holds the lead line. The rain subsides, but the swell keeps tossing us up and down. Lightning flashes behind us. The shoreline has changed completely. Heavily wooded chalk hills break off at the waterline. There are gigantic holes behind a curtain of vines that is moved back and forth by the wind and the surging water. A cape wades out deep into the sea, a small bay retreats inland. It's completely dry again. Fillipus lights his stove and makes tea, the men change on the outriggers.

We keep cruising back and forth until it gets dark, steering far out to sea, then turning and swerving back, and then going about again before the dark steep shore. The ironwood almost grows into the sea here, but there are big scars where the young forest has been hacked away by the people from Larike and Wakasihu who come from Ambon in *tembangans* to take the wood away from Buru. [127] You need a license to cut wood, and you have to pay levies and logging fees. There are many stipulations, and some of them are rather stupid. But no one ever asks for the license of the bootleggers who take the young wood from Buru away in their laden *tembangans*. This is the kind of injustice that embitters the heart and makes life lonely with a loneliness that is bigger than that of the water and the forests. It is the kind of loneliness shared by all Europeans who trade and cultivate the soil on the thousand islands of this country. The wind vanishes along with the sun and we row into one of the small bays. The water grows dark early from the shadows of the forest, it smells of wild soil and *kenanga* [128] flowers. The smugglers' *praos* used to drop anchor here in the old days. The ones from Singapore came with matches, salt, and opium, but stringent control has reduced smuggling a great deal and only salt is still transported in secret.

Fillipus cooks rice and pumps up the big lamp. We dry our cushions and our blankets in its warmth, and we put mats across the soaked mattresses. But before we have completed the preparations for the night, and before the rice is done, the wind comes up again, the good wind from the north. We row out to sea again, the sail stands taut and we sail full speed for the dark cape that reaches far into the sea, and for Wai Tawa that lies behind it. Because it is too dark now to cross to Ambelau, we'll spend the night in this big *kampong*. It still takes hours, because the wind has turned again, and it's blowing across the bow. A heavy rainstorm comes over again, and lightning flashes every three minutes, as regular as a lighthouse. We eat rice with butter and *ketjap*,[129] because Fillipus has to help with the rowing to keep the *prao* out of the current around the *tandjong*, and has no time to bake dried fish.

The children are in bed and I am sitting next to my husband at the helm. The big lamp has been screened off with a mat, and the night stands over the dark water without a moon or stars, momentarily lit up by flickering lightning. We pass so close to Tandjong Makatita that the foam crest of its cliffs splashes back in our faces and we smell the strong smell of its forests. It's ten o'clock before we drop both anchors among the slippery stones before Wai Tawa.

That night we sleep in Wai Tawa's decrepit *passangrahan*,[130] all of us together on the long *baleh-baleh* that has been built across the whole length of the room. Only Heintje and Odeh remain on board.

It is a clear day when I wake up. Fillipus has made a fire between two stones in a corner and is preparing the morning coffee. The smoke spirals slowly up through a hole in the roof, and curious faces are looking at us through the many holes in the wall. We have only to put on our shoes to be dressed. After our coffee we go outside to wash up behind a bamboo thicket, past a bend in the *kali*. Wai Tawa is a big *kampong*, built partly against the hills. Fishermen from Larike have put up a tent on the beach and are smoking fish on little bamboo racks above small fires of coconut shells. All around split coconuts are drying to obtain copra. Small naked boys chase the goats away with stones. An old man is building a *prao* with his two sons. A long row of women climb the road to the *djagung*[131] gardens in the hills, each with a child on her hip and a machete in her hand. Wai Tawa has been settled by people from

Ambelau, and they work harder than the people from Buru and have a better head for business.

We stay in Wai Tawa that day, buying chickens, eggs, *pisang,* and young coconuts, discuss lumber with an Arab and hire a pilot who knows the water around Ambelau. We go on board again at dawn. We slowly float away with the wind from the side. Above the mountains of Wai Lua the sky is a pinkish gray, like the feathers on the breast of a big *kaketu,*[132] but the day quickly soars up, blue and shining with gold, over the wide water, from the high green coast of Buru to the high green coast of Ambelau. The wind dies down almost completely after an hour and we are floating around helplessly, abandoned to the heat and the reflections of the sun on the sea.

The sails do not billow out again until we have come right under the coast of Ambelau. Wildwood grows here from the tidemark to the mountain peaks. We lie stretched out on the mattresses in the deckhouse and, tired from the slow hours on the glistening sea, our eyes are healed by the green of this land. It's high tide, trees bend far over the water, tiger orchids hang down in long branches full of blossoms and there is a smell of *kenanga.* A white *missigit,*[133] its peak covered with zinc, stands between red and yellow shrubs on a small cape that juts out into the sea. Broad steps rise up out of the water, closed off by a low white wall on both sides. We land right in front of the stairs, as if it were a pier. A *koleh-koleh* comes to get us and we walk up the road to the *kampong.* Fruit trees, *nangkas, mangas,* and the big leaves of the *sukun* cover this road with their broad shadows. Dwarf coconut trees barely come up to the roofs of the houses, red and yellow shrubs grow right along the whitewashed *karang*-wall that separates the yards from the road.

It is Friday morning. A loud prayer is recited in the *missigit.* But right across from it, in the *passangrahan,* the *marinju*[134] is waiting for us, quickly arranging a clean *sarong* around his hips. A man has filled a long bamboo with water from the *kali.* Two strapping boys bring wood for the kitchen. After all the capes and currents and whirlpools we have dropped anchor in this haven. After the loneliness of the sea and the loneliness of the forests, this *passangrahan* on forlorn and desolate Ambelau is the small white house from the lost dream we will never return to.

XX

The *koleh-koleh* goes back and forth to the *prao* to get our luggage, mattresses, and kitchen utensils. The *marinju* has a new table brought in and new chairs, and all the old gentlemen in long white jackets come to visit us as soon as the prayer in the *missigit* is over.

We hear that the *kampong* chief has gone to Buru and isn't expected back until next week. Nobody dares decide if the young men can come to work for us after the *hari radja,* the holiday, but five hours rowing down the coast is another *kampong,* and my husband asks for rowers and a small *prao* to make a quick trip there and back. After people have volunteered and the pay has been settled, the old men stay to talk some more. A distant thunderstorm threatens from the sea. Boys are sent up in the rafters to check the roof and add new *atap.* A new wooden bed is carried into the small side room and set up; I have my own bed and my own room now, and I don't have to look for a bamboo grove anymore in order to change my clothes. We are sitting on the verandah and on the other side of the road the *missigit* rises between the bright colors of leaves and flowers, surrounded by old graves like a village church. The sea glistens through the shining green roof of the low coconut plantations. A small river runs loudly over the large stones behind the house. Fillipus is in the kitchen, roasting a fat chicken on a section of braided bamboo.

After the siesta we walk into the *kampong* with the children. The houses are built of ironwood and *gaba-gaba,* their facades are embellished with carvings. People are busily working in their yards, the men are chopping small *praos* from the trunks of *salawaku* trees,[135] and together they are laying the keel for a big *tembangan.* The women sit on the small porches in front of their houses, making pots from clay and weaving mats from small *panan* leaves.[136] The most striking aspect of this *kampong* is the absence of a Chinese *toko.* There is a small cooperative shop, where every man delivers his beams of ironwood every month. The lumber is then taken to Ambon in a *tembangan* and sold there, after which everybody gets his share of the proceeds, paid in *barang* from the *toko.* Chinese are not allowed to settle on Ambelau. "The Chinese take the money away," says the *marinju,* a young man with an open intelligent face.

There are no schools on Ambelau, nobody can read or write or do arithmetic on a piece of paper, nobody has taught these people the advantages of cooperative living, and yet they have all based their trade on that principle in their own primitive way. The district officer visits once a year to collect taxes. They pay promptly with big rixdollars[137] and small half guilders. A bureaucrat always has money. The mountain rises behind the *kampong*. There are some meager gardens, heavily fenced in with *karang* stones. Pigs are a plague here every night. Their tracks run straight through the *kampong* and stop right behind the houses, they poke around in the outbuildings and uproot the newly planted *pisangs*. The *marinju* shows us the soil that has been dug up in his garden; a big pig dug beneath the low stone wall around a young *sukun* tree no more than two nights ago.

We stroll up and down the wide road. The wind rises. In the west, above the mountains of Buru, the morning thunder rumbles. An old *hadji* invites us into his house. We drink coffee and coconut water and talk about workmen and the price of wood. The petroleum lamp is lit and eyes peek at us from behind every curtain. Back in the house the children eat on the porch under the big lamp. The whole *kampong* sits on the low walls around the house and stares at them. It is as if my two small sons are performing on a brightly lit stage. The rain comes down while I am feeding them the last few bites and the audience vanishes.

The next morning my husband sails five hours down the coast in a small *prao* to another *kampong* where it's said that there are workers available. Heintje goes with him, I stay behind with Fillipus, Odeh, and La Runga. I bathe in the river with the children in a place that's deep and protected by two tree trunks that have fallen down from the high river banks. We wash our clothes and spread them to dry on the hot stones. In the afternoon we walk on the beach and the dry cliffs when the tide is out. Odeh holds the children by the hand and they call him *Bapak*. We walk to the distant dark cape where almost no trees grow, which is black and sharp because of immense boulders. On the way back we pick low-hanging orchids. La Runga fells a tree in the forest on the other side of the *kali* to use as firewood for the return journey. My husband sails the *prao* to shore between the reefs, using the last gust of wind before the rain comes. This is the last evening, we are going back tomorrow. It is ten o'clock and very warm already before the *prao* is ready to sail. We bought some wood from the eldest *hadji*, which keeps the *prao* lower in the water and gives it less of a list. There is almost no wind. The Binongkos try to row, but three hours later we can still clearly recognize the *missigit* and the low coconut trees of Ulima. Last night's thunderstorm has moved off to the south, but it will come back when the wind turns.

It is well past noon when we get to Wai Tawa. We put the pilot ashore and buy some fish, and then a gust of wind chases us in the right direction, due north. It has begun to rain before we have passed the big *tandjong* after Wai Tawa, and it keeps raining all afternoon. The heavy cargo of wood keeps us more steady in the water. Sometimes the rain comes inside, and it is cold and wet, but we no longer get seasick. We leave the wind and the rain behind just before the smugglers' bays. We sail into a small bay and light small fires to cook our evening meal and dry our clothes. Night falls over us from the dark steep forest. I don't know how long I've been sleeping when I hear my husband trying to wake up Heintje and Odeh: "There's a wind from the south, in back of us." But they sleep on, dead tired.

We only leave at dawn. The landwind puts us in the right direction. We sit aft on a flat zinc trunk and drink coffee. We have to tack past Batudjongku. We round Tandjong Kajuputih without any trouble and we are able to see Namlea. We could be home by noon. We overtake a small fishing *prao* and buy some *kakaps*.[138] The wind drops but the swell goes up and down like heavy breathing. The sails hang limp and the Binongkos are rowing. The sun is covered by clouds, but the heat is oppressive all the same. The wind has turned when it rises again, it's blowing across the bow. We sail out as far as we can, but it's very hard to turn here in the strong current of the Buru Straits. My husband holds the rudder, the *prao* rears up in the waves, its bow held high. We are cruising back and forth, we tack a dozen times to gain a few yards, but we can't round Tandjong Waät. We can see the hills of Batuboi and the crooked mangrove trees on the reef of our own *tandjong*. Namlea seems to be very close. We wait before Ceit until the wind turns. We lie there all afternoon in the windstill, oppressive heat. We make pancakes and drink tea. The wind keeps blowing from the same direction, but the swell gets up around six. Nonetheless, it's long past midnight before we round the last *tandjong* to the sound of the gong and drop anchor in our own bay.

XXI

A temporary economic recovery and we, as well as everybody else, mistake it for the big turnaround. In May 1936 the prices begin slowly to rise. Large areas of *kajuputih* were destroyed by the fires of last year and the result is a kind of natural restriction. The last few months we sold almost nothing, but as soon as the prices go up we'll get rid of our stockpile.

The increase is not just caused by this temporary shortage, it is also due to the increased demand from Europe. By the end of the year prices have gone up two hundred percent. We are selling four to five times more than we produce every month and we have to buy great quantities of oil from other merchants. We check very carefully and select only the best oil, of the greatest weight and with the right green color. Sometimes we can't deliver because there is not enough good quality oil around. For the first time we are making more money than we need for immediate expenses. We have the *alang-alang* cut on the big plain of the river near Batuboi, along with the river forest. Leaves and branches are piled on heaps to rot, the usable wood is hauled aside, and the useless trunks feed small fires. Among their smoking remnants we put sticks to support growing coconut trees. In the seed beds next to the *gudang* the stiff shoots from the husk fibers of the carefully selected coconuts sprout. Holes have been dug for the *kapok* along the road and six Papuans are working on gutters to drain the soil. We still haven't got all the official documents for our long-lease tenure, it can take years before they have gone through all the administrative channels. But last year my husband spoke to Resident Haga in Ambon about our plans, and the resident fixed the land rent. A few sections of the plain are too swampy to be of use, but we have asked for all the land from Tubahoni to the beach anyway, in order to keep it in one piece.

The rising oil prices have also pushed up the prices of *damar* and copra. Coconut plantations are brought back into production again all along the coasts of the Moluccas, Ceram, Halmahera, and the small islands between Ambon and Ternate. Everybody is recruiting people. Odeh Madi returned from Ambon with two men, while we were counting on twenty. Other merchants are hunting for workmen and they give big advances. We have a very high turnover. Buyers are willing to pay eighty cents for a beer bottle of *kajuputih* oil. It is now very advantageous to work an isolated still and keep back one bottle out of every four. The debt for food and clothing remains about the same, but the belts are heavy with cash. During the bad time, when the oil went for forty guilders a *pikol,* we employed sixty people, and now, when the price has gone up to five hundred we can barely scrape together thirty men. Odeh Madi has taken a crew to Tubahoni, to work two *tungkus* there. The Sulanese operate the big still at Pohon Bulu, together with the Kaus, the Kabaus and Uma Ternates. They're a bunch of crooks and cutthroats and fanatic hunters. There is Saleh Kau with his ripped nose, Adam—the biggest arsonist on Buru, but never caught in the act—Abu with his two wives who alternate being beaten and loved and produce a child every year. A *kampong* has been built for them in the small valley behind Pohon Bulu, and they have been living there for almost a year. We probably keep them happy by asking them to serve as beaters when we go hunting on Sundays when the boat isn't coming. We don't let them join in if their *bluburs* aren't full: no work, no hunting. From the valley of Pohon Kinar, straight across the plain from the river to the hills, they drive the game toward us, yelling and screaming while the dogs bark frantically. Hunters are waiting with their rifles at the crucial spots, a crossing by the *kali,* and in the small ravines between the hills. Success varies, but the catch is divided fairly: pigs for the Christians, deer half and half, and a measure of powder for whoever fires a shot that kills.

The majority of our work force is Sulanese, because we can't get any more people from Ambon. They are also Kaus, Kabaus, and Uma Ternates, who are now all related through marriage. The Papuans live in a house behind the old still in Pohon Bulu. They are Christians and eat pork, also opossums and bats. The Butonese also keep to themselves and sleep by their own still.

Adam and Umar came to talk to Heintje when we had gone with the children to Batuboi for a few days. Gawi Kai has taken off with a Sulanese girl, without first abducting her according to *adat.* The angry father demands a big dowry. Will the Sinjo help them? The whole Kau family put themselves up as collateral, which is no more than an empty gesture. Their combined possessions consist of a dilapidated house, a plot of land in the *kampong,* a coconut grove that's heavily mortgaged, and a still that has been the cause of a lawsuit that has been going on for years. If we refuse they will all go to the Chinese and we'll lose twenty people. We talk about it all evening, and consultations begin again the next day, after the leaves have been weighed. The angry father knocks twenty-five guilders off the price of his daughter. The documents are signed when the lamp has been lit. We sit outside after dinner. The forest and the hills are shimmering in the steady light of a slanting moon. The smoke from the big still drifts away to the river. Someone is tapping a tune with his finger on a deerskin head of a *tifa*. An old man coughs, a dog begins to bark farther away, where the Papuans live. The documents have been signed. All the Kaus and Kabaus and the Uma Ternates will share in this debt, twenty people altogether. We assure ourselves that they will pay it off in a few months. The price of the oil is high and the people make good money. We can look out over the whole plain that has been cleared down to the bend in the river. The work is going well and prices keep rising. We always said that our people would never get into debt, but this dowry business has done it after all. This not a reproach, but the beginning of the end.

I go back to Europe with the two boys and I am a child again in my father's house, but my mother has died and no journey goes far enough to take me back to her. . . .

Even before I arrive in Holland, prices begin to fall faster than they climb. We can't get rid of our big stockpile fast enough. The loss swallows up a year's profit. We can be carefree for a few weeks sometimes, or in a dream perhaps, like very young children, but then the toys break or mother dies or it rains before evening falls and we can go to sleep.

I can only realize a year's losses when I am back in Namlea. Low prices, not much demand, heavy competition, adulterated oil, a big expensive stock, and workers barely able to pay off the debt of the good year with their small wages. But on Batuboi the first feathered leaf unfolds between the straight stiff leaves of the shoots. The *kapok* is growing along the path and stays bright and green in the dusty afternoon. The green manure winds upwards and pushes down the weeds. This is the credit side of that misleadingly rich year: the new green of twelve hundred coconut trees where once only the seeds of the *alang-alang* prospered. The plain measures four hundred acres from Tubahoni, the still on the border, to the tidal forests on the shore that stink of mud and

crocodiles. It will take work, the labor of many years before the
foliage of a plentiful garden folds its cool shadow around the
noonday heat. The only way to make money in this remote district, this cursed and beloved land, is to write about how you can
lose it. Fires and *bandjirs,* the disasters from the heat and the monsoon, illness, bad harvests, pests, and a dwindling market. I have
been living on this island for six years, on this poor, almost barren
soil, but neither adversity nor loss have been able to lessen the joy
of the splendor of this life. Then comes the message from Ambon
that our request for a long lease has been honored, but that the
land rent has been set too low, so we have to pay double the
amount. It has been three years since we requested the lease.
Resident Haga has become governor of Borneo.

I go to Ambon and explain to the resident's secretary that our
land is in a river plain and that the acreage of other tenants is
situated along the coast. And finally I invoke Resident Haga's
promise.

"Do you have it in writing?"

"Unfortunately, my husband was naive enough to trust the
word of a Resident of the Moluccas."

"We shall look into it."

"If the rent is doubled we can't do it because it would be too
expensive."

"You will hear from us."

And we do. We are informed that the governor of Borneo, Dr.
Haga, does not remember having made such a promise. Not illness or loss of money, nor the fear of death and the daily worries
embitter us, but this injustice makes us lonely, resentful, and re-
bellious. Land, land, land! The fields stretch for days on these
islands, uncultivated, all the way from the beach up to the forests
on the hills. Overpopulation, colonization, the "danger of open
spaces," articles in newspapers and magazines and many pro-
posals to open up the thinly populated and uncultivated outlying
possessions before another people do it for us.

Of our own free will we left inhabited regions and we are foolish enough to prefer this withered poor earth to the most fertile
gardens of Java. My two small sons are rowing their little *prao*
over the reefs. They draw ships and cranes in the hard sand at
low tide and they walk barefoot on the stony road through the
plain for two hours. They are the third generation of De Willigens
living on the *tandjong.* The people from Namlea and the Alfurs

from the interior call us "Tuan Tanah."[139] But not a foot of this land will belong to these people; because of the shortsightedness and bureaucracy of a group of strangers they are doomed to remain strangers without land in their own country.

We had a task and it has been taken from us, we have attacked the wilderness and have been abandoned. It's all over, the vision and the labor. On the large plain, weeds will grow again and vermin, the giant python and the gruesome crocodile.

The Counselor H. J. Friedericy

Introduction

H. J. Friedericy's short novel *The Counselor*, based on personal experiences, is one of the best proofs in Dutch colonial literature that an equanimous style is the most suitable literary vehicle for rendering the dramatic intensity of life in the tropics. Its narrative tone is sober, concise, almost lenitive; yet the narrative material is theatrical, expansive, and violent. One finds here an ardent and alien life memorialized by a self-possessed craftsman whose intimate knowledge of his subject made him aware that stylistic hyperbole was unnecessary.

This seemingly incongruous conjunction appears also to have been part of Friedericy's personality. He is said to have been reserved though ingratiating, courteous without obsequiousness, a keen though unobtrusive observer, and a very good listener. In short, Friedericy had the qualities necessary for a writer or a successful diplomat, which, in a sense, he was for the greater part of his life.

His career as a colonial official and diplomat was distinguished. Herman Jan Friedericy was born in 1900 in Groningen, one of Holland's most northern provinces, but spent most of his youth in the southern province of Brabant.[1] He entered Leyden University as a very young man to study "Indology."[2] In Holland one can acquire a terminal degree by fulfilling all the formal requirements for a doctoral degree, except the dissertation. Friedericy obtained such a "doctorandus" degree at the age of twenty-one. In 1921 he entered colonial service and was posted in the most southern peninsula of Celebes (now called Sulawesi) where he remained for eight years, until 1930. That same year he married and left for Holland on a leave to finish his studies. In 1933 he obtained his Ph.D. with an ethnological study of social rank among the Buginese and the Macassarese.

In 1933 Friedericy returned to the Indies and held a variety of posts in the colonial administration in Palembang, a city in southern Sumatra, in the colonial capital Batavia, and with the office of the governor general. After the capitulation he spent more than three and a half years in Japanese concentration camps and prisons between 1942 and 1945. It was in these camps that he, like some other writers of Dutch colonial literature, began his literary career.[3]

Strictly speaking, his diplomatic career began after the war, although being a colonial official in the outer possessions (i.e., any area outside Java) required the tact, patience, and careful reflection before acting that has always been considered indispensable for a career in the foreign service. From 1946 to 1947 Friedericy was head of the political section of the Ministry of Overseas Territories in The Hague. From 1947 to 1950 his diplomatic talents must have been severely tested when he was charged with explaining to Americans the Dutch position toward the new state of Indonesia.

Such experience made him a logical choice for Counselor for Press and Cultural Affairs in the Dutch Embassy in Washington, a post he held from 1950 to 1956. He had a similar position in the embassy in Bonn from 1956 to 1959, and then in London, from 1959 until his sudden death in 1962.

Friedericy published five books. The first was his ethnological study of *Social Rank among the Buginese and Macassarese* (*De Standen bij de Boeginezen en Makassaren*, 1933). In 1947 he published his first work of fiction, a novel entitled *Bontorio*, under the pseudonym "Merlijn." This novel was reissued in 1958, without its final section, under the title *The Last General (De laatste generaal)*. In 1957 he published a collection of short stories, *Kings, Fishermen, and Farmers (Vorsten, Vissers en Boeren)*, which contained work written in the camps, including his first literary effort, the story "The Dance of the Herons" ("Reigerdans"). In 1958 he published his last work of fiction, the novel *The Counselor (De raadsman)*, and in

1961, one year before his death, he published a collection of letters about his first appointment in colonial service, *The First Stage (De eerste etappe)*. These letters provide a picture of his life in Celebes and were written when he was only twenty-three years old.

All five books deal with southern Celebes. Celebes is one of the four great Sunda Islands, east of Borneo and south of the Philippines. Its curious shape somewhat resembles a giraffe, with its longest peninsula, which runs northeast, representing the neck. Three other peninsulas extend from its hub, embracing the large gulfs of Bone, Tolo, and Tomini.

The region where Friedericy was stationed for eight years, and which never faded from his imagination, is the island's southernmost part between, in the east, the Gulf of Bone, and in the west, the Straits of Macassar. This area was historically the most populous and thriving part of the island, and was dominated by two peoples: the Buginese and the people from Macassar. The Buginese realm was that of Bone on the east coast of the peninsula, while that of the Macassarese was the realm of Gowa with Macassar, the largest settlement in Celebes, as its center.

The two peoples, though ancient political rivals, shared many characteristics. Their separate languages have a common ancestor, they shared a distinctive alphabet, and, though both were Muslim, they retained similar indigenous as well as Hindu beliefs. The Macassarese were renowned as traders, and their principal city, the harbor of Macassar (now called Ujung Pandang), was one of the great commercial centers in the archipelago in the fifteenth and sixteenth centuries. Even today the Buginese are considered the best mariners and shipwrights in Indonesia. They sail all over the archipelago and are so skillful that they often still "feel" their way across the seas, relying on natural indicators such as the waves or the wind, disdaining the expensive aids of modern technology.

It was Gowa's principal city, Macassar, that incited Dutch hostility. In the beginning of the seventeenth century the Dutch Trading Company insisted that it had a monopoly on the spice trade from the Moluccas—an adjacent group of islands in the Banda Sea. The most important transit center in the eastern archipelago was Macassar, and the Kingdom of Gowa wanted to maintain both its independence as a trading nation and its jealously guarded maritime sovereignty. In fact, the ruler of Macassar and Gowa was defending an Indonesian version of Grotius's concept of *mare liberum* when he insisted in 1615 that God "divided the earth among mankind [but had] given the sea in common."[4] The result was nearly a century of bitterly fought wars, with the Dutch playing the rival states of Gowa and Bone against one another. Only in 1667 did the Dutch admiral Speelman, helped by the Buginese, manage to defeat Gowa's King Hasanuddin and capture Macassar in a hard fought campaign which testified to the legendary prowess and ferocity of both the Macassarese and the Buginese.[5]

With the subsequent decline of Gowa, Bone's fortunes flourished and the Dutch were forced to check its expansion in turn, even defending Gowa against their former ally. But, in fact, neither realm was ever completely vanquished until the first decade of the present century. The decisive military campaign took place in 1905 and 1906, whereafter both Gowa and Bone ceased to exist as autonomous realms. The king of Gowa died when, fleeing Dutch troops, he fell in a ravine, and the king of Bone was banished to Java where he died in exile. The Dutch dismantled the feudal superstructure of the ruling royalty and nobility, and replaced it with the impersonal rule of a colonial administration modeled after their system on Java. They even confiscated the sacred regalia *(gaukang)*, and then distributed them between museums in Batavia, Leyden, and Amsterdam. By 1910 not only an era but a unique world and way of life had nearly vanished, sacrificed to colonial expediency and the demands of modern progress.[6]

It is clear from his published work that Friedericy's sympathy was with the feudal aristocracy which, when he came to Celebes in 1922, possessed merely a shadow of its former glory. His successful attempt to understand its psychology, its social philosophy, and its former influence was stimulated not only by the practical demands of his job but also, it would seem, by a personal congeniality.

Friedericy knew perfectly well that the old feudal system of Gowanese and Bonese royalty and nobility had been a cruel burden for the common people of what was essentially a society without a middle class.[7] There was a very strict hierarchy which favored the royal house of the king (the *aru* in the Buginese or *karaëng* in the Macassar language), the high nobility comprised of the descendants of the monarchs (the *anakaraëng*), and the class of the chieftains. The nobility lived a life dictated in every detail by ritual and tradition, which regulated clothing (only people of royal descent could wear yellow), marriage, the construction of houses, and one's appearance. A noble lady had a very fair complexion because she was never exposed to the sun and tiny feet because she was carried most of the time. She could only ride a horse if she were sitting on the number of pillows commensurate with her rank (for instance, seven was proper for royalty in Bone).

The nobility's treatment of the common people was tyrannical and often arbitrary. They could impose fines if they felt there had been trespasses against their dignity and, as Friedericy notes, what they considered discourteous was often absurd. They could punish a man, for example, if a corner of his headcloth stood up too straight, or if he built his house on more stilts than he was allowed by rank, covered his house with two roofs, didn't provide a visiting nobleman with the correct number of cups and plates, or didn't have the young women of the household serve his unexpected guest.[8]

Such despotism had been eliminated by the Dutch, yet the disfranchisement of the nobility had left a power vacuum. Friedericy was charged by the colonial government with the task of finding a political compromise whereby the innovations of the progressive European government could be allied with a beneficial reformulation of the ancient power structure. Such a task, as he wrote in 1925, required "study and research,"[9] and two of the side benefits were his ethnological study of status in the realms of Gowa and Bone, published in 1933, and the historical novel *The Last General*.

The Last General was first published in 1947 as *Bontorio*. It was republished some ten years later without the final section, which was considered artistically and structurally inadequate. This shorter version describes the life of a nobleman in Bone from 1870 to 1906. It is a fairly rare example of a Dutch writer's inventing a native existence in an objective fashion without either romantic sentimentality or patronizing indulgence. This life of Mappa, the Aru Bontorihu of Bone, testifies not only to Friedericy's intimate knowledge of the aristocratic past of the Buginese, but it also betrays his unabashed admiration for that particular way of life. That life was a feudal one, one that exulted in physical courage, violence, fealty, unquestioned loyalty to the *Arumpone* (or king of Bone), deer hunting, gambling, court intrigue, and martial prowess.

Perhaps the violence of that life and the manner in which the Buginese accepted it are the book's most striking features and serve to set it apart from Dutch literature proper. The novel contains, for instance, a scene at court where Mappa's father kills a man who has run *amok*. Later Mappa excites himself into a furious trance of loyalty to his king, screaming his readiness to kill anyone his king desires to see dead. The two incidents are related; they both portray the ability of the Buginese individual to induce in himself a state of psychological immunity to prudence or fear that is coupled with a homicidal mania that knows neither quarter nor discrimination. Called "running *amok*," it was best described by Multatuli as a "way of committing suicide in public."[10]

To be sure, running *amok* was a condition associated with all the Malay peoples, wherever they lived. In Java a special kind of pitchfork *(tjanggah)* was kept in the guard houses to subdue that kind of berserkers. But in the nineteenth century the Buginese were considered "by far the most addicted to run amok. I should think three-fourths of all the cases I have seen have been by persons of this nation" (Yule, p. 22). A. R. Wallace in his well-known book on the Malay archipelago states that "Macassar is the most celebrated place in the East for 'running a muck' [sic]." One should remember that this condition is affective and is not necessarily the result of opium or alcohol. Nor is it restricted to any particular level of society, as Friedericy's two novels show. In *The Counselor* one finds several cases of poor people running *amok*, while in *The Last General* it is the nobility who reach that level of frenzy, though their excitement is more like that of the ancient "amoucos" in continental India or of the Japanese kamikaze pilots of the Second World War, in that it is a frenzied emotional pledge of allegiance to their sovereign whereby they gladly sacrifice their lives.

In any case, this kind of violent death is accepted with remarkable equanimity by every class in Buginese society, and the same can be said for their acceptance of whatever punishment was meted out. Besides what must appear to us completely irrational motives for this crazed behavior, the most common reason was a violation of honor, be it personal, family, clan, or, formerly, the sacred honor of the king. To this day, the *sirik* tradition still metes out tragedy in Celebes, where an insult or a death must be avenged by the next of kin in a manner very reminiscent of Sicilian vendetta.

The Last General is a dramatic and vigorous book written in a graphic narrative style with a visual energy not often encountered in Dutch literature. The kinetic style relies on vivid images which are never sacrificed to aesthetic effect but which serve to produce a structural fluidity strikingly similar to cinematography. In fact, *The Last General* and the stories "Blood," "The Dance of the Heron," and "The Gang Leader," in the collection *Kings, Fishermen, and Farmers,* are reminiscent of a number of films by the Japanese director Akira Kurosawa, especially the ones which depict the martial virility of feudal Japan. For instance, Friedericy's description of the battle between the forces from Bone and Wadjo recalls the battle scenes in Kurosawa's most recent film, *Kagemusha* (1979). In Friedericy's story "Blood," Daëng Sisila (the *pamantja* master) and his pupils, who are all artists at killing with *kris* and *badik,* live by an ethos not much different from the samurai in such Kurosawa films as *Sugata Sanshiro* (1943), *The Seven Samurai* (1954), and *Yojimbo* (1961).

Both the stories and the novel are remarkable for the identification of their Western author with the Asian protagonists. It was a congenial symbiosis which vouchsaved an authenticity that is rare in colonial literature. During an interview in 1959, Friedericy said that while on a postwar visit to Indonesia he was approached by an Indonesian who introduced himself as the son of Aru Bontorihu. The author expressed surprise because the character he had created was an amalgam of various people and had never existed in the flesh. The enigmatic reply was "You're the one who knows best."[11]

The interviewer noted how captivated he was by Friedericy's talent for telling a story. A. Alberts was the colleague and fellow author who, in the Suka Miskin prison in Java during the Japanese occupation, encouraged Friedericy to expand a story about Bontorio into a novel. Alberts wrote in a memorial article after Friedericy's death that it was a rare privilege to *hear* him present a tale: "It was quite an experience. He really gave a marvelous performance, walking back and forth, gesticulating and, especially, miming to a circle of people who were breathless with suspense. Short and longer stories, masterfully constructed up to and including the final word."[12] This gift, mentioned time and again by

people who knew Friedericy, may come as some surprise when
one tries to reconcile it with his personality, which was often described as reticent and reserved. However, the diplomat needs to
be a good listener, and this same ability is also a prerequisite for
the storyteller who must gather material for his tales. Perhaps he
learned something of this craft from the professional storytellers
in Celebes, the *pakeso-keso* who, while accompanying themselves
on a kind of violin *(keso-keso)*, are invited at feasts to narrate the
old epics.[13]

Friedericy's work is typical of the best in Dutch colonial literature in that it is written in a style which—as I have emphasized
elsewhere—evolved from an oral tradition and stayed close to
the spoken word. This was never the case in continental Dutch
literature. Du Perron, another colonial writer, once characterized
it as a *parlando* style. *Parlando* is a musical direction indicating that
a passage should be sung or played as if it were being spoken or
recited, and it happens to be the stylistic vehicle best suited to
convey the drama of its material. Friedericy's skill and enthusiasm for telling stories was transferred to his writing. He once said
that "I've found that it is the same thing with smoking as with
writing. Once you really get going, it's very difficult to stop."[14]

Friedericy's narrative talent is at its best in his last work of fiction,
The Counselor, published in 1958. The structure of this short novel
is a series of stories told by an omniscient narrator, clustered
around the central relationship of the young Tuan Petoro (the
second word is a Macassarese and Buginese term for a Dutch official of at least the rank of controller or assistant resident) and the
considerably older and more experienced Tuan Anwar, a Macassarese nobleman in the service of the Dutch colonial administration. The stories are fascinating tales told in a succinct style that
has lost some of the figurative richness of *The Last General*. It is an
appropriately direct tone that allows events and characters their
rightful place without drawing attention to itself.

Yet this narrative is deceptive. In his novel *Die Blendung* (1935;
translated as *Auto-da-fé*) Elias Canetti characterized the novelist
as "an actor with a pen" and Friedericy does not belie this description. The stylistic insouciance is artifice because the paring of
figurative adornment, the constraint of adjectival sentiment, and
the unruffled syntax are used for dramatic effect. This is Friede-

ricy as the storyteller that Alberts described, in full control of his craft down to the last word. The author once mentioned that he rewrote the manuscript of *The Counselor* six times.[15]

Some reflection on the reader's part will suggest that a great deal of emotive power has been insinuated in the text despite the understated quality of the prose. We find here a Macassarese world just as matter-of-factly violent as the Buginese one in *The Last General*. Here too, killings are accepted with the same equanimity by the Macassarese as the Buginese, but to the Dutch they remain serious transgressions of moral and legal laws and they trouble the quiet resolve of the Tuan Petoro. The entire world of Friedericy's previous work is present here, but in muted tones and scaled-down—in contrast with the aristocratic emphasis in *The Last General*—to the level of more common people. Now there is a sense of compassion rather than admiration. Nevertheless, one will find echoes of the virile past—when deer hunting and cattle rustling were honorable activities for men of noble blood—embodied in Sila the robber, or in the quiet dignity of the old Karaëng Manudju. That erstwhile realm is in the distant past now but Tuan Anwar wants to revive it (as Friedericy did too), with its excesses controlled by a more humane authority. We are also introduced to the two antithetical forces of Islam (in the person of the devout Tuan Anwar) and native superstition (in the incident of the dog). There is a reference to a golden *kris*, the sacred *gaukang*, as a relic, an icon of that same irretrievable past, also embodied in the person of the small, old, aristocratic Lady Manudju.

A great deal of love lodges behind the plain facade of the style, so perhaps there is a psychological reason for this sober rendition, as well as a dramatic one. It may be said to serve as a screen, a controlling device to restrain the powerful emotions of affection and sadness. For not only are the legendary realms of Gowa and Bone now only a memory, but the present world of Tuans Anwar and Petoro is also no longer viable.

Tuan Anwar is an anachronism within his own society. He is a Macassarese nobleman without any of the manly attributes that distinguished his class, as exemplified by the heroic portrait of Mappa, the Aru Bontorihu of *The Last General*. He does not care for hunting, has never killed a man (except once by accident), and has tried for a lifetime to improve the lot of his people by a judicious balancing of what was the best in his own heritage and in the policy of his European overlords. He is a kind, compassionate, and wise man, ensnared in a time warp of history. His own past invokes his anger with its injustices but his tireless efforts for the present meet with disdain in the future. Tuan Anwar is a man whose decency and humanity are sacrificed to historical necessity. He is a man overtaken by history.

It may be noted that the Tuan Petoro is never individualized with a name. He is one of many Tuans Petoro who will come and go, while the land of Celebes will remain a reality, individualized in Tuan Anwar, whose name in Arabic means "brightness." It should also be mentioned how carefully each person is accorded his or her proper title as part of a clearly defined world of mutual respect. But that world died in the Second World War. Not only the world of the Tuans Petoro—the world of colonialism that intended to be decent, even if it sometimes failed—but also the world of Tuan Anwar is superseded by a new generation of inexorable forces. By the end of the book, the ruthless dynamism of social and historical necessity have reduced Tuan Anwar to a level as faceless and nameless as the erstwhile succession of Tuans Petoro. His identity, his individuality, his past, and his lifetime of honest and compassionate effort have been negated and reduced to the innominate classification of "collaborator." His counsel goes unheard.

There is pain and sadness in this passing, but Friedericy does not judge or accuse. The former Tuan Petoro has gained the same weary acceptance as his erstwhile counselor. If anything, it is he who is the "son" of Anwar, the son Lady Manudju "adopts," the paradoxical inheritor of the realms of Gowa and Bone. He too is an anachronism. Tuan Anwar's real son, Dr. Musa, represents the new Indonesia which cannot allow itself subtle distinctions in its uncompromising pursuit of a new order and a new freedom. Yet there is one final irony. During the time that the Tuans Petoro and Anwar were in office, the common people of Celebes resented and disliked the Dutch attempt to educate them. Tuan Anwar himself was skeptical about education's efficacy, yet his son, who would not understand his father, was educated in Dutch schools and becomes minister of education in the government of the new nation.

Finally, it should be pointed out again that Dutch colonial literature mirrors not only a specific colonial society but that it also often reflects a more perennial theme, one native to all literatures: the passing of an era, an old order, of a vanishing world that is unalterably different from present reality. Symbolically, it is most often represented by the clash between generations, between fathers and sons, between the element that wants to preserve and the element that wants to inflict change. This ancient struggle that will never be stilled, as inevitable as the cycle of the seasons, lends *The Counselor* a perspective that extends it beyond the historical moment. In the final analysis it addresses human kind.

The Village

Leaving Macassar[1] on the road curving around the most southern point of the peninsula, as a traveler you would first pass the village Djongala—once residence of the kings of Gowa, and, after the death of the last ruler, of the principal members of the noble house of Gowa—and afterward, proceeding toward Takalar, the villages Djeneponto, Bantaëng, Bikeru or Sindjai, and Sunggu-minasa. The total distance would be about seven miles.

Entering the last village, you would find on both sides of the road some houses built on stilts in the Macassar style. After those, some Chinese and Macassar shops, interrupted on the right-hand side by the market with two shelters: cast-iron poles supporting a corrugated iron roof. The road ended in a path, shadowed by tamarinds,[2] demarcating the southern border of the *alun-alun*.[3] To the right, behind a large lawn with some hedges, stood the house of Tuan Petoro: a central building connected on the right with the guesthouse and on the left with the garage.

To continue on your way, you would have to pass the governmental office next to the house of Tuan Petoro: a white building with green shutters and a large cool front porch used for meetings of the native chieftains and the native court of Gowa. Next to that was a small prison with a front yard circled by barbed wire, and in that yard a bronze bell had been hung within a wooden frame, used by the prison guard to mark the half hour and the hour.

To get around the square you had to make a ninety-degree turn to the left. At your right there is first the road further south, then a narrow road leading to the mountains, to Parigi, and, finally, the clinic where the victims of local brawls were the main patients. And finally, on a certain day in April in the mid-twenties, you would have passed an unoccupied house built of stone in which once a hydraulic engineer had lived, and which would later be used by an assistant controller, a "Tuan Aspirang."

The clinic and the empty house were on the east side of the square; beyond them the road continued to Tombolo, but if you made another left turn you found on the north side of the square the white stone house of Tuan Anwar daëng Situdju[4] and next to that a large wooden house in the Macassar style, on stilts, of a Gowa copra merchant,[5] a member of the low nobility, with a wife, fourteen children, and a host of servants.

On the west side there were no houses. Sixteen tall coconut palms grew there as well as a high hedge of red and pink flowers, called "kembang sepatu."[6] It was usually quiet around the square. A single car might be waiting under the heavy foliage in front of the government office, or, more often, horses, shuffling their feet and chasing flies with their tails, waiting for their owners, Gowa native chiefs. In the afternoon once it had cooled off enough, dozens of Macassar boys appeared, among them three or four of the children of the Gowa merchant, and they'd play a kind of soccer there until it got too dark to see the ball.

The Counselor

It was late afternoon, about a quarter past five, and the brief twilight had set in. Tuan Anwar sat silently on his front porch in his high-backed chair and looked in the direction of the low house across the square. He could see the pavilion to the right and the garage to the left, but all that was visible of the main building was the roof with its brown-red glazed tiles. The white facade shimmered behind the hedges on the lawn.

The new Tuan Petoro might arrive any moment. Tuan Anwar had met him for the first time two weeks ago. The new Tuan Petoro, who used to work in the governor's office in Macassar, had paid a visit to his predecessor who had introduced the office personnel to him. The new Tuan Petoro was certainly a very young man indeed to become the highest official, the controller, representing the Dutch colonial government. This would be his first independent post.

Tuan Anwar shook his head just slightly. The governor of Macassar had degraded Sungguminasa to the rank of capital of a subdivision. The division Sungguminasa had been added to the territory of Macassar, with the city of Macassar as the capital, under one assistant resident. Along with the old division of Macassar (consisting of the subdivisions Macassar, Maros, and Pangkadjene), the assistant resident was now also in charge of the subdivisions of Sungguminasa, that is, Gowa, which had the village of Sunggaminasa as its capital, Takalar, and Djeneponto. How would that work? Tuan Anwar shifted in his chair. His youngest son, two years old, tried to climb up his left leg and looked at him with his large dark brown eyes. "Oh, all right," Tuan Anwar said and took him in his lap. "Do you want my watch? Here." From the breast pocket of his immaculate white uniform he took an old-fashioned gold watch on a gold chain and put it in the little hands of the boy. The child held it against his cheek and listened carefully. Tuan Anwar, holding the boy with both hands, kept watching for a car approaching the large house. The new Tuan Petoro did not seem a day over twenty. A subdivision like Gowa, ruled by a child. Under how many Tuan Petoros had he served? Ten? Twelve? Those in Sungguminasa, where he had worked for more than ten years, had all been assistant residents, men of forty or older. And now this. . . . At times he felt he understood the Dutch, but there were always new riddles.

Tuan Anwar was about forty-five, but he looked older. It wasn't that he had many wrinkles, in fact his face was rather smooth and very light of skin. But his hair, shaven, and his curly Macassar mustache were gray, and his almost black eyes behind rimless glasses showed a kind of tired wisdom. At times his face lit up with a childish smile, when for a few moments he forgot his troubles or was grateful for some kindness.

His father had been the prince of a small territory north of Pangkadjene in government lands, in that southwestern part of South-West Celebes which at the time of his birth, around 1880, had for many years been under direct Dutch rule. Gowa, Wadjo, Bone, Soppeng, Luwu, the Adjataparang, and other princedoms had remained nominally independent until the year 1906.

His father had died in 1904, just before the outbreak of war between the Dutch and Bone and Gowa. He had been a progressive man and had sent his three sons to school in Macassar. His oldest son had succeeded him and had become one of the most modern of the native chiefs of the area. His second son had become involved in the operations of a far-flung gang of cattle rustlers and had been in jail for three years. Two years later, when he was thirty-six years old, he had been stabbed to death by the jealous husband of a young woman whom he had never touched. Anwar,[7] the quietest of the three *anakaraëngs*,[8] after his school years had been taken to the Tuan Petoro of Pangkadjene with his father's request to teach him. The Tuan Petoro knew his father as a proud and incorruptible man, and he had not asked him just what he wanted his son to be taught.

The young man had shown himself clever and eager, and after becoming first an assistant scribe and then a scribe, he had become assistant—Tuan Assisten—in Maros. Now he was administrative assistant, grade one, in Sungguminasa. Now he was "Tuan Anwar" and his name was known by all the officials, both the Dutch and those from Macassar, and by many of the native chiefs. He was a very pious man and took his religious duties as seriously as his work allowed him to. He never touched liquor except when he, very rarely, had a bad cold and sent for a bottle of wine from the Chinese in the market. In such cases, a Macassar cleric had assured him, the wine counted as medicine and not as an intoxicating beverage. All through Ramadan, the month of the fast, he did not even swallow his own saliva during daylight hours; when he was in his office he had to spit it out every ten minutes in a large copper spittoon. His most fervent wish was to go soon on a pilgrimage to Mecca.

When he arrived in Sungguminasa, the village had recently been made the capital of what was left of Gowa after the wars with the Dutch. In the previous capital, Djongaja, a few miles from Macassar, there were several dozen large Macassar houses, each standing on twenty-five piles or stilts. They housed hundreds of members of the Gowa nobility with their servants and slaves. The slaves had been freed by the Dutch government but they preferred to continue living in the shadow of their formerly powerful masters.

The princedom, once so powerful and famous, had now been reduced to its old nucleus, the area of the "nine flags,"[9] the nine electors. They were men of lower rank and from the start they had looked up to Tuan Anwar. Not only was he of higher nobility, but he was also the representative of Dutch power in Gowa, the Tuan Petoro.

The last king of Gowa, Kulau Karaëng Lambangparang,[10] had fled from the Dutch troops in 1906 and lost his life when his horse fell into a ravine. Crown prince Mappanjuki, a boy of sixteen at the time, had been exiled to the island Salajar. The princes of the blood and the court nobility had lost both their leader, the king, and their power; no longer could they exploit the people, and many of them sank into poverty. Yet Djongaja still had considerable influence. Once, before the Dutch had taken it away to Batavia, the miracle sword of Gowa, the Sudang,[11] had been kept there. The word of a prince of the blood was still worth more than the word of a thousand commoners. The Dutch might have taken away the power of the house of Gowa, but no matter how poor its members had become, their prestige survived. When Tuan Anwar, now more than ten years ago, began his work in Gowa, everyone from Djongaja had looked down on him. But Tuan Anwar knew his place in the Macassar society. Himself a nobleman, he was always courteous, and he remained so, even in difficult circumstances. After a few years, the most important princes started trusting and appreciating him. He became their counselor in many affairs. But although he was excessively courteous and showed the greatest respect to these embittered, resentful princes, he was afraid of them. Here was a man who, though noble, had never joined a hunt, and had never, after an argument, stabbed anyone with his *kris* or *badik*.[12] Physically, Tuan Anwar was no hero. But at the right moment, in his soft, hoarse voice, in carefully chosen words, he would present his opinion, even if it differed from that of the highest nobility, or of his boss, the Tuan Petoro.

Tuan Anwar saw a large black limousine pull up at the big house. He looked at his youngest son who was trying to eat his watch, smiled, put the watch in his pocket after having dried it off on his sleeve, got up, and called his wife. She was much younger than he, and pregnant. He said, "The new Tuan Petoro just arrived. I will be summoned soon." He put the boy down next to her, and the child grabbed his mother's skirt, her *sarong*.[13]

The New Tuan Petoro

The new Tuan Petoro did not look older than twenty and, in fact,
he was not much older than that. He would be twenty-five in a
few months. He had stayed the last few days with a friend in Macassar, and the friend had driven him to his new post. Together
they were watching how a tall batman, in dark blue uniform with
orange trimming, black velvet *kupiah* and bare feet, carried the
luggage in. Afterward they entered and made a tour of the house.
"A great place," the friend Theo said. The new Tuan Petoro
looked at the empty rooms in which the few pieces of furniture he
had sent seemed lost, and asked, "How'll I get this organized?" It
was almost dark now and the batman switched on some lights.
"I've put your luggage in the bedroom," he said in good Malay.
"Thank you," said the new Tuan Petoro. The batman continued,
"The *djongos*[14] and the cook have also arrived." "Fine," the Tuan
Petoro said.

  Friend Theo said goodbye and was taken to his car. The new
Tuan Petoro slowly walked back, put a little rattan table in front of
the house, just outside the circle of light from the bare ceiling
lamp of the front porch, and asked the batman to bring two rattan
chairs. The new tuan looked at the batman and asked, "Don't
I know you?" The batman answered, "Yes, sir," and smiled,
showing his large teeth, three of which were gold. "What's your
name again?" "Badawi, from Soppeng."[15] The new tuan started
laughing. "Of course! Badawi! How are you?"Badawi had a certain fame with the younger officials of South Celebes. He was a
Buginese, and until two years ago he had been the batman for the
Tuan Petoro in his place of birth, Watan Soppeng. He was a
young man, about twenty-five, born in the class of freedmen, but
he had had the misfortune to fall in love with the beautiful niece
of the Princess of Soppeng, a woman of the highest nobility, and
she had had the misfortune to answer his feelings. On a bad day it
had been discovered that they had slept together, a crime punish-
able by death. But they had immediately put themselves under
the protection of the Tuan Petoro and had thus escaped the death
which the male relatives of the princess were about to mete out.
The native court, under the chairmanship of the Tuan Petoro,
had exiled them both from Soppeng for five years; she had been
sent to Madjene where, uprooted, she had gone downhill quickly; he had been sent to Sungguminasa where he had become bat-

man of the Tuan Petoro once more, married a lovely young Macassar woman, and was now father of a son.

The new Tuan Petoro asked Badawi to go to Tuan Anwar and ask him to come over. He then went into his bedroom. He looked around. There was his iron bed all made up, with mosquito netting closed around it. Between the opening to the side gallery, with dark brown doors, and the window, with a dark brown wooden screen, stood a table with a wash basin and a jug. Above it, a small mirror. Against the wall across from the bed was a darkly waxed cupboard, and in the middle of the room a little oak table with a bare light bulb above it. He studied his serious face in the mirror, combed his strawblond hair, and said to himself: "Now you're a real Tuan Petoro. Best of luck. You'll need it."

Then he went outside, sat down with his back to the house in the chair on the left, and put a box of matches on the table. He saw a man in white enter the right-hand gate to the front lawn, followed by a man in a native *sarong*. That would be Tuan Anwar. He had heard much about him: expert on Gowa, spoke the Macassar language—his mother tongue—but also Malay, Buginese, some Arabic, and Dutch. He got up and walked toward him. He put out his hand, and thought, "Tuan Anwar is older and smaller than I remember him." "Good day, Mister Anwar," he said. "Here I am. Please sit down. Do you smoke?" "No, never, sir," Tuan Anwar said. To the man in the *sarong*, a servant, he said in the Macassar language: "Why don't you go to the back of the house." Tuan Anwar was wearing a *songko*[16] made of horsehair, in which two strains of gold thread had been interwoven. Tuan Petoro lit a cigarette and thought: "It would have been more polite if I had been wearing my uniform—but oh well—in Macassar they don't wear uniforms that much—." He turned toward the front gallery and called, "Abu!" The servant must have been waiting, for he appeared in two seconds. The guest and his host decided to drink orange lemonade, called "orangeade" at that time and in that area.

Tuan Petoro started out by talking about himself. He had studied law in Holland, had arrived in the Indies three years ago and been stationed in Watampone, in Bone that is—you must know the Tuan Petoro of Maros, who plays the piano so well and conducts the Macassar orchestra?—then Sindjai, then Bantaëng, then Macassar, and now Sungguminasa. It was the system of the former governor: assistant controllers were transferred every few months, to get to know the country. Tuan Anwar slowly thawed out a bit. They discussed, very circumspectly, the local chieftains of South Celebes. Tuan Anwar spoke Dutch with a heavy accent, but his syntax, though of a local character, was quite good.

In answer to a question by Tuan Petoro, Tuan Anwar told him that he was once married to a daughter of Karaëng Segeri. She had died. She had given him three children. The eldest, a daughter, was married and lived in Pare-Pare; the middle one, also a daughter, had died at an early age of smallpox; the third, a son called Musa, was now fifteen and went to school in Macassar. Soon he would go to school in Batavia; he wanted to study medicine. His present wife, a niece of the first one, had given him two children: a daughter of five and a little boy of two; she was expecting number three.

After half an hour Tuan Petoro said, "Mister Anwar, I would like to say something this first evening which is of great importance to me. Look—I am young, you are older and very experienced. I have been appointed your chief, but will you help me where you can? Can you, where possible, be my teacher, while I will be your pupil?" He paused. Had that been a good move? He held out his hand which Tuan Anwar touched rather shyly. Then Tuan Anwar said, "Thank you, sir. Certainly, sir. At your service, sir. I understand, sir."

Tuan Petoro felt relieved and said, "I'll let you go then. Tomorrow I'll be in the office at half past seven. I would like you to introduce the entire staff to me once more."

The Poor Groom

About six weeks later, Tuan Petoro and Tuan Anwar were talking in the study of the large house, one of those evenings in the dry season when the heat of the sun continues to radiate into the night from the soil and the rocks. Thousands of crickets were singing in the dark grass. Tuan Petoro had had furniture made by the Chinese carpenter and had invited Tuan Anwar to come and see it; he was rather proud of the result. Tuan Anwar had had a look around and said, "Very nice, sir! Very nice, sir!" Afterward Tuan Petoro had ordered two orangeades and they had started talking. They talked a lot together. Tuan Petoro told about Holland, where Tuan Anwar had never been and where he wanted to send his son to study medicine. But usually Tuan Petoro just listened and asked questions. He loved listening to Tuan Anwar. When Tuan Petoro had said goodbye to the governor in Macassar before coming to Sungguminasa, the governor had told him that the organization of Gowa was a mess. The class which socially, and, in a sense, religiously, belonged at the top, had been eliminated by the Dutch, and the direct rulers were officials whose rank was too low and who had little influence. "You're going to Gowa," the governor had said, "look and listen, and above all, establish contact with the House of Gowa." Tuan Petoro had not told this to Tuan Anwar, but Tuan Anwar was aware of the great interest his chief had showed in the history of Gowa and in the lives of its princes.

During their evening conversations, Tuan Anwar did not wear a uniform anymore, at the suggestion of Tuan Petoro. He wore a loose, gray, thin shirt of Macassar cut and a dark checkered *sarong*. He felt at ease and sat in his wide chair, with his legs crossed. Tuan Petoro was dressed in a cotton robe and listened to Tuan Anwar's description of a brother of the last king of Gowa. This man, Karaëng Mandalle, had the nickname "Lida Padalle," after the forked tongue of the large lizard.

Tuan Petoro soon realized that Tuan Anwar had vast experience in the work of government, and that he would not have acquired this without his profound knowledge of human beings. Tuan Anwar did not seem to be aware of it himself. Tuan Petoro realized that he also knew something about human nature, but where it concerned Indonesians he was wrong in five cases out of ten.

"Yes, sir," Tuan Anwar said, "this man is totally unreliable. He would be ready to poison his own brother."

At that moment, Badawi entered and asked permission to speak. Tuan Petoro nodded. "Here is the head of the *kampong* . . ." and he gave a name which Tuan Petoro did not catch.

"Ask him in." The head of the *kampong* was an old man from Macassar with a gray mustache and a wrinkled face. He had a dirty turban wound around his head. He wore a black coat, which had been buttoned the wrong way, and a red checkered *sarong*, and he was armed with a *kris*. He *salaamed*, bent over, touching first Tuan Petoro's hand and then Tuan Anwar's hand. Both times he followed this by touching his forehead with folded hands. After that, he quickly sat down on the rug between Tuan

Petoro and Tuan Anwar and told his story in one breath. Men had run *amok*. During a wedding meal, a quarrel had arisen, men had stabbed each other. He did not know how many had been killed. He had been there when it started but had soon left for Sungguminasa to get help. His breath came in gasps and Tuan Petoro saw how his hands, on his *sarong*, trembled. Tuan Anwar said, "That *kampong* is not more than two miles from here, sir. Do you want to come along?" "Immediately," Tuan Petoro said. "Badawi! Call Tuan Djaksa and tell him to arm himself. Mister Anwar, let us get dressed quickly. Badawi, you come too. We'll meet in front of the office."

Ten minutes later the men met. Tuan Djaksa, the Macassar public prosecutor, came last. He was a slow, thin, silent man. He carried a shotgun over his shoulder and a *badik* in his belt. Tuan Petoro had also brought a rifle, an old model Beaumont which Badawi had loaded for him, whispering, "Careful, Tuan, sometimes it just goes off by itself."

Tuan Petoro carried it carefully over his right shoulder. He was just about to arrange the formation, when the men somehow left, taking him along in the middle of the group. In front went, on the left, the *kampong* head, in the middle Badawi, also armed with a rifle, and to the right of him a colleague, a little fat fellow, related to the house boy Abu and for mysterious reasons called Prince. He had worked in an office as a boy where he had been baptized "Prince," and at times he was called "Pering," a bastardization of "Friend" (the answer to the challenge from a guard at night crying out, "Who goes there?"). But he liked "Prince" and refused to listen to "Pering." He had no rifle but wore a *badik* and looked as happy as ever.

Behind him came Tuan Petoro, with Tuan Anwar on his right. Both in khaki, without hats, both carrying rifles. Behind them, at the last moment, came the male nurse, Sitahaya,[18] who was a dark, soft man from Ambon, and two men clumsily carrying a stretcher with a first-aid box sitting on top.

They took the road into the mountains and did not try to keep in step. Under the last street lamp, some thousand feet beyond the office, where the deep darkness began, they stopped without anyone having said a word. A dozen curious men from Sungguminasa had joined the group, some, to the surprise of Tuan Petoro, carrying torches which they now lit. Prince got hold of one of the torches and Tuan Anwar cried, "Ajo!," after which they marched on. Prince started talking in an excited voice but Badawi said, "Quiet!" and it was quiet.

Tuan Petoro was worried about what they would find and thought Tuan Anwar must feel the same. Tuan Anwar walked very close to him, their arms touching at times. It was bad going on the narrow, pebble-strewn path, in spite of the red glare from the torches. Tuan Petoro remembered his first day in the service. The evening before he had arrived in Watampone, the capital of the old princedom of Bone, together with the new assistant resident whom he had met on board the ship. The first day the controller, while showing him around, had also made him visit the hospital. In one of the rooms were twenty-four beds and each held a wounded man. Bandaged heads, arms, thighs, and chests. He had asked, quite seriously, "Is this from a traffic accident?"—this in the interior of South Celebes which had no trains, and hardly any roads. . . . The assistant resident and the controller had burst out laughing. "A traffic accident!" People had run *amok*. A wedding, in Udjung Lamuru. After the party, after everybody had gone to bed, one of the guests had farted. Another guest started to laugh, followed by others, and the man who had farted went crazy and ran *amok* in the pitch dark. "Eight dead, as well as this bunch here." The assistant resident, the controller, and the military doctor had made the rounds of the beds and the assistant resident had said gravely: "And there was no reason for the man to feel hurt because no one knew who had really farted."

Tuan Petoro also remembered the Maros murder. He had been in South Celebes no more than a year and a half. He did not remember the precise sequence of events, but he had been visiting the controller and his wife, and suddenly a batman had appeared. The controller and he had run out of the house and, aided by torches, had come to an alley behind the house. An alley between high hedges. There, stretched out on his back, lay a dead man, with a *badik* in his heart. Around the *badik*, in the naked chest, was a tiny blood stain. The man did not look older than thirty. His eyes were open and there was a soft smile under his coal black mustache.

The group walked slowly on. No one spoke. Tuan Petoro remembered another incident. A prisoner had behaved badly, a guard had reported it, and the *djaksa* had recommended ten strokes with the rattan. Two guards tied the man to a pole in the prison yard, his hands high, with pillows protecting his kidneys and thighs. All the prisoners were called out. Two guards had bared the man's behind and had taken turns beating him, calling out to each other "harder, harder," and one of them had laughed. Tuan Petoro had watched it with beating heart, saw the blood appear, and had cursed himself because he had not dared call "Stop!" He had sworn that this would never happen again and now, thank God, the new governor had banned this form of punishment. But why think about it now?

They were approaching the *kampong* and took their rifles off their shoulders. Everything was quiet. The houses were dark. The *kampong* head motioned them to stop at one of the first houses. Tuan Djaksa turned a flashlight on a simple Macassar house, mostly bamboo, on stilts. A light burned in the front room. "This is it, my Lord," the *kampong* head said, and led them around the house.

At first Tuan Petoro could not make out by the light of the torches and the flashlight what was lying among the banana trees. Suddenly he realized and stared at Tuan Anwar. No one spoke. The entire bamboo back wall of the house had fallen over into the yard and on it, arms bent, lay a dead man. "Yes," the *kampong* head said, "this is the oldest brother of the bride. He was against the marriage and he called the groom something unmentionable so that everyone could hear it. The groom ran *amok* and first stabbed the man who had offended him. That man jumped back with such force that he landed in the yard, wall and all."

Tuan Petoro asked if there were more victims. "Probably inside," the *kampong* head said. They returned to the front of the house where they found more than twenty men and women. The women were crying, and some people were walking back and forth, trying to help the wounded. The man who had run *amok* was not to be found and Tuans Petoro and Anwar decided to look through the *kampong* for him. If a man runs *amok* and is not killed, he suddenly calms down and acts as if awakening from a terrible dream. He feels completely exhausted and does not resist arrest. Some report to their chief or, in those days, to the Tuan Petoro.

Tuan Djaksa stayed at the house with his servant to interrogate the people, and the male nurse and his assistants stayed to help the wounded. As Tuan Petoro and Tuan Anwar, with Prince and Badawi, were about to leave, the *djaksa* called from upstairs in a loud voice: "Tuan! Another corpse. The bride!"

Tuan Anwar and Tuan Petoro, led by Badawi and followed by

Prince, slowly and carefully went down the narrow *kampong* paths, their rifles at the ready. Badawi turned out to have brought a flashlight too, a large one which he hung from his uniform button. "Where did you get that?" Tuan Petoro asked Badawi's back. "It's yours, sir," Badawi answered. "I found it in the shed." "Why didn't you use it before?" "*Batarènja ampir mati*—the battery is almost dead," Badawi answered.

He directed the light under the houses, through the stilts, and under the sixth house they found him. The groom was a thin pale boy. He was waiting for them, silent, panting, and exhausted. He had lost his *songko* and *sarong,* and stood there in a white pair of underpants and a black shirt—the shirt of a poor groom. "Come here," Badawi called, and he came, let Prince handcuff him, and then went quietly along to Sungguminasa.

The Shot

The following morning Tuan Anwar entered the office of Tuan Petoro and said, "Good morning, sir." "Good morning, Mister Anwar, did you sleep well?" "No, sir," Tuan Anwar answered and looked shyly at Tuan Petoro. "My wife had a baby last night, quite suddenly." "Not too soon?" "No, sir, but very sudden." He hesitated. Then he said, "When I came home last night, sir, I wanted to unload my rifle. And suddenly, sir, you wouldn't believe it, it discharged! Right through my desk. It scared me but it scared my wife even more and then—Allah, sir!—her pains began." Tuan Petoro did not know what to say. Then he asked, "Everything all right now, I hope, Mister Anwar?" "Oh yes, sir. Another son."

Tuan Petoro and Tuan Anwar looked at one another. They shook hands and started to laugh out loud.

About Death

The first few nights after the *amok* incident, Tuan Petoro had difficulty falling asleep. He kept seeing the dead man on that wall and the tired boy under the house.

He had not often confronted death. The first time, as far as he knew, he had been five years old. He was living with his parents in a village in the southern Netherlands. He had been playing in the attic with a toy clown who was riding a dappled horse. He had heard screams outside and had seen from the window, across the roofs, a woman who was running, her hands in the air. He had run down the two flights of stairs—one, two, one, two, hold on carefully—and at the open front door he had found a small group of people. The only one he recalled was his mother. She had been standing there with a little girl on her arm, a very pale girl with green leaves in her hair and a wet dress. Her head rested against his mother's shoulder and she was asleep. No, she was not asleep. She had drowned in the canal across the street.

Nor would he ever forget the death of his elder brother. He was six, his brother nineteen. His mother had taken him into the front room and had raised him in her arms saying, "Give him a little kiss." His brother was lying there, very white and motionless. It had been nearly dark in the room and he could not see his brother's face very well.

And he had been to only two funerals. No, three, but he did not remember anything from the first except that he had to join his classmates in the funeral procession. He was seven, and it was the funeral of a boy in his class, little Ton Verdonk, who had fallen through the ice. Then a funeral in The Hague, of a great-uncle. All he remembered of that was the cheerfulness of the guests afterward: cigar smoke and port and sherry. He had been eighteen and everyone had laughed because he looked much younger in his top hat and morning coat. He was still ashamed about the aftermath of the third funeral. He had been nineteen. After the funeral in Amsterdam of one of his old professors, he and a friend had started drinking—gin and more gin—and it had gotten to them. At three in the morning, in the center of town, they had been singing so loudly that the police had picked them up, top hats and all.

It was evening again. Tuan Petoro sat behind his writing desk, in a loose white shirt, white trousers, and sandals. The man who had run *amok* was in prison. One of the wounded had died that day in a Macassar hospital. Three slightly wounded were still being treated at the clinic. He was studying the papers of a complicated inheritance case. He could not understand all the statements. He called, "Badawi!" Badawi appeared and said, "Tuan?" "Badawi, please ask Tuan Anwar to come."

Tuan Anwar came. Yes, mother and child were well. Once

Tuan Anwar had crossed his legs under him, and Tuan Petoro
had swung his legs over the arms of his chair, he asked about the
inheritance case. But fifteen minutes later, before the glasses of
lemonade were half empty, his thoughts wandered. He thought
about the attitude of the men of Macassar and of the Buginese
toward death. Toward a violent death. Dozens of people in this
region daily lost their lives through violence. Not violence of
nature or random traffic violence—no, death from the hand of a
fellow man. And how did bystanders react? A mother, a wife,
would cry. A father hid his head in his hands. A brother turned
pale with rage and pulled his *badik*. But all the others just watched
and accepted this as they would accept a leaf tumbling off a tree,
or a cloud passing across the face of the moon.

He fell silent and Tuan Anwar noticed that his thoughts were
somewhere else. Suddenly Tuan Petoro asked, looking at
him, "Mister Anwar, what do you think of death?" Tuan Anwar did not reply immediately. Then he asked, "What exactly
do you mean, sir?" "Are you afraid of dying?" "I think so, sir."
Tuan Anwar waited and then asked softly, "And you, sir?"
"Yes, I suppose so," Tuan Petoro answered. Then he added, "I
am sure."

Tuan Anwar did not look tired, he looked wisely through his
glasses. He said, "But we all die, and I always think, sir, since
Allah lets everyone die, death cannot be a bad thing. Death has to
be good, sir. Here on earth things can go wrong, do you see, sir?
Because of the evil in people. But death has been decreed by Tuan
Allah just like birth. Those two things must be good, sir, but in
between there's often a lot of trouble."

Tuan Petoro smiled and Tuan Anwar smiled too. He continued, "And then, there is a hereafter." He looked searchingly at
Tuan Petoro. "Yes, sir," he said. Tuan Petoro remained silent. He
lit a cigarette, put his arms behind his head, and stared at the ceiling. He asked, "What do you think of the death penalty, Mister
Anwar?"

Again Tuan Anwar waited before answering. He looked at his
folded hands in his lap, while Tuan Petoro watched the smoke of
his cigarette. "Look, sir," Tuan Anwar finally said, "punishing
by death is allowed, allowed under Muslim law, under Dutch
East Indies criminal law, and also under Macassar and Buginese
law. Yet—I think it's terrible, sir."

"I do, too," Tuan Petoro said. "You know what it says in the

Bible, thou shalt not kill, and how would one man dare decide when it is time for another man to leave this earth—." They fell silent once more. Tuan Petoro then asked, "Did you ever kill anyone? I mean—in your youth—because it was a matter of honor—or because of danger—a case of *amok*, perhaps?" "Luckily not, sir," Tuan Anwar said. "And I hope I never will."

Not long after that Tuan Anwar would kill a man.

The Second Shot

Tuan Petoro was about to go to his office when the telephone in his study rang. He picked up the receiver, heard the usual interference, and a distant voice called, "Hello, hello—are you there, sir? This is Anwar—." "Hello," Tuan Petoro called, "How are you?" "Fine, sir, very well, sir, we have a problem, sir."

Tuan Anwar, the *djaksa*, and a new young assistant, Abdulkadir, had gone into the mountains on horseback and were now in the area of the Lompobatang or Big Belly, an extinguished volcano. Here the borders of Gowa, Djeneponto, Bantaëng, and Sindjai came together. They had gone there because rumors had reached them that the notorious Sila, released from jail a year and a half earlier, had formed a new, although small, gang in the area of Gowa, in Parigi to be precise, and that the group was attacking and robbing traveling merchants.

"What is the problem, Mister Anwar?" The telephone rattled and sighed, and finally Tuan Petoro thought he heard Tuan Anwar say that Sila had probably crossed the border to Sindjai. Of course, Karaëng Parigi was with him, but was he allowed to collaborate with the assistants and chieftains of Sindjai? "I'll let you know!" Tuan Petoro yelled as loudly as possible. "Tomorrow!" After that he only heard hissing and crackling.

He phoned his boss, the assistant resident in Macassar, and he in turn called his colleague in Bantaëng. The following morning Tuan Petoro was about to call Tuan Anwar, when Tuan Anwar called him from Parigi. The connection was, if possible, even worse than the day before, but he could immediately tell that Tuan Anwar was nervous. "Something terrible happened, sir," Tuan Anwar said. "Tell me." Tuan Anwar yelled, "I've shot and killed Sila!" Tuan Petoro was quiet for a moment and then asked, "What happened?" "Well, sir, I could not help it, sir."

Tuan Petoro thought about that night when Tuan Anwar had fired a shot by accident, and his wife had promptly had a baby. "Tell me calmly what happened!" he shouted. The connection deteriorated further and he could not hear a word. Finally, he yelled, "Stay in Parigi! I'll be with you in an hour and a half!"

A month earlier Tuan Petoro had bought a secondhand Dodge convertible from a doctor in Macassar, a 1923 model, and ten minutes later he was on the road to Parigi with Badawi beside him. Badawi had brought a rifle, just in case. At one o'clock he stopped in front of the small wooden guest lodge of Parigi. On the front porch four serious-looking men were seated and when they saw Tuan Petoro in his open car—bareheaded ("Very unhealthy, sir," Tuan Anwar had remarked once)—they stood up. They were Tuan Anwar, Tuan Djaksa, Tuan Abdulkadir, the young assistant, and Karaëng Parigi, the local prince or chieftain.

The five of them sat down. The sun was high, shadows were short, and a scent of wild flowers hung in the air. The sky was as bright as molten silver and the mountains were blue in the vibrating air. Yet it was not hot at that altitude and Tuan Petoro felt he was not in a solemn enough mood to match the four men.

Tuan Anwar told his story, occasionally interrupted respectfully by Tuan Djaksa. The four of them, with three followers of Karaëng Parigi, had at seven that morning ridden to a *kampong* a couple of miles from Parigi, having heard that Sila had spent a night there some two weeks earlier. Only Tuan Anwar and Djaksa had carried rifles. On the road Tuan Djaksa had said, "Let's drink some coconut milk," and the seven of them had dismounted in front of a small house on stilts which sat by itself on the high plain with a growth of coconut palms beside it. Tuan Djaksa had handed his horse to one of the followers of Karaëng Parigi and had gone toward the house. When he was about ten feet away, the door opened and a man appeared, a large heavy man, with a full black mustache. His chest was bare and he was wearing a *sarong* but no turban. He had shouted something in a loud voice and waved a *kris*. Karaëng Parigi had cried, "That is Sila!" The man had come down the stairs at Tuan Djaksa, shouting curses. Tuan Djaksa, he did not know how, had fired a shot, surprising himself, but he had missed Sila. "Yes, sir, then I turned around and ran away, and ended up under the coconut palms." "I was quite startled, sir," Tuan Anwar said, and Tuan Abdulkadir smiled and said, "We all were." Tuan Anwar continued, "I just fired a shot, sir, I had no time to aim. And with the first shot—*aduh*—dead."[19] He looked sadly at Tuan Petoro through his spectacles, and sighed. Tuan Petoro considered and asked, "Where is the body?" "In a shack next to the house of Karaëng Parigi," Tuan Anwar said. Tuan Petoro went on, "Are you sure it is Sila?" "Yes, sir," Tuan Djaksa answered. "The man and woman in the house know him. Their daughter was his girl friend. They raised hell." Tuan Petoro asked, "And the gang?" "They've vanished," Karaëng Parigi said, "I've heard they went down to Manipi. I'll be watching." "Well, let's eat together," Tuan Petoro said, "and then I want to see the corpse, and afterward Tuan Anwar, Tuan Abdulkadir, and I will return to Sungguminasa. Karaëng Parigi must take care of a speedy funeral."

Back in Sungguminasa Tuan Petoro reported that same evening by phone to the assistant resident of Macassar and promised a written follow-up. This report was forwarded by the assistant resident to the governor, and one of the men on the staff of that functionary wrote in the margin, "This affair seems to have degenerated into a general shoot-out." Tuan Petoro heard this and over a couple of drinks in the club "Harmony" in Macassar he confided to a few friends and colleagues that he thought the remark was a disgrace. And those young men all agreed that "Macassar" never understood anything.

Nevertheless, the governor ordered an investigation, and thus three weeks later a considerable crowd assembled in the Parigi guest house. Again, as on the day of Sila's death, Tuan Petoro, Tuan Anwar, Tuan Djaksa, and Abdulkadir were there, as well as Karaëng Parigi. But so were the assistant resident and the public prosecutor of the General Court in Macassar. The entire group visited the spot where Sila had fallen and the public prosecutor took statements from everyone, including the followers of Karaëng Parigi. Tuan Anwar was in a sad state. He kept his eyes to the ground and looked like a murder suspect. At the end of the afternoon, the public prosecutor said, "Tuan Anwar, my congratulations, you have been vindicated." Everyone shook hands with Tuan Anwar. For a moment he seemed about to burst into tears, but he controlled himself and at each handshake he said softly, "Thank you, thank you."

Next day, when they were alone in the office, he said to Tuan Petoro, "It's terrible enough, sir—to kill a human being—but then all that fuss too! I'll never do that again!"

Tuan Cashclerk

Tuan Petoro had been about eight months in Sungguminasa, when Tuan Anwar became seriously worried. It concerned the clerk Katwyk who supervised Tuan Petoro's finances and was usually called Tuan Cashclerk. He had already been on sick leave for more than four weeks. He was a skinny fellow with blue-black hair low on his forehead, and an elegant mustache with dashing little points up in the air. This was in sharp contrast to his sad mouth and melancholy eyes. He was not older than thirty-six and suffered from chronic asthma. He was a silent man and until then, as far as Tuan Petoro knew, he had done his work well, and in beautiful handwriting. A month earlier he had written Tuan Petoro an extremely polite letter: he could not come to the office because of a serious asthma attack, but he had the books at home and would continue his task as well as possible. Tuan Petoro had visited him a few times, and Katwyk had indeed looked terrible, pale and tired, and his face was even thinner than before. He had spoken hoarsely and was short of breath.

One evening when Tuan Petoro was reading in his study, Badawi came in and announced Tuan Anwar. Tuan Petoro got up and walked toward his visitor. Between the old and the young man a bond of mutual trust had come into being and they often discussed matters that even men who call themselves friends leave untouched. Tuan Petoro immediately saw that Tuan Anwar looked solemn, and once they were seated, he asked, "What is it, Mister Anwar?"

"Yes, sir," Tuan Anwar said, and thoughtfully stroked his gray mustache. "Yes, sir,—difficult, sir." Tuan Petoro waited. Then Tuan Anwar polished his glasses and carefully put them back on. He looked at Tuan Petoro. "It's about Katwyk, sir," he finally said. "What about Katwyk? Did he die?" "Oh no, sir, oh no— you see, you and I thought he had asthma, and he does, but I have learned, reliably, that he sends for a taxi from Macassar almost every evening and then arrives back home, in another taxi, quite late. Expensive, sir. And he often takes his, excuse me, sir, his trull, I mean that Javanese con—con—" "Concubine," Tuan Petoro said. "Exactly, sir, he takes her along."

Tuan Anwar stopped and Tuan Petoro tried to hide his confusion by lighting a cigarette. What to do? He asked, "And what do you think Katwyk does in Macassar?" Tuan Anwar said, "He gambles, sir."

Tuan Petoro pulled at his cigarette and slowly blew out smoke. Yes, what to do? He felt guilty. He had not paid enough attention to Katwyk, and that, of course was because he was not interested enough in the finances of his office. Or rather—he did not understand them and was too lazy to bother. His high-school teacher had been right when she had shaken her gray head and announced, "You'll never make a good accountant, Carel." She had been right. There he was.

"All right," he said after another moment of quiet smoking. "All right. Tomorrow I'll send for Katwyk and inspect his books. I thank you, Mister Anwar."

Tuan Anwar left and Tuan Petoro felt so down that he decided to go visit one of his friends in Macassar. The yearly *Pasar Malam*[20] was in full swing that Friday evening, and he felt he had earned some distraction after this blow. It was Friday night, and the first friend he called on was immediately ready to go with him. They wandered around in the glare of dozens of arc lights and hundreds of lamps, amidst the tents and stalls. Thousands of people pushed them along. Tuan Petoro led his friend to the merry-go-round; even as a small child he had loved those, especially if they had white horses with large staring eyes, flaring nostrils, and beautiful accouterments with little mirrors stitched on.

The friends were contentedly watching children and grown-ups whirling around, each in his or her own dream. Suddenly Tuan Petoro said, "Well, dammit all!" "What?" his friend asked, raising his voice above the noise of the fair. Tuan Petoro had seen Katwyk whirl by. There he was again, elegant on a fiery horse, dressed in an immaculate white suit closed at the neck, a white cap at an angle on his head. He looked happier than Tuan Petoro had ever seen him. And on the other horse sat his, excuse me, sir, trull, sidesaddle. A young Javanese woman, in *sarong* and *kabaja*, a pink veil chastely covering her face. Tuan Petoro hastily turned his back and left the place with his friend, making for the club to recover from all of this.

When Badawi appeared the next evening at eight o'clock in Tuan Anwar's house and asked him to come over, he had been expected. Tuan Anwar was worried about his young and inexperienced boss. That morning, Tuan Petoro had summoned Tuan Cashclerk, who had appeared, deadly pale and panting. What had happened thereafter in Tuan Petoro's office, Tuan Anwar could only guess. Cashclerk had first gone back home and reappeared with a pile of ledgers. Then he had come out of the office and searched in his own desk for a stack of papers. All that time the office personnel had kept as quiet as mice. The clerk Ponggawa, the scribes, and assistant clerks had hardly looked up. On the front porch, Badawi and Prince kept silent; even Prince did not feel like chatting.

At a quarter past ten, the assistant resident of Macassar had arrived in his black Oldsmobile. Tuan Petoro must have telephoned him. He and Tuan Petoro had dispensed with the usual smiles when they greeted each other. Tuan Anwar had heard the assistant resident say: "A fine affair, young man!" Cashclerk had stayed at his desk, his head in his hands. After some time, Tuan Anwar had been called in. Tuan Petoro, seated behind his desk next to the assistant resident, had pointed at a chair; his face was beet red. The assistant resident had asked: "Mister Anwar, have you deposited monies with Katwyk while he was ill?" "Yes, sir, I will get the receipts." Tuan Anwar had gone to fetch them and given them to the assistant resident, who had dismissed him after a few more questions. After that, Katwyk had been in there for more than an hour. Around three o'clock, the assistant resident had left and Tuan Petoro had slowly walked back to his house.

Now Tuan Petoro was calling him and he hurried to the house of his boss. Tuan Petoro did not speak, gestured toward a chair, sat down and got up again, and lit a cigarette. "Mister Anwar," he said with forced calm, "it's very bad. When I checked Katwyk's books this morning, I immediately found a deficit of more than six hundred guilders. Now I don't know much about this kind of thing, but the assistant resident who interrogated you and Abdulkadir found that Katwyk has also received monies at home and did not book them—like the money you deposited." "All I deposited," Tuan Anwar said, "was money in lieu of *corvée* labor."[21] Tuan Petoro continued: "All right. It is stupid, and Katwyk has stolen, and I am guilty for not keeping a better eye on him, but the worst part of it is that he says he handed all the money over to me, and that I put it in the safe and that I should know where it has gone!" Tuan Petoro's voice broke and Tuan Anwar was visibly rattled. He got up, went over to Tuan Petoro, touched his shoulder for a second and said in a hoarse voice, "But sir, no one will believe that!"

Tuan Petoro nervously stubbed out his cigarette and lit another. The phone rang. "No," he answered, "no, not tonight,

really not, I am too busy—I am not acting—go to hell yourself—
bye." To Tuan Anwar he said: "A friend, I don't feel like going to
Macassar tonight. And then—the assistant resident is coming
back tomorrow, on Sunday morning"—he sounded disgusted—
"at eight o'clock."

Tuan Anwar left Tuan Petoro. He was worried about him, but
there was little he could do. How could he have warned his boss
without any proof? Yet, once he learned that Katwyk spent his
evenings in Macassar—.

Next evening Tuan Petoro asked Tuan Anwar over at dusk. It
was warm. Tuan Petoro and a friend who had arrived just then,
soaking wet from a bicycle trip all the way from Macassar, were
sitting in rattan chairs around a small table on the lawn, drinking
Scotch and soda in the light of a table lamp. Tuan Petoro took
Tuan Anwar inside and told him that the assistant resident had
established a shortage in cash of four thousand four hundred
guilders. Cashclerk insisted he had given the money to Tuan Petoro. Tuan Anwar sighed and said it was terrible, but he was sure
it would all come out well. They shook hands and Tuan Anwar
returned to his wife and children, and Tuan Petoro to his guest.
He said, "Let's do some serious drinking."

About an hour or so later—when Tuan Petoro had cheered up
considerably—Badawi appeared in the circle of light and said,
"Tuan Katwyk's *njai* wants to talk to you." Tuan Petoro repeated,
surprised, "Tuan Katwyk's *njai?*" Badawi muttered: "She has
brought a rifle." Tuan Petoro said, "What next," and went to the
house.

She was a small woman and very beautiful. She apologized for
the interruption, but Katwyk had been drinking in his room all
afternoon and then he had loaded the rifle and said, "I'll put an
end to all of this." After that he had entered his bedroom and
fallen asleep on the bed. She had taken the rifle, and here it was.
Tuan Petoro should be careful, it was still loaded. He thanked
her, and she hurried away into the darkness. He unloaded the rifle, and then telephoned the assistant resident. He reported the
story and suggested a house search the next morning at Katwyk's, for instance by the subcommissioner of police in Macassar. His suggestion was approved; De la Court would be on the
spot at nine.

It was five minutes to nine the next morning when De la Court
got out of his car in front of Tuan Petoro's house. Those two knew

each other and laughed when they met. A minute later Tuan Anwar appeared. Tuan Anwar and De la Court had known each other for years and slapped each other on the shoulder.

De la Court was a big fat man, hailing from Rotterdam. He had left the Dutch East Indies army, where he had been a sergeant-major, some ten years earlier to enter the police force. His white, buttoned uniform collar enclosed a solid neck; a weathered, red head had twinkly little eyes behind an old-fashioned lorgnette. He said, "Boys, what an affair. Shall we send for Katwyk?" He looked around. "The assistant resident told me everything. Is that the gun?" He picked it up and put it back in the corner. "A piece of junk. Still, good enough to blow your own head off."

Fifteen minutes later, Cashclerk appeared, looking even more miserable than the day before. It was early and not hot yet, but his white forehead was wet with sweat. He had dark blue bags under his eyes and was audibly panting, his mouth half open. He looked like a deer at bay. Tuan Petoro asked him to sit down and said, "Mister Katwyk, Mister De la Court here of the Macassar police, has been summoned to do a house search—" He stopped, because Cashclerk held up both hands and then said hoarsely, "Oh, sir, sir, no need—don't bother—I confess." He shouted, "I confess!" And softer, "I stole it all—lost it all." His hands dropped between his thighs and he started coughing. When he had finished his coughing spell, he kept his head down. No one spoke. Tuan Anwar sighed and looked at Tuan Petoro with a little smile. Finally De la Court said in a military voice, "Katwyk!" Katwyk looked up. De la Court pointed at the rifle in the corner and asked, "Is that yours?" Katwyk looked, nodded, and muttered, "That goddamn whore."

Tuan Petoro said, "Well, Mister De la Court, let's go. Mister Anwar, will you stay here with Mister Katwyk?"

In the wooden Macassar house of Tuan Cashclerk everything was very neat. The young Javanese woman received them and then vanished to the back of the house. De la Court went over everything very professionally but found nothing. A few school notebooks he put aside. He went through them at the end of the visit; one was empty, but in the other he started to read, leafing through it and finally crying out, "Well, I'll be damned!" He went up to Tuan Petoro and said, "Look at this, on page number one, 'Ode to God.' On page number two, another poem but rather different, 'Jack the Tickler.' But now hear this, a letter, 'My beloved sister—' " De la Court read the whole letter out loud, standing in the middle of the room, and Tuan Petoro couldn't believe his ears. It was full of religious sentiments and Jesus was repeatedly invoked. But the strangest thing was, it sounded like a letter written from prison. "Signed," shouted De la Court, "Billie!" He howled with laughter. "And where is this letter from?" He looked triumphantly at Tuan Petoro. "From Semarang! Semarang prison! This is Billie! Billie Katwyk! How could I have been so dumb! I never thought of Billie! But," he added apologetically, "Celebes is full of Katwyks."

That evening Tuan Anwar went over to Tuan Petoro on his own initiative. Tuan Petoro had come back from Macassar, where he had gone with Katwyk and De la Court. Katwyk's confession had been duly taken down. Tuan Petoro told him about the search and the letter from Semarang. Tuan Anwar sat with his mouth wide open in astonishment. "But sir, none of us knew Cashclerk had been in prison. Why was he?" "Fraud," Tuan Petoro said. "Some eight years ago, in Pontianak.[22] He served two years. After that, his record was expurgated. They just found out in the governor's office in Macassar."

Four months later, Katwyk got another two-year sentence. At the end of the year, Tuan Petoro got what he had expected: in the jargon of officialdom, a bad mark was made on his record. And this quite apart from the fact that he had to make up for the lost money.

The Miracle

Toward the end of the dry season, in the same year which saw Tuan Cashclerk enter prison for the second time, something happened that would remain the topic of conversation for Tuan Anwar and the office personnel for years to come. Tuan Petoro would tell the story to his children, although he could not know that at the time.

One morning in the office Tuan Anwar passed the room of the new Tuan Aspirang, who had settled with his wife in the house of the hydraulics engineer who had been transferred. He was seated behind his desk, his face toward the open door to the porch, where Tuan Anwar was passing by. On the floor, in front of him, a man from Macassar was seated, in peasant clothes.

Tuan Anwar looked inside, and Tuan Aspirang smiled and called, "Mister Anwar! Mister Anwar! Come in for a moment."

"This man," Tuan Aspirang said, "announces that he is not a thief." "Yes, sir," Tuan Anwar said. "Look," continued Tuan Aspirang, "look at those two *ubis*[23] in front of him. He says, if someone announces he has stolen them, that's a lie. That's what he has come to tell me." Tuan Anwar looked at the man. He had the appearance of a peasant back from the field after a rough day; his hands, his clothes, and his turban were filthy. He looked at Tuan Anwar with glittering eyes and repeated, beating the mat on which he was seated, "I did not steal these *ubis*. I am not a thief."

Tuan Aspirang said, "Do you know what I think, Mister Anwar? That this man has a fever. That he is suffering from malaria." "Very clever, very clever for such a young man!" Tuan Anwar would later say to Tuan Petoro.

Tuan Petoro was called and since no one had a better theory, Prince took the man to the clinic and put him in the hands of the Sitahaya, the male nurse. Sitahaya put him in bed, covered him up, and took his temperature, to the amazement if not terror of the poor fellow. He was running a high fever and Sitahaya gave him some quinine and told him to go to sleep. That was at half past twelve in the afternoon.

Around five, after his siesta, Tuan Petoro opened the blinds in his bedroom which looked out on the garage. That same moment Badawi appeared, a nervous grin on his face, carrying the rifle of his tuan, which sometimes stayed in the car. He ran toward Tuan Petoro's bedroom door, banged on it, and cried, "Tuan! Tuan!" Tuan Petoro opened and Badawi rushed toward the drawer, took out some cartridges, and stuffed them in his pocket. Tuan Petoro stared and finally asked: "What's going on?" Badawi said, "*Amok*, Tuan," and disappeared, to call a friend and guest of Tuan Petoro, Lucien,[24] who was staying in the pavilion and owned a large revolver, as Badawi told Tuan Petoro later.

It turned out that the malaria patient, in a delirious fever, had run away from the clinic at the moment when, across the way, the prison guard was changing. This was done very informally: the gate with its barbed wire remained open while the previous and the new guards made a round of the cells, and they left their *klewangs* hanging on the garden bell. The patient had entered, taken a *klewang* in each hand, and run back out into the street, enjoying his power and bellowing a war cry. The first person he saw was fat little Mrs. Sitahaya, who had just left the clinic with her three children for an afternoon stroll. They took to their heels, screaming, and the patient, waving his *klewang,* had sort of danced on, toward the house of Tuan Petoro.

Neither Tuan Petoro nor his friend knew what was happening until they had arrived in front of the house, each in his bathrobe. Badawi joined them and the three went, bent over, across the lawn toward the road where the man who had run *amok* approached. Tuan Petoro—no one would ever understand why— was unarmed. Lucien's revolver was empty but neither he nor anyone else knew that. Badawi had trouble loading his rifle, not surprisingly, as he had brought the wrong cartridges. But they did not know this as they were facing the enemy.

In the meantime the village was in full alarm. In the market, the threatening signal was beaten out on the *tong-tong:* "Someone has run *amok.*" The two prison guards, minus their *klewangs,* were lying in the grass, half kneeling, and throwing stones at the crazy man from a safe distance.

Then came the unforgettable moment. From the house beside the clinic, blinking against the sun in his spectacles, Tuan Aspirang appeared, walking calmly toward the man running *amok.* In his hand he held an antique Indonesian sword as if it were an umbrella. The handle of the sword was shaped like a little Buddha.

The three on the lawn, still thinking that two of them were well armed, held their breath. But Tuan Aspirang jumped the ditch and onto the road, and called out in his best Malay: "Throw away your arms!" Although the madman only spoke the Macassar language, he obeyed, and came to a halt, staring in front of him. Tuan Aspirang smiled at him and was just about to pick up the *klewangs* when Badawi and the two prison guards jumped forward and knocked the man down. From the village came the sound of a hundred naked feet and men appeared, waving lances and *krisses.* Tuan Petoro cried as loudly as possible, "Don't kill him! Don't kill him!" but they only heard and repeated, "*Bunuh!* Kill! Kill!"

At the last moment, the two tuans, Petoro along with Aspirang, and Tuan Anwar, who had appeared with a rifle at the ready, managed to get between this mob and the poor madman. Tuan Petoro shouted at Badawi. "Leave him along, dammit! Take him to a cell and let Sitahaya take care of him."

Later Tuan Petoro said to Tuan Aspirang, "You shouldn't have done that, you could have been killed." Tuan Aspirang looked at him very seriously and said: "But he knew me, didn't he?"

Little Mother Manudju

During the first monthly meetings on the cool front porch of the office, where Tuan Petoro presided with Tuan Anwar on his right and, later, Abdulkadir on his left, he had noticed a silent, young-ish man who had a slight squint. When he and Tuan Anwar were discussing the most important chieftains of Gowa one time, Tuan Anwar had said, "That Karaëng Manudju is really a good chief, sir. He doesn't say much. He really never says anything. But he feels for his people, he knows every tree in his area and is good and just with the *kampong* heads. His colleagues respect him. He is also brave, sir. Two years ago he captured three dangerous robbers in a little house in the mountains, just he and a fourteen-year-old boy who worked in his stables."

"Next month I want to make a tour in Manudju," Tuan Petoro said, "and I want to take you and Tuan Abdulkadir along. Tuan Abdulkadir and I haven't been here long; you can explain things to us. We will take the car to where the main road enters Manudju and go on from there on horseback—about five days in all."

"Then you must call on his mother," Tuan Anwar said. "His mother?" "Yes, she is one of the most remarkable people in Gowa. I think the people respect her more than anyone. In her younger years she was highly popular at the court of the king of Gowa. She, as well as her husband—." "Her husband? Is he still alive? Is he the father of Karaëng Manudju?" Tuan Anwar smiled. "Yes, he is seventy-three. Three years ago he decided to abdicate and his only son became Karaëng Manudju. He looks sixty, has a young wife, and spends all his time with her or deer hunting. During the last rainy season he came to a river in flash flood. He took off his clothes and swam across. And back, for he was doing it for fun." Tuan Petoro laughed and said, "Well, I'll meet him when I visit the old lady." "No, sir," Tuan Anwar answered, "the old Karaëng rarely sees the lady. He lives with his young wife." "Well," Tuan Petoro said, "then I'll see him there. I do want to meet him, in any case."

A few weeks later Tuan Petoro, the young Karaëng Manudju who had waited for them on the main road, Tuan Anwar, Tuan

Abdulkadir, Prince, and three servants had set out, proceeded by
the official lance carrier of Karaëng Manudju. When they stopped
their horses at the house of the old karaëng, they learned that he
was not home. He had been gone for a week, on a deer hunt, and
the old retainer who told them this did not know when he would
be back. Thus they went on to the *kampong* where the young karaëng lived. They were expected there and would spend the
night. The young karaëng was less silent now, and showed a
gentle sense of humor. That evening they were all his guests at
a large meal. During the conversation they learned that, strange-
ly enough, they were not in the house where in an attic the *gaukang* of Manudju, a gold *kris*, was kept. The *gaukang* was in the
house where his mother lived, together with a male priest in
women's dress, who had to take care of it.[25]

The following morning they all rode on to the village of the old
lady. The fiery Macassar horses danced along the stony mountain
paths, the sun shone from a cloudless sky, a mild wind blew
through the dark canyons, and the mountains were blue-green.
After two hours the path turned in a complete half circle around a
high black rock. "There is the house," Karaëng Manudju said.
Tuan Petoro saw a field full of white flowers, with a small path
cutting through it, and behind it a long black-brown house on
many stilts, against a green hillside.

They crossed the field and dismounted. Tuan Petoro asked Karaëng Manudju to go ahead, then he climbed the stairs, followed
by Tuan Anwar and Abdulkadir. The old woman was awaiting
them in the middle of the large living space. A small thin lady
with white hair pulled together in a bun, she was standing
straight as an arrow. She wore the simple, long black dress of a
Macassar woman; under it a pleated red and green silk *sarong*
showed.

Tuan Petoro went toward her and held out his hand. She took
it with both her hands and pressed it against her chest. She had a
small wrinkled face and a mouth without teeth, but her large dark
eyes, with a hidden smile in them, had something girlish about
them. She sat down on a mat and invited the men to sit down,
too. They would spend the night, and Prince put up Tuan Petoro's camp bed in one of the rooms. When the old lady noticed
that, she got up and ordered him around: here was a draft, there
his head would point in the wrong direction. That day she stayed
away because she was arranging things, but they were aware of

her presence. That evening, when Tuan Petoro got under his mosquito netting, he found not only his own pajamas but also a rough linen pair of shorts and a large *sarong* which, he later heard, belonged to the young Karaëng Manudju. The old lady had not understood what he would be doing during the night in the things Prince had spread out for his tuan.

Next day Tuan Petoro asked to see the *gaukang,* the golden *kris.* The priest led him and the Karaëng Manudju up the steep ladder to the attic. There they saw the little house that held the relic, and after burning incense and muttering holy words, the *sànro* unwrapped the *kris* from its white cloth. Thus Tuan Petoro and the old lady developed a kind of friendship without saying much. Half a year later he attended a large festival in her house on the occasion of the ritual cleaning of the *kris.* She played a leading role in that, for she knew and directed the traditional ceremonies and rituals of centuries ago.

During the farewells after the festival which had lasted six days, she held Tuan Petoro's hand for a long time and looked solemnly at him. Then she said: "I now take you as my son." She waited, smiled, and added: "Now I have two sons." Tuan Petoro just nodded and would have liked to kiss her wrinkled cheeks, but he did not dare.

The Ghost in the Holy Tree

It had been a busy week. Tuans Petoro and Anwar had come to the mountain village Parigi to judge a number of connected thefts, in conjunction with the Native Court of Gowa. That was ten days ago. From nine in the morning until late at night, by the light of storm lamps, the court had been in session every day except Sunday, and hundreds of witnesses had been waiting in the guesthouse. Besides the cattle thefts, the court had had to deal with a murder and a case of manslaughter.

During an interrogation, one of the witnesses—a pretty young woman who was relating how her father had been threatened for months by his murderer—had suddenly stopped, looked in pain, and put her hand against her body. She had bent her head and the men behind the table could no longer see her face. Tuan Anwar had waited and then asked her gently to go on. She had whispered something which had surprised him and the other members of the court, and Karaëng Parigi had jumped up and called the mother of the woman, who had been waiting outside. "Hurry! Hurry!" Tuan Petoro had asked, "What is all this about?" Tuan Anwar had smiled and announced, "She is having a baby. Yes, sir."

The court had continued with other witnesses. Half an hour later a broadly smiling Prince had brought in a nervous young man, who asked permission to speak and announced that his wife had just given birth to a daughter. The members of the court congratulated him. The young father stayed on his mat and then said with a radiant face, "And we will name her Base Kántoro,[26] because she was almost born in this office."

Now it was evening. The girl Base Kántoro was four days old, the murderer had been sentenced to twelve years, two-thirds of the cattle thefts had been dealt with, and now Tuan Petoro, Tuan Anwar, Tuan Abdulkadir, and a young Dutch official, who was on an inspection tour and was staying for one night in Parigi, were sitting together. They were talking and smoking by the light of an oil lamp.

It had rained heavily for several hours and through the windows and doors of the simple guesthouse a cool mountain wind wafted in.

Tuan Petoro was telling about his friend, the Tuan Petoro of Takalar. Late one evening, alone on his porch, the Tuan Petoro of Takalar had become aware of a high whistling sound from somewhere—it seemed to come from high up in the air. It didn't come closer nor go away. It was a shrill whistle. He had called his *djongos*, who appeared shaking and trembling. Yes, the servant said, his wife and some guests had already heard it for an hour. They did not dare leave. Tuan Petoro Takalar had gone outside. His batman had vanished. "He's afraid," the *djongos* had said, "so he's sitting with us."

Tuan Petoro Takalar sent for a storm lamp and for his batman, and together they made the rounds of the house. At a certain moment he thought they were approaching the source of the noise. It seemed to come from the shed that housed the little train that ran from Macassar to Takalar. Could it be the engine? They woke up the station master who opened the shed, and there they found two little engines. One had sprung a steam leak and was producing the high whistle.

They all laughed and Tuan Anwar said: "People are easily

scared. Superstitious, sir." Tuan Petoro lit a cigarette and in the ensuing silence they suddenly heard from outside, but quite clearly, a long drawn-out plaintive cry, as of a person dying. They looked at each other. After a few seconds of total silence another cry, which seemed to fill the whole house. It started softly, became louder, and died away. Tuan Petoro got up and walked to the back door, where Prince was sitting on a bench, talking with two followers of Karaëng Parigi. "Prince," Tuan Petoro asked, "do these men know what that sound is?" Prince passed the question on and one of the men said, "That is the *sètan* in the *waringin,* the holy fig tree."[27] The second man, who was preparing his *sirih* chaw, looked up for a moment and said pensively: "It is *malam djum'at*—the evening before Friday,"[28] as if saying that that was the time when ghosts appear. Again the cry was heard. Tuan Petoro wondered if his old wish would be fulfilled and if he would finally see a ghost. He turned around and said, "Do you hear that? It is a *sètan* in the *waringin* tree." "Yes, sir," Tuan Anwar whispered and Abdulkadir did not say anything.

In front of the guesthouse stood a centuries' old *waringin* tree, and the sound seemed indeed to originate from there. The men looked at each other and Tuan Petoro said: "I'm going to see." "Don't, sir," Tuan Anwar said hastily. "I'm going to," Tuan Petoro said, and went to get a flashlight from his bedroom. He called Prince. A small cortege formed: Tuan Petoro in front with Prince, behind them the followers of Karaëng Parigi, and in the rear Tuan Anwar and Abdulkadir. They were in pajamas and *sarongs,* and without weapons. They knew that weapons were useless against ghosts.

They followed Tuan Petoro's light and walked on as soundlessly as possible, to their left the guesthouse and to the right a pile of wooden beams under an *atap*[29] lean-to. The cry sounded again, clearer and more frightening than before. In front of them the shape of the tree loomed up, black against the night sky. Slowly Tuan Petoro approached, with only Prince beside him. He shone the flashlight over the mighty foliage, over the motionless air roots, and over the maze of branches and leaves. The cry sounded again, now not as if coming from the tree itself but as if it were reflected by it. Tuan Petoro turned around and said, "I don't think we'll find anything here." They made way for him and he shone his light first on the guesthouse and then on the pile of timber. Suddenly he saw two eyes light up and at the same time they heard the drawn-out cry once again. Prince called, "It's a dog!"

Next to the beams a dog lay dying.

The men went back in without speaking. Finally Tuan Anwar said in a voice which showed his relief, "No devil, sir."

Abdulkadir entered the room he shared with Tuan Anwar and came back out again with a rifle. He and Prince, who carried the flashlight, left the house. A shot sounded, and after that it was still.

The Gifts

Tuan Petoro had been in Sungguminasa for more than a year when Tuan Anwar announced the young Karaëng Manudju. They exchanged greetings and Karaëng looked shyly at Tuan Petoro. "Tell him," Tuan Anwar urged. "My mother sent me," Karaëng Manudju said. "She is quite ill. She has a fever, she has headaches, and she coughs." He fell silent and looked away. "Say everything," Tuan Anwar urged. "And now she asks you—." Tuan Anwar interrupted, "as her son—." Tuan Petoro started laughing and they laughed all three. "She asks you—" Karaëng Manudju spoke slowly, obviously repeating what he had learned by heart, "to send her one bottle of cough medicine, one bottle of eucalyptus oil for a massage, and one crate of condensed milk." He stopped and did not know where to look. Tuan Anwar said, "She loves sweetened milk and it will fortify her. Sometimes the king of Gowa also sent her a crate."

Tuan Petoro gave Karaëng Manudju his best wishes for his mother's recovery and within half an hour Badawi was on the way in the car (he had learned to drive in a reckless fashion), with cough medicine, specially made by Sitahaya, a large bottle of eucalyptus oil from the Chinese shop, and a crate with twenty-four cans of condensed milk from the supply room. The village head whose *kampong* on the main road was nearest to the house of Little Mother Manudju (as they called her from then on) would take care of the final stage of the transport.

Less than two weeks later young Karaëng Manudju came to report that his mother had recovered. She was going to send his father to thank Tuan Petoro personally. Tuan Petoro did not pay too much attention to this, although he was struck by the fact that Little Mother Manudju would send her husband, the former karaëng. After an hour's talk—about the harvest, the number of absentees in the new and unpopular people's schools, cattle thefts, and the roads and irrigation systems in Manudju, the young Karaëng Manudju said goodbye.

Eight days later Tuan Petoro was reading Dutch newspapers in his study, after his siesta, when Badawi entered and said in a respectful voice, "Tuan Anwar is coming, bringing the old Karaëng Manudju." Tuan Petoro went to the front porch, happy that he had planned a visit to Macassar and so was not wearing a robe but a white shirt and flannel trousers, and shoes rather than sandals, although no tie.

From the right a slow procession approached. Tuan Anwar and the old karaëng were in front. Tuan Anwar, at the karaëng's left, was in uniform and had on a white pith helmet with a black and gold emblem. The seventy-three-year-old karaëng strode straight and proudly, next to Tuan Anwar, his large mustache and bushy eyebrows a silver gray. He was in court dress. He had on a black, horsehair *songko* with a wide gold band around it, a jacket of purple gold brocade with velvet buttons and close-fitting sleeves, and a wide, gauze skirt with an embroidered belt which, in front, held a gold *kris*. He was followed by six boys in the same costume, though simpler, with *songkos* made from a white starched material. Tuan Petoro advanced, led the old karaëng to the porch and made him sit down. He also offered Tuan Anwar a seat, but he refused and remained standing. The boys sat behind their master on the rug, spread their gauze skirts out, and whispered with each other behind their hands. Badawi and Prince stood in the back. They did not want to miss this spectacle for anything in the world. Prince started babbling, softly but excitedly, but Badawi put his hand over Prince's mouth.

The old karaëng sat up straight, looked Tuan Petoro in his eyes, and made a speech in a subdued voice in which he thanked him for what he had done for his wife, without which she doubtlessly would have died. He wanted to offer Tuan Petoro a present. He made an impatient gesture toward his followers and suddenly he held in his hands an antique Chinese vase of almost transparent white porcelain, painted with blue flowers and birds. He stood up with difficulty. Tuan Petoro got up too and accepted the vase. Then they both sat down again and Tuan Petoro answered, saying how happy he was with the recovery of the karaëng's wife, and that he would gratefully keep the vase all his life as a memento.

Abu appeared as if summoned and whispered into his master's ear: "Orang sherry?" Tuan Petoro nodded. Abu must have had it ready, for he immediately appeared with a tray and three glasses of orangeade. One for Tuan Anwar, one for the karaëng, one for Tuan Petoro. The followers did not count. But the old karaëng took a sip and handed the glass to one of the boys, who took a sip in turn, and passed it on, until it came back to the hand of the master, still half full.

The karaëng coughed and said: "To bring you fortune, sir, I am presenting you with the most famous fighting cock from the mountains of Gowa. He is called 'The Fortune of Baringing,' the *kampong* of his birth." The old man made another gesture toward his followers and there was the cock (Tuan Petoro never understood how he could have remained invisible until then). He was a white cock, his feet and beak tied up, staring angrily out of his round eyes. It was the largest cock Tuan Petoro had ever seen. He accepted the heavy bird. He saw Badawi smile radiantly at Prince: a fighting cock in the yard of Tuan Petoro opened up undreamt-of possibilities. He beckoned Badawi, gave him the bird, and asked him to take it to the yard. The karaëng continued: "This bird, sir, is a very special cock. He will defeat not only all other cocks, but he is so brave that he also attacks human beings. He will defend your garden against intruders."

From the backyard they heard loud screams. Tuan Petoro looked at Tuan Anwar who showed a resigned smile. The cock had been set loose and was pursuing the cook and the *babu*.

Again Tuan Petoro thanked the old karaëng. But that was not the end of the gifts.

"Finally," the karaëng said, "I brought you one of my sons," and he put arm around a boy about ten years old, dressed neatly in a black buttoned jacket and colorful *sarong*, and with a black *kupiah* on his little round head. Tuan Petoro really only saw him now, sitting next to the karaëng (had he been hidden like the cock and the vase?). "I give you, my lord, this son of mine." Tuan Petoro knew he looked bewildered. "He will be your son and you his father. I hope you will raise him and send him to school. One day he will honor your name."

Tuan Petoro was afraid to look at Tuan Anwar. "Thank you, oh karaëng, for this signal honor. I will raise him and have him schooled and try to be a good father." He thought desperately, "What am I going to do with him?" The poor boy couldn't help it either. He would discuss it with Tuan Anwar. He kneeled down, took the boy's hand, and smiled. The child looked terrified.

That was the last present and after another round of orange-ades, the karaëng asked permission to leave. After they had said farewell Tuan Petoro called Abu and told him to take the boy to the back of the house, where the servants were. Tuan Anwar, who had seen the karaëng off, came back immediately. He laughed more loudly than Tuan Petoro had ever seen him do and said: "Yes, sir, there's always something."

As a result of their discussion Badawi was sent out to fetch Tuan Abdulkadir, the young assistant. When he heard the story, he howled with laughter too and said, grinning broadly, "A child just like that, sir, without a woman." Tuan Anwar started laughing again, and Tuan Petoro too, but weakly. Then he said, "Well, I must accept the consequences of receiving this boy. But I can't take care of him, you know that. Can I board him out to you, Mister Abdulkadir?" "Certainly." "Good," Tuan Petoro said, "and then we'll send him to school here right away. You are a father or you aren't." He looked suddenly at Tuan Anwar and asked him: "Is this a son of the old karaëng?" "Yes, sir. By yet another woman."

And thus little Hussein was boarding with Abdulkadir and went to school in Sungguminasa. But five days later Abdulkadir entered Tuan Petoro's office with a wide grin on his face and said: "Your son has run away, sir." "Run away?" "To Manudju. My wife and I expected it." "Now what?" Tuan Petoro asked. "Let's call Tuan Anwar."

The three men decided that nothing at all should be done. Honor had been satisfied. The old karaëng had offered a son as a gift to Tuan Petoro, the highest honor. And Tuan Petoro had accepted, the only possible course of action. No one was to blame for the son running away to go back home. Without doubt all parties were now satisfied.

Three months after this, Tuan Petoro and Abdulkadir rode on horseback into the *kampong* where Little Mother Manudju lived. Three naked boys were playing and when they saw the horsemen they screamed and fled into the bushes. Abdulkadir said, "There goes your son, sir."

The "Fortune of Baringing" also gave trouble. In the beginning he attacked not only Tuan Anwar and Abdulkadir but all the other inhabitants of the house as well. He always attacked from the rear, dug his spurs into a man's or woman's behind, pecked them between the shoulder blades, and hit the arms of the victims with his wings. On the third day, at the risk of their lives, Badawi and Abu got him into a cage. Later he got used to Abu, his wife Kenna, the cook, Badawi, Prince, the housekeeper, and the gardener. Sometimes, when she noticed friends coming who she didn't want to see just then, the cook would open his cage.

He was to follow Tuan Petoro to Watampone when he was transferred, and there "Fortune" ruled a harem of twenty beautiful leghorns. He died four years later, dramatically, found dead early in the morning by Tuan Petoro's local batman, Samaila. He had died of chicken pest. It was on the very day that Tuan Petoro and his wife were going to Holland on leave.

The Chinese vase went with Tuan Petoro and his wife to Watampone, then to Holland, then back to Palembang and to Batavia. There it was lost during the Japanese occupation.

Pekaieng

Year's end approached and Tuan Petoro had already been more than eighteen months in Gowa. Assisted by Tuan Anwar, he had steadily improved his connections with the foremost members of the noble house of Cowa.

One of the younger karaëngs of pure blood, Karaëng Katangka, was gradually taught how to govern the realm, in preparation for a reformulation of Gowa rule. This had the full support of the patriarch of the noble house of Gowa and of the former crown prince.

In spring, Tuan Petoro and Tuan Anwar had received strange reports from some of the larger Gowa *kampongs*, which were within easy reach of Macassar. The first one came from Barombong, a *kampong* almost on the border of the Macassar subdivision. One morning toward ten o'clock, a stranger had entered the house of the chieftain. He had not identified himself but had authoritatively ordered the head to call all the men of the village together. He had an important announcement. The astonished head had obeyed, sent out a helper, and asked the guest (who spoke the Macassar language with a heavy Javanese accent) to sit down and have some coffee. The man had slowly sipped from his cup and not said anything about his purpose. He had asked the head how many children he had, and on the answer, "Four," he had nodded solemnly. The helper returned and reported that about a hundred men, young and old, were assembled. He was panting, and no wonder, for he had had less than half an hour to collect such a crowd. They were now waiting in the yard of the house where the chieftain lived. The stranger had gone outside and faced them. He looked at them and then made a long speech. No one could recall what he said precisely, but it was agreed that he had talked with great passion, and that he had predicted a great change in the making: the Dutch would leave the country and never return; an endless period of happiness and prosperity would begin; no one would have to pay taxes, no one would have to do unpaid labor, the harvests would be bigger, and everybody would get more money.

The stranger had then asked if this was all clear to them and if anyone had any questions, but the people had remained totally silent. Then the stranger had said goodbye to the head, had picked up his brand-new bicycle which was leaning against one of the stilts of the house, and had slowly pedaled away in the direction of Macassar, while everyone stared after him. The head had waited a moment, then ordered his *bendi*[30] and had gone to Sungguminasa to inform Tuan Anwar of what had happened. Together they had gone to Tuan Petoro where the story was told one more time.

"Why did you obey this man?" Tuan Petoro had asked. The chieftain said that he thought the man somehow belonged to the government. Until he heard his speech, of course. "Oh yes," he added, "the man said that 'Pekaieng' would rule the country." Tuans Petoro and Anwar did not understand. After the head had left, Tuan Anwar said, "It's like Sangkilang, sir. He was the runaway slave of a prince of Bone and around the year 1770 he pretended to be the king of Gowa, Batara Gowa II, who had been banished by the Dutch to Ceylon. Within a few months he had many followers around him. Even two sons of the king and princes of Sanrabone and Tello believed in him. Finally he was so powerful that the legal king of Gowa had to leave his country and put himself under the protection of the Dutch merchants in Macassar. People believe anything, sir."

Next morning Tuans Petoro and Anwar drove to Karaëng Katangka, the future chief of Gowa, to discuss various things, and Tuan Petoro mentioned the appearance of the stranger in Barombong. Karaëng Katangka immediately said, "That can be very dangerous, sir." In the following week three more reports came in about visits by strangers in the *kampongs* near the Macassar area. In all cases two strangers had shown up, one speaking Malay with a Javanese accent, one a Macassar man.

It had also become clear that the strange word the chieftain had reported, "Pekaieng," was a slurred pronunciation of PKI, Partai Komunis Indonesia, the Indonesian Communist Party.[31]

After reporting all this to Macassar, Tuan Petoro was advised by Tuan Anwar to go on a major tour and visit as many *kampongs* as possible within the next three weeks. They talked to the men there and asked them why they thought they had to pay their four or five guilders a year in taxes. An old man from Macassar had answered, "Half goes to Macassar and half to the queen of Holland." Most of the men had remained silent. Then Tuans Petoro and Anwar asked if they did not realize how expensive the irrigation works were which gave them a larger rice harvest? More expensive than all the taxes coming from Gowa? And the new bridge which made it easier to get their wares to the market? And the roads on which they could now take a bus? And the roofing over the market protecting their wares against the rains? And the clinic, where they got medical treatment? And the large hospital in Macassar, which was free? — No, not a cent went to Holland.

After the tour, Tuan Petoro went back home both tired and dispirited. What was the use? Most of the chieftains must understand how the tax monies were spent! Didn't they tell their assistants? Didn't they then tell the villagers? He had not even mentioned that the badly attended village schools were also financed from the taxes—these were already unpopular enough.[32] He had felt better when the head of a large *kampong* on the road to Limbung, where he and Tuan Anwar had spent the night on their tour, came to report a visit of the two strangers, and told him that when the Javanese had wanted to give his speech, both he and the Macassar man with him had been beaten by the villagers.

After that, nothing was heard of the PKI in Gowa for half a year.

Then, one afternoon in November, Tuan Anwar came and told Tuan Petoro an astounding story. Tuan Anwar had been visited by an old man from Tombolo, who had assured him that that same evening the electrical power station would be attacked. This station was about a mile from Tuan Petoro's house and served both Macassar and Sungguminasa. The son of the head of *kampong* Kassi was involved and would attack with a large group of men from Kassi and perhaps from other *kampongs*. Moreover, Tuans Petoro, Anwar, and Djaksa would be killed.

"I know the son," Tuan Anwar said. "He is a good-for-nothing, a gambler, and he runs after whores, if you pardon me, sir." Tuan Petoro got up and called Badawi to bring the car. He got in, took the wheel, and said to Tuan Anwar, "Well, I'm off to Macassar, I'll be back as quickly as possible." Tuan Anwar looked at him and said, "Yes, sir." Tuan Petoro turned around to Badawi and said, "Take a rifle along." "It's in the back, sir."

In Macassar the assistant resident said he was almost sure the attack would not take place, because—and this was top secret—because of the large activity of the communist party in the last few months, especially on Java and Sumatra. Plans of the party had been leaked and there would be major arrests at midnight of communist leaders and procommunists. But yes—that would not be until midnight. For extra security he would ask the military commander for soldiers for duty in Sungguminasa after dark; however, he did not think he would get more than twenty men.

On the way back Tuan Petoro called on Karaëng Katangka, who had already been informed by Tuan Anwar. He told him that probably a detachment of soldiers would appear in the early evening. "Twenty is not enough," Karaëng Katangka said. He lowered his heavy lids over the slanted eyes and slowly turned a large diamond ring around his slender finger. After a few moments he stopped this and looked uncertainly at Tuan Petoro. "I don't know if you want this," he said softly, "but in the Limbung area is a *kampong* whose men in the past had to protect my uncle, the king of Gowa, when asked. Because of that, they did not pay taxes or perform unpaid labor. I am sure these men are still completely reliable. If you permit me, I will call on them to guard the power station this evening, and no one will get near it." He smiled. "In that case, you can keep the soldiers in reserve near your house." Tuan Petoro thanked him and accepted the offer.

Then Tuan Petoro visited the Dutch director of the power station. He and his wife remained completely calm. The director said, "I'll put on some more arc lights in the yards." And his wife said, "We'd better stay up tonight, eh, boy?"

Tuans Petoro and Lucien also prepared themselves. They both had revolvers, and since Tuan Petoro did not know much about

them, Lucien checked and loaded them. After that, Tuans Anwar, Djaksa, and Abdulkadir were called in. It was agreed they
would stay home to protect their families. They were still talking
when the phone rang: the assistant resident. After dark, twenty
men led by a second lieutenant would arrive by bus at Tuan Petoro's house. The men would be at his disposal until the following day.

When the others had gone, Tuan Petoro and Lucien held a war
council. They decided to keep the building in the middle fully lit
until midnight. The soldiers would stay in the dark, on the front
porch of the office. They themselves would keep guard in the
dark pavilion.

A few minutes after dark the bus arrived with the officer
and his twenty men. The house was still dark and Tuan Petoro
asked, staring into the dusk, "Where is second lieutenant Van
den Broek?" "Here," a voice called and a large man appeared in
front of him. Tuan Petoro told him softly what had happened so
far and that the power station would be guarded by men from
Macassar. . . . The lieutenant asked, with surprise, "From Macassar?" "Yes. Local men," Tuan Petoro said, and explained the situation very quickly. He asked the officer to be on guard on the
porch of the office. There were plenty of chairs, and the boy
would bring a large pot of coffee. They laughed, and the officer
took his men along. Then Tuans Petoro and Lucien drove to the
power station. The entire area was brightly lit and at least a hundred local men, armed with lances, *krisses*, and *badiks*, stood in
corners and in the dark under trees. The director and his wife
were quietly drinking weak Scotch and sodas in their living room
and acting as if they were used to regular attacks by communists.

When they were back, Tuan Petoro put his car next to the garage and Lucien put his next to the pavilion. Badawi sat behind
the wheel of Tuan Petoro's car and the gardener, although he
could not drive, sat proudly in the other car. If there was any
alarm, they would turn on the headlights and illuminate the lawn
in front of the house.

After that, with one building brightly lit and two in the dark,
there was nothing left to do but wait. Abu and Prince were going
back and forth all night with pots of coffee. Toward sunrise Tuans
Petoro and Lucien drove to the power station and found a pale
but cheerful director and his pale but cheerful spouse. The director would somehow drum up some nice food for the Macassar

guards, and Tuan Petoro would call off the emergency as soon as he knew more.

They drove back and visited the officer and his soldiers, all looking spruce. Tuan Petoro could only think of bed. The officer suggested "having a look in that *kampong*." "All right," Tuan Petoro said, "and we'll take Tuan Anwar along." Badawi, still able to run after a long night, dashed off to get him. Tuan Anwar was visibly exhausted and kept saying, "Yet the information was reliable, sir." Tuan Petoro nodded sleepily. "Let's go now," he said.

The bus with the soldiers drove in front and behind it was Tuan Petoro's car, with the top down, Badawi and Tuan Anwar in front and the two Dutchmen in the back.

As they entered the prosperous *kampong* Kassi with its many large houses and hundreds of coconut palms, Tuan Anwar called out in his hoarse voice, "Sir! There's not a man in sight!" Not one man. In the morning sun, women were walking and children were playing in the light under the palms. They drove right through without finding one man. The bus stopped. Badawi stopped and the officer came out and approached the car. Tuan Anwar said, "The men are having a meeting somewhere outside of the *kampong*." "Couldn't they be in the houses?" Tuan Petoro asked. "Let's see," the officer said. They did: no men. Tuan Anwar said, "Let us see if the chief is around, sir."

He was. He was an old bent man, with white hair, fine white eyebrows, and a narrow, noble nose. He was probably about to go bathe at the well, for he was only wearing an old *sarong*. His chest was bare and the wrinkled brown-yellow skin hung loosely around his ribs. He was startled when he noticed the group of men at the bottom of his stairs. Tuan Anwar asked, "Aren't there any men in the village?" "No," the old man said, shaking his head desperately, "I don't know anything about the men."

A few minutes later the bus and the car left, loudly honking their horns. But an hour later they came back, very quietly. The men had returned. They were standing and talking in little groups and stared with surprise at the bus and the car gliding by. The vehicles stopped in front of the chief's house. The old man still looked as if he were about to go take his bath. He was even more startled this time. Tuan Petoro asked, "Where is your son?" He answered, almost inaudibly, "Gone to Macassar." Tuan Petoro, Tuan Anwar, and the officer went up the stairs, while the soldiers surrounded the yard.

They searched the house while Badawi watched over the old man. The rooms were empty. In the attic was nothing but a large pile of unhulled rice. Suddenly Tuan Anwar noticed something and pointed. The rice was moving regularly; someone under it was breathing. "Come on out!" Tuan Anwar called. The son appeared. He was breathing heavily, hatred in his small eyes. He was a thin creature, tiny, with a narrow chest and rings under his eyes. They took him along. When they passed the old man, he looked with heartbreaking sorrow at his only child. The son did not look back at his father.

The investigation showed that Tuan Anwar's reports of the previous day had been correct. The son of the Kassi village head had received instructions to knock out the power station with his followers by killing the director and the men working there and stopping the machines some way or other. Another group was to kill the Tuans Petoro, Anwar, Djaksa, and Abdulkadir. The son had discussed this with more than a hundred men of Kassi. However, toward the evening of the fatal day, the son had visited all the men, going around on his bicycle, and called off the attack. The following morning at a meeting in the forest, he had threatened them with death if they ever gave away what had happened.

Most men of Kassi were never prosecuted. Nothing showed that they would really have participated in the murders or in the attack on the station. Nine men were sent to prison for two or three years. One got four years: the son of the chief who until the end refused to say who had given him the instructions and who had canceled them. His father asked and got permission to resign and died within two months.

About Freedom

Tuan Petoro had decided at the age of fourteen—that is to say, eleven years earlier—while in the second grade of a high school in southern Holland that he wanted to be an official in the Dutch East Indies. His Dutch language teacher had given him a little book which he had read through three times, in his own room at home, concentrating as hard as he could. He had put it in his bookcase and never looked at it again. But he stuck with his decision: he would study at Leyden University and go to the Indies as a government official. His family had no ties with the Indies and he knew they would be upset about it. At the age of sixteen, he became friends with a boy whose father had been a military man in the Indies and who then became an official in Holland; he often went to his house and the family had shown him their photo albums and told him about the country. At that time he told his parents his plan and contrary to what he had expected, they did not protest much.

In Leyden he had met and made friends with Indonesian students and they often talked in each other's rooms all night long. He had been interested in what they said about the country and themselves, and each evening they told jokes and laughed uproariously. Some of his fellow students, Dutchmen fresh out of high school, had theories about the way the Dutch East Indies should be run. For them the future was not at all "a closed book." He himself had usually remained silent. Not because he was too prudent to say what he thought politically; that wasn't it. He had not spoken because he did not know. What did he know about the Indies? He would find out once he was there. And he had said to his Indonesian friends: "I don't know anything—not yet. Wait six years or ten years, but don't mistrust me."

Now his student life lay five years in the past, and in the silence of the tropical night, behind his desk in the official residence of Sungguminasa, he was bending over documents relating to a major cattle theft. His thoughts were wandering and suddenly he heard the voice of Onno, a medical student, who slowly and speaking through his nose, in a strong provincial accent, shouted: "You guys are going to the Indies as officials, you're going to play at being little kings. You have inferiority complexes which you'll get rid of on our brown brethren. Believe me." Tuan Petoro had been astonished to see the veins on Onno's forehead swell. He had listened, but his friend Hein, in whose room they were, had gotten up and said, "You've gone crazy! Get out of this room, dammit, or I'll kick you out!"

Before leaving for the Indies at the age of twenty-one, he had had some experiences which would always remain with him. In his sophomore year he had gone to a lecture by a former clergyman of his village, who had given him Bible classes and whom he had always admired. This man had gotten into trouble during the First World War when he preached pacifism in his sermons and told men to resist being drafted. Then he became a political

writer. After the lecture, Tuan Petoro-to-be had joined some el-
derly ladies to go and shake hands with the speaker. He had
laughed at the man and said, "Greetings, Reverend. Remember
me? I am Carel." The man had looked at him and said, "I hear
you are going to the Indies as a government official." He had answered, still laughing, "Well, I hope so." The former minister
had turned away from him without another word.

The second experience had been of similar nature and also concerned a clergyman. This one had given him Bible classes in high
school. He had gone to say goodbye before his voyage to the Indies. The minister had taken his hand between his own two
hands, had looked at him with worry in his light blue eyes under
reddish eyebrows, and asked, "Carel, boy, do you know what
you're doing?" "I think so, Reverend." And the clergyman had
said, "You, with your character, can't possibly approve of our
suppressing those people. I know—you are going because you
love art—the Borobudur Temple—Bali—." Carel had pulled
back his hand, reddened, and stammered: "Of course I don't
want us to suppress the Indonesians! In the long run, they
should be free!" The vicar had cried happily, "Thanks be to God!
I knew you would feel like that!"

The third experience had been one week before his departure.
He had dropped by one of his Indonesian friends in Leyden and
they had talked for an hour. He had said he would prefer to work
on one of the outer islands rather than on Java; he thought there
would be more to do there. On most of those islands Dutch rule
was not more than twenty years old and he had heard that people
were more modern there and more progressive. The other man
had said, "Why? Come to us, to the Sunda region. Lovely." He
was just about to leave when another Indonesian arrived, a boy
who had just arrived in Holland. After the introductions, he had
said goodbye, first to his friend, then to the new arrival. The first
goodbye was very friendly, with a hug and a promise to get together; to the second boy he had said, "See you in your country."
The boy had glared at him and answered, "One of us in front of
the bars, the other one behind them." A painful silence. His
friend had said, "Oh come on, don't be like that." He had been
shocked, and smiled painfully. "All the best," he had muttered,
and left.

Now he had been in South Celebes for four years. Had he ever
been sorry about his choice? Never. Had a dream of power

brought him here? No. Were his friends and colleagues voluptuously engulfed in the respect the simple population paid them? Perhaps one or two. Had he been moved by idealism? Partly. Looking for adventure, longing for the mysterious East? Yes, certainly. That search and desire were the strongest motives. But desire to rule, to dominate—no.

More than four years in South Celebes—what had he found? No nationalism, neither organized nor unorganized. He had found Buginese and Macassarese, still more or less grouped in tiny princedoms, a feudal world. A world that assuredly had lost its glamour and excitement. The princely houses, if not overthrown, had not much power anymore, there were no little wars, no gangs of robbers, the nobility had increasingly fewer chances to milk the people, slavery had been abolished, so that, in general, justice was served.

He called Badawi. Badawi had been sitting outside, talking softly with Abu. He appeared immediately. "Would you call Tuan Anwar for me?"

Tuan Anwar appeared. While they slowly sipped their customary orangeade, they discussed the cattle case, and then Tuan Petoro suddenly said, "Mister Anwar, I often think about your future." As usual when Tuan Petoro said something he considered strange or unexpected, Tuan Anwar did not move a muscle and answered, "Yes sir."

Tuan Petoro was used to that and he continued, "With that, I mean in the first place the future of Indonesians and in the second place, specifically, of the people of these regions." "Yes sir," Tuan Anwar said. Tuan Petoro asked, "Do you, personally, desire to be free now, free, you understand? Free from the Dutch?" Tuan Anwar quickly answered, "Personally: yes, sir. Begging you pardon, sir, but—." "Not at all," Tuan Petoro said. And he asked slowly, "What would happen if the Dutch left now, Mister Anwar?" Tuan Petoro would never forget the answer. After thinking for half a minute, Tuan Anwar answered, "The British would arrive. Begging you pardon, sir, but that's my opinion." Tuan Petoro was silent and thought, "Well, what do you know, Carel. Tuan Anwar reads the Koran, the little local paper, and all sorts of miserable official letters, and he comes up with this." He continued aloud, "All right—but suppose they didn't." "Then," Tuan Anwar said, "everything will collapse. Begging you pardon, sir. Wars between Bone and Wadjo, and Gowa and Bone, and robbers—as it was thirty years ago, sir—." Tuan Petoro asked, "Are there many local people longing for those old days?" "Members of the ancient nobility, many, sir. Not the little people. They want our protection." "Ha," Tuan Petoro thought, "Now he says, 'our.' " Tuan Petoro said, "But, in my opinion, it cannot take more than another generation before Holland and the Indies part ways." He said "generation" and thought, fifty or sixty years. He remembered what his governor had told him: "Carel, our duty is to govern this country so well that the unavoidable separation, which is not as far off as most Dutchmen think, takes place without violence. And that we remain friends." The men were silent. Tuan Petoro lit a cigarette and Tuan Anwar said, "Yes sir." "Another orangeade, Mister Anwar?" "Yes, please, sir." Tuan Petoro called Abu, who brought a beer and an orangeade. "Mister Anwar," Tuan Petoro asked, "What do we have to do?" Tuan Anwar hesitated only a moment and answered, "The country is unhappy, sir." Tuan Petoro knew he meant the country of the Macassar people. "Unhappy because the most important princely houses have lost their power, begging you pardon, sir. We should reestablish them, but under our control. I hope you understand me. And the young karaëngs and chieftains must get a first-class, a first-class, education. Because they are the natural leaders for the people from Macassar and for the Buginese. There are a lot of scoundrels among them, but also fine men. Sort them out carefully, if you'll pardon me, sir." He stopped, took a clean handkerchief out of his pocket, and rubbed his glasses. Then he blinked at his young chief, in a friendly manner, and said, "I should know, sir. I am the son of a karaëng." "And the ordinary people?" Tuan Petoro asked. Tuan Anwar answered, again without hesitation, "Irrigation, agriculture, sir." "And schools?" Tuan Anwar waited, put his glasses back on, and said, "Yes—also schools."

Father and Son

Tuan Petoro had met Musa, Tuan Anwar's son, but perhaps not more than five times during the year and a half of his stay in Sungguminasa. He had only talked to him twice. Musa was big for his age, seventeen, a head taller than his father. He was a quiet boy, with a thoughtful expression on his face. The few times that Tuan Petoro had talked to him, he had smiled but he had given very short answers to such interested questions as, "Do you like school? Are you doing well? Are you happy that you'll be studying in Leyden in just a couple of years?"

Tuan Petoro did not think father and son were very close. Tuan Anwar was proud of his son at times—Musa was number two in his class, Musa was a member of the school soccer team, goalie—but there was little intimacy noticeable between them. But, Tuan Petoro had thought, perhaps that is even more rare here than in Europe.

Musa was always simply but well dressed. At times he wore a Macassar *songko* with the gold thread, at times a black velvet *kupiah*. At times he was in European trousers and jacket, at other times in a *sarong*. He had the movements of a nobleman. His eyes looked freely and boldly into the world, and he was never humble or falsely polite.

One evening, shortly after the trials of the Kassi conspirators, Tuans Petoro and Anwar were talking in Tuan Petoro's study, about some *kampong* head accused of fraud.

Tuan Petoro had rarely seen Tuan Anwar in a state of anger or temper. Once Tuan Anwar had become angry, during the interrogation of the son of the chief of Kassi. Afterward he had said shyly, "Well, the poor father, I pity him, sir." Another time he had berated Karaëng Mandalle, a congenital liar, who had spread dirty rumors about some of the most prominent members of the House of Gowa. That morning Tuan Petoro had heard Tuan Anwar shout in the office. Now, sitting in an easy chair, he had said, "Yes sir, I was really angry this time. That *kampong* head had not only stolen tax money, he had collected more than he was allowed to, sir."

Tuan Petoro looked searchingly at him. He seemed to have aged in the last few days. His eyes looked tired behind his glasses and he seemed to sigh almost inaudibly.

Tuan Petoro waited awhile and then in a moment of silence he asked, "Something wrong, Mister Anwar?" Tuan Anwar looked at him, looked down, and said softly, "No sir." They were silent and Tuan Petoro lit another cigarette. He watched the smoke and heard Tuan Anwar say, "Yes—youth, sir."

Tuan Petoro looked at him and Tuan Anwar stared ahead and said, "It's my son, sir—I'll tell you—difficult, sir."

Softly and hesitantly Tuan Anwar told his story. Musa had

been home on vacation—Easter vacation—and he seemed to be a different boy. He did not say much, that was not it, but he criticized his father. Not rudely, surely not, but he had asked why his father worked in the government. First, Tuan Anwar had not understood and he had explained it all minutely: first assistant scribe in Pangkadjene, then scribe, then assistant. He could not have become karaëng because of local law regarding inheritance. Musa had asked why his father had not become something else then, a merchant, for instance. Didn't he think it was terrible to serve under the Dutch?

Only then had Tuan Anwar understood what was going on in his son's head.

Tuan Anwar looked sadly at Tuan Petoro and said, "Difficult, sir."

"Very difficult," Tuan Petoro answered. "Can't you explain to him that you are working for the best of this country and these people?"

"I didn't try," Tuan Anwar said. "I got mad." He sighed. "Musa started talking about the Kassi affair, and he said the motives of the son of the *kampong* chief had been noble. The means had been wrong, but the goal was noble." "Which goal?" Tuan Anwar hesitated a long time and then said, "I trust you, sir." Tuan Petoro nodded. "The goal was to chase out the Dutch. I got very mad. That boy doesn't understand what that would mean— he got angry, too, and told me he'd never work for the Dutch—."

Tuan Petoro remembered his Leyden conversations. Musa was now seventeen and still in high school. In a few years he would be strolling down the main streets of Leyden. And a few years after that he could be one of the young local leaders. Would he ever understand his father, who also worked for his people—in his way?

Tuan Petoro did not quite know what to say. Seventeen—. He stood up and Tuan Anwar followed his example. Tuan Petoro looked at Tuan Anwar and said, "The more you tell him about our work, the better, Mister Anwar—. Or so I hope, anyway."

The Farewell

It was very early in the day and the red of the rising sun appeared behind the roof of the house of Tuan Aspirang. A thin mist hung above the empty lawn, looking like blue smoke. A deep, dream-like silence, with the cry of a single bird. Tuan Anwar sat down in one of the comfortable rattan chairs on his porch and looked around. He took off his glasses and wiped them clean with a tip of his white jacket. A female servant brought him a cup of steaming coffee. He put his glasses back on and stared ahead. He had been awake for hours. At eight o'clock Tuan Petoro would go to Pare-Pare, with his wife, stay with friends, and the next day go on to Watampone. After three years, he had been transferred to the old capital of the Bone empire, and from Tuan Petoro Gowa he would become Tuan Petoro Bone. Much had happened in the past few months. In September of the previous year, Tuan Petoro had come into his office one day and said, "Come with me, Mister Anwar." And he had been shown a large picture of a young girl, with dark serious eyes. Tuan Petoro had held the picture far in front of him and announced, "This is the woman I am going to marry."

Tuan Anwar had opened his eyes wide and said, "Very young, sir. Very much a minor, sir." He had looked worried, and finally asked in his hoarse and hesitant voice, "Aren't child brides illegal in Holland?" Tuan Petoro had laughed and said, "Yes, she looks very young, true, but she will be twenty-one soon."

Some four months later, they were married in Macassar, and had gone on a honeymoon in Boronggrappoa, high in the mountains of Bulukumba, and from there they had made their entrance into Sungguminasa. Tuan Petoro and his bride had returned, suspecting nothing. Tuan Djaksa Takalar (the subdivision Takalar had been added to Gowa), Karaëng Katangka as representative of the House of Gowa, Tuan Abdulkadir, and he himself had formed a kind of committee and they, months before the wedding, talked with Tuan Aspirang, who had talked with the assistant resident in Macassar. It was agreed that voluntary contributions from the chiefs, high and low, would be used to buy a present for the young couple. The present—a silver tray with an inscription—had been presented during a big party in the garden of Tuan Petoro's house. It had been full of tents and stalls. The chieftains had given eight water buffaloes to be slaughtered. Little Mother Manudju had come to stay in Tuan Petoro's house and she herself had donated two buffaloes. The festivities had lasted six days and nights, drums were beating, dancers dancing. Including the dance of the herons,[33] Tuan Petoro's favorite.

After the festivities, the committee had written a letter to Tuan Petoro's parents in Holland and each of the members had kept a copy. It was a beautiful letter.

Tuan Anwar got up. It was six o'clock and the sun had risen.

He entered the house and from a drawer he took a flat decorated wooden box, with silver adornments. In there he kept his papers and also a copy of the letter. He took it to the porch, he asked for a second cup of coffee, and slowly read what he and his colleagues had written.

After that, he looked at the big house across from him. Tuan Petoro's parents would surely be happy with the letter and Tuan Petoro himself, when he was in Holland on leave in two or three years, would read it and think again about the friends he had left behind in Gowa.

Tuan Anwar got up; he had to get dressed.

San Francisco

At the bar in the restaurant of San Francisco's airport, two Indonesians were sitting with a Dutchman. The Indonesians were students; the Dutchman was he who once had been known as Tuan Petoro. Tuan Petoro no longer was a Tuan Petoro. The Gowa years were long gone. His work, since about two years after the end of World War II, had been in the United States. With much pain and suffering on both sides, Holland and Indonesia had been separated. He often recalled what his teacher in Macassar had said, "For us, Carel, the first duty is to rule so well that the unavoidable separation, which is not as far away as most of us think, will be without violence. And that we remain friends." He had not taken into account, had not possibly been able to take into account, the enormous changes resulting from the war.

He had discussed these matters the day before, with a small group of students and professors at Stanford University. After his lecture and the lively debate that followed, several students had come to him to introduce themselves and ask further questions. Two had clearly been Indonesians, and after a few words in English they had laughed and switched to Dutch. He had invited them to lunch in his hotel the next day and they had come. When they heard that he was flying off to Chicago in the late afternoon, they had asked if they could come and see him off. And here they were, the three of them, drinking cold beer at the bar.

Against a background of engine noise and public speaker an-
nouncements, they were still talking animatedly. One student, a
little man from Sunda with a cheerful face, who spoke very fast,
came originally from Bandung;[34] the other, with lighter skin, was
from Menado and was much quieter.[35] He looked at his friend as
if he wondered why he was so open with a Dutchman. They were
both studying political and social sciences. They seemed optimis-
tic about collaboration between Holland and Indonesia. The man
from Bandung said with a smile what he thought of the new government. "Certainly not anti-Dutch," he announced, "not anti-
Western. More neutral, you see. Between the two big powers.
That is shown by its composition. Prime Minister—." Suddenly
the name Musa was mentioned. A Dr. Musa was Minister of Education in the new government. "Oh!" the man from Bandung
cried, "This will interest you! He is from Macassar!"

It took a moment before the name registered with the Dutchman. Musa—Musa—the son—maybe the son of Tuan Anwar?
He asked, "Do you know anything about his father?" The man
from Menado said, "I think he was in the local government."
"You mean, assistant?" "I guess so, sir."

The son of Tuan Anwar, now minister. After his departure
from Sungguminasa he had seen Tuan Anwar twice. Once on a
boat, the *Van der Wyck*, when he and his wife and one-year-old
son had left Macassar to go on leave to Holland. The members of
the Aru Pitu, the royal council of Bone, and the Tuans Anwar,
Djaksa Takalar, Abdulkadir, Karaëng Katangka, and other members of the House of Gowa had seen him off. And when he had
returned to his parents, after eight years, he had been moved
when he read the letter about the festivities at his wedding, written by his Gowa friends. "We are writing you all this," the letter
ended, "to show you how much we love your son. When he
comes home on leave he can read this himself."

After that he had exchanged a few letters with Tuan Anwar.
Musa, Tuan Anwar had written him, had not gone to Leyden but
to the medical school in Batavia. After the war and more than
three years in Japanese prisons and concentration camps, Tuan
Petoro—in 1947—had visited Macassar and immediately asked
after Tuan Anwar. Yes, he was told, Tuan Anwar was alive and
still in Sungguminasa.

He would never forget their reunion. One of the departments

of the East Indonesia government had lent him a car, and he had driven to Sungguminasa, the same old place, to the left and right the Macassar and Chinese shops, to the right, the market. He had told the driver, "To the left—to the right—stop." Where Tuan Anwar's house used to be there was a large new Macassar dwelling, the residence of the new king of Gowa. At the top of the stairs, he was welcomed by Karaëng-ri-Gowa, whom he had known years earlier. After fifteen minutes he had asked, "And Tuan Anwar?" "He is waiting for you," the king had said, "I will send for him."

Then, five minutes later, Tuan Anwar had entered. Very old, very small. He had cried, in his hoarse voice, "My Tuan Petoro! My Tuan Petoro!" And they had stepped toward each other and embraced and Tuan Anwar had cried and he also had had tears in his eyes. The king of Gowa had turned away, and he had asked Tuan Anwar, pointing at his turban, "You have been to Mecca?" "Yes sir," Tuan Anwar had said with a radiant face, through his tears. "Yes, sir, just before the war."

He had not been able to stay long but had promised to be back the next year if at all possible. But when he came back, Tuan Anwar had died and no one in Macassar knew where his children were.

"Musa," he thought. "Musa—the son of my counselor."

He turned toward the Indonesians and said, "I knew Musa when he was sixteen or seventeen. A nice boy. His father was one of the best Indonesian officials I ever knew."

Outside the engines were roaring. The Indonesians and the Dutchman fell silent. "Fine," he thought, "this is all over," and he emptied his glass. He wanted to pay because it was time to leave, but he hesitated a moment—was the man from Menado trying to say something? Just then a woman's voice said on the public address system, "United Airlines—Flight 192 to Chicago and New York—gate four—all aboard, please."

Above the roar of plane engines and the woman's voice he heard the voice of the man from Menado, "If you'll permit me, sir —but in our eyes Musa's father was one of those collaborators who have done our country much damage."

The Dutchman paid and got up. The woman said through the loudspeakers, "United Airlines—Flight 192 to Chicago and New York—gate four—all aboard, please." He shook hands with the Indonesians, and they smiled.   January–June 1958

Notes

The Last House in the World

Introduction

1   Hannah Arendt, *The Origins of Totalitarianism,* 2d enlarged ed. (Cleveland and New York: The World Publishing Company, 1958), pp. 189, 187, 186, 186–88.

2   Ibid., p. 209.

3   Robert Louis Stevenson, *Works,* 24 vols. (New York: Charles Scribner's Sons, 1900), 12:186. Italics added. Motility, with all its possible connotations, is definitely at the heart of adventure literature. One more example is found in the writing of Robert Byron who, in his travel book *The Road to Oxiana* (1937; reprint ed., New York: Oxford University Press, 1982), dreads the end of his travels: "At Paddington [station in London] I began to feel dazed, dazed at the prospect of coming to a stop, at the impending collision between eleven months' momentum and the immobility of a beloved home" (p. 286).

Motility is, of course, an important aspect of romanticism too. Multatuli, who I have characterized elsewhere as a romantic author as well as a writer of colonial literature, phrases it this way in chapter eleven of *Max Havelaar:* "Nature is movement. Growth, hunger, thinking, feeling, is movement, immobility is death! Without movement no grief, no pleasure, no emotion!"

That there is a connection between adventure literature and Dutch colonial literature has been noted, if only indirectly, about other colonial writers. See Menno Ter Braak, *Verzameld Werk,* 7 vols. (Amsterdam: Van Oorschot, 1950–51), 7:129–30 (on Van Schendel, a writer published in this series); 357–63 (on Alexander Cohen, a writer excerpted in the anthology in this series). Also, see E. Du Perron, *Verzameld Werk,* 7 vols. (Amsterdam: Van Oorschot, 1955–59), 2:604, 633–34. See also J. H. W. Veenstra, *Multatuli als lotgenoot van Du Perron* (Utrecht: Reflex, 1979), p. 20, and E. M. Beekman, "Dutch Colonial Literature: Romanticism in the Tropics," *Indonesia,* no. 34 (October 1982), pp. 17–38.

Toward the end of the last century Lodewijk van Deyssel, writing under the pseudonym "A.J.," published a brief study about Multatuli wherein he characterized Multatuli as an adventurer who was, by virtue of this fact, incapable of living a normal quotidian existence. See A. J., *Multatuli* (Bussum: J. C. Loman, Jr., 1891), pp. 59, 62, 87–91. See also my essay on Multatuli published with his novel *Max Havelaar* in this series: Multatuli, *Max Havelaar* (Amherst: University of Massachusetts Press, 1982), pp. 338–86.

4 Stevenson quoted by Robert Kiely, *Robert Louis Stevenson and the Fiction of Adventure* (Cambridge: Harvard University Press, 1964), p. 214.

5 Paul Zweig, *The Adventurer: The Fate of Adventure in the Western World* (1974; reprint ed., Princeton: Princeton University Press, 1981), pp. 7, 4.

6 Stevenson, *Works*, 13:238.

7 Kiely, *Stevenson*, p. 40.

8 The claustrophobia of the landscape is suggested more clearly in the original text because Vuyk repeats the adverbs "verstard" and "beklemd," words that she also used for describing the Javanese mountains in *Thousand Islands* and in "Fulfillment and Return" ("De vervulling en de terugkeer," 435).

9 Theses writers are important for the link they make between the literature of adventure and colonialism, and are discussed as such in Martin Green, *Dreams of Adventure, Deeds of Empire* (New York: Basic Books, 1979). In the original Dutch text the work which, I think, is meant to be Scott's is printed as "Rob en Roy." I assume this is a misprint for *Rob Roy* (1817) by Sir Walter Scott; see Green, pp. 97–128, and Zweig, p. 189. For James Fenimore Cooper, see Green, pp. 129–63. Frederick Marryat is represented in the original text by "Stuurman Flink," which I assume refers to *Masterman Ready* (1841); see also Green, pp. 214–16.

10 Rimbaud used this phrase to describe the tropics in the text "Démocratie" in *Illuminations*. Rimbaud was in Java in the summer of 1876, after enlisting in the Dutch colonial army. He deserted three weeks after his arrival. In an aesthetic as well as a psychological sense, one could make a fascinating case for Rimbaud's being an "adventurer" for whom motility was also one of the most important aspects of life.

11 Colors give Vuyk's Moluccan world that bright surface quality that, as Zweig points out, is also evident in the greatest adventure story, *The Odyssey* (Zweig, pp. 21–24, 31).

12 The alliterative adjectives in the original are "de groene, geurige kajoepoetiholie" (157, 185), while the original of "the wild, green scent of adventure" is "de groene, wilde geur van het avontuur" (230, 254, 256).

13 Details of distilling kajuputih oil are from P. A. Arends, "Waarom kajoepoetih groen is," *Moesson* 26, no. 10 (1981):8–9.

14 Kipling, *The Seven Seas* (New York: Appleton and Company, 1896), p. 209.

15 Zweig, p. 81; see also pp. 23, 32, 81–85, 93–96.

16 There are some curious resemblances between "Way Baroe" (258–69) and R. L. Stevenson's story "Will O' the Mill" (*Works*, 7:69–103). Both stories are about impassive men, who are immovable as if transfixed by the exuberance of life. Both protagonists once recognized life as a form of adventure, but both rejected it as such. Both cease to care about life, and both come to a living death because they reject life as a form of adventurous motility. One could investigate both stories in terms of the interplay of images of movement and images of stasis.

17   The prodigious as normality is emphasized again and again by Vuyk. This is, of course, what makes each day an adventure. In the sixteenth section she describes the daily event of buying fish from *praos*, and ends the passage with a paean to adventurers.

18   Joseph Conrad, *Within the Tides: Tales* (1915; New York: Collier, 1925), p. viii.

19   Stevenson, *Vailima Letters: Being Correspondence Addressed by Robert Louis Stevenson to Sidney Colvin*, 2 vols. (New York: Scribner's, 1906), 2:127. Stevenson's exultation of physical work in the tropics is very similar to Vuyk's (1:27–28). His ability to make ordinary events into adventures is mentioned by Gavan Daws, *A Dream of Islands. Voyages of Self-Discovery in the South Seas* (New York: Norton, 1980), p. 175.

20   Zweig, pp. 227–28.

21   Stevenson quoted by Kiely, pp. 173–74.

22   Zweig, pp. 61, 71.

23   Willem Walraven, *Brieven aan familie en vrienden 1919–1941*, ed. R. Nieuwenhuys and F. Schamhardt (Amsterdam: Van Oorschot, 1966), pp. 608, 624.
    Beb Vuyk had the good fortune of being praised quite early in her career by some of the best and most influential writers and critics of her time, and Walraven (who is included in the anthology of this series) was one of them. E. Du Perron (1899–1940), who was the most prominent colonial writer in the two decades preceding the war, also admired her work; see his *Verzameld Werk*, 6:190–93, 419–24. Menno Ter Braak (1902–1940), Du Perron's close friend, concurred; see Ter Braak, *Verzameld Werk*, 6:383–88; 7:309–14. The last is a review of *The Last House in the World*, and Ter Braak briefly refers to Vuyk's work as adventure literature, noting that "adventurers are rare in our literature, at least the true ones, for whom adventure is something different than a source for good copy" (314). Finally, the critic and writer of colonial literature Rob Nieuwenhuys (born 1908) also praised her efforts. See Nieuwenhuys, *Oost-Indische Spiegel* (Amsterdam: Querido, 1972), pp. 473–85. This literary history of Dutch colonial literature is published in this series as *Mirror of the Indies*.

24   Zweig, pp. 227, 239, 114.

25   Walraven, p. 496.

26   Ibid., pp. 639, 608.

27   Ibid., p. 556.

28   Arendt, p. 123. Arendt refers specifically to the three decades between 1884 and 1914, but this is just as true of Holland and its colonies during and after the Second World War, particularly because Holland had been spared the horrors of the 1914–1918 war.

Notes to the Text

If a Malay word is not discussed in the notes, refer to the glossary.

For practical reasons the old Dutch spelling of Indonesian words and phrases has been kept. Not only is this treatment appropriate to the age when these texts were written, but it also will aid a student of this literature in finding other sources pertaining to this genre. All such secondary literature will have this spelling, including dictionaries, atlases, and other references. For those who would wish to follow the modern orthography of Bahasa Indonesia, the following changes should be noted:

The old spelling tj [tjemar] is now c [cemar]; dj [djeroek] is now j [jeruk]; ch [chas] is now kh [khas]; nj [njai] is now ny [nyai]; sj [sjak] is now sy [syak]; and oe [oedah] is now u [sudah]. Only the last change was adopted in this series because the diphthong [oe] is not familiar to readers who do not know Dutch.

Not every Malay or Moluccan name for flora and fauna has been identified. One reason is that there is an enormous variety of names, derived from various languages and local dialects (if not specific localities), while the Dutch used their own version of some Malay nomenclature. Variant spellings add to the problem, as well as a paucity of systematic reference works. Nevertheless, all the Indonesian words in Vuyk's original text were kept. Removing them and substituting general words such as "tree," "plant," or "boat" would violate her artistic intention.

A number of works were frequently used and referred to. They follow in alphabetical order and will be cited in the notes only by author and page number.

Beekman, E. M. *The Poison Tree: Selected Writings on the Natural History of the Indies.* Amherst: University of Massachusetts Press, 1981.

Bickmore, Albert S. *Travels in the East Indian Archipelago.* New York: D. Appleton and Company, 1869.

Broersman, R. *Koopvaardij in de Molukken.* Batavia: Noordhoff, n.d.

Encyclopaedie van Nederlandsch-Indië, 4 vols. and 3 supplements. The Hague: Martinus Nijhoff, 1917–1932.

Hoëvell, G. W. W. C. Baron Van. *Ambon, en meer bepaaldelijk de Oeliasers.* Dordrecht: Blussé en Van Braam, 1875.

Ludeking, E. W. A. "Schets van de Residentie Amboina." *Bijdragen tot de Taal-Land-en Volkenkunde van Nederlandsche Indië,* derde volgreeks, derde deel [3d series, vol. 3] (1868), pp. 1–274.

Wallace, A. E. *The Malay Archipelago.* 1869. Reprint. New York: Dover Publications, 1962.

Wilkinson, R. J. *A Malay-English Dictionary.* 2 vols. 1901. Reprint. London: Macmillan, 1959.

1   Buru is one of three important islands that separate the Ceram Sea from the Banda Sea. The other two are the largest island Ceram (about 5,000 square miles) and the historically important Ambon (the smallest of the three at about 2,000 square miles). Buru is about 2,600 square miles, and lies to the west of Ceram. The Manipa Straits separates it from Howamohel, a peninsula of Ceram. Almost all Buru is circled by coral reefs. Considerable sections of the coast are sand beaches

and/or swamps with mangrove forests. With the exception of a large plain behind Kajeli Bay, there are few large open spaces. The greater part of the island is mountainous, rising 3,000 feet or more above sea level.

The main locale for the book is Kajeli Bay, on the northeast corner of the island. It is the largest bay and natural harbor of the island, some seven miles long. Entrance from the sea is between two high capes—Tandjong Karbau and Tandjong Waät, both mentioned in the book—some three to four miles apart. Further south down the coast is Tandjong Kajuputih. The shores of this bay have low alluvial land, and going inland from the bay is the largest savannah on the island. Through this plain flows Buru's major river, the Wai Apu, which is navigable for two days going upriver. Of the three islands mentioned, Buru has the only lake, high up in the Mala Mountains, called Wakolo or Rana Lake. Buru's two main towns lie across from each other: on the north side of Kajeli Bay, the town of Namlea, and on the southern shore, the town of Kajeli.

The original inhabitants were the 116 different tribes of Alfurs (see n. 41). The first foreign people to occupy the coast were the Malay. Ten years before the Portuguese arrived, around 1520, the sultanate of Ternate subjected the island to its rule and introduced Islam. In 1652 the sultan of Ternate signed an agreement with the Dutch, who had replaced the Portuguese, to eliminate the clove trees on the island in order to insure their monopoly. The inhabitants rose up in revolt and waged war against the Dutch. In 1657 the hostilities were terminated, the clove trees destroyed, and the coastal population was forced to move to Kajeli Bay, where they could be kept under control by Fort Défensie.

Practically nothing was known of what lay beyond the coast until an expedition in the last decade of the nineteenth century, and Buru was not really exploited until twenty years later.

The small island of Ambelau, mentioned toward the end of the book, lies southeast of Buru. It is very mountainous and its small population cannot grow enough to feed itself. It gets most of its sago from Buru's southern coast. It is heavily forested and has a large population of wild pigs.

Buru's major export article was the *kajuputih* oil. The oil was derived from the *Melaleuca leucadendron* tree or, more correctly, from the small bushes that grow from the extensive root system of the tree. Those roots grow in such number that, during the war, the soil was hard enough to serve as landing strips for Australian planes without having to construct runways. The oil was primarily used within the archipelago as a sudorific, as a stimulant, and as an antispasmodic. Yule (Henry Yule and A. C. Burnell, *Hobson-Jobson* [1903; reprint ed., New Delhi: Munshiram Manoharlal Publishers, 1979]) mentions that in India the oil was taken internally as a remedy for cholera. The value of the oil was in its cineole content. Cineole is an ether that smells like camphor and has a pungent and cooling taste. *Kajuputih* export to Europe was greatly reduced when it was discovered that eucalyptus oil was easier to obtain, was cheaper, and contained a greater percentage of cineole.

For Buru see Bickmore, pp. 253–97; Wallace, pp. 293–99; Ludeking, pp. 6, 30, 79–80; *Encyclopaedie*, 1:336–39; for the geology of the island see K. Martin, *Reisen in den Molukken, in Ambon, Den Uliassern, Seram (Ceram) und Buru*; part 3: *Buru und seine Beziehungen zu den Nachbarinseln* (Leiden: E. J. Brill, 1903).

For *kajuputih*, see P. A. Arends, "Waarom kajoepoetih groen is," *Moesson* 26, no. 10 (1981):8–9. See also Ludeking, pp. 104–5; Broersma, pp. 40–41; and Supplement 6 of the *Encyclopaedie*, s.v. "aetherische oliën."

2   The Ambonese are the people who live on Ambon, a small island in the southern Moluccas, a group of islands located in eastern Indonesia. Although it is by far
the smallest of the three main islands—Ceram above and to the east of it, and
Buru to the west—Ambon is historically the most important as the seat of colonial
government. The Amboina District included the entire Banda Sea, with all its
islands. Ambon was the first island where Dutch authority was established in
1600, and was the home of Rumphius, the seventeenth-century naturalist whose
work is represented in this series with *The Poison Tree*.

3   KPM is the acronym for the shipping line, the *Koninklijke Paketvaart Maatschappij*, or the Royal Packet Company. It is clear from the present work that the KPM
was an indispensable factor of life in the archipelago, and anyone who lived in the
Indies after 1900 will concur. I kept the Dutch acronym in the text because it was
very much part of the colonial Indies. The company was established in 1888 by the
Dutch government to counteract foreign competition and to open up the vast
realm of islands by means of a regular and dependable service. Actual service
started in 1891 and by the second decade of the present century it had realized its
goal. By that time the line serviced an area roughly equal to Europe by means of
fifty-six different routes. The fleet consisted of some forty different types of ships
to accommodate different cargoes—from coal to coolies—and different geographical needs. There were small boats equipped with paddle wheels to negotiate the
shallow rivers of Sumatra and Borneo, and there were the once ubiquitous *kapal
putih*, fast ships, resembling yachts and painted white (hence their name, for *kapal*
means "ship" and *putih* means "white"). A journey from Sabang, the most northern port near Sumatra, to Merauke in New Guinea, a distance of 3,400 sea miles,
would take eleven days.

There is no doubt that the KPM was an important economic factor in the Indies.
Its tariffs were high, but one reason for this seems to have been that the line maintained unprofitable services to places that were lucrative neither in terms of commerce nor in terms of passengers. The line made indigenous shipping obsolete
because the KPM steamships could sail in any monsoon, had larger cargo holds,
could reach the most remote islands, and could be depended on. For the Moluccas, for instance, the KPM was a boon. When around the turn of the century there
was a sudden demand for copra and copal, its ships had just established dependable routes to those islands and this made it possible for the Moluccas to compete
in the world market (Broersma, p. 23; see also *Het Indische Boek der Zee*, ed. D. A.
Rinkes et al. [Weltevreden, Java: Drukkerij Volkslectuur, 1925], pp. 93–111).

4   In the original, "paddling" is *pagaaien*. This Dutch verb was derived from the
Malay word *kajuh*, a single-blade paddle, and its verb *penkajuh*, to use such a
paddle.

5   *Alang-alang* is the commonly used Javanese word for a very tough tall grass
(*Imperata cylindrica* or *arundinacea*), also called *lalang* in Malay and Balinese. It is
very common, will grow anywhere where the forest has been cleared, and is a
serious threat to agriculture. One way to control it is to burn it down and have cattle eat the young shoots. Wilkinson, under "lalang," gives some striking expres-
sions in Malay that reflect the nature of this grass. For instance: *tanah lalang*, or
"land overgrown with [this] grass," meaning worthless land; *api makan lanang*, or
"fire eats the lalang grass," referring to things you cannot control; and the fine
metonym, *bunga lalang*, which means "lalang in bloom," referring to "spears

waving pennons," derived from the fact that the grass has a long plume on top of silky, silvery hairs.

6 *Air putih* literally means "white water"; *air*, also spelled *aer* and *ajar*, means "water." It refers to a violent and dangerous surf often encountered in these islands.

7 The *ketapang* or *katapang* tree *(Terminalia catappa)* is a tall tree that grows throughout Indonesia, most often near the coast. The seeds are sometimes used instead of almonds in baked goods.

8 *Suanggi*, also spelled *suwangi* or *swangi*, is the Moluccan word for either a witch or a malevolent ghost. Wilken derives the word from the Javanese *wengi* or Macassarese *bangi*, meaning "night." Among the Alfurs of Ternate and Halmahera the *suanggi* represented a kind of vampire that flew around at night as a winged head, looking for victims. An older text identifies the *suanggis* as female ghosts who dance by the light of a full moon (Ludeking, p. 159). Van Hoëvell translates *suanggi* as "magician" and notes that entire settlements could have bad reputations for being adept at black magic. The town Kajeli on Buru was one of them (p. 120). See also G. A. Wilken, "Het Animisme bij de volken van den Indische Archipel," *De Indische Gids* 6, no. 1 (1884):945–55.

9 *Aren* fibers, I would assume, refer to the black "hairs" one will find between the leafstems of the *aren* palm or sugar palm *(Arenga saccharifera)*. These strands, resembling horse hair, are woven into a kind of rope. The *aren* palm produces the well-known *saguer* wine and *aren* sugar, better known as *gula djawa*.

10 Surabaja is the chief city and harbor of east Java.

11 Priok is an abbreviation of Tandjung Priok, the harbor of Batavia (now Jakarta), some five miles north of the city. It was built toward the last quarter of the nineteenth century after the Suez Canal was opened in 1869. The construction started in 1877 and the harbor was in use by 1886. It was connected to the former colonial capital by canal, railway, and highway.

12 Macassar was and still is the chief city of Celebes (now Sulawesi) on the "foot" of the western "leg" of that island. Historically the city was very important as the center of power in the Moluccas and Celebes, and as the driving force of opposition to Dutch colonial rule. See *The Poison Tree*, pp. 147–53.

13 Leksula is a town on the southern coast of Buru.

14 *Barang* is one of those words Vuyk used to give her narratives authenticity. Commonly translated as "luggage," *barang* really means something more: it refers to anything that can be carried, from chickens to fruits.

15 The *orang badjo* or *badjau* were a people said to be part of a larger group called *orang laut* or "sea gypsies." The difference, it seems, is that the *badjos* lived primarily in the eastern part of the archipelago. They were an itinerant people, primarily fishermen, who preferred to live on or near the sea. They were excellent mariners but from time to time performed unskilled labor as coolies in exchange for food and other necessities.

16 *Gaba-gaba* is the midrib of the sago palm's leaves, and is used to construct walls, floors, and attics of native houses.

17 Organ-pipe coral is formed by the *Tubipora* or *Hicksonia* polyps, which leave a

crimson-colored skeleton of upright tubes, somewhat resembling the pipes of a church organ.

18   *Karang* is the general Malay word for "coral."

19   *Tandjong* is the general Malay word for "cape," and *karbouw* is the Dutch spelling of *kerbau*, the gray water buffalo used everywhere in the Indies as a work animal. Hence the two names mean: "Cape Kajuputih" and "Cape Buffalo."

20   *Sinjo* was a term of respect for a male descendant of European or mixed parentage. It was derived from the Portuguese *senhor*, and one could translate it with "master," a form of address for a young man. *Nonnie* was an abbreviation of *nonna*, probably equivalent to *sinjo*, indicating a young girl. It can be translated as "Miss."

21   The *waringin* is the *Ficus benjamina* tree, found all over the archipelago. Its trunk grows very thick and the tree becomes very tall. It has an extensive crown and can grow to be extremely old. It does not have aerial roots and is considered a holy tree.

22   Ternate is a small island off the western coast of the island of Halmahera. As was the case with its equally small neighbor, Tidore, the sultanate of Ternate wielded power disproportionate to its size, controlled the spice trade before the Portuguese came, and became an ally of the Dutch voc in the seventeenth century. It was the destructive rivalry between Ternate and Tidore that allowed the Europeans to play one off against the other and insinuate their own authority. During the seventeenth century Ternate ruled a vast colonial empire of islands in the southern Moluccas (including Buru) where it exacted tribute and demanded obedience to its rule. The ruthless monopoly policy of the Dutch reduced Ternate, Tidore, and other Moluccan islands to indigent vassal states. See *Poison Tree*, pp. 148–51.

23   Binongkos are people from the small island Binongko, one of the Tukangbesi Islands that lie east of the island Buton (or Butong), which lies southeast of the eastern "leg" of Celebes. Binongko is a rather desolate island with little vegetation. Its people lived primarily from seafaring and hiring themselves out as laborers on other islands.

24   *Manga*, also spelled *mangga(h)*, is the *Mangifera indica* tree. It has a dense crown with small leathery leaves. It is cultivated for its egg-shaped fruit, which is usually yellow or green with orange, rather fibrous meat. Depending on the variety, the fruit can either be quite pleasant or taste like turpentine. It is frequently used to make a kind of chutney.

25   *Melati*, one of the most common flowers of the Indies, is the *Jasminum sambac* shrub. It has long branches, light green and shiny foliage, and clusters of three white flowers that have a beautiful fragrance.

26   The *antjak* tree is described by Vuyk as a wild fig tree. I have not been able to identify it.

27   A *koleh-koleh* is, specifically, an *orembaai* with outriggers. The *orembaai* is a Moluccan type of boat with a keel and, normally, without outriggers. Its stem and stern rise high above the deck, somewhat reminiscent of gondolas, and are usually finely carved and decorated. If an *orembaai* was primarily intended for fishing the thwarts would run lengthwise, leaving a space for nets amidships. Such a boat

was propelled by sixteen to twenty men with paddles, and it was also steered with a paddle. If used for transporting passengers, it would have one or two sails and a deckhouse.

28   The breadfruit tree is the *Artocarpus communis* tree, called *timbul* in Malay and *kaluwih* in Javanese. It is more familiar to readers as the fruit that the early mariners in the Pacific longed for after many months at sea.

29   Sago was the staple food of the Moluccas, particularly on Ambon, Ceram, and Buru. As Vuyk makes clear, sago was so easy to obtain that people had little incentive to work for their daily food. Wallace calculated that one tree could provide a man with a year's supply of food (p. 292). The sago tree is a palm, the most commonly used variety is the *Metroxylon Rumphii*, named after the great seventeenth-century naturalist Rumphius. Ludeking (p. 85) lists seven varieties of the sago palm, of which two (*sago utan* and *sagu duri* or *babuwa*) are found only on Buru. It grows between twenty and thirty feet high and has very large leaves that cover the entire trunk. Between the tenth and fifteenth year of growth the tree produces, in Wallace's words, "an immense terminal spike of flowers," which signals its impending death. Before it has fully flowered, the tree is cut down for harvesting. It is cleared of its leaves, the trunk cut into manageable segments, and a broad strip of bark is removed from the top in order to expose the pith or marrow (*ela*). This pith is loosened from the tree by beating it with a wooden club (*nanni*) that has a piece of rock at its end, or, these days, an iron blade. This activity, which takes some time and must be done with care so as not to lose any sago, is known as "beating the sago," in Dutch, *sago kloppen*. When all the marrow has been loosened, it is carried in baskets made from the tree's leaves to the place where it is "washed." The trough (*goti*) is made either from the leaves or from an emptied section of the trunk. The marrow is tossed into this trough, water is poured over it, and the *ela* kneaded and pressed against a strainer to separate the finer "meal" from the marrow's woody fibers. The reddish mixture of sago and water passes to another trough where the meal is trapped and the water removed. The residue that remains after the sago meal has been collected is called *ampas ela* and is used for fodder. It was Rumphius who taught the Ambonese how to obtain this farinaceous meal from the palm.

   This meal (*sagu mantah*) can be prepared in several ways. Most commonly it is baked in small stone or clay ovens that are divided into six or eight compartments. These are filled with the sago, covered with a part of a sago palm leaf, and baked for a short time. The result are cakes called *sagu lempen*. They can be eaten right out of the little oven with sugar and grated coconut, and are then called *sagu kalapa*. These same cakes dried in the sun for several days can be kept for a long time. When they are to be eaten, they are soaked in water until soft and then roasted. Mixed with fish, salt, hot peppers, and lemon juice, the sago dish represents the main meal for the people of these islands. If the sago is not baked in the little stone oven but in sections of bamboo (the way the Alfuran chief has it done in section 5) and then cut into small pieces, it is called *sagu tutupolah*. It was also often eaten as a cold or hot porridge called *papeda*.

   Nothing of the tree is wasted. The outer trunk is used for containers and the trough; the leaves are used for plaiting rough baskets (*tumang*) to transport the sago meal; the *tumang* is also a rough measure of weight, since such a bundle weighs about thirty pounds. The long thick midribs of the leaves are used as a building material. These midribs (*gaba-gaba*, see n. 16) are twelve to fifteen feet long, and can be as thick as a man's leg. They are light but very strong and take the place of bamboo in the Moluccas. Remaining pieces of the leaves are used to make *atap*, the thatch for roofing in the Indies, while the peel of young branches is made into a rope called *hahesi*. While rice is the main staple everywhere else in Indonesia, on Ambon, even today, it is a "snob food"; see Shirley Deane, *Ambon: Island of Spices* (London: John Murray, 1979), p. 18. One can find some contemporary photographs of making sago meal in Mochtar Lubis, *Het land onder de zon* (Alphen aan den Rijn: A. W. Sijthoff, 1981), pp. 130–31.

30 The *lubi-lubi* is probably the *lobi-lobi* tree, also called *tomi-tomi* in the Moluccas. It is a tall fruit tree, *Flacourtia inermis*, that produces fruit too sour to eat raw but which, when prepared in various ways, is considered a sweet. A recipe for this kind of candy can be found in J. Kloppenburgh-Versteegh, *Wenken en Raadgevingen betreffende het Gebruik van Indische Planten, Vruchten, Enz.* (1911, rev. ed. 1934; reprint ed. Katwijk aan Zee: Servire, 1981), pp. 355–56.

31 *Sukun* is the seedless variety of the breadfruit tree.

32 *Djeruk nipis* is a fruit tree *(Citrus aurantifolia)* cultivated all over Indonesia for its fruit, which resemble yellow limes. It is used in Indonesian cooking, as a shampoo, and to clean one's hands.

33 The *Kapok* or *kapuk* tree *(Bombax pentandra L.)* grows tall, thrives in just about any soil, and has few leaves. The word *kapok* also refers to the silky threads around the seeds. This was once known in English as silk cotton and was used chiefly for stuffing pillows and mattresses.

34 *Terong* is eggplant *(Solanum melongena L.)*.

35 *Kasbi* is cassava, the edible roots of the *Manihot utilissima* plant. In Malay the plant is also known as *ketela pohung*, as well as by other names. Dried roots are known as *gaplek* and are ground into *gaplek* meal. Something similar to this meal is used to make tapioca.

36 *Bilangun* wood refers to a very durable wood from various kinds of *Calophyllum* trees which prefer coastal regions. The wood is reddish brown and can withstand water very well.

37 Rumahtiga ("Three Houses") is a village on the northern peninsula of the island Ambon, a peninsula known as Hitu.

38 *Dusun* can mean a settlement, village, or a piece of cultivated land. In the northern islands of the archipelago, off the northeast coast of Sumatra, *dusun* means the permanent gardens outside a town; on the Sumatran east coast it means hills. It can also be used to indicate inland peoples of Borneo in a negative sense, i.e., yokels or boors. In Ambon and surrounding islands it almost always means an orchard.

39 Atjeh is the name of a region and sultanate in the most northern section of Sumatra. The people of Atjeh were devout Mohammedans and fiercely anti-Dutch. They were also indomitable fighters. Atjeh was the last region in the Indies to be "pacified," but it was involved in almost continuous warfare from 1873 to the beginning of the Second World War. Obviously the colonial government needed manpower for these military campaigns and they recruited soldiers all over the archipelago. This is what Vuyk is referring to. For a recent critical examination of these campaigns see Paul van 't Veer, *De Atjeh-oorlog* (Amsterdam: Arbeiderspers, 1969).

40   Bara is the name of a bay, mountain range, and town on the northwestern coast of Buru.

41   *Alfur* is a troublesome term because it was used in a general sense and did not really refer to a specific ethnic group. The word derived from the language once spoken in northern Halmahera; *halefuru* meant "wild terrain" or "jungle." Its derivation, Alfur, came to mean "bushman" or aborigine and was used by more "civilized" people living on the coastal areas of Celebes and the Moluccas to refer to the indigenous peoples living inland, especially in the mountains. It was meant to be derogatory, having a general meaning of uncivilized people, boors, yokels. It also came to refer to "pagans," i.e., anyone who was neither Christian nor Muslim.

The Alfurs, especially on Ceram, were head hunters; this activity was called *potong kapala*. Up to the turn of the century they wore nothing but a *tjidako*. Bickmore described this as "a strip of the inner bark of a tree beaten with stones until it becomes white and opaque, and appears much like rough white paper. This garment is about three or four inches wide and about three feet long. It passes around the waist and covers the loins in such a way that one end hangs down in front as far as the knee" (204). Black rings on the *tjidako* indicated how many heads a warrior had taken. An enemy's severed head was brought back because it was believed to house the soul, hence possessing a number of heads increased not only the warrior's regard in the community and made him eligible for marriage, it also added to his soul-stock. The Alfurs were animists, believing that just about everything in nature was inhabited by spirits. This worship included the spirits of their forebears, called *nitu-nitu*. Anything they could not comprehend was attributed to these spirits. Any object that the Alfur found impressive, such as a tree, a large rock, parts of forests, or rivers, were called *pamali* or *pemali* and were said to house spirits. Most often large stones were declared holy and were then called *batu pamali* or *pohon pamali*. When Vuyk mentions a "small *pemali* house" one should probably understand this to be a *huma sikit*. This was a small structure built on stilts some six feet off the ground. It was no more than a covered space where the Alfurs kept the skulls of their ancestors arrayed on plates or dishes. They would go there every so often to offer food, weapons, cloth, and other things to ensure their good will. In earlier times the Alfurs gathered the skulls of their enemies in a place in the forest called a *baileo*, that had an *astana*, or a stone slab resting on four other stones like a table, and a place to sit, several feet off the ground, called a *para-para*.

The history and ethnology of the two types of Alfurs on Ceram (called the Patisiwa and Patilima) is somewhat complicated and can be studied in Hoëvell (pp. 148–59) and Ludeking (pp. 53–80). But two aspects of their lives need to be mentioned. Before and during the time of the Company the men were united in a secret society called the *kakian*. Originally the *kakian* was established to protect the Patisiwa against such enemies as the Patilima, but in the middle of the seventeenth century its main objective was opposition to the Dutch. For a description of its ceremonies see Ludeking, pp. 67–78. Members of the *kakian* called each other "brother," or *pella* (also *pela*). Hoëvell asserts that a practice called *pela* derived originally from the *kakian* society. *Pela* bonds were created between different communities on the same island, or even between different islands. These were alliances of friendship, with two settlements helping each other in every possible way, even with fighting. Such a *pela* bond was sacred and absolute. Since the Alfurs believed in vendetta, the existence of a *pela* bond between two villages meant that a man who had committed a criminal act at the cost of an inhabitant of either of the two villages would be hunted down by both populations. These bonds still exist today; for modern Ambon, for instance, see Deane, pp. 131–37; Hoëvell, pp. 157–59; Ludeking, pp. 59–60. Ludeking reports, like Vuyk, that the Alfurs, whom he had observed personally, were shy but proud people, mostly hunters. He also notes the plates, mentioned in Vuyk's book. For the Alfurs, porcelain plates represented wealth and were greatly desired. They especially coveted large plates *(kena patu)* from the days of the seventeenth-century Dutch Trading Company, or VOC, which were usually Delft blue (Ludeking, p. 65). Although Bickmore describes the Alfurs from Buru as "mild and inoffensive" (p. 272), he called those from Ceram "fiends in human form" (p. 206).

42 *Bubara* refers to a large fish I have not been able to identify. There are said to be close to a thousand varieties of fish in the Moluccas.

43 The *bubu* is a fishtrap used along coasts that have cliffs and reefs. It is an open basket woven of bamboo with an inverted cone at each end, each apex the smaller opening. Weighed down with stones they are lowered into deep water of thirty feet or more and hauled up every two or three days. They somewhat resemble New England lobster traps.

44 Fernand De Willigen is called the Sinjo Tandjong, which means here something like "Young Master of the Cape."

45 The *turie* tree is cultivated everywhere. It is a small tree with a short lifespan *(Sesbania grandiflora)*, and is used for various purposes. The bark is used as a remedy for intestinal complaints, the sticky sap is used for fishing lines, the leaves are used for fodder, and the white flowers and pods are eaten as a vegetable. There is a variety with red flowers, but I don't understand why Vuyk calls them "useless." Perhaps a different tree is meant?

46 *Patjolling* is a transcription of the verb *mempatjul* which means to use a *patjol.* The *patjol* is the ubiquitous Indonesian version of a hoe.

47 *Bajem* is a generic name for various kinds of vegetables eaten like spinach. Most likely the variety meant is either *Amaranthus tricolor L.* or *Amaranthus spinosus L.*

48 In the original, "school" is *volksschool.* These schools were the result of the colonial government's attempt to bring at least rudimentary education to the common people. In 1907 they were ordered to be established everywhere with a curriculum adapted to local needs. To finance this organization, Governor General Van Heutsz ruled that local governments would pay for their own school and could therefore charge a modest fee. The government would provide financial aid but was to refrain from disturbing the local character of the institution.

49 One must be careful with *guru* because the term does not have to mean a religious teacher as is now popularly assumed in the West. Although it could and can, of course, mean a spiritual guide, it was more commonly used for any kind of teacher, particularly a schoolmaster. In this text it is meant in both a religious and a pedagogical sense.

50 I am assuming that "red sugar" is *gula merah* (*gula* means "sugar" and *merah* means "red"), the Indonesian version of brown sugar. It is also widely known as *gula djawa,* which means literally "Javanese sugar." The most common variety of *gula djawa* is made from the male flower stalks of the *aren* or sugar palm, hence also

known as *gula aren*. Then there is the sugar called *gula tebu*, made from sugar cane, *gula kalapa* made from coconuts, and *gula siwalan* made from the *lontar* palm.

51   *Kenari* (or *kanari*) pits refer to the seeds of the tall *Canarium commune* or *Canarium indicum* L. tree. These seeds can be eaten raw and are said to taste like either walnuts or filberts. Crawfurd (*History of the Indian Archipelago* [London, 1820], 1:383) states that "it is one of the most useful trees of the countries where it grows. The nuts are either smoked or dried for use, or the oil is expressed from them in their recent state. The oil is used for all culinary purposes, and is more palatable and finer than that of the coconut. The kernels, mixed up with a little sago meal, are made into cakes and eaten as bread."

52   *Anak piara* or *anak mas* refers to a native child that has been adopted by a family to be a playmate of a single child or to help with the household. *Anak* means "child"; *piara* means "to bring up"; and *mas*, which normally means "gold," is in this context a title.

53   The *sarong* or "skirt" of the Indies is worn by both men and women. The word *sarong* (or *sarung*) was more commonly used by Europeans, while *kain* was the general word used by the native population with countless combinations, so that *kain sarung* would probably be more correct. A kind of jacket, known as a *badju* (*baju*) was commonly worn with the *sarong* by both men and women. It traditionally was meant to cover the upper body from the neck to the knees. A *badju* (or *baadje* in Dutch) that reaches just below the hips is called a *kabaja*. This is fairly loose, open in front, with long and narrow sleeves fastened at the wrists. The front does not have buttons and is closed by three brooches connected with little chains, often silver, called *kerosang*. Because the combination of *sarong* and *kabaja* is both elegant and comfortable, it was adopted by European women as a relief from the unpractical and stifling European dresses.

54   *Bapak* literally means "father." It is used here for the captain—i.e., the population called him "Father Captain," as a term of respect because he was older, but also because of their affection. Calling him Tuan Tandjong was out of respect for his position because, certainly in the days of Captain de Willigen, *Tuan* meant "lord" or "master," hence "Lord of the Cape."

55   *Radja* does mean "king," from Sanskrit *radjan*, but one must be careful not to assume that everyone called *radja* was a king. In this case in particular and all over the archipelago in general, even a village head was called a *radja*.

56   *Adat* indicates indigenous "custom" in its most comprehensive sense, including native law, rules, and behavior. It is a very complicated concept and was separate from European jurisprudence.

57   The Utrecht Mission was a Protestant missionary organization that began to spread the Gospel on the southern coast of Buru in 1885. It also had the not very enviable task of trying to convert the Papuans of New Guinea. The hazards of this Sisyphean endeavor were described in a work of fiction: F. Springer, *Schimmen rond de Parula* (Amsterdam: Querido, 1966).

58   *Wa* is the Burunese word for "river." The Apu River disembogues in Kajeli Bay, and flows through what is the largest area of savannah land on the island.

59   *Soa* is the Alfur word for "village," and *kepala* is Malay for "chief," hence *kepala soa* means "village chief."

60   *Damar* is the general word used by the native population for any resin they

could burn. The resin was collected from various large trees and there seems to be little information on how it was collected. The Moluccas constituted one area in Indonesia where resin was shipped out as merchandise. Copal, often confused with *damar*, is properly speaking the resin tapped from the *Agathis alba* tree (*damar putih* in Malay). The *damar* mentioned in the present text was probably collected from the *Shorea* and *Hopea* species of trees. The resin flows either from the trunk or from the branches and could also be found lying on the ground.

61   *Kepala* means "head," hence this refers to the still head.

62   The *hinolong* is constantly itching. Bickmore (p. 271) mentions that the Alfurs of Buru suffered from ichthyosis, a congenital skin disease where the skin flakes off in large scales, hence also called fishskin disease.

63   *Pinang* is the Malay word for the tree and the nut of the Areca palm. Whereas elsewhere in the archipelago the main ingredient of *sirih*-chewing (the Indonesian equivalent of our chewing tobacco) are leaves of the *sirih* plant, in the southern Moluccas, according to Hoëvell (p. 168), the main ingredient was the *pinang* nut, which was chewed with a little lime or tobacco (or cloves to substitute for the tobacco). This custom was called *makan pinang*.

64   In the original "cunningly" is *pienter*. This common Dutch word is derived from the Javanese *pinter*, meaning "learned" or "clever."

65   *Pusaka* connotes a great deal. It can be translated as "heirloom," but more correctly it means any object that is venerated by an individual, a community, or a royal house. In other words, an object that is said to be *pusaka* is holy and should be respected. It is never sold or bartered, and for an Indonesian to do so would indicate a dire need.

66   *Kapal putih* ("white boat") was the common name for a speedy KPM boat (see n. 3).

67   In the original, "degree in colonial administration" is *bestuursschool*. This school was founded in Batavia in 1914 to instruct both aspiring Dutch officials in the civil service and native officials already employed but desiring promotion. The school had a two-year curriculum.

68   Deli was a large district on the east coast of Sumatra. It became famous for its tobacco and rubber plantations and infamous for the conduct of its European planters. The planter's life was portrayed critically by Madelon Székely-Lulofs in her best-selling novels *Rubber* (1931; English trans., 1933) and *Koelie [Coolie]* (1932; English trans., 1933), and in a book by her husband, Ladislao Székely, originally published in Hungarian, translated into German as *Tropenfieber* in 1937, and then translated into English. It was first serialized in *Harper's Monthly Magazine* in 1936 and published in book form in 1937 under the title *Tropic Fever: The Adventures of a Planter in Sumatra*. This was recently reprinted by Oxford University Press (1979).

69   Malang is the name of a district and its capital in east Java, south of the mountain Gunung Butak. Its elevation of over 1,200 feet gives it a healthy climate. In colonial times it was also a large military base.

70   *Mangi-mangi* refers to the mangrove trees of the family *Rhizophoreae*. The more common name for mangrove trees in Malay is *bakau*.

71   Brain coral is the hemispherical *Meandrinas*. Bickmore says that "when the soft polyps are removed, small fissure-like depressions are found winding to and

fro over its surface, making the raised parts between them closely resemble the convolutions of the brain" (p. 285).

72   The *nipa* palm is the *Nipa fruiticans*, a palm either with or without a very short trunk. It grows among mangroves in brackish water. Its leaves were primarily used to make *atap*, the most common roofing material.

73   *Pantjoran* refers to the once ubiquitous bamboo conduit that brought water to the *mandi*-room where one bathed. Here the word is used in the general sense of "conduit" or "pipe."

74   Ajer Buaja literally means "crocodile water."

75   Rumphius was the great seventeenth-century naturalist Georg Everard Rumpf (? 1628–1702) who lived for almost half a century on the island Ambon, east of Buru. He was particularly famous for his book on shells *Amboinsche Rariteit-kamer*, published in 1705, and for his main achievement, the seven-volume *Ambonese Herbal*, published between 1741 and 1755. Annotated selections of these two works, with an introductory essay, were published in this series under the title *The Poison Tree*.

76   Thomas Josephus Willer (1808–1865) was an official in the colonial civil service from 1832 to 1858. He was first stationed in Sumatra but went in 1846 to the Moluccas. In 1847 he wrote reports about Buru and about the Alfurs on Ceram and Halmahera. These works were published in 1849. Vuyk is probably referring to a shorter work that was also printed in 1849, which dealt with the possibilities of economic developments on Buru.

77   The Wakanos and Serhalawans are probably Alfuran tribes.

78   *Sitsjes* was a colloquial word for cheap cotton fabric.

79   The Buginese are a people from a region north of Macassar. They are a maritime people and gradually replaced the Javanese and Malay as seafaring traders.

80   A *slametan* (also *selamatan*) is a religious feast. It can be given for any number of reasons—death, birth, marriage, nightmares—and is always held in the evenings and is only attended by males. The food is prescribed according to the occasion, incense is burned, the host gives a formal speech to present the reason for the gathering, and a prayer is chanted. *Slametans* are still very much a part of life in Indonesia; see Clifford Geertz, *The Religion of Java* (1960; reprint ed., Chicago: The University of Chicago Press, 1976), pp. 11–85.

81   *Tuan* [mister, sir] *djahat* [bad or evil] *tetapi* [but, however] *njonja* [madam, a married woman] *hati* [heart, center of feelings] *baik* [good, nice]. Hence: "The Tuan is nasty but (his) lady has a good heart (or soul)."

82   Mangoli, also spelled Mangole, is one of the Sula Islands, to the north of Buru, in the Ceram Sea. Directly north of Buru is the island Sanana, situated vertically. Mandole is right above Sanana, horizontally, as if forming the upper bar of a *T*. The Sula Islands are very mountainous and were for the greater part of their history subject to the sultanate of Ternate. They were once favorite hiding places for pirates. The Sulanese were traditionally the stokers for the *kajuputih* stills on Buru.

83   The word *anachoda* derives from the Persian for "shipmaster," hence it can mean skipper or captain. The way the term is used in Vuyk's book it seems to mean leader or foreman. In the Moluccas it could also mean a cargo clerk, some-

one who was a trader not for himself but for a third party.

84   Halmahera is the largest island of the northern Moluccas. It resembles Celebes somewhat in that it, too, is formed by four peninsulas. It lies to the east of the most northern tip of Celebes, and west of the most northern tip of New Guinea.

85   Bula refers to Bula Bay on the east coast of Ceram. In the beginning of this century oil was discovered there, but it was not shipped from Bula Bay until 1915. There were refineries in that bay until 1926.

86   *Tembangan*, also spelled *tambangan*, a general term for a flat-bottomed boat intended for transporting people or goods for a short distance. The name means in effect "ferry boat." If used on the open sea it has a triangular sail and can also be rowed.

87   *Trompong*, also *terompong* or *teropong*, means literally a "tube" or a "tubular appliance." Here it refers to the cooling pipe of the *kajuputih* still.

88   *Menari* night here means "night for dancing," although the *menari* was also a specific dance from the Moluccas. Hoëvell found it exceedingly boring (p. 168), and when Bickmore witnessed a performance only young women danced: "They were arranged in two rows, and their dance, the minari, was nothing more than slowly twisting their body to the right and left, and, at the same time, moving the extended arms and open hands in circles in opposite directions. The only motion of their naked feet was to change the weight of the body from the heel to the toe, and vice versa. During the dance they sang a low plaintive song, which was accompanied by a tifa and a number of small gongs, suspended by means of a cord in a framework of *gaba-gaba*, the dried midribs of palm-leaves" (pp. 189–90).

89   *Katjang idjo* is one of the most common and desirable beans in Indonesia. *Katjang* is the word for any kind of bean, and *idjo* is the Javanese equivalent of Malay *hidjau*, both words meaning "green." The *katjang idjo* is the *Phaseolus radiatus* plant. The small, round, green beans are eaten as a vegetable, ground into a kind of meal to make cookies *(satru)*, and if allowed to germinate, the beans produce the little white and yellow shoots known to anyone familiar with Chinese cooking as *tao ge* (bean sprouts). Kloppenburgh-Versteegh (see n. 30) informs us that a soup of *katjang idjo* and chicken broth alleviates melancholy, while *katjang idjo* was also officially used as a remedy for beri-beri because the bean contains a large number of vitamins (p. 58).

90   An aerometer is an instrument to determine the weight and density of gases or air.

91   *Puasa* refers to a fast, especially the fasting month of the Islamic year, the ninth month called *Ramedan*, also called *Ramelan* on Java. At the end of this fasting period comes the Great Feast known as *Hari Raja Puasa. Hari* means "day," and *hari raja* means a "holiday."

92   Rilke's untitled poem (its first line is: "In diesem Dorfe steht das letzte Haus"), which gave Vuyk's book its title, is from the section "Von der Pilgerschaft" in the collection of poems called *Das Stunden-Buch* (1905). Rather than attempt a poetic translation, which would have done violence to the original, I provided a literal prose translation.

93   BPM was the acronym for a Dutch petroleum company known as the "Bataafsche Petroleum Maatschappij."

94   *Kumang* is the hermit crab. This crustacean was described by Rumphius (*The Poison Tree*, pp. 41–44).

95   The *tatu* is the coffer fish (of the genus *Ostracion*) which has a bony armor that encloses its body.

96   *Windhout* means literally in Dutch "wind wood." I have not been able to identify it, but I wonder if this is a misprint for "wildhout," a term used in the Indies for any wild forest that did not consist of *djati* (teak) trees.

97   *Kunjit* is the *Circuma domestica* plant, cultivated for its roots. When grated, these orange rhizomes are used to make curry.

98   *Kankung* is a creeping herb *(Ipomua reptans)* that likes to grow in damp places. Its leaves are used as a vegetable.

99   Martaban jars were large glazed, earthenware jars, which were originally made in the town of Martaban in Pegu, a region in Burma.

100   Boldoot is a Dutch brand of an eau de cologne.

101   *Tempanjangs*, also spelled *tempajan*, were large earthenware vessels for keeping water.

102   *Guritas* is the *ikan guritas*, an octopus that prefers to live on the bottom of the sea where there are rocky formations or coral reefs.

103   Nils Holgersson is the hero of what used to be one of Europe's most famous children's books, *The Wonderful Adventures of Nils* by Selma Lagerlöf (1858–1940). It is the story of fourteen-year-old Nils who becomes very small after he has tormented the dwarf mentioned in Vuyk's book. The dwarf was old and had a wrinkled, beardless face. The book narrates Nils's adventures when, on the back of a gander, he travels with a flock of geese all over Sweden. The book was first published in Sweden in 1906, and translated into most European languages. The English translation appeared in 1907.

104   *Tonkol* (also *tongkol* or *tjakalan*) is a kind of tuna frequently found in Moluccan waters.

105   *Ikan asar* refers to "smoked fish"; *ikan* means "fish," and *asar*, "to roast." Smoked fish was not common in the Indies and the people of the Moluccas were somewhat unusual in preparing fish this way. In most other places it was salted. The method of smoking described here and elsewhere in the book seems to have been unique to these islands and had been used for centuries. The fish was clasped between two small frames of bamboo *(waja)*, and then held above a smoky fire. Particularly two kinds, *ikan djulung* and *ikan komu*, were always prepared like this and sold on the market *(pasar)* still between the bamboo frames as *ikan waja*. Fish treated like this can be kept for twenty days (Hoëvell, p. 211).

106   *Djulung* is a fish resembling a pike *(Belone* fishes). They are slender and their jaws are long and thin. In Javanese they are called *lontjong*.

107   *Sonko* (or *songko*) is a brimless hat about as high as a fez, usually made of black velvet, and worn by Muslims.

108   *Takalele* or *tjakalele* is an ancient Alfuran war dance. Usually the participants have a sword, a long shield (called *salawako*), and a copper helmet topped by feathers of the bird of paradise. While standing on one leg, the performers or warriors jump toward each other and then jump back. This dance, which originally

had a religious significance, was only performed at very important festivities and ceremonies.

109   *Tandak* as a verb is used correctly here in that originally *tandak* meant short brusque steps made by a few warriors in front of the regular troops when they were about to engage in combat. To use *tandak* as a verb, simply meaning "to dance," was popularized by the Dutch. The Javanese word for dancing is *djoge-dan*, while the common Malay word is *menari* or *tari*. Dancing as a refined form of art was practiced particularly on Java, while in the Moluccas dancing was, and still is, one of the most favored pastimes.

110   Feast of the Thirty-first refers to the Queen's Birthday, which was a national holiday that was celebrated in the Indies also. Since the ruling queen during the time of this book was Queen Wilhelmina (1880–1962), this holiday fell on August 31.

111   *Haagsche Post* was a popular weekly magazine, once printed like a news-paper on pink paper. Now it is a news weekly in the format of *Time*.

112   *Sate (saté* or *sateh)* is a native dish resembling miniature shishkabob. Small cubes of beef, pork, or goat's meat *(sate kambing)* are skewered on small sticks and roasted over a charcoal fire. It is often sold by street vendors.

113   *Krupuk* is the Indonesian version of chips. They used to be deep fried in large pieces and then broken up while eating *rijsttafel*. Usually they have a pink color and a delicate flavor. They can be made with beef rind, eggplant, or seeds from certain trees, but the most common variety is made with shrimp *(krupuk udang)*.

114   *Katjang goreng* are fried peanuts.

115   *Dansi-dansi* refers to an evening of dancing; a corruption of the Dutch verb for dancing, *dansen*.

116   *Rokki,* also spelled *roki,* means skirt and is a corruption of the Dutch word for that garment, *rok*.

117   *Sitsen* is a cotton material printed with small figures against a bright back-ground. Originally it was made in the Indies and is still used there.

118   Buitenzorg is the name of a city south of Batavia in the mountains, some 800 feet above sea level. In Dutch the name means "without care" and the city is now called Bogor. It was the seat of colonial government, the palace of the governor general was there and so were the offices of government departments. One of these was the Department of Agriculture, referred to here. The city also contained the famous botanical garden with its experimental stations and laboratories.

119   Menado was a city and district in Celebes, situated on the farthest point north of the top "leg" of the island that stretches out horizontally to the east.

120   *Tita* (or *titah)* is the important word in this Malay sentence. It means anything that is prescribed, commanded, or ruled, by either individual or government.

121   "Tuan Allah punja mau" means literally "It is Lord Allah's will." *Mau,* how-ever, indicates a future tense, hence, "It will always be Allah's will."

122   Marsman was one of Holland's finest modern poets. He was born in 1899 and died in 1940 when the ship he was taking to England was torpedoed by a Ger-man submarine. He was one of the most prominent prewar poets, moving from

expressionistic verse to an idiosyncratic form of vitalism. He was a major influence on the generation of poets that followed him. His later and most mature poetry was shaped by a combination of philosophical reflections on Christianity and a Mediterranean paganism. The poem Vuyk mentions specifically, "In Memoriam P.M.-S.," is from his second period of development, between 1929 and 1933. It is too long to be translated here, but it commemorates a woman "for whom the sense / of life only began forever / shortly before her death and grew with that death." It is certainly understandable that, given the narrator's plight, she would think of this poem. For that matter, Marsman wrote a great deal about death. The poem can be found in H. Marsman, *Verzameld Werk* (Amsterdam: Querido, 1960), pp. 59–63.

123 I use "foredawn" because Vuyk uses the Dutch term *nanacht*. This means the last part of the night, the beginning of dawn. The English "foredawn" refers to the same time of night.

124 *Ketupat* is cooked rice wrapped in coconut leaves or in the leaves of the *pandan (pandanus)* tree. These small bundles protected the food and were easily transportable.

125 *Sambal* is a hot condiment made from *tjili* or Spanish peppers. There are countless varieties.

126 "Beach tobacco" in the original is *strandtabak*. I have not been able to identify it. Perhaps *Ximenia americana* or *bidara laut?* There are numerous littoral trees and shrubs in Indonesia.

127 Trading in wood and the injustice of the colonial administration connected to this enterprise were also the subject of Vuyk's next novel, *Bara's Wood* (1947).

128 *Kenanga* (or *kananga*) is a tree *(Canangium odoratum)* cultivated exclusively for its fragrant flowers. It is ubiquitous in Indonesia, the Philippines, Australia, and Polynesia.

129 *Ketjap* is the Indonesian equivalent of soya sauce.

130 A *passangrahan* was a building erected at the government's orders in most villages, meant to lodge government personnel traveling through. It could also be used by private individuals.

131 *Djagung* is the general name for "maize." The plant was introduced by the Dutch because it is not native to the archipelago.

132 *Kaketu*, also *kakatu* or *kakatua*, is the Indonesian word for "parrot."

133 *Missigit* or *mesigit* is the name for the parish mosque in a village or town. From the Arabic *masjid*.

134 *Marinju* is the Ambonese word for a deputy village chief.

135 I've not been able to identify *salawaku* wood.

136 I wonder if *panan* leaves is a misprint for *pandan*. The latter refers to the *Pandanus* tree, which can be found everywhere in Indonesia. Its leaves are used for basket weaving.

137 Rixdollars *(rijksdaalders)* are coins worth two-and-a-half guilders.

138 *Kakap* is the *ikan kakap* fish, called "cockup" in India, a marine fish also found in the mouths of tidal rivers. It is the *Lates calcarifer*, called *kaalkop* in Dutch (which

means "bald head"), and is much sought after for its excellent meat. It can grow quite large, up to eight feet or more.

139 "Tuan Tanah" means literally "lord of the land" and was once used in our sense of "landowner."

The Counselor

Introduction

Some of the following information is derived from two works by Friedericy: *De eerste etappe* (Amsterdam: Querido, 1961), abbreviated as *Etappe;* and *De standen bij de Boeginezen en Makassaren* (The Hague: privately printed, 1933), abbreviated as *Standen*.

1 The biographical information is based on a variety of interviews and commemorative articles in Dutch newspapers and journals from the fifties and sixties, including the article by Rob Nieuwenhuys, "Herman Jan Friedericy," in *Jaarboek van de Maatschappij der Nederlandse Letterkunde 1969–1970* (1971), pp. 119–26.

2 The academic training for a position in the colonial administration is described by A. A. J. Warmenhoven in "De opleiding van Nederlandse bestuursambtenaren in Indonesië," in *Besturen overzee: Herinneringen van oud-ambtenaren bij het binnenlands bestuur in Nederlands-Indië*, ed. S. L. van der Wal (Franeker: T. Wever B. V., 1977), pp. 12–41. The same volume contains a description of a Dutch official's task in South Celebes, the area where Friedericy worked, by H. J. Koerts, "Bestuursambtenaar in Zuid-Celebes," pp. 45–72.

3 Two other writers of Dutch colonial literature who began their writing careers in Japanese camps were A. Besnard and R. Nieuwenhuys. It is ironic that perhaps the most important Indonesian novelist of today, Pramudya Ananta Tur, began his writing career in a Dutch prison and that his most important novels were written on the island of Buru where he was imprisoned for fourteen years by the Indonesian government.

4 The Indonesian *"mare liberum"* quote from G. J. Resink, *Indonesia's History between the Myths* (The Hague: W. van Hoeve, 1968), p. 45. For a study in English of these seventeenth-century wars in Celebes, see Leonard Y. Andaya, *The Heritage of Arung Palakka: A History of South Sulawesi in the Seventeenth Century* (The Hague: Martinus Nijhoff, 1981).

5 Hasanuddin is a local as well as a national hero in modern Indonesia. His tomb is near Sungguminasa, the town that is the setting for *The Counselor*. The airport of modern Macassar or Ujung Pandang is named after him.

6 For the demise of those realms, see Friedericy, *Etappe*, pp. 150–53; see also Friedericy, *Standen*, pp. 1–2.

7 Friedericy asserts that there was practically no middle class in *Etappe*, p. 151.

8 These supposed trespasses are given in the article on "Boeginezen" in *Encyclopaedie van Nederlandsch-Indië*, 7 vols. (The Hague: Martinus Nijhoff, 1917–1939), 1:323–31. See also Friedericy, *Standen*, pp. 124–30.

9 Friedericy, *Etappe*, p. 152.

10   On the derivation of *amok* and illustrative passages see the entry "a muck" in Henry Yule and A. C. Burnell, *Hobson-Jobson* (rev. ed. 1903; reprint ed., New Delhi: Munshiram Manoharlal Publishers, 1979), pp. 18–23. See also A. R. Wallace, *The Malay Archipelago* (1869; reprint ed., New York: Dover, 1962), p. 134. Wallace's book is a favorite of the modern Indonesian writer Mochtar Lubis who has some comments on the *sirik* tradition in Celebes in his recent work, *Het land onder de zon: Het Indonesië van nu* (Alphen aan den Rijn: A. W. Sijthoff, 1981), pp. 153–56.

11   From an interview in *Het Vaderland,* April 9, 1959.

12   A. Alberts, "In Memoriam H. J. Friedericy," in *De Groene Amsterdammer,* December 1, 1962. Friedericy's narrative talent was also mentioned in articles about him in *Het Vaderland* (April 9, 1959, and November 23, 1962) and by Nieuwenhuys in his article in *Jaarboek,* pp. 120–21.

13   For the *pakeso-keso,* see *Standen,* p. 71.

14   From an interview in *De Telegraaf,* February 3, 1960.

15   Ibid.

Notes to the Text

1   Macassar was, during the time of the novel, an important harbor with a population of about 50,000 people. Joseph Conrad had known the port during his years as a merchant marine officer. He described it as follows: "At that time Macassar was teeming with life and commerce. It was the point in the island where tended all those bold spirits who, fitting out schooners on the Australian coast, invaded the Malay Archipelago in search of money and adventure" (Joseph Conrad, *Almayer's Folly* [1895; reprint ed., Harmondsworth: Penguin Books Ltd., 1978], pp. 9–10). Macassar was the city where Almayer met Captain Lingard. Celebes figures prominently in Conrad's story, written in 1897, "Karain: A Memory," published in the collection *Tales of Unrest* (1898). My surmise is that the name of the main character is modeled after the word *karaëng,* which is a title of a king or prince, as Karain is in Conrad's story. However, he is said to be a Buginese and in their language such a person would be referred to as *aru.* Other details in the story ring true, including the obsession for revenge.

2   The tamarind tree is the *Tamarindus indica* tree of the *Leguminosae caesalpinae* family. It was a favorite shade tree along avenues. The Javanese name is the *asem* tree.

3   *Alun-alun* is a large open square in a city or town.

4   Daëng is a title of nobility in both the Macassarese and Buginese languages, and was used all over southern Celebes. Every male member of the high and low nobility assumed that title when he was around fifteen or sixteen. Friedericy notes that there often was a tenuous correspondence between a person's first name and his "daëng name"; for instance "Marewa daëng Barani" literally means "Courageous daëng Brave." Daëng was used before the higher title of karaëng (*Standen,* pp. 57–58).

5   Copra is the dried flesh of coconut. Because of its high fat content it was (and is) exported to Europe where it was used in the manufacture of margarine.

6   "Kembang sepatu" refers to a common, very beautiful flowering shrub, the *Hibiscus Rosa-sinensis*. The Malay name means "shoemaker flower" because the petals were once used to polish shoes (*kembang* means "flower" and *sepatu* means "shoe"). It was also called *bunga raja* (the "great flower") or Chinese rose.

7   Friedericy did have an assistant named Anwar (*Etappe*, p. 154), but the figure in the novel is an amalgam of several people he knew.

8   *Anakaraëng* means "royal child" in Macassarese, the child (*anak*) of a karaëng.

9   Nine flags were part of the regalia of Gowa (see below), called *Batesalapang* in Macassarese. *Bate* is the word for flag.

10   *Karaëng* was originally the Macassarese title of the king of Gowa, and may be translated as "lord." Only the male descendants of princes of the blood and the highest nobility could assume this title. It was usually followed by the name of the district or appanage belonging to the karaëng. The Buginese equivalent of *karaëng* is *aru* (*Standen*, pp. 56–57).

11   The sudang is, like the "golden kris" mentioned later, a *gaukang* or part of the regalia—royal emblems—of the rulers of Gowa and Bone. They were held sacred and were said to possess magic powers. The Malay equivalent for this Macassarese and Buginese term is *kabesaran*. Although this tradition can be found anywhere in Indonesia, it was once particularly prominent in Celebes. One could call these objects fetishes that were thought to impart authority to the monarch and were believed to contain such great supernatural power that they were displayed in order to negate bad harvests, cure epidemic illnesses, and minimize natural disasters. They were always kept either in the attic of the ruler's house itself or in a house solely built to store them. These regalia did not need to be precious artifacts such as cannons, *kris*, or jewels. They could be all manner of things—flags, stones, vases, plates, cups, gongs, a lock of hair, or a brush—which had some kind of relationship to an eponymous ancestor. There is no doubt that at one time it was believed that the ruler obtained all his power from these regalia. These ornaments were never guarded but were taken care of by priests called *bissu* in Buginese and Macassarese, or *sanro* in Buginese, and *pinati* in the Macassarese language.

The *bissu* was a peculiar individual. The word seems to mean "dumb" or "denial of certain things," such as marriage. Most of the *bissus* were men who dressed like women and were usually homosexual. They lived together and had access to the women's quarters of a ruler. Their ranks were filled with boys who were thought to look effeminate at an early age and who were then raised and educated by the *bissus* themselves. This class no longer exists in Celebes, their importance having been undermined first by Islam and then by the modernization of Indonesian society. See *Standen*, pp. 48–55, 68–69; G. A. Wilken, "Het animisme bij de volken van den Indischen Archipel," *De Indische Gids*, 6, part 2 (1884): 60–63; and the entry on "priesters" in *Encyclopaedie van Nederlandsch-Indië*, 3:508–9.

12   *Kris* is the ubiquitous short sword worn by men in the Malay archipelago, used as a weapon, as an indicator of superior rank, or as a sacred object. The Buginese and Macassarese held that the *kris* is the inseparable companion of a man because it represents the missing rib on the left. Forging these weapons used to be circumscribed by a very complicated set of rules and rituals. The nomenclature for the various components of the weapon, for the forging itself, and for the countless

varieties was very elaborate. Relatively little has been written on the subject of the *kris*. Perhaps the most useful study is the recent one by J. Engel, *Geschiedenis en algemeen overzicht van de Indonesische wapensmeedkunst* (Amsterdam: Samurai, 1980).

The *badik* is a knife, unique to southern Celebes. It has a blade between eight and twelve inches long; its back is straight and the cutting edge is convex. The *badik*'s handle curves at a right angle to the cutting edge and usually has some silverwork at the top. The sheath used to be made of two dark brown pieces of wood held together by silver bands, and was often inlaid with silver coins. There were two kinds: the *badik sosoro*, which had a blade of watered steel and was used only for combat, and the *badik pateba*, which was also used as a tool.

13   *Sarong* is the "skirt" worn by both men and women in Indonesia, fastened around the waist and coming down to the ankles. The correct term should be *kain sarung*, and the root of the word means "sheath." It is of interest to note that, though it was a common garment among them, the Macassarese and Buginese did not use this word. In their languages they called it *lipa*, presumably derived from a root word for "folding over," "double."

14   *Djongos* was the word for a male servant who worked in the house. The word is a corruption of the Dutch word *jongen* which means boy.

15   Friedericy had a servant named Badawi (*Etappe*, p. 154).

16   *Songko* is a kind of skullcap typical of southern Celebes. For the common people it was woven from the rib of a leaf from the lontar palm, while for the upper classes it was woven from horsehair with an edge fashioned from gold thread. It has now been completely replaced by the *kupiah*, the black velvet cap worn by men to indicate they're Muslims.

17   "Lida Padalle" was the eldest brother of the thirty-third and last king of Gowa. When Friedericy met him he was sixty-four. He was resented and disliked by the nobility of Gowa because he collaborated with the Dutch during their final military campaign in 1905-6. Since no one trusted his word he was nicknamed "Karaëng Lida Padalle" which means "the forked tongue of the Lizard," to rhyme with his own name "Karaëng Mandalle" (*Etappe*, pp. 162-63).

18   Sitahaya is also based on a real person, a male nurse (*Etappe*, p. 154). The scene described here is based on real experience in 1922 (ibid., p. 30).

19   *Aduh* is a Malay exclamation of pain or grief, from the verb *mengaduh*, to mourn, to grieve.

20   *Pasar Malam* was a well-known Javanese feast that lasted for a week. It resembled a fair and was celebrated at night. *Pasar* means "market" and *malam* (in Javanese, *malem*) is "evening." It was particularly associated with the religious feasts connected with the Muslim "ramadan" or month of fasting.

21   *Corvée* labor (i.e., *herendiensten*) refers to the labor the common man owed to his native overlord and to the Dutch colonial government. This labor was most often exacted for public-works projects such as maintenance of roads, dikes, dams, and the like. Gradually, during the second half of the nineteenth century and the first two decades of the twentieth, the labor was replaced by a tax.

22   Pontianak is the name of a town on the west coast of Borneo. It is a strange name because the same word indicates the greatly feared ghost of a woman who died in childbirth. The place where the town was built was considered a gathering

place for these spirits. Abdul-Rahman, who founded Pontianak, is said to have bombarded the spot for two hours with the cannons of his ships in order to scare the *pontianaks* away. He then leaped on shore by himself and began hacking at the underbrush with a machete. Only after that would his followers join him (G. A. Wilken, "Het animisme bij de volken van den Indischen Archipel," *De Indische Gids*, 7, part 1 [1885]:55).

23   *Ubi* is a general name for all kinds of edible roots and tubers.

24   Lucien was Lucien van Wehly, Friedericy's fellow administrator and friend in Celebes (*Etappe*, p. 150).

25   For a discussion of *gaukang* and male priests in women's dress, see n. 11 above.

26   *Base*, as it is used in the present context, indicates that the child was female.

27   *Sètan* comes from the Arabic *sjaitan*. Although in Arabic it always indicated a malevolent spirit or devil, this is not the case in Indonesia, where the word can also refer to benevolent spirits.

The *waringin* tree is the *Ficus benjamina*, a large, tall, shapely tree which was used everywhere to grace the *alun-alun*, or village square, because the tree was held to be holy. The Malay thought that the *waringin* was a gathering place for spirits. The tree referred to here is the other variety of *Ficus*, the *Ficus Kurzii*, which has airroots; the *Ficus benjamina* does not have any.

28   *Malam djum'at*, also spelled *malam djumahat*, is Thursday evening.

29   *Atap* is a roof covering made from the dried leaves of the nipa palm.

30   A *bendi* was a small horse-drawn carriage with two wheels.

31   The episode about the representatives of the Indonesian Communist Party is based on reality and took place during 1926 (see *Etappe*, p. 161). The Partai Kommunis Indonesia was founded in May 1920 in Java and was one of several political parties striving to gain independence for Indonesia.

32   Village schools (*volksscholen* in Dutch) represent the attempt by the colonial government to bring at least rudimentary education to the people. At first the government thought to finance the establishment of thousands of schools entirely from the treasury, but this proved too costly. Ironically, it was the conqueror of Atjeh, the controversial Governor General Van Heutsz, who in 1907 ordered that the schools were to be established to provide elementary instruction adapted to local needs. To finance this organization, Van Heutsz ruled that local governments would pay for their own school and could charge the parents a modest fee. The colonial government would provide financial aid but was to refrain from disturbing the local character of the instruction. It was the taxation that the people from Celebes were objecting to.

33   The dance of the herons from southern Celebes had a great fascination for Friedericy. He mentioned it expressly in his letters (*Etappe*, pp. 196–97), made it the subject of his first literary effort, the story "The Dance of the Herons," and refers to it again in this novel. In one of his letters he mentions that the dance was quite old, that the dancers who performed it were called *pakondobuleng*, and that "though I don't understand the origin or meaning of this dramatic dance, it never fails to move me." The action concerns a lame hunter who stalks a heron. When he finally shoots the bird, the hunter discovers that he has killed his own son. The

only accompaniment was provided by drums *(ganrangs)*, played by the *pagan-rangs*. These drummers, according to Friedericy *(Standen,* pp. 70–71), were highly regarded by the Buginese and Macassarese because of the difficulty of their art. Friedericy described the dance itself, beginning with a description of the dancer who portrays the heron.

The dancer had a narrow, light blue cloth around his shoulders. He held its ends between the fingers of his extended and closed hands, his arms spread wide like wings. Stretched from the inside by means of a couple of little bamboo sticks, a second light blue cloth covered his head completely and, alternately lit by the moon and the fire, it had a remarkable resemblance to the head of a large bird.

Supported by the voices of the drums, the heron floated majestically over the green land. Everything was at peace. Every so often a stately beat of the wings, every so often a barely perceptible reeling immediately corrected by a twisting of the feathers, every so often a searching of what lay below to see if perhaps a shining little fish might jump from the liquid mirror of the rice fields.

The drums spoke softly of sailing clouds, of slumbering dark green villages, of scorched brown mountain sides. Suddenly they sounded worried. Something unknown was approaching. They raised their voices. They spoke excitedly, afraid. Beating its wings rapidly, the heron looked in all directions. And there was the hunter, the lame hunter who made the large-eyed children in the front row move away in fear. The drums enveloped the hunter and the bird with their voices. Bird and hunter were driven by the *ganrang* couple. The hunter could do nothing but slink closer, dragging his leg, limping to the dull insistent beat which drove him to his goal. And the heron could do nothing but flee, and yet return again to where the danger was, descend in wide circles, and alight. And the hunter was not to see the bird while he, all the time limping along more wearily, had to peer around him with blind eyes.

I had seen it many times before and I knew how it would end. The hunter would finally kill the heron. He would hobble up to his prey and discover to his horror that the heron was his own son.

The drums held their breath for a moment. The men by the fire grew silent. The moon shone through the palm trees as if it were behind a graceful cast-iron grate. The children, who had laughed at the lame hunter, looked scared. The hunter had seen the bird but the bird had not seen the hunter. A thundering blow resounded from the head of one of the drums. The heron struggled to rise. A few fruitless wingbeats barely moved him one step. The raised bird's head turned helplessly from left to right, the large beak half open, breathing with difficulty. The wings hung down. A second shot. The ponderous bird made one other heartbreaking attempt at flying. But the drums were almost struck dumb. They hardly breathed. And the heron lay down, so weary, so very weary, to rest. He stretched, trembled, and was dead. And now the lame hunter jumped forward. He kneeled next to the lifeless bird and after he had bent over the corpse he burst out in a loud wailing. "It is my son," he moaned, "my son." (H. J. Friedericy, *Vorsten, Vissers en Boeren* [Amsterdam: Querido, 1957], pp. 41–44)

34   Sunda is the western section of Java. The greater part of it is mountainous. Bandung is a well-known city in that part of Java, over 2,000 feet above sea level.

35   Menado was a district in the northeastern part of Celebes's northern peninsula which juts out eastward, just below the Philippines. It is also the name of the
principal city there.

Glossary

Unless otherwise noted, the words are Malay. If the word or phrase is not listed in the glossary, consult the notes.

agas   tiny stinging gnats. They are usually near water and sting during the day as well as the night.

alang-alang   a tall, tough grass.

atap   thatch; a roofing material made from the leaves of various palms.

baleh-baleh   a bench to sleep or rest on.

bandjir   violent flooding of rivers.

blubur (belubur)   a bin; here a storage bin to keep the *kajuputih* leaves for fermentation.

copra   the dried kernel of the coconut. It is an export article that provides coconut oil.

dendeng   thin slices of dried meat, similar to our jerky.

djeruk   the general term for citrus fruit.

djongos   Javanese for houseboy. It may be a corruption of the Dutch word *jongen*, which means "boy."

dusun   here means orchard.

gudang   warehouse, or any place where goods are stored.

guru   in this book it refers to both a teacher and a religious leader.

hadji   a Mohammedan who has made a pilgrimage to Mecca.

ikan   general word for fish.

kain   the general word for fabric, cloth, or garment.

kali   although a Javanese word, the most common word for river.

kampong   Malay for "village." It can also indicate a neighborhood or section of a large town.

kasbi   cassava roots.

katti (kati)   a measure of weight about one and a quarter pounds. One *pikol* equals one hundred *kati*.

kebon   gardener.

klambu   mosquito netting put over a bed.

klewang (also *kelewang*)   a single-edged Indonesian sword that becomes wider toward the point. The cutting edge is straight. To be distinguished from the *parang*, which is a machete.

kontjo   buddy, friend.

mandur   from the Portuguese *mandador*, refers to a native overseer.

mantri   a native official of a lower rank. Used in combinations to indicate official status, such as *mantri* nurse, which is a male nurse employed by the government.

nasi goreng   fried rice. *Nasi* means rice.

parang   the Indonesian machete.

pasar   market.

patjol   the Indonesian hoe.

pikol   a weight measure, equivalent to roughly 120 pounds.

pisang   banana. *Pisang goreng* means fried bananas.

pondok   hut, temporary shelter.

prao   the general Malay word for a boat with outriggers.

radja   in this case, "chief" or "head of a village."

sukun   breadfruit tree.

tandjong   cape.

tangsi   military barracks.

tjot   hill. The word is originally from Atjeh. Also used in soldier's slang in the colonial army.

toko   a shop, usually run by Chinese, that could contain the most amazing variety of goods.

toppi (usually spelled *topi*)   hat.

tuan   mister or sir. Used particularly by the native population when addressing a European.

tukang   a workman, but one who knows a trade, such as carpentry. A *tukang* is not an unskilled laborer or coolie.

tunku   here the oven of the *kajuputih* still. Originally referred to the hearthstone of a stove.

warong   Javanese word for a stall or booth in a market.